THE FRACKING WAR

THE FRACKING WAR

MICHAEL FITZGERALD

MILL CITY PRESS, MINNEAPOLIS

Mill City Press, Inc.
322 First Avenue N, 5th floor
Minneapolis, MN 55401
612.455.2293
www.millcitypublishing.com

ISBN-13: 978-1-62652-706-5
LCCN: 2014903001

Cover Design by Will Sweeney of New York
Typeset by Mary Kristin Ross

Printed in the United States of America

Acknowledgments

This book would not have been possible without the unwavering support and encouragement of my editor, wife, and best friend, Sylvia Fox. When I announced in the summer of 2012 I wanted to write *The Fracking War*, her response was simply, "What can I do to help?"

She was the first reader when the manuscript was completed and the last set of eyes on it when it went to the publisher. Without her steady belief in the book and my ability to complete it, *The Fracking War* might not have made it past my daily ranting about how much hydrofracking for natural gas threatens all of our futures.

There are many other people to thank, especially the "beta" readers who reviewed the first draft of the manuscript—Sylvia, Jennifer Noble, and Brynne Betz. Each of them, in their own way, contributed to changes and emphases in the book that resulted in a more complete novel for readers.

It was their unanimously voiced belief that the book should move from manuscript to print that gave me the confidence to move ahead with publication.

A special acknowledgement goes to Wrexie Bardaglio, who carefully proofread the manuscript three times. Wrexie went above and beyond the call of duty in her review, catching a number of structural and stylistic faux pas I would not have wanted in the book in your hands.

My thanks also goes out to the incredible activist community in the Finger Lakes —especially Yvonne Taylor and Joseph Campbell of the group Gas Free Seneca—whose brave actions and non-violent protests against hydrofracking and its related industries provided me with inspiration throughout the writing process.

And my thanks also goes out to author, biologist and environmental activist Sandra Steingraber of Ithaca, New York, who reminded me that "It's time to play the 'Save the World Symphony,'" in an interview with Bill Moyers just days before going to jail for her role in a gas-related protest. "I don't know what instrument you hold, but you need to play it as best as you can and find your place in the score."

Her words validated what I was thinking when I started drafting *The Fracking War*. My instrument was my keyboard. My place in the score was to write a novel to ignite a sleeping citizenry and reignite the passions of activists.

Lastly, I want to thank my children, Jason, Anne, Dustin and Dylan, and all of my friends around the world who have encouraged me through this writing, editing, and publishing process, always cheerfully asking, "How *is* the book going?"

They have their answer now.
Done.

Watkins Glen, New York,
November 2013

PREFACE

I first became aware of the oddly named natural-gas-extraction method called hydrofracking in 2007 when I spotted a handful of roadside signs in upstate New York that boldly exclaimed "No Fracking!"

It immediately reminded me of the television program *Battlestar Galactica*, in which the word "frack" was a futuristic epithet used liberally.

I thought the signs might be some kind of joke.

But it didn't take much research into hydrofracking technology for me to recognize what a powerful threat it poses to the environment, to health, and to the social, political, and economic fabric of communities.

As I write this preface to *The Fracking War* in the fall of 2013, a bibliography of the articles detailing out problems caused by hydrofracking would run into the hundreds—perhaps thousands—of pages.

There have also been a number of excellent non-fiction books about hydrofracking published, most notably Tom Wilber's *Under the Surface: Fracking, Fortunes and the Fate of the Marcellus Shale.*

But these non-fiction tomes use a classic, even-handed journalism approach that informs and only rarely inflames.

While journalism reports on what has happened, it rarely looks at what *might* happen. And news reports can't state what most of us believe— that exempting hydrofracking from federal clean water and clean air laws is a violation of government's responsibility to protect its citizens.

In the fictional setting of *The Fracking War,* flames, passion and what *could* happen are on display for the reader.

The inspiration for this work of fiction came from daily news reports from around the nation and the world. But it also sprang from conversations heard (and overheard) in various parts of the Finger Lakes region as people debated the wisdom of hydrofracking in town hall meetings, village conferences, in schools, barbershops, beauty salons, restaurants, saloons and wineries.

Anytime the topic came up—whether pro or con—I felt the tension in the room become palpable.

Just weeks before *The Fracking War* was dispatched to the printer, members of several Canadian First Nations in the province of New Brunswick faced off with the Royal Canadian Mounted Police in what turned into a violent confrontation eerily similar to some events in the piece of fiction that lies beyond this introduction.

Many more such incidents are likely on the way as the citizenry rallies to protect the planet from a litany of bad decisions by our governments.

PRELUDE TO WAR

Rockwell Valley, Pennsylvania
New Year's Day

Delbert Dogg thought he heard something a fraction-of-a-second before the bullet slammed into his right shoulder, spinning him sideways and dropping him to the rock-hard icy ground by his parked utility pickup truck.

Lying on his back, he turned his head and tried to focus on the edge of the woods two hundred yards away from the raised concrete pad where he had been checking gauges and pipe connections on a newly "fracked" natural gas well owned by Grand Energy Services, an energy conglomerate with headquarters in Missouri.

The snow on the winter-frozen terrain, a few miles south of the Pennsylvania-New York border, was humped up in spots, spoiling a clear view of the stand of trees from the ground.

Deer hunters, Dogg thought. *Deer hunters. Some stupid-ass hunter missed his shot. Jesus H. Christ!*

The thought stayed with Dogg as he assessed his burning shoulder, not wanting to move, but knowing he needed to get to the cell phone in his truck. He tried to get more air as his breathing contracted. His heart was pumping so hard he could hear it pounding in his eardrums.

His eyes were closed tight as the pain in his shoulder spread down to his ribs where he had landed hard when he fell. Then he heard the crunch of boots on the hard-packed snow headed towards him.

"Call an ambulance you fucking moron! I'm hit. You shot me. You bastard!"

As the crunching stopped, he opened his eyes, expecting to see a hunter in bright orange hurrying towards him.

"What the HELL?"

Two men stood a hundred feet away, dressed head-to-toe in winter-white camouflage, both carrying scoped rifles.

Their faces were covered with white ski masks, with slits for eyes, nose holes, and ragged mouth openings.

For a moment, Dogg watched the steam of their breath rising out of their masks, as if they were smoking. They were standing stock-still, like spooked deer.

"I'm hit, you idiots. Call a fucking ambulance!" Dogg screamed, the pain made worse by the exertion.

Dogg simultaneously saw the flash from the rifle's gun barrel and felt the impact of the second bullet, this one going straight through his forehead, exiting the back of his skull, digging deep enough into the ground that it took sheriff's deputies hours to find it the next day.

Delbert Dogg, 51, known to his Pennsylvania neighbors and gas company co-workers simply as Dogg, would come to be known in the history books as the first casualty in the conflict most people eventually came to call *The Fracking War*.

Horseheads, New York
March

The second box Jack Stafford opened had all his journalism notebooks, memorabilia, and his favorite photo of Amelia—Amy—his wife of twenty years who had died six months before.

Jack had been transitioning from a successful but intense career as an investigative newspaper reporter to teaching at a rural junior college in Northern California when Amy's digestive system stopped working and the doctors found cancer in her colon.

Swift and merciful, they said, Jack thought. *Swift and merciful? Maybe for her.*

He stared at the photo of them taken on a ferry to Catalina Island off the California coast shortly after they were married. A Japanese tourist snapped it for them, the city of Avalon in the background.

Amy's smile was wide, her arm tightly holding onto Jack, whose smile was even wider. They had even seen half-wild buffalo on the island on that trip.

He shook his head to clear the thought, and arranged his new Apple laptop computer, a massive paper dictionary, and a new copy of *The Associated Press Stylebook* on his desk at the *Horseheads Clarion*, a twice-a-week tabloid newspaper that was defying the trend of most newspapers, which were cutting back so much on staff and quality that they were becoming irrelevant in their communities.

The *Clarion* was still alive and thriving, thanks to Walter Nagle, its 75-year-old owner and publisher, who had given Jack his first newspaper job writing about local high school sports more than thirty years before.

Jack was coming full-circle, back to the small town where he grew up, went to high school, and worked after earning a state college degree in American Literature and English.

He had escaped the snow when he landed a newspaper job in San Francisco, then found another in San Diego a few years later.

"Miss the smog and traffic?" Walter asked.

Jack looked up to see Walter standing in the doorway of his 10' x 10' glassed-in corner office. The office and furniture looked like relics out of the 1930s film *The Front Page*, with newspapers stacked four feet high on the floor and a roll-top desk piled with file folders. A half-dozen mugs stood on top of a bookcase, probably harboring dried-up coffee and tea. The office hadn't had a deep cleaning since Jack had been out chasing high school football results.

"No, I don't miss California, too crowded. I do kind of miss the Colorado air. You could see for miles."

After Amy died, Jack found he couldn't face his English and journalism classes. All the sympathy from the students and his colleagues, as sincere as it might have been, suffocated him. And so with only two months left in the fall term, he resigned. A week later, he headed out to Colorado to stay with an old friend from high school who had retired early and spent most of his days drinking his way through life in several Aspen bars.

Jack spent a few weeks at the bars with him, amazed at how much two drinks at that altitude could affect a person. Then one afternoon he was cornered by a cute 40-year-old academic-journalist-turned-environmental activist named

Devon Walsh who sold him—with the help of two glasses of wine on her tab—on the dangers of hydrofracking for natural gas.

Colorado was one of many states in the United States that had gone into hydrofracking big-time, without knowing exactly what it was getting into.

Jack's interest was piqued when Devon laid out a damning case against fracking and rattled off the names of a half-dozen likely carcinogenic chemicals used in the process that were starting to show up in the groundwater. He had read bits and pieces about fracking, but California was just starting to see news reports pop up about it—all negative.

Jack had spent his first couple of years as a reporter in California writing about the dangers posed by nuclear power and the penultimate issue—what do to with all that radio-active waste. No one really knew how to dispose of spent nuclear fuel, so they just warehoused it in Nevada, among other places, hoping for the best.

He had moved to California just three years after the near-meltdown of the Three Mile Island nuclear power plant in Harrisburg, Pennsylvania had put the brakes on construction of more nuclear power plants across the country— an environmental near-miss less than 200 miles from Horseheads.

But to Jack, this hydrofracking technology seemed potentially much worse than nuclear power, compounded by the unbelievable greed of the natural gas exploration companies. The tales Devon told him about broken landowner leases, toxic chemical spills, sick people, dead animals, and officials being bribed raised his blood pressure enough that he started researching instead of hanging out at the bars.

For a while he wrote some freelance articles for regional newspapers, and an article for a magazine or two, hammering at hydrofracking problems. Then Walter called him and said he needed Jack back in Horseheads.

"I am not getting any younger, JJ, plus, these damn college kids I hire aren't as smart as you were coming out of school," Walter told him on the phone. "Come on home. All your friends here are getting old, too. We all want you here."

It helped that the day Walter called it had just snowed two feet and Jack's soft-core California winter wardrobe was inadequate for the 15-degree Colorado temperatures. Plus, his California-purchased snow boots had been no match for slippery sidewalks and he had gone ass-over-teakettle twice just going out for a cup of hot tea that morning.

Not that Horseheads would be much warmer. But it would be home—literally home—if he moved back into the family home he inherited when his father passed away.

Walter had also dangled the idea of making a new position at the newspaper—investigative columnist—with the freedom to take a hard look at hydrofracking.

"There's a war brewing here and down in Pennsylvania, I swear. And a lot of strange stuff going on that needs somebody with your talents," he'd said.

Being called by his nearly forgotten New York growing-up nickname, JJ, helped, too.

Jack's full name was John James Stafford, one of the Irish Staffords, part of the clan that traced its roots to the time of the Norman invasion of England. Jack's ancestors had fled England for Ireland long before his great-grandfather came to New York City on a boatful of other Irish immigrants.

Jack looked a lot like his grandfather, just over six feet tall, with broad enough shoulders that he could have worked in the construction trade like his father had for years if he had wanted to.

Walter stood outside his office watching Jack unpack his boxes, weighing how much to tell Jack—and how soon—about what he suspected was already happening in New York, and what was about to happen.

"When you get settled in at that big desk, let's have some of that still-fine diner coffee across the street at Millie's," Walter said. "Millie died ten years ago, but it's still the morning hangout around here. Some gas company guys are there most days. Most of them knew that guy who was murdered New Year's Day down in Rockwell Valley."

Jack looked up at Walter, marveling that at 75 he still stood ramrod straight to his six foot height, and didn't have an ounce of fat on him.

"I'm with you. But I gave up coffee, Walter. Bad for my stomach. I'm a tea drinker these days, but I definitely still need the caffeine."

PAGE 1
The *Horseheads Clarion*

New staff member joins the Clarion

Jack Stafford, a veteran newsman from California, Colorado, and the Southern Tier of New York, has joined the staff of the *Horseheads Clarion*, editor and publisher Walter Nagle announced today.

Stafford, 55, will be the newspaper's first investigative columnist, focusing on the region's environmental and political issues.

"Jack started his career at the *Clarion* more than 30 years ago, right out of college, and comes back to us with a wealth of knowledge," Nagle said.

Stafford's resume includes stints with the *San Francisco Daily News,* the *San Diego Express,* and several newspapers in Central and Southern California.

Most recently he worked with several Colorado newspapers and magazines, writing articles about the push for hydrofracking for natural gas in that state.

Immediately before that, he was teaching college-level journalism in Northern California.

Stafford grew up in Horseheads, graduating with honors from Northside High School, where he captained the wrestling and track teams.

He holds a bachelor of arts' degree from SUNY Buffalo and

took coursework at the University of California at Berkeley in environmental justice.

"Jack's coming to us to help in good part with our coverage of the big push for natural gas wells in the state by gas exploration companies," Nagle said.

"He's had lots of experience in covering environment and legal issues in California and wrote a series of articles on the California Environmental Quality Act that is being published in a journalism textbook."

Stafford said he is very pleased to rejoin the staff of the newspaper and will reside in his family's home, which he inherited two years ago when his father, James Stafford, passed away.

When hydrofracking for natural gas first burst onto the energy scene, it seemed like it was almost too good to be true, especially for the economy of the region, Walter thought.

All that natural gas that had been unreachable for so long was suddenly available for companies to extract and sell.

And like so many things, it was too good to be true

in many ways, though most people—journalists like Walter included—didn't seem to want to look too closely, at first anyway.

Walter watched Jack pause in front of Millie's Diner across the street, wondering what was going through Jack's mind now that he was back at the *Clarion*.

On his desk, Walter had amassed stacks of file folders full of information about how hydrofracking gave natural gas companies a way to get at the gas buried thousands of feet below the earth's surface, where it was locked in tiny bubbles in shale rock formations.

A geologist friend told Walter that gas companies had known for years about the rich deposits. But unlike normal natural gas wells, where drillers would hit a pocket of gas and release the pressure, this natural gas was locked deep in the shale and was stubborn, existing in tiny bubbles in the layers of rocks rather than caverns or pockets.

Gas companies developed a process to inject water and chemicals under high pressure into very deep wells that not only went down vertically to hit the rock strata, but spread out horizontally for thousands of feet, and sometimes farther.

The chemical-laced water was injected with such force that it caused fractures in the shale (thus the term fracking) that released the gas bubbles back up the pipes.

Walter's friend had reluctantly admitted that yes, hydrofracking actually creates small earthquakes to crack the shale and release gas. But he argued it was not a problem. What were a few miniscule earthquakes thousands of feet below the surface of the earth when compared to the bonanza natural gas represented?

But one file folder on Walter's desk was full of clippings

and reports that it was a big deal for residents of Ohio, Colorado, New Mexico, and Louisiana, where they had already experienced damaging earthquakes for the first time in their histories. And outside the United States, earthquakes in the United Kingdom and other nations were prompting bans on fracking.

Environmentalists were flooding newspapers with letters and emails, sounding the alarm about everything relating to hydrofracking.

A retired Rockwell Valley high school teacher had written a letter to the editor to Walter just the week before, dragging global warming into the fray. "Here is yet another technology aimed at grabbing a finite natural resource which will add more carbon to an already overheating planet," Celice O'Malley had written. "University researchers say all that leaking methane from the hydrofracked wells is going to be the number one contributor to global warming. We are headed for disaster. An environmental apocalypse."

Walter was a little surprised she had neglected to cite what environmentalists called "the Halliburton Loophole," which was an amendment to the Safe Water Drinking Act, a bill signed into federal law by President George W. Bush in 2005. The Halliburton Loophole exempted natural gas and oil companies from having to reveal what chemicals they were using in the hydrofracking process, an exemption that made Walter's blood pressure rise a few points any time he thought about it.

But the Halliburton Loophole—so dubbed because of then-Vice President Dick Cheney's role in getting the amendment inserted into the Act and signed by President

Bush—was credited with launching the 21st century gas rush by freeing up the companies from much environmental oversight.

It also kicked off enough financial speculation in gas lease and gas company stocks that at one point it looked like it might eclipse the speculation in real estate blamed for the big economic crash of 2008.

Walter had stacks of letters from landowners, too, most of whom were leasing out their land and hoping to become millionaires.

The nation's media had been slow to recognize the trend, except for a handful of financial reporters curious about the investing activity. After all, investing activity was hardly sexy news in depressed rural areas of Pennsylvania and New York. Most media ignored hydrofracking, that is, until an amateur film maker from Pennsylvania got a lot of attention with a short movie that included episodes showing people turning on water taps that ignited because their wells had been poisoned by hydrofracking.

Walter laughed the first time he saw the burning water tap in the movie. He had seen that trick performed many times at homes in Pennsylvania, where natural methane intrusion into wells had been a fact of life for as long as he could remember.

But now the gas was showing up nearly everywhere a drill rig started to poke. And because the wells were fanning out horizontally for such long distances, wells a mile from a drill site were showing methane, too.

Walter flipped through the most recently submitted letters to the editor to another one from a gas-drilling supporter, claiming that hydrofracking had been going on for many years and besides, it would mean jobs, lots of jobs.

He set the letter aside. As much as Walter wished for a more prosperous economy, the few new jobs related to gas drilling were being taken by roughnecks from Oklahoma and Texas, adding some interesting accents and interactions to upstate New York and Pennsylvania conversations.

Walter put another letter focusing on the million gallons or more of fresh water required for each hydrofracked well in a stack to run sometime in the next week. He was growing more and more concerned with the toxicity of the water from the drilling process. And, so far, no one could figure out how to clean up the water.

The letter was from a resident of Dimock, Pennsylvania, hydrofracking's ground zero, just a couple of hours south and east of Horseheads, and well outside the circulation of Walter Nagle's *Horseheads Clarion*. But the letter writer was one of the people whose well was fouled and now received daily deliveries of clean water trucked in courtesy of the gas company that had drilled a well a half-mile from his house.

Many people in Dimock, the letter writer claimed, had also discovered their wells were full of methane and toxic chemicals, poisoning the water and making people, pets, and livestock sick in the process.

In the conference room of the *Clarion*—the room Walter Nagle had nicknamed the "war room" the day Jack Stafford agreed to leave Colorado and come to work for him—a map with yellow pushpins marked more than a dozen communities, including Dimock, where residents said they were getting sick from polluted wells and polluted air. Many of the same people also said they had been lied to and were being cheated by the gas companies and their flim-flam sales people, the landsmen who talked them into signing mineral leases.

Another set of pins, red in color, marked locations where people said there had been toxic frack water and other chemicals dumped into rivers and creeks by the gas companies, resulting in dead fish, dead animals, and dead vegetation.

A third set of black pins marked where there had been deaths that were being blamed directly on hydrofracking.

A fourth set of blue pins marked where police reports indicated incidents of vandalism and weird events happening to gas company properties or to employees.

A single bright orange pin marked Rockwell Valley, Pennsylvania, just across the New York border from the *Clarion*'s office.

Walter placed the orange pin a few days after New Year's when he learned that a gas company worker named Delbert Dogg had been found dead at a drill rig. Dogg had been shot twice, police reports said, though details were sketchy and the case was still under investigation.

A few days later, Walter received a handwritten note, slipped under the front door of the newspaper. He hadn't shared it with anyone, but planned on showing Jack Stafford.

> We have had enough. People are dying because of the greed of the gas companies. The environment is being destroyed. Enough. Enough. Enough. We are going to fight back.
>
> MWG

J ack sipped his second cup of hot tea at Millie's Diner, sitting at the same stained Formica lunch counter that had been there thirty years before. And it looked like it still had the same Bunn coffee makers and tea kettle—ancient, he thought, even when he drank coffee here as a sports writer.

Walter had dispatched Jack ahead of him, saying he wanted to pull some documents from the conference room to chat about over coffee.

Walter had been a great reporter and could have made it in Washington or New York City had he wanted to. Instead, he said, he was content being the publisher and editor of the *Horseheads Clarion*.

And the entire area was a better place because of it. More than a few politicians had felt the sting of his reporting and editorials over the years.

He once told Jack his favorite sound was the "hiss of a punctured politician."

When Jack was a young reporter for the *Clarion*, Millie's was the hangout for most of the area's workers, from mill workers to cops to state staff. And mornings it was always the scene of a coffee klatch of local old timers, mixed with up-and-coming leaders.

On this late March morning, with spring in the air and most of the snow melted and gone, the breakfast crowd was leaving as the coffee klatchers arrived to set up their informal conferencing in a horseshoe corner booth that gave a great view of the main downtown intersection.

There didn't seem to be any gas company people in Millie's—or if there were, they weren't wearing Grand Energy Services work shirts.

Behind the lunch counter, a slim girl who looked to be about 18 years old was taking orders, hanging paper slips on a rotating stand for the kitchen staff behind to grab. There were no computers at Millie's. Even the NCR register was circa 1985.

"Were any Grand Energy guys in this morning?" Jack asked as she refilled his mug with hot water and offered him a fresh tea bag.

The young woman's nametag said "Shania" and Jack had a flash of her mother and father meeting at a Shania Twain concert.

"Yup, you just missed them," she said. "Just one group today. Five guys. All eggs, bacon, and hash browns almost every day. I remember orders but not names."

She gave Jack a shy smile as she grabbed a coffee pot to take down the counter to a couple in their seventies having breakfast. He made a note to remember her name and to be sure to tip her well. Waitresses in places like Millie's were as valuable as secretaries in government offices when it came to having information. They saw and heard a lot. And they frequently loved to tell what they heard, particularly if they didn't think they would be quoted.

When she came back through with the hot water a few minutes later, she asked Jack for his name. "Otherwise I'll have to call you 'Lipton with lemon,'" she said, laughing.

"It's Jack, Jack Stafford. I grew up around here and just started working across the street again. At the *Clarion*? You probably see my boss Walter Nagle in here all the time."

Shania placed the hot water pot carefully up on the tabletop before answering.

A thinker, Jack thought. *Probably top of her high school class.*

"Walter's a sweetie," Shania said. "But the gas guys complain about the gas stories in the *Clarion* all the time. I think if Walter weren't so old, they would beat the shit out of him. Sorry! I mean crap."

While Jack pondered that, the door swung open, bringing the moist smell of early spring with it as Walter came in. He waved Jack over to a corner booth at the opposite end of the small diner, away from the coffee klatch and away from the people finishing breakfasts.

Shania brought Walter's favorite coffee mug from the New York Newspaper Publishers' Association and filled it for him as Walter slid into the booth.

"How are your classes going at the community college?" Walter asked.

Jack revised his age estimate of Shania upward to maybe 19 or 20. Then he saw Walter write the number 24 on his paper napkin, smiling at Jack.

"Good. But I'm not doing so hot in English," Shania said. "I don't read enough, my professor told me. But I don't have time."

Walter gave her a grandfatherly look and waved a book he had carried in with a stack of file folders. "My friend Jack here is going to read this classic, I think. But when's he's done, I think you'd like it. Your professor would, too."

She looked at the cover and smiled, heading back when she heard plates banging on the chef's window counter ready to go out to customers.

"You want her to read *The Monkey Wrench Gang*, Walter? Really? That book's getting a little long in the tooth and Edward Abbey wasn't any James Lee Burke when it came to writing style."

Walter sipped his coffee and slid the book across the table to Jack, with a slip of paper sticking out of it—the note he had received back after Delbert Dogg had been shot.

"You're right about style. But it's content Jack, content. I'm not sure, but I think some of the people who are fighting hydrofracking have read it and might be using it to get a little inspiration."

Jack pulled the piece of paper out of the book and read it carefully.

"Oh boy… this is why you wanted me back here, wasn't it Walter?"

He signaled to Shania for more tea and a menu.

"Walter, it's been years since I read this. But in *The Monkey Wrench Gang* nobody shot anybody."

Walter stirred his coffee and looked out the window.

"Walter, what else aren't you telling me?"

Jack had read Edward Abbey's *The Monkey Wrench Gang* after leaving New York for California.

Published in 1975, *The Monkey Wrench Gang* had been the inspiration behind the formation of the famous environmental group Earth First. In California, it was often talked about in newsrooms, though more as a caricature of environmental action than a guidebook.

The main characters in the novel were out to disrupt the mining industry in the southwestern United States, among other industrial enterprises, in order to protect the desert environment.

And to have fun raising hell and blowing stuff up, Jack thought.

Jack remembered liking the book, but found it difficult to believe, even as a novel. He had the same problem with some of Joseph Heller's work, particularly his famous novel *Catch 22*.

But one of the Earth First's founders, Dave Foreman, was so inspired he later published a well-read manual for direct action entitled *Ecodefense: A Field Guide To Monkey-wrenching*.

How seriously activists took the book was never really studied. But a lot of owners of trucks and pieces of equipment all over the United States found sugar and sand in their gas tanks after both *The Monkey Wrench Gang* and *Ecodefense: A Field Guide To Monkeywrenching* were printed.

After his conversation with Walter at Millie's Diner, Jack took Walter's copy of the book back over to his desk at the *Clarion* and started to skim it, deciding he should read it line-by-line if it might factor into some future stories or columns.

In fact, he thought his first column might take a closer look at *The Monkey Wrench Gang*, kind of a quasi-book review, comparing it to the sketchy reports of vandalism Walter said were trickling in.

Jack had scanned the bulletin board in the conference/war room and was surprised at how many acts of vandalism and odd incidents had taken place. But he was more interested in the number of people who claimed to be sick because their wells were contaminated and had blamed it on hydrofracking.

He was more than a little skeptical of the note Walter had received from MWG. Still, Walter was a good newsman, and often spotted trends and news stories months before other journalists who were content to wait for a press conference or some official to tell them what was going on. Or wasn't.

The balance of the *Horseheads Clarion* staff included a bookkeeper named Martha Pickney, who had been there before Jack had left, two just-graduated reporters, Stanley Belisak and Jill Nored, a combination reporter/computer wizard/photographer named Eli Gupta, a small cadre of part-time sports reporters, and several commission-only advertising staff members.

They were all at their desks, tapping on the keys of shiny new Apple computers.

Gupta's tall, thin frame towered over his desk while he sat. He moved his hands over his keyboard like a concert pianist but at a speed most typists would envy. Walter had told Jack that Eli was generally quiet but brilliant, and had been a catch for the *Clarion* to hire several years before.

Walter also relied on a network of freelance writers for the two issues of the *Horseheads Clarion* he put out each week on Tuesdays and Fridays. The freelancers were mostly retired or semi-retired journalists who had known Walter for years and liked to keep their skills honed by writing occasional stories.

I guess I'm just around the corner from joining that *group,* Jack thought.

Jack didn't officially start work until the beginning of the following week. But when Walter found out that he had arrived in town, he pressed Jack to come in to the office to get settled.

Jack was just thinking about leaving and walking the three-quarters-of-a-mile back to his inherited family home when Walter burst in through the front door of the newspaper, his face red from hustling across the street to talk to Eli.

"Eli, I need for you to get up to Watkins Glen right away. Over on west shore highway. I just heard there's been a propane spill. The police are spooked about propane on the highway," Walter said.

"Want to go, too, Jack?" Walter asked.

Jack hesitated for a moment as Eli streaked past on his way out the door.

Then Jack grabbed his coat, reporter's notebook, and *The Monkey Wrench Gang.*

"Sure... but how about putting me on the payroll starting today instead of Monday?"

Jack got a grin and a thumbs up from Walter in return as he headed towards Eli's SUV pulling up in front of the newspaper's office.

Walter's bookkeeper scowled at Walter and shook her head.

"It's my money, Martha," Walter said. "Forget it. Like Captain Picard used to say, 'Make it so.'"

The propane spill turned out to be a tractor-trailer rig that had ended up lying on its side on Route 14 on the west side of Seneca Lake. About forty worried volunteer firemen from three towns surrounded it, concerned that at any moment there would be a huge hiss and liquid propane would be pouring out, which would then flow downhill a quarter-mile to the shores of the lake.

No propane actually ever leaked out because it turned out the truck was almost empty and deadheading north to pick up a load.

Had the tanker been full and its load leaked out, it

could have left a cloud of propane mist floating lightly on the water surface—an ongoing local nightmare scenario.

The specter of that happening had been dragged out at virtually every public meeting, protest, and gathering when people talked about proposals for increasing propane storage in tanks or in old salt caverns.

Various gas company experts said it couldn't happen. People opposed to adding propane storage admitted it was unlikely. But if it did, and a sufficient volume of propane gas blew down the lake towards Watkins Glen, the results would be catastrophic.

Jack played with that scenario in his head as he drove south from Horseheads to Rockwell Valley a few days later, tucking it away as a possible future column. It sounded like a disaster movie and he wondered how he could write it in such a way as to make it believable. He hardly believed it himself. But Walter had shown him an analysis done by a friend, a retired geologist and engineer, that was as persuasive as it was chilling.

The engineer had even included some photos of what the city of Dresden in Germany looked like after its fire-bombing in World War II.

But Jack was working on his first column idea as he introduced himself as the *Horseheads Clarion's* new—and first—investigative columnist.

The widow of Delbert Dogg, the gas company employee found shot to death New Year's Day on the well pad at a Grand Energy Services natural gas well, was willing to chat with Jack.

Jack knew it would to be difficult, even though he had spent many hours in his career talking with people who had lost loved ones.

Muriel Dogg had sounded quite calm on the phone. But what piqued Jack's interest, at first, was that Grand Energy Services was blocking payment of the widow's life insurance benefits, benefits she should have picked up without question, it seemed to him.

She hinted that GES was in financial trouble and that some of the wives of other workers were telling her that paychecks weren't being deposited directly on time and that health insurance claims were also very slow in being processed through the main offices of the company. And although there had been a few newspaper stories about GES and some of its bad investments, the bonanza of shale gas production and ebullience seemed to overshadow everything in all the media reports.

So a column in the *Horseheads Clarion* that could show that hydrofracking, at least at GES, was an example of a crumbling financial Ponzi scheme could be a booming start for Jack.

Walter loved the idea and had pulled together a stack of GES financial data going back to the first days when the company started hydrofracking in Pennsylvania.

But the more Jack thought about it, the more he thought the column might focus more on Muriel Dogg herself.

He knew he was on the right track when he called Sunday afternoon to confirm that he would be coming the next day to visit her at her Rockwell Valley home, a few miles down the road from where her husband had been killed.

Muriel Dogg said she wasn't feeling too well, but still wanted Jack to come. Her bladder cancer, diagnosed not long before her husband died, was giving her a lot of pain. But she knew pretty much what to expect, she said.

She knew because her next-door-neighbor—and a woman who lived on the farm a half-mile away—had also been diagnosed with bladder cancer in the last year.

"GES told me it has nothing to do with the gas wells we got all around here," she told Jack on the phone. "I think that's a load of gas company bullshit."

Walter reread Jack's first column again, his third go at it, though he and Jack had agreed that there would be no heavy-handed editing of Jack's columns.

At 75, Walter felt as strong as he had twenty years before, but had no illusions that he would live forever. And because of that he wanted to use his last breath, and his last dollars, fighting what he thought was likely the greatest environmental and political threat he had seen in his lifetime.

"I just want to make sure we nail these hydrofracking bastards solidly, Jack. Solidly."

But Walter was still a little uneasy that Jack's first column out of the box would hit the gas companies hard with claims that their hydrofracking chemicals, and the air pollution caused by gas wells, were the most likely cause of the cancers of the widow of the murdered Grand Energy Service's worker and two of her nearby neighbors.

All three women were also heavy smokers and drinkers and would be easy targets when the gas companies started to howl about how there could be a half-dozen other factors involved in causing their cancers.

"Three women living within a half-mile of each other get cancer in less than a year, Walter? And just two years after the gas wells were put in? And the same damn cancer?

Please. We are looking at the Love Canal here. But now it's Pennsylvania, Ohio, Colorado, and everyplace else."

Walter had witnessed the Love Canal debacle in the 1970s, where newspaper reporters had tested sump pump water in basements of the Love Canal neighborhood in Niagara Falls, New York, finding toxic chemicals.

Their work ignited a firestorm of local residents' protests and lawsuits when it was clear that a housing development had been built on the site of a huge toxic waste dump. The reporters' stories and subsequent EPA cleanup had also helped make the dangers of a chemical called dioxin a household word.

"You're right. I hired you to kick some gas company ass," Walter said. "And this certainly does it. Let's send the file to Eli and have him show you the redesigned layout I made up. We're going to run your column on the front page and call it *Column One*, just like the *Los Angeles Times*. I only steal ideas from the best, Jack."

From the *Horseheads Clarion*

Column One
The Horseheads Clarion

Three women, three cancers
By Jack Stafford

ROCKWELL VALLEY, Pennsylvania — Three women, three cases of bladder cancer—and they all live within a half-mile of each other.
Coincidence?
Doubtful.

The women's homes all sit atop the Marcellus Shale, the rock layer thousands of feet below their houses which is being mined 24-hours a day for natural gas by Grand Energy Services, a natural gas company.

Grand Energy Services says the three cancers are tragic. But the company denies that the 14 natural gas wells in the two-square mile area, drilled using the hydrofracking process, have any connection with these women's illnesses.

One of the women isn't so sure.

Muriel Dogg, who just turned 50 in February, is a widow. Her husband Delbert Dogg, a GES employee, was 51 when he was found shot to death New Year's Day near a GES well not far from their small three-bedroom home on Rockwell Valley Road.

Police are still investigating months later but have concluded the shooting was not a hunting accident as they first speculated.

Mrs. Dogg was diagnosed with bladder cancer a month before her husband died.

And though the news of her

cancer came as a huge blow to her and her late husband at the time, she was already all-too-familiar with the disease. She has been helping her next-door-neighbor deal with bladder cancer, and both of them were helping a mutual friend who lives on a farm just over the crest of hill behind her house with *her* bladder cancer.

Three women, three diagnoses of bladder cancer within a few months of each other.

Of the three women, only Mrs. Dogg has any direct connection to GES. The other two women, who asked that their names not be used in this column, have been trying to sell their homes for more than a year because they said they feared exactly what has happened.

Their fear?

That the toxic chemicals used in hyrofracking—or the air pollution from the wells—would make them sick.

Since the new technology for hydrofracking for natural gas was launched in the last decade, its effects on the environment and people's health has been debated and studied. Most readers of this newspaper are quite familiar with the controversy in Dimock, Pennsylvania, an ongoing nightmare for residents on both sides of the issue.

The federal Environmental Protection Agency's on-again, off-again concern has been as maddening as it has been ineffective at helping the Dimock people.

Residents with polluted well water and breathing unclean air are getting sick. People who want to boost Dimock as a great place to live are finding it's nearly an impossible task.

Who wants to buy a home or invest in a business in a town that has become synonymous nationally with water pollution and chemical-induced illnesses?

For Dogg and her two ill neighbors, the whole mess is being compounded by Grand Energy Services, they say.

Since her husband was killed, Mrs. Dogg has been unable to tap a GES fund set up for survivors of gas company accidents. The company says because there is an ongoing police investigation, they won't disburse any money. She fears they will never pay her.

And all three women say their various doctors and health care providers are complaining that GES' in-house health insurance isn't paying for their treatments.

GES, by the way, threatened to file a lawsuit against the *Horseheads Clarion* if this newspaper in any way implied Muriel Dogg's bladder cancer, and that of her neighbors, was somehow linked to the toxic chemicals used in hydrofracking, the toxic waste water that is often trucked right by their homes to a disposal site, or air pollution.

Lawsuits are scary.

But so is bladder cancer for Muriel Dogg and her two friends.

Jack Stafford is an investigative columnist and reporter for the Horseheads Clarion *and has worked as an investigative reporter for metropolitan newspapers in California and Colorado. His Column One will appear every Friday. He can be reached via email at JJStafford@HorseheadsClarion.com.*

Jack reread his column early Friday morning, grabbing a copy from the back of the delivery truck stacked high with the freshly printed newspapers.

Walter had sold his Goss printing press fifteen years ago to an Ohio newspaper when he realized it was cheaper to have the *Horseheads Clarion* printed at a daily newspaper in central Pennsylvania instead of having to pay a full-time pressman and maintain the aging equipment.

His decision was also prompted by the death of his longtime press operator, who dropped dead of a heart attack while running the press one winter day.

Jack was pleased with the final edited copy of the column, which Walter touched so lightly Jack could barely see where it had been changed.

He had originally included a section that referenced the Love Canal but pulled it out. He and Walter agreed this opening-shot column was good as is, hit all the right buttons, and would establish not only Jack's writing skills and reporting credibility, but would show the *Horseheads Clarion* was going to ensure that the public knew everything Jack could find about hydrofracking.

It would show that GES was a corporate bully, quite willing to pressure even sick widows.

Walter's Tuesday and Friday routine was to walk across the street and drop off a few free copies of the newspaper at Millie's Diner, his way of salting the conversation there.

But today he suggested that Jack might want to take the copies of the *Horseheads Clarion* over first and then stay for breakfast.

After the paper had been sent to the printer the day before, Walter and Jack had charted out a series of columns for the next few months, including a piece about the Pennsylvania gag rule that kept doctors from talking about the health effects of fracking.

Most of the doctors in Pennsylvania were upset by the law and the fact that they were seeing all kinds of weird illnesses they suspected had links to hydrofracking chemicals.

The gas industry public relations people claimed that the law did no such thing. But Jack had found three doctors—by making three phone calls—who said that the gag rule did, in fact, prevent them from speaking out.

And they would be happy to chat with him about their experience, off the record and with a promise of anonymity, of course.

"It's pretty amazing that we know more about what's in a can of diet soda than what they are injecting into these gas wells," Walter said. "People whose wells have been contaminated don't even know what to test for."

A column on the complexities of testing well water—and the roadblocks thrown up by the gas companies—seemed like a natural, too.

Jack scanned the rest of the newspaper as he waited for Walter to get off the phone. Jack thought he might drive up to Seneca Lake over the weekend and check in on some old friends, including his best friend from high school, Oscar Wilson, a winery owner.

The weather forecast called for the possibility of a late season snowstorm, a reminder to Jack that he needed to check out the sales rack for some good boots and shoes before the summer stock of sandals, swimsuits, and shorts came in.

In California, clothes were clothes and weren't as seasonal. In different parts of the state you could find any climate you wanted, nearly any time of the year, and you didn't really change your wardrobe. You just layered up.

Jack was ready to walk out the door to Millie's when Walter stood up, the telephone still in hand, and waved for Jack to come into the office. His face was a mixture of grin and concern, touched with a cocked eyebrow that Jack had learned years before meant that Walter was hearing something that was likely to turn into a story.

In this case, Jack figured it might also be a column.

"Yes, yes, yes, sure, sure. No. Anonymous. You bet, Rudy. Thanks. Keep your head down, okay?" Walter said, as he hung up the phone.

He plunked down into his chair and exhaled while Jack sat down across from the desk.

"Good news or bad news?" Jack asked. "Or both?"

Walter held up the front page of the paper and pointed to Jack's column, smiling. "I just heard from a guy whose son works for Grand Energy Services. He and I go way back. Anyway, he said his son was told yesterday by his boss, all very hush-hush, that GES guys are now allowed to carry handguns when they travel in GES trucks. In fact, he said his son thinks the GES folks want their people to carry weapons. They're talking about terrorism being a threat to the gas supplies."

It was a stretch to go from vandalism and pranks like those described in *The Monkey Wrench Gang* to terrorism, but it fit with the gas company's normal pattern of overreaction to any kind of criticism or protests.

Jack had a fleeting vision of a gunfight at a natural gas

well and then realized why Walter had held up his column for him to see.

"You've already written the headline, haven't you Walter," Jack said. "'Guns and gas don't mix.' Ha! Jaysus. I'll get started making some calls after we go to Millie's."

Sometimes finding news is simply a matter of being in the right place at the right time.

Even the most successful investigative reporters will tell you that many of their biggest stories came about not because of Herculean research efforts, clever thinking, or even determination, but because of dumb luck—stumbling onto just the right person to talk with, or finding a long-buried government document.

Walter was always threatening to write a book about his lifetime of news experiences and call it *The Accidental Journalist*.

When Jack was starting out as a reporter at the *Horseheads Clarion*, Walter lectured Jack that newspaper reporters needed to be curious and ask lots of questions, even if they seemed annoying. And reporters always needed to pay attention to detail.

"They say the devil is in the details," Walter would offer. "I say the news is the details."

Jack had made a career following Walter's advice and was paying close attention as he and Walter walked together into Millie's. Three GES gas workers were sitting at the lunch counter finishing up big breakfast platters.

Jack dropped off a half-dozen *Clarion*s in a bin by the front door for patrons to pick up for free to read while they ate. Then he made his way back to the corner booth where he and Walter would have an unobstructed view of the main intersection and most of the diner. Walter never liked to sit with his back to the room anywhere. He said it was from watching too many cowboy movies.

Walter had a file folder with him labeled *Monkey Wrenching Incidents,* tucked in with a copy of the day's newspaper.

One of the GES workers got up and picked up a *Clarion.* He showed it to his two co-workers at the lunch counter who gave Jack and Walter sidelong glances.

Walter waved to Shania who smiled back but looked nervously at the GES workers.

Jack heard one them swear as he read the front page. From across the diner, he couldn't see for sure if it was his column that drew the epithet, but if it was, it made him happy. The worst thing for a newspaper columnist was to not get any reaction.

Shania made her way from behind the counter, juggling a coffee pot, Walter's favorite coffee mug, and Jack's tea set up on a tray. She had fixed her blonde hair up in kind of bun arrangement this morning and looked like she was a college student dressing up as someone from the 1950s.

"Anything important I need to read in today's paper?" she joked, smiling at Jack who had the *Clarion* spread out in front of him and Walter. Walter was already marking things up with his pen—stories to follow up on, headlines he didn't like, and ideas for layout changes for the Tuesday issue.

Jack looked past Shania and could see that the three GES workers were looking across the room at him and Walter, while handing the newspaper back and forth, the front page obviously the object of their attention.

After much debate, Walter had convinced Jack that the *Clarion* should publish his photo each Friday, along with the column on the front page. "It's not like it's any secret that you work here, Jack. Christ, half the people in this town know you already—though you do look a lot older. Sorry. Let's say more mature. I bet when you wrote that business column in San Diego they had a photo of you."

Jack protested, arguing that he didn't want to become a media personality. "I don't need a date or any groupies," he said.

But Walter argued that the *Clarion* would benefit by making Jack, and his column, into icons, telling all about hydrofracking and its ills.

"And you know, one of these days a social date wouldn't hurt you either, Jack. For sure you need a woman to dress you. I swear that sports coat is the twin of the one you wore to basketball games when you were right out of college. It was out of style then, too."

Jack finally gave in and Eli, wearing his staff photographer hat, took a set of digital photos, offering Jack the opportunity to pick the mug shot he wanted to run on the header of his Friday columns.

Eli's work was impressive. By adjusting camera angles and lighting he had produced a dozen photos in which Jack thought he looked pretty good—a few years younger for sure. And Eli had even gotten Jack to smile for most of the shots.

"You know the high school kids here call the place the Village of Horseshits, don't you? What's that make them, huh?"

Jack was thinking about another joke Eli had told him—

something like nothing rhymes well with Horseheads—when he heard his name called as Shania finished pouring his tea. She turned and moved out of the way, giving him an unobstructed view of the three GES workers who were now standing by their counter stools, money in their hands as if to pay their bills.

"Do you get paid to write lies?" the shortest of the three workers asked in a loud voice while looking directly at Jack.

"DO YOU?" he asked, more loudly. His face was screwed up in a scowl and even from across the room, Jack could see that while he was short, he had broad shoulders and his hands were large and calloused.

Jack reached down for his teacup, looking away while he studied his copy of the *Clarion* on the table. Jack had spent too many hours in too many bars to not see that the GES worker was hoping to provoke something.

And if Jack made direct eye contact and stared back, the challenge would be on and there might even be a few fists thrown.

The GES worker strolled over, with a slightly rolling sailor's gait. He still held his bill and money in his hand, waiting for Jack to look up.

But just as Jack started to raise his eyes, Walter spoke up and made sure he spoke loudly enough for the whole diner to hear.

"I pay him," Walter said. "I pay him to write his opinions. I don't pay him nearly enough, by the way. But let's keep that a secret. Okay, um, Tom, is it? I see that on your company name tag."

The GES worker named Tom, who Jack could see

now wasn't much taller than 5 feet 5 inches, looked at his nametag as if he had forgotten it was there.

Oh God. And he probably has a Napoleon complex, too, Jack thought.

"Well, whatever," Tom said. "You pay him too much if you pay him anything. His story is total bullshit. Bullshit."

He turned around, mumbling to himself and his coworkers, and walked back towards the door, dropping his money on the counter next to the cash register.

The other GES workers grabbed their coats, dropping their copy of the *Clarion* on the floor by the register, stepping on it as they walked out the front door to their truck.

Once in the truck, they glared through the windshield, then sprayed gravel across the parking lot as they pulled out too fast into the intersection.

"I guess they won't be signing up for *Clarion* home delivery anytime soon," Jack said to Walter, whose hands were shaking slightly when he lifted his coffee mug.

"No, they won't. But the gas companies are bringing in goddamn thugs," Walter said. "We've had more crime in the county in the last two years than the last ten. Fights. Vandalism. Burglaries. That's stuff we just don't usually see around here."

Jack waved to Shania to bring more coffee and hot water. He put his hand on Walter's arm.

"Well, it might get worse. Your buddy was right. Did you see when they put their coats on? One of them had a small pistol strapped in a holster inside his coat.

"Definitely a *Column One* topic, Walter. 'Gas and guns don't mix,' right?"

That weekend, Jack thought, he would take a leisurely drive up to Seneca Lake to visit Oscar Wilson, one of Jack's oldest friends still living in the area. Instead it turned into a stay-at-home, stay-at-the-office session with stacks of research materials and hours on the Internet.

While the lake and Oscar's fast-growing Lakeside Winery north of Watkins Glen beckoned, a late-season snowstorm unceremoniously dumped twelve inches of snow over two days, iced over the roads, and generally made travel treacherous.

Jack had driven in snow when he was young, and then was reintroduced to it in Colorado. But his nearly twenty-year-old Nissan SUV had lived most of its life as a California highway car and its street tires were a little worn. He had visions of sliding off the highway and not even having proper gloves for his hands while he shoveled himself out of a snow bank.

Plus, Jack knew he needed to read up on hydrofracking and get some rest.

The local bars beckoned but he declared Saturday and Sunday as AFDs—Alcohol Free Days.

And now sitting at his desk late Sunday afternoon, Jack watched the snow blow by, the tail end of the storm that would probably become a front-page story in the Tuesday edition of the *Horseheads Clarion*. In the Northeast, the weather is always news.

Two days of reading, emails, and phone calls had filled Jack's notebooks to overflowing.

The *Clarion* office had an incredibly fast Internet connection and Jack had read reports from various environmental groups, as well as pro-hydrofracking outfits, scanning for column ideas, but he was still trying to get his mind wrapped around how the people had bought into this foul and dangerous gas extraction technology.

The corrupt federal government path connection between former Vice President Dick Cheney and Halliburton was as easy to see as a yellow line in the middle of a repaved highway. But what puzzled Jack was how easily government officials at all levels seem to embrace it, even after the pollution problems started showing up.

He made a mental note to himself: *check local campaign contributions.*

Pennsylvania was the poster child for lack of regulation and oversight in the Northeast. But a new report coming out of Texas stunned him.

The gas companies across the nation had long held that they would not reveal many, if not most, of the chemicals they put in the fracking fluids pumped into the ground as part of the process to extract the gas. In the million gallons or more per well, Jack knew there were many chemicals deemed toxic to humans and animals but kept secret thanks to the Halliburton Loophole.

When pressured by public and environmental groups, the companies said the names of these chemicals, and the amounts used, were trade secrets.

In Texas, he read, the trade secret rubric was claimed nearly 20,000 times the year before by companies, rendering any attempts to determine what was being pumped into the ground meaningless. But it made him think about Dimock, Pennsylvania and the sick children he had seen in photos.

Jack reread a report listing just of few of the chemicals and their effects on humans, along with some environmen-

talist commentary. He felt a headache coming on and started
to rethink his alcohol-free policy.

Earlier Sunday, Jack had gotten an email response from
a water specialist at a biochemical laboratory in New York
City. He had tried to get several Pennsylvania water-testing
labs to talk to him, but as soon as he identified himself
as a newspaper columnist, the labs said they would not
comment.

```
Mr. Stafford:
    I don't have much experi-
ence dealing with hydrofracking
chemicals but I can tell you
that it's a nightmare for any
testing labs. The gas companies
won't say what they are using,
and as you know, they are exempt
from most disclosure require-
ments. So when any lab tests,
it's like blind men trying to
describe an elephant. Even
the most thorough lab workup
will miss things. And a lot of
the compounds they use are in
such tiny concentrations, they
are virtually immeasurable.
But they are still dangerous
because they can accumulate.
Hope this helps. And Mr. Staf-
ford, please, DO NOT quote me
on any of this. Even though
```

```
we aren't actively involved
in the hydrofracking testing
business, we feel pressure.
    E. Thayer
    Water Technician II
```

Pressure from who? Jack wondered.

Jack thought back to his interview with Muriel Dogg and conversations with her two neighbors, all suffering from bladder cancer, cancers everyone except for the gas companies were quite sure were caused by the chemicals leaching from the fracked gas wells into the water, or from air pollution.

He dialed Walter's cell phone and left a message.

"Walter, this is Jack. I want to hold off on the guns and gas column idea for a while. It will keep. I just read this report out of Texas and I think I want to hit the toxic chemicals in fracking fluids Friday. And, no news to you, probably, but I just watched a truck drive by the office with Pennsylvania plates that is probably hauling fracking wastewater to somewhere around here. Water was leaking out onto the road and leaving puddles. We can talk tomorrow."

Jack powered down his computer and headed across the street to Millie's for a late afternoon lunch that would probably double as his dinner. With any luck Shania would be there to chat with and it wouldn't be too busy.

Walter had confirmed she was 24—still less than half his age—but she was easy to talk to.

Plus, there were no GES trucks parked out front, so a peaceful meal seemed likely.

Lindy Karlsen opened a bottle of Oscar's Boot, a wildly popular Riesling produced by Lakeside Winery on the east side of Seneca Lake, where Lindy worked as a self-described "wine wench," pouring tastings for tourists.

Her nickname at the winery was Mo, pronounced mau, short for Mouth because she was often argumentative with customers, so much so that winery owner Oscar Wilson would have fired her if she wasn't so popular with most of the locals, who treated his winery like a neighborhood tavern.

Plus, she was his niece.

And after she hurt her knee playing basketball at college in Buffalo and dropped out of school, Oscar hired her for the tasting room, knowing that it would make his younger sister very happy. Having a gorgeous nearly six foot tall, 22-year-old blonde behind the plank was also a good business move.

Lindy took a tiny taste of the Boot to make sure it was good, twirling it in the glass to check its "legs."

It was nearly 6 p.m.—closing time on a Sunday night—but with Boot selling for $39 a bottle, she had strict orders to make sure no tourist ever got a bad sip. There were only two people left tasting, a young couple from New York City who had braved the snowstorm that had kept most people away over the weekend.

She considered having a full glass of Boot for herself, but corked the bottle instead.

She heard the pickup truck coming into the parking lot off NY Route 414 fast and throwing gravel before she saw it. It told Lindy that either she had someone arriving who had already been tasting too much wine elsewhere on the Wine Trail, or some gasbags were coming in.

"Gasbags" was the nickname given to the roughnecks hired by the half-dozen natural gas exploration companies who had been sniffing around the area for several years, buying up leases in anticipation of using the technology known as hydrofracking to get at the natural gas-rich Marcellus and Utica shale formations thousands of feet below the fertile farmland used mostly for growing grapes.

The gasbags were working on several plots of land to the east, closer to Cayuga Lake, moving in trucks, tanks of toxic chemicals, compressors and big drilling rigs, while laying gas pipelines and building sludge ponds for what they expected to be a bonanza of natural gas, most of which would be eventually shipped off to China.

GES was already doing some drilling that company spokesmen had labeled "exploratory," which had most of the rural neighbors up in arms.

The week before, Lindy had refused to serve a trio of gasbags who came in filthy from their job site and reeking from beer they had already consumed, probably in the company truck on the way. They caused enough of a row after she refused to pour them wine that she pretended to call the Sheriff's Office. When they saw her calling, the three gasbags stormed out into the parking lot, stopping just long enough to urinate on a tourist's car tires before roaring out on the highway.

"Hello! Sorry! We're closing," she shouted as three men in Grand Energy Services' uniforms pushed in roughly through the glass doors. The young couple moved aside to let the men have a clear path directly to the center of the bar behind which Lindy stood.

"Tasting time is over. Sorry, boys," Lindy said, the smirk on her face offering just enough of a hint of defiance that the shortest man in the group made a big show of tapping his wristwatch, putting it six inches from Lindy's nose, his hand balled in a fist.

"You know, I paid a lot of fucking money for this watch. And you know what? It works great. And it's ten minutes before your closing time, sweetheart. Ten minutes. We'll have three glasses of that stuff by your hand."

The young couple from New York City who had been considering buying a bottle of Oscar's award-winning merlot and possibly some Boot as gifts instead waved goodbye as they headed for the door.

"We'll be back," they said, almost in unison, nearly tripping in their haste to get out.

Lindy squared her shoulders and waved back, knowing it would be futile to try to get the couple to stop. Her own heart was beating pretty fast, though the three men in front of her were actually not as big as the typical fleshy big gasbags she saw in the winery and around the village.

"Look, um, Tom is it?" Lindy said, making a big show of reading his nametag. "I don't make the rules here. But really, I can't be serving you right at closing time, and if you check that watch again, there are only a couple of minutes before I have to lock the door. Sorry. Really. Another time."

Lindy took the bottle of Boot off the bar and turned her back on the three men, ducking down to put the bottle in the bar cooler where all the tasting bottles were kept.

She silently congratulated herself on her diplomacy and was hoping to hear them shuffling towards the door. She fully expected to hear them swear at her a few times on their way out, of course. *Goddamn gasbags*, she thought.

But instead her heart skipped a tiny beat.

"Hey blondie. You're the bitch that threw my friends out last week, aren't you?"

E ven when he was in junior high school, people underestimated Oscar Wilson.

Teased because he was much bigger—including his girth—than all of his classmates, it was only a matter of time before he broke a few noses in schoolyard scuffles. The boys on the east side of Seneca Lake quickly learned that Oscar wasn't really fat at all.

He was strong, strong like Polynesians from Samoa or Tonga, where most of the men and women are the size of double-door Kenmore refrigerators.

Local legend has it that in high school a friend was pinned underneath a Volkswagen Beetle when a car jack slipped. Oscar lifted the front end of the car by himself so that his friend could be pulled to safety.

Later recountings of the tale had him lifting it with one hand. But Jack Stafford had witnessed it and it was definitely a two-handed hoist.

Oscar was in great demand around harvest time, too, as he could toss bales of hay all day and barely break into a sweat.

At this moment in the winery, a tired 55-year-old Oscar was sweating profusely in the back room, getting a shipment of two-dozen cases of wine ready for pickup when he heard Lindy shout.

"Oscar. Front please. NOW!"

Her voice gave off enough strain that Oscar grabbed a short steel pry bar he kept in the back room as he went through the double doors. Daytime robberies of wineries in the Finger Lakes were unheard of. But since the gas companies had started buying up leases and moving in equipment, there had been a rash of nasty vandalism and numerous barroom brawls in the seedier saloons in Watkins Glen, Horseheads, and Elmira to the south.

At home and in his pickup truck, Oscar now kept a baseball bat, calling it his Louisville Slugger security system. He made a mental note to put a bat behind the bar in the tasting room.

The three men at the tasting bar, all wearing Grand Energy Services uniforms, looked surprised when Oscar came out. It was difficult to tell if it was because of his 6 foot 4 inch height, his solid, if fleshy, build, the pry bar in his left hand—or that he was there at all.

"What's up Lindy? These guys want to buy some Boot? None out here?"

Oscar was about fifty feet from the three men when he looked at the pry bar in his hand as if he had forgotten it was there.

"Sorry! I was opening some crates in the back," he said, breaking into the big friendly smile for which he was known all around the Finger Lakes.

He didn't get any smiles back. The shortest of the men stared malevolently.

"I was just telling these boys here that we're closed," Lindy said. "It's 6 p.m., actually 6:02 now. Ha, look at that. This guy Tom has a great watch, Oscar. You should look it at it. Really cool. But what's really amazing is how well he can tell time."

Oscar closed his eyes for fraction of a second as he gripped the pry bar a little tighter. Then he glared at Lindy for an instant before he spoke. He wondered what in the name of God had happened before he came out.

"Um, gentlemen, I'm afraid you'll have to come back tomorrow for a tasting or to buy a glass or bottle. Can't do anything after 6 p.m. except lock the doors. Sorry about that."

And for a minute, it looked like that was it.

Tom smiled, looking at his watch for a moment as carefully as a child learning to tell time.

He even gave a forced smile in Lindy's direction, the kind of smile a fraternity boy makes that's really more sneer than smile.

But as the three men sauntered to the double doors, they stopped while Tom turned and came back, walking up to Lindy at the bar.

He spit directly in her face, leaving a big dripping goober of snot on her left cheek.

He turned immediately towards a stunned Oscar, holding up his hands high in the air like a suspect in front of a cop, backing away from the bar and moving very quickly. He walked backwards towards the doors where the other two men were already outside and moving quickly to their truck.

"You gonna hit me with that bar for spitting?" he jeered. "You'll go to jail for that. I promise."

Lindy held up her hand towards Oscar before Oscar could move.

"Let the little pissant and his gay friends go, Oscar. He's right. You don't need it. I just wish I had served him some wine. His spit smells like he gargles with skunk piss."

Jack had forgotten the pace of a short-staffed newsroom.

Monday was a crazy day, with Jack having to help out with everything from writing to editing to page layout for the Tuesday issue.

The Tuesday paper had to be sent electronically to the printer by 5 p.m. on Monday and so it was a scramble to get the storm covered, the regular news, and a short item about a GES truck that had exploded and burned over the weekend.

A friend of Walter's in the fire department in Rockwell Valley said it might be arson. But the company said it had been caused by a gasoline leak.

"Sounds plausible, doesn't it?" Walter asked. "Except that I am pretty sure most of the GES trucks run on propane."

And when Jack came up for air Wednesday, it was time to pen his next column and answer emails from his friends at Seneca Lake who had discovered he was back in the area.

A newspaper column with your photo running with it makes it hard to hide.

And it was time to see longtime friend Oscar Wilson. When Jack, Oscar, and a local fellow named Butch Boison were teenagers, they had gotten into enough trouble that the local police called them the Unholy Three. Sometimes the cops also called them the Three Stooges. Butch had a slight stutter that made him the target of bullies—before he grew into a gangly six-foot frame and filled out to 200-plus pounds. Plus, it wasn't a stretch even for low-I.Q. teenagers to figure out Boison rhymed with poison.

Butch might have had a stutter, but even as a skinny kid he won the lion's share of fights, and the bullies stopped teasing him.

Oscar now had a successful winery. Butch still drove a tow truck for pulling big rigs out of trouble. Both men wanted him to come up to the lake as soon as he could get away for a little reunion.

It was certainly on Jack's agenda. But he was waffling about his column for Friday.

He had thought about a column detailing the known toxic chemicals in hydrofracking fluids and spent time amassing basic information. But the fact that the government allowed companies to pump poison into the ground—much of which remained there—and let them take what poisoned water they recovered to ill-equipped water treatment plants was unfathomable.

"Even most dogs know better than to shit in their own back yard," he had told Shania at the diner.

Walter had shown him a file that intrigued him—a file full of incidents that Walter thought were part of a loosely organized effort to annoy the gas companies with pranks. But when Jack read the file—and some of the things Walter called pranks, he wondered if Walter was right about a war of sorts in the offing.

"What's on for Friday, Jack?" Walter called from across the newsroom. "I have two dozen letters to the editor about your column from last week that I'm trying to figure out how to squeeze onto the editorial page," he continued. "Maybe

I'll run them all on the web and put two or three in print."
One of the letters was on the official letterhead of Grand
Energy Services from a vice president in charge of chemical
safety.

It read, in part:

> The lack of documentation in
> Friday's front-page column
> by Mr. Stafford is appalling
> and beneath the standards of
> even an unprofessional tabloid
> newspaper like the Clarion.
> Exploiting the widow of a
> valued GES employee is a new
> low, even for your newspaper.
> Shame on you.

Jack looked at the papers scattered about his desk and
decided perhaps it was time to give the alleged Monkey
Wrenchers a little ink to stir things up.

"I'm going to exploit Edward Abbey this week, Walter.
I'll have something to show you in a couple of hours."

Walter stood up straight, smiled and gave a fist-pump in
the air as he turned back to walk into his office. "Shame on
us, Jack. Just shame on us. Ha!"

From the *Horseheads Clarion*

Column One
The Horseheads Clarion

Sometimes life does imitate art

By Jack Stafford

ROCKWELL VALLEY, Pennsylvania — Grand Energy Services is dismissing a series of recent destructive incidents as simple pranks, played by either miscreant teenagers or in some cases disgruntled former (or current?) GES employees.

Some of incidents can reasonably be labeled as pranks. For the most part, GES has been reluctant to officially report them to authorities at all, perhaps afraid that it might inspire copycats.

On the prank side, there have been a lot of broken windows at various GES offices and air let out of tires on GES vehicles and vehicles owned by employees.

But some of the things labeled as pranks are getting expensive.

Four gasoline-powered GES trucks in the last three months

have had sand or sugar poured into their gasoline tanks, their door locks filled with some kind of superglue adhesive, and in three cases, electric control panels at natural gas wells were covered with spray paint so the company had to shut the wells down.

The control panel spray-painting stunt required fire departments to stand by in case of a fracking fluid spill or the unplanned release of natural gas.

Once hydrofracked, the wells mostly operate automatically, requiring minimal supervision. But without being able to read the gauges, the operators were flying nearly blind.

In all three cases, the wells were shut down without incident, GES says, though the expensive control panels and electrical systems are in the process of being replaced.

How expensive? GES won't say.

These are all criminal acts, but mostly well inside the misdemeanor range, according to Pennsylvania police and sheriff's deputies.

The same goes for New York

where GES has had similar problems with its operations near Cayuga Lake. In New York though, someone managed to steal a GES service pickup and drive it down a hillside and into the lake. The water ruined the truck engine and expensive electronic monitoring equipment.

All of these—except for maybe the truck-in-the-lake—are nasty, but still might be considered petty and easily dismissed.

But GES is not the only natural gas developer/provider having trouble. Other gas companies in Texas, Colorado, Ohio and Michigan are quietly stepping up security, too.

Very quietly.

If any of this sounds vaguely familiar, it could be because you might have read a classic novel published in 1975 called *The Monkey Wrench Gang*. It was the work of the late Edward Abbey and was a wild, fanciful tale about how a small group of people upset with the mining industry in the southwestern United States started pulling pranks to show their pique. Those fictional pranks helped launch the very real eco-terrorism movement in the United States.

"Pranks" included sand in fuel tanks of bulldozers as well as other attacks on industrial equipment. The characters in the book got more serious as the book developed—including blowing a few things up.

Remember, this was a novel, a work of fiction, though it inspired the formation of an environmental group called Earth First. And the people who put Earth First together shared a value with today's anti-fracking protesters: They didn't trust the government to do the right thing.

Check out the signs at any anti-hydrofracking protest if you don't believe me.

I am not trying to draw a straight line from *The Monkey Wrench Gang* to the woes of GES today. Even a novelist would hesitate to suggest there was a shadowy Monkey Wrench Gang "cell" sitting around in basements reading *The Monkey Wrench Gang* excerpts, plotting some guerrilla assault against an industrial gas company enemy.

But real life is sometimes stranger than fiction, such as in early January when this newspaper received this cryptic note, printed in its entirety here:

We have had enough. People are dying because of the greed of the gas companies. The environment is being destroyed. Enough. Enough. Enough. We are going to fight back.
   MWG

Yes, police were notified back in January. No, there have not been any more notes.
   Because *The Monkey Wrench Gang* was just a novel, after all. Remember?

Jack Stafford is an investigative columnist and reporter for the Horseheads Clarion and has worked as an investigative reporter for metropolitan newspapers in California and Colorado.

The first phone call Friday morning to Jack came from Devon Walsh in Colorado, the environmental activist who had gotten him hooked on writing about hydrofracking and the entire natural gas imbroglio in the first place.

Computer wizard Eli had loaded the last of the stories on the website late the night before, about half of them copy-protected unless a person had a subscription.

Jack's column, however, was going online in its full glory, free for anyone to read since Walter wanted to use it to build subscriptions as well as promote the column in general.

Jack was pleased Devon was calling. Though there had been no hint of romance when they had shared drinks and notes in Colorado, she was smart in a confident way without being arrogant, easy to talk to, and he liked her dedication to a cause.

She reminded him a little of his late wife, something about the way she gently touched his arm when she wanted to make a point—and to make sure he was paying complete attention.

She was dark-haired, attractive in a very wholesome way, and tall. She had gone to college on a volleyball scholarship and done two seasons with the rowing team.

As Jack researched hydrofracking, they met often, meetings Jack realized he looked forward to, just like when he found excuses to email Devon or call.

When he said he was moving to New York to the job with Walter and the *Horseheads Clarion*, her disappointment was hard to miss. But they had parted on good terms, with Devon offering she would likely be coming through upstate New York sometime in the summer.

"Wow. That was some column today," Devon said. "I mean, last week's was good, too. But Jesus, Jack, have you been keeping track of what's been happening in Missouri?"

Jack had to rumble through the back of his brain to remember that Grand Energy Services corporate offices were in Missouri, somewhere near a gaggle of other natural gas exploration firms.

In all of his researching the week before, he hadn't noticed anything coming out of the GES main offices other than the normal corporate PR drivel.

"What did I miss? And by the way, it's great to hear your voice, Devon, really."

Jack looked across the room and saw Walter cock his eyebrow.

"So, tell me. Does the Monkey Wrench Gang have a chapter in Missouri?" Jack asked.

Jack started tapping on his computer keyboard while Devon told him about an incident at the GES corporate offices the week before. No note was left to take credit but it was nasty.

"GES kept it out of the local newspapers and the TV stations didn't have any film, so it was kind of non-news for them," Devon said. "But there is an anti-fracking website that was started about a year ago that has GES in its sights. Have you seen it? They have the basics of what happened. Read it and call me back, OK? Oops, got another call. Ciao."

Devon hung up before Jack could get the full name or actual Internet address for the website and so it took him more than a few minutes, even with Eli's help, to find the website, which turned out to be appropriately titled *Monkeying with Hydrofrackers.*

How the hell did I miss that over the weekend? Jack wondered.

MONKEYING WITH HYDROFRACKERS

FLATHEAD, MO — A top GES vice president was burned early this week in the restroom of the executive suite at GES headquarters in Flathead, Missouri.

When he went to wash his hands, presumably after using the toilet, he pushed the soap dispenser and used the granulated soap in it to wash his hands.

The problem was the granulated soap was not soap.

The VP was rushed by paramedics to Flathead General Hospital, where eyewitnesses said his hands looked like they were bleeding through the thick bandages placed by the paramedics who responded to a 911 call at the offices. He was taken by ambulance to the hospital.

An anonymous caller to the hospital the next day told a nurse that the burns came from a mixture of well-known drain cleaner and regular granulated soap.

Police say they are investigating.

Jack reread the piece twice, then forwarded the link to Walter before calling Devon back.

He saw Walter check his email, then follow the link, then look out of his office to Jack, his face of mixture of disbelief and sadness.

Jack simply nodded his head and decided that tonight he would drive up the lake to see Oscar and some of the old gang. The snow had all melted and he needed to be around some friends. It was definitely not going to be an alcohol free day.

Devon picked up on the first ring when he called back.

"Hey Devon, thanks for the depressing story. But really, thanks. Is there more to all this?"

He could hear Devon take in a short breath before she answered.

"Oh yes. You have no idea how much, Jack. No idea."

"So you are telling me that you want to bring this Devon Walsh here to Horseheads. Put her on our staff to help you?" Walter asked, his hands laced on top of his head as though he was trying to keep his skull from exploding.

"Jack, really. How many weeks are you into this adventure with me?"

Monday morning production was well underway and Walter looked more than a little harassed.

Jack shifted slightly in the chair in Walter's office.

"That's it, Walter. Exactly. I'm over my head, doing this alone. I can write good columns about local stuff. Eli is a great researcher to help. But really, this story is national. Christ, it's international. And that's the problem. That's why nobody gets it. That's how these companies are getting away with all of polluting and dumping and the other shit. Sorry. But no one news organization is painting a big picture. Earthquakes here, sick kids there, some dead livestock. All little stories that the gas companies can dismiss."

Walter sighed.

"And you think we can do that here? Be the big dog. Really?"

"Yes, we can," Jack said. "But I really need Devon Walsh. She's got the connections, the science, and some great ideas, Walter. Really."

It was late Tuesday before Jack and Walter sorted out what a Jack Stafford-Devon Walsh reporter-research team might look like.

So when Jack called Devon back Wednesday, they talked for nearly two hours non-stop. Devon had started tracking incidents of vandalism across the country—and more serious anti-gas company activities—and thought she saw a lot more than just isolated people getting frustrated.

She said she wasn't ready to say aloud there was a national coordination of these incidents. But clearly something was going on when you studied reports from virtually every state where hydrofracking was in use.

"The vandalism looks similar, which might mean that vandals aren't very creative," Devon said. "Or it could mean that someone is giving some advice on how to monkey-wrench. In Colorado, the sugar they are finding in the gas tanks of gas trucks? Police said it's unrefined raw sugar crystals. Think about it, Jack. Organic vandals. That might make you a whole column. That could even be funny. Or sort of funny."

And when it came to stories about dumping toxic chemicals, people getting sick, and real estate becoming worthless due to gas wells in the area, there were occasional stories in small town newspapers but no big bangs to get national attention.

"You're also describing the problem of media in general," Jack said. "You can say most of those same things about politics or education or anything. Mass media has become the Internet. And it might be because I am getting cynical, but I wonder how much people believe, or even care."

Before they hung up, Devon and Jack agreed. The *Horseheads Clarion* website could become a voice of reason, collect stories, and get the word out nationally, provided Walter would agree. It was a shift from a local newspaper and website perspective to one that would challenge an industry that had billions of dollars at its disposal.

"You and Walter could put out the number one fracking newspaper and news source in the country, Jack. Really."

Jack hung up, excited and wondering if it was because of what Devon had said or because she might be coming to New York.

He had barely broken the connection and shook away that thought when Walter plopped into the chair by Jack's desk.

"So Jack, let me ask you…" Walter said.

But before Walter could get out a question, Jack raised his hand.

"If it's about her credentials, they are great. Science degrees from Berkeley. She taught there, too. Worked for a San Francisco magazine writing mostly environmental stuff. Now she works with a clean water and clean air foundation in Colorado. That's what got her involved with the hydrofracking. But she told me she thinks she might be able to connect the dots on people doing stuff like that caustic-cleaner business at GES headquarters."

Walter shuffled some papers on his desk and leaned back.

"Get her on the phone, I want to talk to her. After that, let's talk again. I stretched a little to bring you here, but what-the-hell."

Jack grinned and suggested that instead of a phone call, they use Skype so they could all three talk face-to-face.

"You're telling me she's good-looking too, Jack? Oh God. Here we go. But let's make it Friday. We've a paper to put out. Okay?"

Jack saluted and headed back out into the newsroom to help write some headlines and edit a story about a GES company car that was found floating in a farmer's pond the night before.

The Skype conference call went on for more than an hour behind the closed door of Walter's glass office, using Walter's new 27-inch screen Apple McIntosh computer on their end.

Devon chatted from her home on her computer in Colorado but without video for the first fifteen minutes.

In their enthusiasm, Jack and Walter had overlooked that it was only 7 a.m. in Colorado and Devon needed at least one cup of industrial strength coffee to get her moving in the morning.

When they called, her coffee pot was just starting to brew. And she said she couldn't talk politics in her nightshirt.

Jack could see that Walter was impressed right away. By the time they broke the Skype connection, Walter said he would talk more with Jack. But Jack knew that Walter would agree to bring Devon on as a consultant to the newspaper.

"Devon Walsh? You know her?" Eli asked when Jack told him whom they had talked with. "She's pretty famous. She might come here? Woo-hoo!"

Jack and Walter had chatted briefly after the Skype call and Walter said he would call Devon back later in the day, offering her a six-month contract to be a special projects editor at the newspaper. And she would start as soon as she could wiggle loose of her Colorado duties.

Eli and Jack sketched out some research that Jack knew Devon would want right away about incidents of vandalism at gas companies and hydrofracking sites. Jack also set Eli to researching New York State gun laws for a future column about GES workers carrying weapons.

He also made a note to himself to call the GES headquarters about the caustic chemicals-in-the-soap dispenser incident, maybe to tie into the same piece.

If someone was trying to hurt people, having GES workers carry guns to protect themselves might not be as crazy as it seemed at first.

And then there was still that Delbert Dogg shooting.

Jack made another note to call the police. It had been more than four months since Dogg was found dead. The police had a theory. Jack just needed to get it out of them.

He looked across the street to Millie's where the parking lot was emptying out as the breakfast crowd left, the lull before people starting showing up for lunch at about 11:30

a.m. A cup of Millie's tea served by Shania was in order, as was more planning.

Jack knew that Shania lived with her mother in an old four-bedroom house not too far from the center of town and the newspaper. She might be willing to rent a room to Devon while Devon looked for a more permanent place for six months.

Jack's own house had plenty of space. But if they would be working together, he didn't think it would be a good idea to move Devon in, even temporarily.

Walter had been right when he said Jack could use some female companionship. But Jack also knew that the loneliness that filled him in quiet moments meant he was likely to fall hard for any female between 18 and 80 who showed him an ounce of compassion.

And Walter was right about Devon. On top of being smart, quick-witted, funny, and cute, she had a big heart, and not just for environmental causes.

And people with big hearts like that are compassionate, Jack thought.

When Devon arrived two weeks later, her Toyota sedan was filled with file boxes and her 6-year-old Labrador Retriever named Belle.

Jack had punched out two Friday columns while waiting for her to make her way east, and had Devon all set to bunk in the house with Shania and her mother. Both women were pleased to have her, plus the money would help Shania with her community college tuition and costs.

Devon told Jack if she had any time at all, she would help tutor Shania if she wanted it.

Jack's column about an overturned truck and fracking fluid spill on the state highway only two miles from the home of Muriel Dogg in Rockwell Valley drew another round of expected criticism from the top management of Grand Energy Services.

Walter's headline on Jack's column was "Toxic—and tipsy—truck travel."

> The GES truck driver told the state highway patrol officer who responded that the water his unit was leaking all over the highway was sparkly clean and on its way to another hydrofracking gas site, where it would be mixed with chemicals and used to frack a new well.
>
> Sounds reasonable, except it wasn't true.
>
> The highway patrol officer got suspicious when the truck driver insisted on taking the time to put on special heavy-duty chemical-resistant boots before walking through the puddles caused by the rapidly leaking truck.
>
> GES declined to comment on the spill or that the driver was cited for driving under the influence, saying that to do so would be "premature."

GES was eventually cited by the highway patrol for illegal dumping on the highway, and Pennsylvania state environmental regulators were threatening to cite the company because at least 500 gallons of the toxic fracking wastewater had run into a roadside ditch and then down to Little Rockwell Creek, where several hundred fish went belly-up within hours.

But on top of that column, the company was still smarting over Jack's repeated phone calls to the main corporate offices to get more details about the men's washroom incident.

The GES official position was that a privately-contracted janitor (not a GES employee) had made a mistake and accidentally put some caustic cleaner in the soap dispenser.

There was no attack on GES, just human error, a spokesman wrote in a press release and in letters to the editors of newspapers.

Jack had failed in attempts to talk with the vice president who had been hospitalized overnight with second-degree burns on his palms.

The VP worked in the finance department and had no real connection to the operations side of hydrofracking, so the attack that GES said was not-an-attack was likely just some monkey-wrenching of a serious kind, Jack thought.

GES declined to comment when Jack asked them about the company policy allowing employees to be armed on the job.

But local Second Amendment Rights groups got wind of the column—probably from GES—and wrote and telephoned in big numbers, implying that Jack was a liberal gun-control proponent.

Walter said not to worry.

"They've been after me for years, claiming I support the government taking away their guns," Walter said. "Half of these wing nuts probably shouldn't be allowed to own guns, but they are just as likely to shoot themselves in the foot as shoot someone else."

Jack hoped he was right.

From the *Horseheads Clarion*

Column One
The Horseheads Clarion

Guns and natural gas don't mix

By Jack Stafford

Guns and natural gas just don't mix.

I'm not talking about the natural gas you might use to cook and heat your home. I'm talking about a recent confidential memo from the Grand Energy Services' main corporate office that says it's all right for GES employees nationwide to pack a pistol with their lunch when they leave the house in the morning.

That's a feeble attempt at humor.

But there is nothing funny

about encouraging the hundreds of GES employees in New York—plus thousands more just across the border in Pennsylvania—to carry a gun. The men working on gas drilling rigs, driving hydrofracking fluid tanker trucks, or even sitting in control rooms running computers frankly don't need to play Dirty Harry.

It's a recipe for disaster.

Two things might have prompted GES to tell employees that carrying a weapon to work—and keeping it on them while working—was okay.

The first is the ongoing and escalating vandalism incidents around the area.

While GES is downplaying the incidents, someone has been busy, though little of the activity seemed to be directed at people. The vandalism has been crimes against property. This newspaper has detailed what's going on, and we don't need to repeat it all here, not now.

The operant word is "was" crimes against property.

That changed earlier this month when a vice president at GES corporate headquarters went to wash his hands in the men's room. Instead of getting a handful of soap at the sink, the dispenser plunked some unknown caustic agent on his palms that reacted with the water on his already wet hands.

He ended up in the hospital with painful second-degree burns. He is still out of work.

This incident has officially been labeled by GES as merely an accident caused by a janitor who mixed up some containers.

That is one possibility.

The other is that someone angry at GES for hydrofracking, the toxic chemical spills, and any one of the litany of woes frequently recited by opponents of the use of hydrofracking technology, has ramped up tactics from slashing tires to going after people.

That might seem almost like an argument in favor of having GES staff carry guns.

Absolutely not.

Encouraging people working on drilling rigs or driving trucks to carry loaded weapons will most likely end in tragedy. Some GES employee, for example, could decide that an unarmed, peaceful protester at a GES drill site poses a threat. In the waving of a loaded pistol to chase them off, the odds are in favor of a bad result.

The county sheriff's department has asked GES to reconsider its memo, though the department says if the guns are properly documented and the men carrying them have proper permits, it's legal.

Legal? Maybe.

Smart? God no!

The GES VP whose hands were burned would not have been spared his pain by executing a quick-draw maneuver in that men's room in Flathead, Missouri.

If GES is really concerned about worker safety, a much more reasonable approach would be to hire additional security guards to patrol. Right now, the company has approximately 100 private security guards watching out for more than a thousand natural gas wells spread over hundreds of miles, along with supposedly protecting thousands of GES employees and the company's trucks and equipment, valued in the millions of dollars.

GES employees should leave

their guns at home and let
police and paid security staff
do their jobs.
 Guns and gas just don't mix.

*Jack Stafford is an investi-
gative columnist and reporter
for* The Horseheads Clarion *and
has worked as an investigative reporter for metropolitan
newspapers in California and
Colorado.*

In Devon's first hour in the office she had already drawn up a list of stories that needed heavy researching, posted a graphic matrix of column and story ideas on the wall of the conference room across from Walter's pin-filled map, and had computer whiz/photographer Eli following her around the newsroom like an overgrown puppy, refilling her coffee mug like a waiter.

"Eli, thanks for the help but I think Walter and Jack need you sitting at the computer over there. When we get together for a strategy meeting at noon, we're going to need some of that research in front of us," Devon said.

Eli looked slightly hurt, but sprang back over to his computer to start researching about reported earthquakes and their connection to hydrofracking for natural gas. He also had marching orders to get information on gas leases.

Devon had slipped into the office that morning just after Jack and Walter had wandered across the street to Millie's for their daily chat out of the office. She figured that she could become part of that klatch if she wanted, but it seemed like Walter and Jack might need the time for just the two of them.

Her degrees in physics and environmental preservation had given Devon great organizational skills. And getting a good handle on the damage being done by hydrofracking for natural gas across the country was going to take all of her skills, she knew. While her science was her strength, her ability to comprehend politics was not nearly as well developed.

That was probably why she thought working with Jack would work so well. He could watch a dozen people in a meeting and predict what was likely to happen within a few minutes. She usually had to watch an entire debate and then check the vote to find out the outcome.

And so as she drew up the research ideas and her matrix, it seemed natural for her to chase the science and environmental side of hydrofracking while Jack could go after the politics and the human impacts.

Devon thought that Walter's idea to have Jack use his column as a reporting war club was brilliant. Most major newspapers—and politicians—cowered when the big gas companies threatened. How long Walter would stand up to it, and how much influence the *Horseheads Clarion* could muster, was a big question.

"Um, Devon," Eli called out from his terminal across the room. "Are you sure Jack is going to want all this data on gas leases? He doesn't really like to sort through stuff like this. He can. But I think he would rather have someone else do it."

Devon gave Eli a big smile and he smiled back. But then he realized that her smile was because she wanted Eli to dig through the records and do a summary. What she hoped to find was anyone elected or appointed to a government post with a gas lease on his or her property. It was the start of a long process at finding out how much corruption existed at the local level.

And she was sure that as they moved up the ladder through the state and perhaps even nationally, they would find an astonishing web of conflicts of interest. Some reporting had been done on it already, but like most hydrofracking stories, scattered and never with big impact.

New York State law was murky at best on conflicts of interest—all the more reason, she thought, for the *Clarion* to shed some light on who might be voting in favor of fracking, hoping for a big payday if New York's governor caved in to pressure and allowed it. So far, he was holding firm and asking every month for more study, more data.

"Eli, I know you probably already know this, but some of these gas leases might be in the names of husbands or wives, and not just the elected people. Better check spouses, too."

Eli waved his hand to acknowledge but was intent on his screen, moving the mouse around as fast as a computer gamer, which he was.

Devon looked out the window across the street to Millie's, where she saw Jack and Walter step lively to avoid a fast moving GES truck that swerved dangerously close to the two of them as they stood on the edge of the sidewalk.

She saw the driver give Jack and Walter the one-finger salute as he drove off, the truck moving way too fast for the crowded main street.

"Eli, how hard would it be to build a database of local GES employees?"

Jack was so involved with researching for columns about politics and natural gas-related money (and corruption) that he had almost forgotten about the monkey- wrenching activities that had become nearly daily occurrences out there in what he and Devon had started calling Frackland.

But Devon's linear mind, with her excellent record-keeping skills, was hard at work putting together lists of incidents from Pennsylvania and New York, rating them on a sort of fracking Richter scale.

Within just weeks of her arriving, she had already documented that Grand Energy Services had nearly a fourth of its trucks taken out of service because of vandalism or theft.

In one particularly daring incident, a two-month old, $85,000 Audi belonging to a GES executive was stolen from the parking lot of GES headquarters in Flathead Missouri.

Police found the car three days later near Chicago with an 8" by 11" manila envelope taped to the steering wheel with a binder inside. GES officials asked the police to keep the contents of the binder confidential. But the officer who found the car had looked at it and already told his wife that it was some kind of manifesto from a group demanding a stop to some new gas drilling technique called hydrofracking.

His wife told her best friend, who in turn told her sister, whose husband was a producer for a small-market suburban Chicago television station.

Eli had seen an online-posted video of the television station's brief report via Facebook, and forwarded it for Jack, Devon, and Walter to watch.

"I don't think the *Clarion* is going to have a lot of clout with the Chicago PD, but let's call and see if we can get a look at what they wrote," Walter said. "This might be what you're looking for Devon… not just locals. Audis are way-overpriced, by the way."

The puzzling thing for Devon was why this group of monkey-wrenchers would use something as low-tech as paper to get their message out—and leave it in a car stolen from the very bastards they were trying to topple.

"It just doesn't make much sense, really," she said. "I mean, come on, the Internet? Arab Spring? Cell phones. Twitter. Good grief. We have organic vandals in New York using an unrefined sugar to wreck trucks. Now the Luddites print their demands out on paper instead of blasting it across the Net? This is weird."

Devon, Jack, Walter and Eli had started having daily meetings for a half-hour, sometimes longer, to talk about hydrofracking coverage. Walter insisted that they had a lot more to publish in the newspaper and thought the one-topic sessions could actually keep fracking from overwhelming the rest of the newspaper.

Jack frowned at the Luddite comment. He didn't think the people trying to stop hydrofracking opposed technology at all, just this Frankenstein-like example. And he was no fan of vandalism. But he had to admit a grudging admiration for the continued harassment of GES. It was taking its toll, if the mood of the GES people having breakfast at Millie's was an indication. Plus, the price of natural gas was plummeting. Some gas companies were already saying they were going to cut back on new wells and shut down some others.

Overproduction was the problem. But no company wanted to slow down because they all had their eye on selling the natural gas to Asian markets.

One dirty financial not-so-secret secret Devon uncovered was that gas companies were selling investors on hydro-fracking using gas production figures from the first few days or weeks of well operations.

"But after that, they don't put out near the volume. I mean, they're dropping by 40, 50, 60 percent or more," she said. "All the projections about the gas bonanza are probably crap. One Wall Street investment house is telling people to get out of natural gas stocks now. They see a crash coming, like housing."

Eli had brought in his personal laptop and, as usual, was tapping on the keys while they chatted in the meeting. It irritated Walter, but frequently Eli could answer their questions in a few keystrokes without having to run back out to the computer on his desk.

Walter liked to point out that when the late Steve Jobs ran Apple Computer, he wouldn't allow computers in the conference room, preferring instead to use a white board and colored pens when brainstorming.

"But Steve Jobs didn't run a newspaper either, Walter," Jack said. "We go to Millie's to brainstorm, right?"

Eli's daily and often nightly Internet scanning was providing all the data that Devon and Jack could handle—too much in most cases. Narrowing things down to digest-ible, understandable news bites was hard, even for a data cruncher like Devon.

Still, the big picture that they had set out to find was becoming clear. And it was one ugly panorama of greed, incompetence, lack of compassion, ultra-toxic pollution, and indifference to the environmental damage caused by hydrofracking and its associated activities.

As they wrapped up their meeting, Walter asked Eli to

start poking around about the Audi theft to see if he could come up with some theories about who the people might be who stole the car from GES.

"Troll those crazy websites you always try to show me, okay?" Walter said.

Eli nodded his head and flipped his computer around for Walter to see as they started to leave.

"This popped up while we were talking."

MONKEYING WITH HYDROFRACKERS

FLATHEAD, MO — It seems even our monkey-wrenching heroes have a heart when it comes to destroying pretty things.

Chicago Police found a brand-new and very expensive stolen Audi belonging to a Grand Energy Services VP safely parked on a suburban street with a note taped on the steering wheel.

(Note, this is NOT the car that was owned by the VP who washed his hands with the caustic powder and ended up in the hospital.)

A local TV station labeled the note a "manifesto" from a group demanding that gas companies quit hydrofracking.

The manifesto is being kept confidential by police as evidence, but someone did get

```
a peek at the document and told
us the document was signed
"Wolverines."
     Several news organizations
are demanding that the docu-
ment be released immediately
and are threatening to sue the
police to make them release it.
```

"Wolverines?" Walter asked no one in particular. "Wolverines?"

Jack closed his eyes and then asked Eli to keep searching for other references to the manifesto and to also cross-reference the name Wolverines with Devon's reports on monkeywrenching incidents.

"Life imitates art, remember?" Jack said, looking at a very puzzled Walter. "Think about it, Walter. It will come to you."

RED DAWN

From the *Horseheads Clarion*

Column One
The Horseheads Clarion

The need to hide under the covers

By Jack Stafford

HORSEHEADS, New York — If you think reading the news can be depressing, consider what the people who compile it for you go through.

In recent months, the *Horseheads Clarion* has been struggling to provide you with the best and most accurate information about hydrofracking for natural gas from all standpoints: economic, social, political, and environmental.

At the same time, the

Clarion has also been keeping up with arguably normal news, the births, deaths, triumphs, and tragedies of the community, region, state, and nation.

And sometimes the *Clarion* covers the world, too, like last week's story about earthquakes in the United Kingdom caused by hydrofracking.

Taken in total, it's enough to make most people want to go back to bed and pull the covers up over their heads. I know this because sometime in the last week, that's exactly how I felt after researching some of the latest incidents of Pennsylvania water wells being poisoned by hydrofracking fluid. Add to that the release of the official police report about the shooting death of Grand Energy Services' employee Delbert Dogg near Rockwell Valley.

The well poisonings—which GES continues to claim have absolutely nothing to do with their nearby injection of millions of gallons of toxic fracking fluid into the rock strata—are blamed for killing nearly all the animals (including several family pets) at a 75-acre farm only three miles as the crow flies from the home of the late Mr. Dogg.

The family that owns the farm fared better as they don't drink the well water. It's only for the animals now. But the family's 4-year-old daughter is in the hospital with a painful bright red rash over her entire body, a rash doctors say is consistent with chemical poisoning. But because they don't know what chemical contaminant —or contaminants— might be in the water in which the child has been bathing, they are having trouble coming up with a proper treatment.

Thanks to Pennsylvania's gag law about such things, the doctors are reluctant to talk about the child's skin rash and likely poisoning —even to her parents.

Ready to go back to bed and pull the covers up over your head yet?

Here's more.

The official law enforcement report about the death of GES employee Delbert Dogg says what people have suspected for months—he was murdered. The report says he caught a bullet in the shoulder, probably from a distance of 100 yards or more. But the second bullet went straight through his forehead and was fired at closer range, maybe as close as 100 feet.

And both bullets came from high caliber rifles.

Yes, rifles. Plural.

In comparing the bullet they dug out of Mr. Dogg's shoulder to one they found later in the ground, sheriff's deputies discovered that there were two high caliber rifles involved.

It was snowing most of the day before Mr. Dogg's body was found by a GES worker after he failed to check in with the main office. But there were enough tracks in the snow to indicate that at least two people had been near the site where he was shot and killed. Maybe several.

Authorities used the word assassination in the report.

If there is any link between this shooting and the vandalism (and various other attacks) on GES equipment, no one is saying anything publicly about it.

But by all accounts Delbert

Dogg had no enemies, lots of friends, and was doing his best to care for his wife Muriel, herself a self-described victim of the ongoing gas well exploration and pollution around her house.

Mrs. Dogg took a turn for the worse this week and has been moved to the Rockwell Valley Hospital intensive care unit because of complications from her bladder cancer.

One of her two neighbors—also diagnosed with bladder cancer—died last week on the day Mrs. Dogg entered the hospital.

Now you can go back to bed and pull the covers up over your head.

Jack Stafford is an investigative columnist and reporter for The Horseheads Clarion *and has worked as an investigative reporter for metropolitan newspapers in California and Colorado.*

Oscar Wilson went back behind the bar at Lakeside Winery to grab another bottle of his best Riesling.

The small group that had just watched the 1984 film version of *Red Dawn* on Oscar's new 60-inch flat screen television was silent, reflecting individually on the Reagan-era film—labeled as jingoist nonsense by most critics—that had later become a cult classic.

The 2012 remake of the film was so bad and so unbelievable Oscar could barely watch the trailers for it, and had turned down offers to even take a peek at pirated copies of the movie.

Oscar had gotten a call from his childhood friend Jack Stafford the day before, asking if Oscar still had a copy of *Red Dawn* handy for viewing, or if not, could he and a small group of people from the *Horseheads Clarion* come by after hours Friday night and run the movie off Jack's laptop through an online movie-viewing program?

"Of course, amigo," Oscar said on the phone. "I got your email when you first got back. Which by the way, was months ago. I've been waiting for you to break loose and come up and visit. But I see your byline and columns all the time. Giving them hell, of course. Still a workaholic, but never an alcoholic, right?"

Jack laughed at the joke they had shared since they were in their early twenties. When Oscar had started working for a winery and received free wine as a side benefit, Jack was tending bar in Elmira a few nights a week to supplement the small salary Walter was paying him at the *Clarion*.

Both Oscar and Jack agreed even then that neither of them should ever have that easy an access to alcohol, given their proclivities to pound down beer, wine, or most other liquors any chance they could.

"I still declare alcohol free days," Jack said. "Keeps me from having to become a twelve-stepper. Probably need a week right now, though."

Oscar had pulled out his best wines for Jack, Walter Nagle, the young computer nerd-photographer-reporter Eli, Oscar's niece Lindy, and a woman named Devon. Oscar thought Devon was striking enough in a very wholesome, no-makeup sort of way that when they arrived he had bolted into the back room to grab a clean Lakeside Winery shirt to replace the one he was wearing that already sported some merlot from an earlier tasting.

Jack had mentioned he was bringing a woman who was working at the newspaper, but he neglected to mention how attractive she was.

"So my friends, I hope you are enjoying the wine and the film," Oscar said, a bottle of Riesling in one hand, a merlot in the other. "Jack told me *Red Dawn* is part of a story the paper's working on. Not top secret, I hope."

Walter raised his glass and offered a toast before answering.

"Here's to Oscar's wines and his hospitality," Walter said. "We could have done this in our office but we needed to get out to think. Plus I haven't been up to the lake in years. Easy to forget how beautiful it is here. Thank you, Oscar, from all of us."

Walter signaled Eli to get started with the conversation. Eli looked nervous, a combination of being away from the office and the two glasses of wine that would calm most people but tended to agitate him. He reached over to his laptop and connected a cable so that his display would show up on the big screen TV.

When it popped up, the classic photo of C. Thomas Howell holding up a gun and shouting "Wolverines!" practically jumped off the screen at the group.

"Um, first, I have to say that in most of my searching I found a lot of data about animals and references to this movie," Eli said. "I know Jack and Devon have been poking around too, so maybe they found something I didn't."

Eli's comment got a big laugh. If he couldn't find web references to wolverines that tied somehow to the vandalism against gas companies, it was unlikely Jack or Devon would do much better.

"But I did find that in a lot of cases, okay, wait... maybe ten...whoever wrecked a truck or set a fire or did something else left a note of some kind. But we don't know what the notes say, that hasn't been published or released. I didn't have time to track down each police department or sheriff to ask. Besides, that's really up to Jack and Devon, right Walter?"

Oscar raised his hand like a student.

"Wait, wait, wait. Are you guys telling me you think somebody is using *Red Dawn* like a guide to terrorism or something? The movie gets my blood going. But really?" Oscar said.

Eli flipped from the image of C. Thomas Howell to a list of the incidents from New York to California in which there was some reference to a document being left at the scene or being received later, either by the gas company or a police agency.

In none of the cases was any information released to any media outlets.

"I don't know if any of these are connected to the note or manifesto or whatever you want to call it that was left in that Audi in Chicago," Eli said. "The one that was signed 'Wolverines?'" As Eli got ready to expound further, Oscar heard a loud rapping on the glass front doors at the other end of the winery.

Three men in GES uniforms were there, making motions like they wanted to sample of glass of wine.

"Excuse me for a minute," Oscar said. "Some freeloading gasbags have arrived and I need to tell them we're closed."

Monday morning at the office of the *Horseheads Clarion* the combination staff and news meeting was subdued, as they ran through the stories, photos, and other details that needed to get done for Tuesday's paper.

Walter thanked everyone and then asked Jack, Eli, and Devon to stay behind for their short fracking meeting.

The wine-and-film evening at Oscar's had gone on for hours, and Walter made a note to send a formal newspaper thank you to Oscar for hosting, providing several bottles of wine, and joining in.

Walter remembered Oscar as a sharp young guy when Walter had first hired Jack. Oscar would come by to chat, sometimes plopping into the chair in Walter's office—a pretty confident young man.

Friday night, listening to Oscar's near-encyclopedic knowledge of the film *Red Dawn* had been fascinating.

Walter also made a note to be sure that Lakeside Winery got a free subscription to the *Horseheads Clarion*.

"Let me say first that I think we need to be pretty careful here," Walter said. "I think Eli is definitely onto something. There's a lot we can speculate on. But honestly, we have to walk a little softly. And all of you—don't look at me like that. I am not backing off on anything."

Eli's theory was simple on one level, but byzantine on others.

The lack of a big Internet splash was because the Wolverines, as he called them, were likely some of the same people who were opposing hydrofracking for natural gas in very public ways. "Obviously, right?" he said.

But those methods—the protests, petitions (on paper and via internet), email campaigns, phone calls, a handful of lawsuits and arrests at demonstrations—were not making much of a dent in slowing down the rate of gas drilling across the country.

Even in California, state regulators who should have been alarmed at a technology that was likely to cause earthquakes seemed relatively unconcerned. As in the rest of the nation, the gas companies simply told any nervous politicians or citizens not to worry. They knew what they were doing.

Then at some point the idea of monkey-wrenching caught on, simple harassment for the most part, though it was certainly costing some companies some money and time having to deal with the problem.

"The monkey-wrenching, really, I think is all about provoking a reaction," Jack said in the staff meeting. "Sounds like Saul Alinsky. But I don't think anybody believes some sugar in a gas tank is going to stop GES from drilling. But some might be thinking it will push GES into doing something stupid. You know, like telling employees it's okay to carry guns. Oh, wait, they did that, didn't they?"

But the part of Eli's theory that gave Walter sleepless nights on Saturdays and Sundays was that he believed a group within the monkey-wrenchers had decided to move past pranks and lightweight vandalism and maybe start a real campaign against the companies doing the drilling.

The wine Saturday night had made Eli bold enough to use the word "war."

"I don't think this movie would inspire me the way I'm talking about," Eli said. "But I don't think that name Wolverines just popped out of somebody's mouth. I think some anti-fracking people are organizing secretly and planning something big. I can't prove it. But look at all the stuff going on."

Eli showed a TV news report on Oscar's TV from a winery in Bakersfield, California. A young news anchor reported a truck owned by a natural gas exploration company had been found the day before, its hood and driver's door riddled with bullets in a ditch alongside a country road.

Two workers had checked the truck out of the company headquarters that morning and were missing.

"The police say they are investigating. You know, the usual response," Eli said.

A fter Saturday night's movie and the conversation that followed, Jack and Devon had stayed behind when Walter and Eli left, chatting with Oscar and Lindy until nearly midnight. Jack was mostly interested in reliving old times, Devon was interested in figuring out more about Jack, and Oscar was interested to see if Devon was interested in Jack.

Much more wine and I'll be asking her to marry me, Oscar thought.

Part of their conversation circled around to local

problems with GES workers around the lake. Jack relayed the shouting episode at Millie's Diner; Oscar told them about the spitting incident with the GES worker named Tom and his niece Lindy.

Since that night, Lindy said she thought she had been followed several times when she left the winery.

But Oscar had had just enough wine—and was charmed just enough by Devon —that he confided that he was noticing more and more small knots of locals in the winery talking privately, almost conspiratorially.

"Normally I wouldn't think much about it or notice," Oscar said. "Christ, some of these guys gossip like junior high school girls. But some of them are pretty pissed off about the possibility of fracking happening near their land. They're farmers and they're worried—especially the grape growers. And when Lindy tells our friends here about that guy who spit on her? Jesus. I hope that shrimp doesn't come in here again when any of those guys are around. They'll rip his head off and shit down his neck. Um. Sorry, Devon."

Devon shook her head and waved off the last part of Oscar's comments.

"I've heard a lot worse," she said. "Jack, too. And said worse, right?"

Jack nodded and held up his glass in a toast.

"Tonight, I just want say one last thing before we navigate back to Horseheads, hopefully without getting a DUI," he said. "To the Wolverines."

Oscar raised his glass and offered a second toast.

"How about some Shakespeare, too, Jack? I think 'Cry havoc and let slip the dogs of war!' about covers it."

J ack sat in Walter's office, waiting for Walter to finish proofing the final page for the Tuesday issue before it was sent to press.

The staff meeting about fracking coverage went from a calm business meeting through a stage of voices getting louder and louder until Walter finally signaled for Jack to close the door as the handful of other staffers in the office were starting to look nervously toward the ruckus.

"Listen, this is simple," Walter had said. "I don't want any one of us—myself included—using the word 'war' publicly, or even around here so the other people working here can hear it. I'm not willing right now to stick our necks out that far. We're way out there as it is. Let's keep getting proof about how bad this fracking is. Let's keep publishing and hammering at these people. And if we can confirm Eli's 'war,' then so be it. When we can confirm more than just a theory."

Walter pulled Jack aside after that meeting and asked him to come by his office later in the day. Walter's face was red enough that Jack was worried.

And now Jack sat in Walter's office wondering if advertisers were starting to put pressure on him. Walter had been a careful publisher and made a lot of money over the years. But even at that, the payroll and printing costs might be too rapid a drain on the paper without solid ad revenues.

Walter was never one to lose money, even during several recessions when he kept employees working when he could have laid them off.

When Jack had worked at the *Clarion* thirty years before, the Chamber of Commerce had orchestrated a boycott of the *Clarion* because the newspaper ran a series of articles about corruption in city government. The series pointed out the unhealthy alliance between the chamber and the mayor, all of which was tangled up in some legally questionable land swaps.

The female president of the Chamber of Commerce was married to the mayor, and when the pair left town to take up residence in Washington D.C., the boycott disappeared with them.

Walter came in and plunked down in his chair, looking like a tired 75-year-old.

"Close the door, will you Jack, I'm too tired to get back up."

Walter had suffered a heart attack fifteen years before, giving his late wife Andrea the chance to get him to clean up his diet and put him on an exercise routine.

When Andrea had died two years ago, he stayed with both, for the most part, more out of habit than conviction.

"Walter, I understand what you were saying at the staff meeting. We all do. Really. It's just that Eli got us stirred up. Plus, if we ever could really find out there was a conspiracy, it would be quite a story," Jack said. "Bigger than anything I've ever tackled."

Walter pursed his lips slightly but nodded in agreement. He waited long enough to speak that Jack started to get worried that Walter was about to say something uncomfortable for both of them.

But when he spoke, the Walter that had gotten so upset in the staff meeting was gone and the editor/publisher Walter who had brought Jack—and later Devon—in from out of state to take on hydrofracking was back.

Even his face color was back to normal.

"I didn't say it very well today, Jack. And I wanted to apologize. I probably need to apologize to Eli and Devon, too. You three are doing good work and finding good stuff. But what I was afraid of...what I am afraid of...is our reach exceeding our grasp. There might be a huge national conspiracy of people who are monkey- wrenching. Maybe the same group is about to start building pipe bombs, I don't know. But I think either calls for a level of resources we don't have."

Jack leaned forward, happy that Walter was just showing his upstate New York conservative streak and not backing off. Jack had seen several publishers in California cave in to pressure from advertisers and from politicians when they didn't need to.

He had left one job after the newspaper held up his story for twenty-four hours because the publisher was afraid of angering a major national discount house chain. But while Jack's newspaper took a pass for a day on the story, the local radio station and then a competing newspaper got wind of what Jack was going to publish and went ahead.

Jack's paper looked foolish. Jack waited a few weeks then turned in his resignation.

"Walter, I hear you. I just want to keep all our options open and be ready to move. I think Eli will keep on it, even if you told him to never look for the word wolverine again. And Devon's good. She's more interested in the environmental aspects and the pollution."

Walter smiled.

"Okay, good enough. Now that Tuesday's paper is on the way to the printer, I have a present for you, if you want it, for this week's *Column One*. We're running a story in

Friday's paper that I have one of the college kids working on. It's pretty simple, mostly a list, but screams for comment."

Walter handed Jack a file folder with a label that said *Public Officials and Natural Gas leases – NY and PA.*

"We found about seventy-five elected and appointed people with gas leases on their lands or lands their families own. It's not exactly a smoking gun, but it's interesting, especially the last page. By the way, I started calling and they are all refusing to comment. I love it."

Jack flipped open the folder and went right to the last page where there was a list of the elected and appointed officials, which gas company, the approximate amount of money they were paid to sign the lease, and if they had voted in favor or in opposition to hydrofracking cases.

"You read it right, Jack. Every single one of them has voted against any attempts to ban or control hydrofracking. You had laws against that in California, didn't you?"

Jack snapped the file folder shut and stood up to leave.

"We sure did Walter. Some smart-ass columnist might suggest we should have a law like that here. And Walter. Did you notice the name of the Pennsylvania judge? We might be glad we live in New York when we publish."

All talk of hydrofracking—and the under-the-table, hushed discussions about Eli's notions of a national conspiracy to take on gas companies—was eclipsed Wednesday morning when a teenage boy shot up a high school chemistry classroom across the Pennsylvania border in Rockwell Valley.

A female chemistry teacher was killed and five students

wounded when 17-year-old Roy Bonder Jr. walked in and calmly started shooting with a Bushmaster rifle, the same gun used in the famous Newton, Connecticut school massacre.

Jack, Eli, and Devon drove to the high school as soon as they heard, finding a chaotic scene with police, television camera crews, and even a Sheriff's Department helicopter flying overhead an hour after the shooting.

As best Jack could piece together, Bonder had gotten into a heated argument with the teacher over the chemical composition of the fluids used in hydrofracking. The teacher told the class that there were dangerous toxic chemicals in the fluids that were injected into the wells. She also said some of those fluids were likely leaking into water wells at the nearby homes. Bonder argued that his father wouldn't work there if fracking fluid wasn't safe and then got so belligerent that the teacher sent him to the principal's office.

He skipped the stop at the principal's office and drove home to grab his father's gun.

The police hadn't officially released Bonder's name, but two young girls outside confided it to Devon, along with the information that they thought Bonder's father worked for Grand Energy Services.

Bonder had already been taken into custody and was being held at the Rockwell Valley Police Department. But all the continued police action was because the police were afraid that the shooter might have had an accomplice.

"Since Columbine, police just don't take any chances," Jack told Eli.

Eli was shooting both still photos and videos, getting glares from police, but his style was low-key compared to several regional television stations that had shown up with large vans and set up mobile studios on the grass in front of the brick building.

"Television journalist, that's an oxymoron if I ever heard one," Jack mumbled to himself.

Across the wide lawn, Devon was standing at a yellow police tape blocking off the front door of the school where two ambulances were standing by.

Behind the tape were the journalists, parents, some of whose children were still inside the school, and many gawkers who had heard about the shooting or were just driving by.

Jack had heard on the police scanner that the body of the teacher, Anne Kovach, was still in the classroom where she had been shot, along with the five injured students. A medevac helicopter was on the way, but the five students were considered in stable condition and had local EMTs with them.

Jack had covered a school shooting in California in which a teacher—upset that she was going to be denied tenure at her Southern California elementary school — brought her husband's Glock handgun to school, killed the principal, and then shot out the windows of the cafeteria.

Police shot and killed her as she walked out of the school two hours later. She had held several teachers and a classroom of kindergarteners hostage. She refused to drop the gun in her hand as she walked out. It was the first time Jack had witnessed "suicide by cop."

Devon came over to Jack, her notebook filled with scribbled notes. Most of her reporting experience before this had been data mining and record chasing from safe offices.

She had little experience in the field asking questions. And never at a shooting.

But when Jack saw she had confirmed that the shooter was the son of a GES worker and that she had his full name and the full name of his father—Roy Bonder Sr.—he gave her a hug.

A big hug.

From the *Horseheads Clarion*

Column One
The Horseheads Clarion

Teach your children well

By Jack Stafford

ROCKWELL VALLEY, Pennsylvania — Another school shooting in our country, this one right in our backyard.

By now the details have been blasted across the planet, but here's a quick summary.

Anne Kovach, a 26-year-old chemistry teacher at Rockwell Valley High was killed Wednesday in her classroom. Five students in the class were injured, but are expected to recover. All of them were hit with bullets sprayed out of the end of a Bushmaster rifle fired by one of their classmates, Roy Bonder Jr., a recent transfer to the school from Pittsburgh.

Bonder's reason for the killing and shooting spree?

His teacher told him that the fluid used in hydrofracking for natural gas is toxic and polluting water wells, causing health problems for anyone drinking the water or bathing in it. But because Bonder's father works for Grand Energy Services, he didn't believe it.

This tragedy, like all the school shootings we have seen in recent years, was probably preventable. I say probably because the young man—labeled a murder suspect by police—has a serious temper problem, according to high school officials from his former school in Pittsburgh. When the Bonder family moved to Rockwell Valley four months ago, the youth had been suspended from his Pittsburgh school for an assault.

There's plenty of potential finger pointing to go around here: Bonder's access to a semi-automatic weapon, Rockwell Valley High's administration not warning his teachers about Bonder's record, Bonder's being able to walk out of school unnoticed and walk back in unchallenged cradling a loaded automatic weapon.

It was a perfect storm of missteps and carelessness, all of which is easy to see in retrospect but not so clear prior to Wednesday morning.

What is clear is that a teacher is dead, five students were badly hurt and the community needs some time to heal. It also needs some time to look at uncomfortable issues like gun control and the effects felt in our community from the wave of new residents in the last two years.

Those new residents are mostly employees of one of several natural gas exploration firms drilling gas wells—using hydrofracking technology—around the area. Certainly there are many hardworking, honest people among them moving in to work in this industry.

But it's undeniable that there has been a dramatic increase in crime and tension in Rockwell Valley since the beginning of what some people call the Gas Boom.

Police documents show that barroom brawls have become commonplace most weekends, burglaries tripled in the last year, and three women were arrested in the last three months for prostitution.

Prostitution?

The community will be mourning the death of a popular young teacher for a long time. The other students at the school will be adjusting to the tragedy, praying for quick recoveries for their five classmates.

But we should remember that the tension that contributed to this is still there, just below the surface.

Roy Bonder Jr. didn't kill his teacher because they disagreed about poetry.

Jack Stafford is an investigative columnist and reporter for The Horseheads Clarion *and has worked as an investigative reporter for metropolitan newspapers in California and Colorado.*

Jack finished reading his published column for the second time and looked across the room at Devon, who seemed to be looking at her computer screen, but was actually stealing glances at Jack when she thought he wasn't looking.

Since Wednesday, when he had gripped Devon in a bear hug at the high school and nearly kissed her in his excitement, the two of them had been doing a courteous professional dance in which their exchanges seemed perfectly normal for two co-workers, but stiffer than the way they interacted before.

Even Walter wondered what was going on. He thought they had had some kind of disagreement.

Jack and Devon had slowly been becoming good friends since she came to New York. She was spunky, and what she lacked in newspaper news experience she more than made up for with hard work and by being fearless.

Plus, she listened to Jack when he talked. Lately he had begun to slowly, haltingly, bring up memories about his late wife Amy. Devon generally only nodded, as if she understood when he talked. She knew how badly wounded he felt from her death.

But whenever Jack's thoughts started drifting anywhere beyond Devon being a co-worker, the pain of Amy's so-sudden death would come back. Jack thought that he and Amy had been as much been in love the day she died as the day they met. At least that's the way he wanted to remember it.

Right after Amy died, Jack had gone to a counselor in California, a young psychologist who was short on real experience with patients, and long on textbook learning. He told Jack about the stages of grief and was constantly quoting Kubler-Ross. After a few sessions, Jack gave it up and took up serious drinking instead. He finally left California, landing in Colorado.

He had tried to get in to talk with the Catholic priest at the church near his house, but the priest always seemed too busy. Jack was pretty sure that was because he told the priest he hadn't been inside of a Catholic church since he was a teenager.

Devon had helped him more than the counselor in just a few conversations in the Aspen bars, the counseling mixed in with her proselytizing about the need to stop hydrofracking. But Jack's professional armor was covering up his heart quite well. He was all too aware how vulnerable he was. And so he mostly let the alcohol fuel the numbness while he grieved silently and alone.

All that led him to accepting Walter's offer to work in New York and take on hydrofracking. Jack knew if he threw himself into his work, he could avoid thinking about Amy's death.

But Jack felt a tickle of emotion at the school when he hugged Devon. He realized that her finding the shooter's name and the connection to GES was certainly a reason to celebrate. But at the moment he held Devon, he felt a surge of happiness for the first time he could remember since Amy had died.

That's how he thought of it. *Happiness.*

And now watching Devon watching him, both of them pretending not to be watching each other, he realized that a tiny piece of that happiness was still floating around in his mind.

No, not my mind, Jack thought. *In my heart. That's what*

Amy would have said. Your heart is happy, Jack. Let it be happy.

Jack looked across the room at Devon again who now was staring at him quite straightforwardly. She wasn't smiling, but she wasn't frowning either. A tiny smile started to appear as she started typing quickly on her keyboard.

A moment later a chat message popped up on Jack's computer screen.

Your lips were moving like you were talking to yourself. What are you writing?

She raised her eyebrows in a quizzical look and typed again.

Need to talk about it?

Jack felt a tiny bit of moisture in his eyes before the tears actually started to well up. He rubbed his eyes and nodded 'yes' to Devon.

He was glad it was Friday. He had the weekend to sort some things out. And he felt like he needed to do some sorting.

In the end, Devon and Jack tossed a coin during tea at Millie's Diner—heads, drive up to Seneca Lake and visit Lakeside Winery and take in the sights—or tails, drive down into Pennsylvania and drive around for a quasi-work trip as they might stumble across ideas for more stories and columns.

Between them they already had enough information

collected to write several books. But there was always the personal angle to things and the stories that people had.

Plus all that information really needed to be digested. And most of it was so upsetting for so many reasons that it gave both of them indigestion to even read about what a mess hydrofracking was and how much it was hurting people and the environment.

The coin toss—a Mexican 10-peso piece Jack had brought back as a souvenir from a vacation to Puerto Vallarta with Amy ten years before—landed so that a trip to Seneca Lake and a visit with Oscar was on for Saturday. Sunday might end up being a trip to Pennsylvania, they decided.

Since Devon's arrival, Jack and Devon had generally gone their separate ways on weekends, though occasionally both ended up in the office of the *Horseheads Clarion* on Saturday or Sunday—or sometimes both—working on stories or in Jack's case, columns.

While those Saturday and sometimes Sunday conversations were nearly 100 percent work-related, Devon had gotten to know Jack more than he knew, and he could recite things about Devon's career and personal life that would have surprised him if he thought about it.

When they talked about marriage one afternoon, Devon seemed uncomfortable, though she said she had been engaged twice. Jack was surprised to hear a change in her voice when she talked about the engagements.

Devon's parents had died a few years before, just months apart. Her two single sisters, both divorced, had moved into the family home on Vashon Island, near Seattle.

Now sitting in the corner booth that Shania the waitress at Millie's had dubbed the Horseheads Press Club, Jack and

Devon were making more eye contact than they had in three days.

"So, it's Seneca Lake tomorrow?" Devon said, studying the gold-colored 10-peso coin. "You could really cheat with this. I can't tell the head from the tails."

Jack laughed, taking the coin back, slipping into his wallet.

"I did cheat actually. I want to go up to the lake and visit with Oscar again. We can go to Pennsylvania on Sunday. Maybe. But really, I need to flush my mind about this stuff."

They sipped their tea in silence for moment.

"It will be a nice drive up to the lake," Devon said. "Plus, I haven't ever tasted Riesling as good as Oscar's. Ever. And I lived in the Napa Valley for a few years."

Jack laughed again.

"You know what they say around here? The Finger Lakes means wine. Napa means auto parts. Think about it."

The drive up from Horseheads to Seneca Lake along NY State Route 14 winds through beautiful small towns with names like Pine Valley, Millport, and Montour Falls.

Jack had driven the two-lane highway many times when he was young, but had forgotten how beautiful it was, more so now in the late spring with summer hinting that it was only weeks away.

And with Devon, it was like having a young child in the car, she got so excited when she would see interesting things. And everything seemed interesting.

Near Pine Valley she made Jack stop at a fruit stand that had greenhouse vegetables and some early crops already for sale. Jack knew that by late summer the place would be mobbed every day, their bins overflowing with squash, tomatoes, and locally grown sweet corn.

"No GMO stuff here either," he told Devon. "These people are the real deal when it comes to homegrown. It's not all organic. But if they can avoid using Monsanto seeds, they do. And they rarely use any pesticides. I wrote a story about them for Walter thirty years ago. Same family still owns the farm."

They drove along past Pine Valley, paralleling Catherine Creek where fishermen were casting lines. At one section where a bicycle/pedestrian trail was just off the shoulder, a Cub Scout troop was picking up trash while their older companions—Boy Scouts—were wielding brush cutters and rakes, cleaning up the overgrown vegetation that needed attention.

Jack and Oscar had spent many hours doing the same sorts of chores as scouts growing up, eventually becoming scout leaders. That all changed when they were old enough for driver's licenses and got their first motorcycles, then cars. The lure of adventure via motorcycle and car was too strong, even though the motorcycles at 100cc were really more motor scooters than true cycles.

At a spot just before Millport, Devon had Jack pull over at a shop that had hundreds of concrete statues and figurines for sale. Everything from Mickey Mouse to Jesus was there, some small enough for a mantelpiece, others six feet tall. Some items were painted. Some were plain gray concrete.

"We should get Walter a present," Devon said. "I've never been to his house. Would he like a concrete sculpture? Maybe a St. Francis of Assisi for his garden? Does he even have a garden? Do you know…?"

Jack held up his hands while Devon peered closely at a beautifully painted three-foot tall Snow White statue.

"Devon, Whoa! One at a time. Okay? Should we get him a present? Maybe. But I haven't been to his house since I've been back. I'm not sure how many people visit since his wife died. She was the socialite in the family."

The mention of Walter's late wife slowed Devon down. Within a few minutes, she declared she'd seen everything she wanted to and headed back for the car.

As they pulled out, Jack realized that when Devon suggested a gift for Walter, she had said, "We should get…" not "Would Walter like…?"

A small thing? Just an accident of words?

Maybe, Jack thought.

But he was sure of one thing. When she said, "We should get…" that feeling of happiness tickled him again just for a second, even if it was accidental.

He was still smiling and driving a good fifteen miles per hour over the 25 mph speed limit when he went though Millport five minutes later, and only pulled over when Devon pointed out there was a police car right behind them with its rooftop party lights blazing.

Small towns in upstate New York depend on people speeding to balance their budgets. But most of them prefer to do so on the backs of tourists, not locals. And so Jack was able to talk his way out of a speeding ticket, partly on the basis of being well known for his *Horseheads Clarion* column, partly because the young officer was immediately charmed by Devon.

The cop's lecture on speeding was perfunctory and most of their roadside conversation was about the newspaper and what life was like in California and Colorado, both places the police officer dreamed of moving to.

Jack recommended California over Colorado if the officer was serious about getting out of the snow. Devon countered that there were parts of Colorado that were as beautiful as Millport.

On the way through Montour Falls and then Watkins Glen, Jack kept a closer eye on the speedometer while he and Devon laughed at how the young officer's speeding speech turned into a fan session.

"You must have some female groupies out there, too. Really," Devon said. "That picture of you on top of your column is pretty movie star stuff. Did Eli take that or was it a studio thing? I bet all the old ladies love it."

Jack winced a little at the old ladies comment. He didn't pay much attention to his age but at that moment he was painfully aware that he was fifteen years older than Devon's 40. When he had taught junior college, before Amy died, he liked working with the undergraduates. He thought it helped keep him young.

It was already noon as they started up the highway on the east side of the lake. Jack slowed down so Devon could get a good look at Hector Falls. She had seen them briefly when they whizzed by the week before for the showing of *Red Dawn* at the winery.

"I know it's total tourist, but take a picture on your iPhone of me in front of the falls, will you? I want to send it to my sisters on Vashon."

Several other cars had pulled off on the bridge, too,

everyone snapping photos madly and enjoying the fast-flowing water. By the time Devon had found a spot where she could get her photo taken alone, a car pulled in nearby and the driver and his wife offered to take a photo of Jack and Devon together in front of the water.

"Sure," Jack said. "That would be great. It's just my phone, but it's good."

Jack stood on Devon's right, his arms straight down at his sides, feeling slightly dizzy. He watched Devon out of the corner of his left eye as he heard the man with his iPhone holler at him to get closer to Devon.

"You guys need be closer. That's it. Yeah. A little closer. Yeah."

Jack was aware of how close Devon was and then in a motion as casual as if she and he had been having their photos taken in front of waterfalls for years, Devon slipped her arm through his and leaned her head on his shoulder.

"That's it! Perfect. Perfect." the man said, snapping off several shots. "Very nice. You guys look great. Will you take one of us, too?"

Ten miles up the road, four wine tastings and a long late-luncheon at a bistro in a winery overlooking Seneca Lake, Jack and Devon checked into the Bended Bow Bed and Breakfast Inn near Lodi as the sun was heading down.

They agreed when they pulled safely into the parking lot that neither of them should drive another foot. And instead of waiting for the afternoon's worth of Riesling buzz to wear off so they could drive back, they agreed they had earned a night away from Horseheads. They also agreed that if they didn't head home, there would be no chance of getting itchy and slipping into the office and work.

At the front counter, the teenage daughter of the owners said they were lucky. The B&B had just one room left for the night, a spacious upstairs two-room suite with a view of the lake and a veranda with easy chairs.

"It's our best room. Really," she said.

Devon slipped her arm through Jack's just like she had done in front of the waterfall.

"It sounds lovely," Devon said. "We'll take it."

It was dark when Jack woke up, his back sore from the beautifully ornate but lumpy couch in the sitting room.

He looked at his watch and saw that it was after 8 p.m. The girl at the front counter said they served wine and light snacks from 5 to 7 p.m. for guests.

"My dad always makes way lots of food so if you're hungry and don't want to go out just come down," she advised.

She had also promised that if Jack and Devon napped too long she would set some food aside.

When Devon and Jack looked at her with raised eyebrows, she offered up that every B&B near the wineries was quite used to people coming in with the need to catch some sleep and stay off the highway after wine tasting.

"And besides, Mr. Stafford, my dad and mom read your column every week. They'll be thrilled that you are here."

The last thing Jack could remember hearing when he laid down on the couch was Devon shouting from the bedroom. "Groupies! I knew you had groupies."

Groupies or not, Jack looked in at Devon who was still asleep. She had matched him wineglass for wineglass at lunch and at the wineries. Impressive, he thought. But he was sure he weighed at least seventy-five pounds more than she did and could soak it up much easier.

He couldn't wait to tell her that she snored.

He went downstairs to round up some of the offered food, and despite Jack's repeated protestations, the owner and his wife insisted that he take a bottle of their favorite Riesling back upstairs along with a tray of cheese and apples and crackers.

"You and your wife have a nightcap on us. And if you don't drink it, consider it a gift. Your newspaper is about the only one around here doing anything decent on this fracking stuff. Keep it up. Please. We need more people like you."

When Jack turned the key and slipped quietly into their room, Devon was sitting on the same lumpy couch where he had napped, her hair with a case of serious bed- head. Her face wasn't smiling, but it wasn't frowning either.

She looked at the wine bottle and the food tray, and then up at Jack who had stopped mid-stride into the room, surprised she was awake.

Then she smiled and patted the couch next to her to come and sit down.

"I'm hungry. And Jack. Isn't it time we talk? Please?

Jack's felt the tears in his eyes coming and let them go.

His hands were full and Devon was already there, taking the food and wine bottle out of his hands before he knew it.

Devon looked at Jack's rumpled clothes and saw their reflection in the mirror, sitting next to each other on the bed.

"You know, if we were in a movie, we would have had wild sex all night," Jack said. "All night."

The early morning light was just beginning to come in through the windows and it looked like a bright sunny day ahead.

"That's true. That's Hollywood. I think talking was even better," Devon said. She reached for his hand and squeezed it.

"Oh shit, I'm sorry, Jack. Here's a Kleenex."

They had talked on and off all night. They would fall off to sleep on the bed, then wake up again. Jack did most of the talking. Most of it was about Amy and her death. Some of it was Devon's careful solace.

A lot was about Jack's guilt over feeling attracted to Devon when Amy had been dead less than a year. Devon let Jack ramble and talk all he needed, trying not to inject too much, knowing that this was his time and that this conversation had been brewing in his head, maybe even since they met in Colorado.

It certainly had been brewing since Devon arrived and they started running around like Batman and Robin for the *Horseheads Clarion*.

Devon told Jack she thought he had a hole in his heart—a void put there by the death of Amy. It was the suddenness of it. And maybe the hole was there for a long time—maybe even from the death of his father two years ago.

And that hole was hurting all the time, sometimes worse than others.

What kept Jack tearing up, in part, was that Amy had told him the same thing many times—even using the same expression, "hole in the heart," to describe how working as a journalist desensitized most people, but only on the surface.

"You have a big heart and that big heart gets wounded when people are in trouble and bad things happen. Especially when people are bullied," Devon had told him in the middle of the night. "I think that big heart is what attracts me to you. Why I love working with you. You're a good man. And that you were willing to come back to help Walter in this crusade? God, Jack. Really. You're Don Quixote with a keyboard."

Devon thought about what she had said for a minute. "So, I guess that makes me Sancho Panza."

They had finally fallen asleep a couple of hours before dawn. They paid no attention to clocks or time passing, only their conversations.

At times Devon pulled Jack to her and cradled him. Other times they lay on their backs looking up at the ceiling. Sometime in the night they started to whisper when they realized their voices might be carrying in the house.

Jack blotted up the moisture around his eyes and suggested that they go down for breakfast as the smell of bacon started to waft up to their room.

"I can't believe we ate that whole tray of food last night, too, and I'm still hungry," Devon said.

She stood up and motioned for Jack to get up.

"This is not about sex. Just give me your pants and shirt and let me see if I can get some wrinkles out of them. I saw an iron in the closet."

Jack complied meekly, handing them over, and headed into the bathroom to wash up.

"Oh, and Jack? I'll let you explain to your groupies downstairs that we aren't married."

Jack's cell phone rang at the breakfast table, just as Jack and Devon were laughing at yet another story told by the owners about people who ended up there after a long day of wine tasting who could barely scrawl their names in the guest register.

On rare occasions, the owner would have to half-carry them upstairs.

Devon had performed clothing magic on Jack's shirt and pants, and her blouse and skirt looked like they came freshly out of a hanging closet.

And despite virtually no sleep, both of them had been alert enough to carry on a lively conversation with the owners, California transplants who had moved to Seneca Lake just the year before.

"Jack, I tried your house phone," Walter said, sounding a little groggy on his end of the phone. "Sorry to bother you on such a beautiful Sunday morning but I knew you would want to know. Muriel Dogg died last night at Rockwell Valley Hospital. The death notice just came in from the funeral home and they asked us to put it up on the website."

Jack thanked Walter and told him he and Devon were up at the lake having breakfast but could stop by the office later in the day, if he wanted one of them to write the web obituary.

"That's probably a good idea," Walter said. "Given your column about her and those other women, I would like you to do the web version. You can do a full piece for Tuesday's print edition.

"And Jack, in the pile of mail that came in yesterday, there was a big envelope for you, postmarked Wednesday from Rockwell Valley. It's from the late Mrs. Dogg."

Jack waved breezily to the same police officer who had stopped him for speeding the day before. This time Jack was cruising through Millport at just the speed limit, even though he wanted to tromp on the gas and get home.

He and Devon had made their apologies quickly to the B&B owners, wolfing down the balance of their breakfasts before hopping in the car to head back to Horseheads and the *Clarion* office.

Walter had opened the letter from Muriel Dogg and read the highlights to Jack while he was finishing his meal.

It explained in emotional detail her late husband's unhappiness-turned-to-anger at Grand Energy Services after she was diagnosed with bladder cancer.

But what had Jack and Devon rushing to the office was a list she had included—the chemicals that GES had been using in its particular hydrofracking chemical cocktail in the gas wells around the Dogg home in Rockwell Valley.

This list was on a delivery receipt as part of a shipment of chemicals sent to the main Rockwell Valley drill site and had some directions for concentrations of chemicals for the next wells to be drilled and fracked.

The delivery manifest was signed by one of Dogg's supervisors, accepting the chemicals.

"Walter just skimmed the letter, but she hints that she has, well, I guess I should say, *had*, other documents, too," Jack said as they drove by the stand selling concrete statues. "When I interviewed her, she didn't say anything about papers. Mostly she was angry with GES. She blamed her cancer and her husband's death squarely on them."

Devon was already making a list of people they needed to contact for Tuesday's paper: Muriel Dogg's doctor, GES to try to get them to admit the list was authentic, and some of the anti-fracking folks who were screaming that gas companies be required to reveal all chemicals used in hydrofracking.

Jack made a mental note to contact the woman with bladder cancer—the only one still alive of the trio he had interviewed for his column earlier in the year.

"Most of these chemicals and gases, like benzene and toluene, we've known about," Jack said. "But there's a couple on that manifest we haven't heard much about. I remember Walter said hexane and xylene. We'll need to track those down too for some medical comment."

Getting medical comment from doctors in Pennsylvania was tricky at best.

Between patient confidentiality laws and the state's own gag rule, it was hard to get doctors to talk, even if they were certain that fracking chemicals were the cause of a patient's illness.

"I think we need a constitutional amendment outlawing confidentiality agreements," Devon said. "I talked with one Pittsburgh doctor a few weeks ago who was treating a child with a tumor on his ear. The doctor said she had signed one of those agreements and because the chemical she thought had caused the tumor was part of the gas company trade secrets, she couldn't say anything. In fact she hung up on me, she got so exasperated just trying to talk around it."

Jack could feel his sense of well-being and contentment slowly slipping away mile-by-mile as they got closer to Horseheads. In a half-hour, he would be at his computer in the office, writing an obituary for a woman who died because she lived too close to a natural gas well, created with the use of toxic chemicals.

And reports of illness and deaths associated with these chemicals—either through water pollution or air pollution—were stacking up like cordwood while state and federal regulators stood by, allowing the gas companies to crow that there were no "definitive studies" proving groundwater contamination or violations of air pollution standards.

"Do you know why they vent their gas wells at night?" Jack asked, just letting off his own steam because he knew Devon probably was quite aware. "The flare stacks and other stuff they let off goes up high in the air. The gas and chemicals are lighter and warmer than the outside air and there's not much wind. If they let it off during the day, the wind can carry the smell towards houses. Lots of people complain about it in the daytime. At night people downwind just get slowly poisoned."

Devon and Jack drove most of the rest of the way in silence, both digesting their talks of the night before and mixing them with what they would be writing relative to hydrofracking in the coming week.

Jack had a kernel of an idea for Friday's *Column One*. As usual, he envisioned the headline first, then fleshed out the details as he drafted the column.

"What do you think about something like 'Pennsylvania gag orders are lethal'?"

Devon looked up from her notebook.

"Sure. Or maybe 'Don't-tell rule is a killer.'"

As they pulled up in front of the *Horseheads Clarion*, Walter was outside on the sidewalk, sweeping up broken glass from a shattered window.

On the other window someone had sprayed-painted, "GES rules."

From the *Horseheads Clarion*

Column One
The Horseheads Clarion

Gagging over abuse of law

By Jack Stafford

ROCKWELL VALLEY, Pennsylvania — If you get sick in Pennsylvania and you suspect it might have something to do with exposure to hydrofracking chemicals, either in water or in the air, your doctor can get information about what chemicals you might have been exposed to, to help them come up with a treatment plan.

But your doctor can't tell anybody else, because in order to get the information, they have to sign a confidentiality agreement.

This might be old news to you. The Pennsylvania law that said doctors could demand to know—and get information about—what toxic chemicals companies are putting in hydrofracking fluid cocktails has been in effect since early 2012. But they can't talk to anyone about it.

So in this case, the rule of law protects the gas companies from exposure and liability.

Most of the people who sign a gas lease also sign away their rights to ever comment on any aspects of the drilling, the damage done to their properties, or even if their water is fouled by the hydrofracking process or some other gas-company activity associated with it.

If they do speak up, they are liable—legally—for damages.

Yes, it's crazy. And it's crazy that people sign these documents. Many people who have problems with gas company drilling have said they regret signing. But that's about as specific as they ever get. Why? They are afraid of being sued.

Tuesday the *Clarion* published the obituary for Muriel Dogg, the wife of murdered GES worker Delbert Dogg.

Muriel died from complications associated with bladder cancer. The bladder cancer, she was sure, was caused by hydrofracking chemicals used in the drilling of gas wells in the area around her house in Rockwell Valley.

Any death is a tragedy. But in this case, Muriel Dogg's passing has also sparked a potentially ugly court battle. Hydrofracking opponents, members of a group called Stop-GasPA, have demanded, in documents filed with the courts, that there be an autopsy. At the same time, Grand Energy Services has announced it will file suit to stop the autopsy. Part of its claim will be that the results of any autopsy, which would be contained in a public document, could reveal trade secrets.

What trade secrets? Well, the names and concentrations of the various chemicals used in the fracking cocktail that might show up in the body of the late Mrs. Dogg.

But wait. GES and other gas exploration companies have been consistently maintaining that hydrofracking chemicals are not getting into the water supply and are not being vented into the air.

Ever.

So the autopsy shouldn't show any benzene, toluene, hexane, xylene or any other of 100 or more chemicals often used in the toxic stew that Stop-GasPA and others say is causing damage to health.

You might even think that GES would want the autopsy to prove its point.

It doesn't.

The county coroner told me this week that if an autopsy is performed, she will not be signing any confidentiality agreements before determining what might have killed Muriel Dogg.

Or signing anything afterwards, either.

And her report—like other autopsy reports—will be a public document, as least as far as she is concerned, unless a court order says otherwise.

Let's hope the court rules in favor of the public.

Jack Stafford is an investigative columnist and reporter for The Horseheads Clarion *and has worked as an investigative reporter for metropolitan newspapers in California and Colorado.*

Jack reread his *Column One* again early Friday morning, then folded the newspaper up and put it in the stack he kept next to his desk before the newspaper opened for the day.

At the last minute, he had decided to remove any references in his column to the documents Muriel Dogg had sent to him, a move Walter and Devon agreed with.

Instead, they were going to have various scientific experts go through the papers to determine the toxicity of the chemicals and examine the amounts being put into the fracking-water cocktail.

It was likely a story would run Tuesday, if the experts could work that fast.

But time was also working against the *Clarion*.

The minute GES got wind of the documents, the company would be in court trying to stop publication, or claiming that the documents were stolen from GES. Either case would drag the *Clarion* into a battle that couldn't be fought on its news and editorial pages, where the newspaper had a clear home field advantage.

Walter plunked down in the chair next to Jack, putting his copy of Friday's *Clarion* on the desk. It was marked up with circles and arrows, part-critique, part-planning tool for the next issue.

"Another prizewinner, Jack. In print, the columns always look so much more impressive than on the computer screen. The GES people are going to crap," Walter said, laughing. "Just crap. It's pretty hard to argue that your chemicals aren't harmful and then try to stop an autopsy."

Except for Walter and Jack, the office was deserted, allowing the hum of computers and equipment to provide a background noise you didn't hear at all during the day.

Eli, Devon, and the two young reporters had been working on tracking down experts to give their opinion on the chemicals in the documents Muriel Dogg had mailed to Jack. Eli and Devon knew about the planned story, which would run without a byline by a reporter. But they didn't tell the other reporters about the document, and wouldn't, until just before the paper was published.

"You know what a can of worms this will kick over, Walter. I went through this twice in California. And I don't know New York law. Dogg might have stolen the papers. Even if he found them in a trashcan, GES will claim that he stole them. We had a reporter spend a night in jail once for receiving stolen property."

Walter leaned back in the chair and smiled.

"That's why we are buying insurance by not putting a byline on the story. If anybody has to sit in the county jail for a while, it will be me. I'm the publisher and ultimately responsible. Besides, you guys are doing 90 percent of the work around here. I could use a vacation."

Jack corrected him.

"Actually, I would say 95 percent, Walter. But if we do get hit with a lawsuit, we will all be named eventually anyway. Just call Devon and me Jane and John Doe."

Both men turned when they heard the beep of the electronic card lock on the front door—a new lock Walter had installed just that week after the front window was smashed and someone had tried to break in through a side door.

Devon and Eli came in together, heading straight for the coffeemaker and the electric teakettle in the conference room.

"I have some news for our fracking meeting later—or I can share it now," Devon said. "Oh hell, I can't wait. Sometime last night someone hijacked a truck full of fracking wastewater on its way to Ohio. Apparently, even with the earthquakes, there are still some places that will allow injecting this stuff into wells. Anyway, I heard it on the scanner. It was a GES truck from Rockwell Valley and it was near the Ohio line."

Jack pulled up a Pennsylvania map on his computer screen as he was listening, trying to figure what route a fracking wastewater truck might take from Rockwell Valley to central Ohio.

"You heard it on the scanner?" Jack asked. "That's kind of weird. Most of the police use their cell phones now and don't go on the air with much. And the Ohio line is a long way for local cops to be talking about it."

Devon smiled over her steaming tea mug.

"I know, I know. But it might be because of who was driving the truck. I think the company wants to keep tabs on him. It was Roy Bonder. Bonder, Sr.? The father of the 17-year-old kid who killed the chemistry teacher at Rockwell Valley High School? I told Eli on the way over. Eli's car is broken down again so I gave him a lift."

Eli was already furiously tapping the keys on his computer and then suddenly waved his hand in the air like a kindergarten student who needed to use the bathroom.

"The Pittsburgh newspaper has a three-paragraph story up on its website. Just says that there is a gas company wastewater truck missing and that police think it was stolen. Very sketchy stuff. But they don't say hijacked—just missing."

Walter stood up and held his coffee mug up in a toast.

"God Bless the Internet. Let's get our story up about Mr. Bonder and the missing truck. Might as well throw in some details about where his son's case stands, too. This is not going to be a good morning for GES."

From the *Horseheads Clarion* website:

Hydrofracking waste-water truck missing

BUTLER, PA (10 a.m. EST) — A bright-yellow truck carrying nearly 5,000 gallons of waste-water from a hydrofracked natural gas well near Rockwell Valley has been reported missing by Grand Energy Services, the natural gas exploration and drilling company headquartered in Missouri.

The truck was reported miss-ing late Thursday night when it did not make it to its destina-tion in Ohio to dump its load at a hydro-injection disposal well just over the Pennsylva-nia-Ohio border.

It was expected to show up by 11 p.m.

The last confirmed sighting of the truck was at a truck stop outside Butler, where surveil-lance cameras show the driver getting coffee and a sandwich about 8 p.m.

The driver is believed to be Roy Bonder Sr., though GES has refused to answer media inquiries about the missing truck or confirm the name of the driver.

Nationally, this is third hydrofracking wastewater truck to go missing in the last month. The other trucks were in Colorado and Texas.

In both those cases, police said the trucks have not been recovered and the drivers are still missing.

Bonder's son, Roy Bonder Jr. was arrested earlier this month and charged with murder after he allegedly walked into a classroom in Rockwell Valley High School and killed 26-year-old Anna Kovach, a chemistry teacher. Bonder Jr. was carrying a Bushmaster rifle when police arrested him at the school shortly after the shooting. Five students in the classroom were wounded in the shooting incident but are recovering.

Bonder Jr. is currently undergoing evaluation in a private psychiatric facility after entering a plea of not guilty in the shooting.

Jack and Devon headed to Millie's Diner after the story was posted on the web. Walter promised to join them, but said he wanted to place a call to the *Clarion*'s lawyer in Syracuse about the documents and what kind of exposure the *Clarion* might have with using the information.

"We're publishing the story. Don't worry about that. Just helps to know what direction someone might shoot at us from," Walter said.

He was smiling, but the smile had some worry lines showing around his mouth.

Now sitting in their familiar corner booth at Millie's, Devon asked Jack if he was worried at all about the safety of the newspaper staff.

"The broken window was one thing. The spray paint pushed it up one notch," Devon said.

"Walter hasn't said anything. But I think he's been getting phone calls on the company message phone. I've seen him deleting them in the morning."

Shania came over right away with their hot water and tea, even though nearly every seat in the diner was filled.

She and Devon had become good friends since Devon moved in with Shania and her mother. And Devon's Labrador Retriever Belle was practically a family member now. Most nights Devon and Shania ended up sharing a glass of wine and chatting when Devon would get home early enough from the office. The age gap didn't slow the friendship. It made Devon like a big sister to Shania, who spent a lot of nights filling Devon in about Horseheads and New York.

She also shared what she knew about Jack from her mother. Shania's mother was only a few years older than Jack and had known his family.

After Shania put down the cups, she sat down on the edge of the booth for a moment and touched Devon's arm.

"Did you get a chance yet?" she said, looking at Devon, then Jack. "Oops. Ha! Sorry. Later."

She popped up and headed back over to the lunch counter where several GES workers were having breakfast.

Jack looked at Devon quizzically but remembered the friendships his late wife Amy had with some of her girlfriends in California. He liked the idea that Devon and Shania had gotten close so quickly. And he liked Shania and thought it wouldn't be long before she outgrew life as a waitress in the diner. He hoped so, anyway.

"So, big secrets?" Jack asked. "Does Shania want to borrow my car? It's hardly worth it."

Devon put her hand on Jack's arm then pulled it back when she realized that one of the GES workers at the lunch counter was staring at her. "No. That car of yours is quite safe. Shania and her mom have been getting some phone calls. Heavy breathing kind of stuff. You know. Could be high school kids doing pranks. Anyway. I told them if they were worried that it had something to do with me and the newspaper, I'd find another place to live while I'm here. They've been great, though. Really. Shania's mother seemed quite relieved when I suggested maybe I move out. Maybe they're tired of a house guest."

Jack sat back in the booth and took a long look at Devon.

He had been rolling around the idea of asking Devon to move in to a spare room in his house since their wine tasting and B&B adventure up the lake. But really just as roommates and colleagues, he told himself.

And Belle was welcome, too, of course.

"You know. Well, you know. Christ." Jack said. "My brain is scrambled eggs about things and Amy, I don't want to step in it here. But my house is a fortress when it comes to security. My dad made damn sure of that. You and Belle would be comfortable, safe. And you could walk to the newspaper. We could commute on foot together."

Devon looked over at Shania who was watching the conversation from the counter, where she was pouring coffee.

Devon gave Shania a brief thumbs-up signal, drawing a grin from Shania.

"Jack. I appreciate it. And it means we're roommates, you, Belle and me. All three of us."

Jack lifted his teacup to make a toast.

"Roommates and colleagues."

They had just clinked their teacups together when Jack looked across the room and saw a GES uniformed worker heading their way.

He swallowed his tea and edged closer to the outside to allow him to get out of the booth.

The GES worker approaching the table was clutching that day's edition of the *Horseheads Clarion* and looked angry.

And although it had been several months before, Jack was pretty sure it was the same GES worker he and Walter had words with in the diner when Jack had first arrived.

Then he saw his nametag up close.

"Tom. Haven't seen you in here in awhile," Jack said, standing up. "What's on your mind?"

Jack sat on his front porch Saturday morning facing the street, waiting for Devon and Eli to show up.

Devon had bought one piece of furniture since she'd arrived, a computer desk that required transport by pickup truck, and Eli was quick to offer that he could borrow one and help out.

Jack's left hand clenched into a fist when he thought about the day before at the diner, then relaxed.

The GES worker named Tom vented for a few minutes while Jack did his best to stand as tall as possible so he could loom over the much shorter man. Jack finally told Tom he should walk across the street and talk to the publisher about his gripes with Jack's column.

"He's the boss. He's the only one who can give you any satisfaction here."

Tom huffed off muttering, shaking his head as he walked back to his breakfast at the counter.

But neither he nor any of the other GES employees looked at Jack and Devon again until they left, giving sideways glances.

Still, Jack was half-expecting Tom to take a poke, but was happy to see that Tom seemed to be just a classic bully. Jack learned that if you confront them head on, showing no fear, they usually back down quickly.

Usually, Jack thought.

Years before, just a few months before Jack had moved to California, three men had confronted him in an Elmira bar, the middle-aged fathers of high school football players who thought Jack's stories about their sons being suspended from the school team had insulted the boys and been unfair.

The suspension was in response to the boys being

arrested for drunken driving. The story laid it all out in detail, including the boys' names and where they lived. All three were 18 years old and the police released their names without any fuss.

That night Jack had been hanging out with Oscar and their friend Butch, talking about Jack's plans to move west. But Oscar and Butch left together to head home for Seneca Lake, leaving Jack to sip the last of his beer.

The three men confronted Jack at the bar when they saw Oscar and Butch had left. Jack raised his hands and said he was just doing his job. He slid off the bar stool, pushing past the men, and headed out the front door.

But one of them jumped him from behind just as he was opening his car door.

The rest of the sequence was fuzzy for Jack, even when he was telling the police later.

As soon as he felt the first punch land on his neck, he spun around and did a classic wrestling takedown of the first man, who, when he fell, knocked down the two other men standing closely behind him in what probably looked to some necking spectators in the parking lot like a Three Stooges' routine.

The three men were quite drunk and Jack moved away from them, hoping that he could get to his car and simply escape.

But the three got to their feet and rushed him all at once.

At the hospital the next morning he remembered thinking what he had learned from his street-smart, construction-worker father when Jack was only 10 years old and had to deal with a 13-year-old, twenty-five-pounds-heavier bully.

"Don't be afraid to poke someone in the eye, to bite

an ear, bite a nose," his father had said. "Forget that movie stuff about punching in the jaw. You'll break your hand. Just take him down any way you can. Do what you have to do to protect yourself."

Jack's head and face were bandaged from the bar fight. But police said the three men who jumped him were missing a couple of teeth and in one case, a nearly crushed larynx. The couple who'd witnessed the fight backed up Jack's claim that he was attacked.

Jack's father drove him home from the hospital and said he was glad Jack was okay, and equally glad that he hadn't hurt any of the men any worse than he had in the brawl.

Or poked out one of their eyes.

"You let the demon out to save yourself and that's a good thing. But Jack? Now you know it's inside you, like we knew when you were 10. Bury him again. Deep. He has a way of sneaking out once he's been let loose."

Now sitting on his dead father's porch—now Jack's porch—Jack took a deep breath and realized that if the GES worker named Tom had taken a poke at him and threatened Devon, that demon might have come out swinging, biting, and kicking, right there in Millie's.

Months of working on the hydrofracking stories had Jack's anger right at its peak. It was something he would have to be careful about.

"Hey, old guy in the rocker! Can you help with these boxes? They're heavy," Devon shouted from the curb. She and Eli were stacking things up, with Belle dancing around them as if she knew it was her new home.

Jack snapped his head up. Had he been asleep? He didn't know. He was groggy for sure.

But he knew he was glad Devon and Belle were moving in. It made him forget the rest of everything, even if only for the moment.

People who knew Jack marked the weekend Devon moved into his house as B.D. and A.D.—before Devon and after Devon.

Jack's sometimes-morose, sometimes-cynical attitude was still lurking, but definitely leavened by having Devon in the house, a smart, bright, humor-full star in what had been a very dark universe since the death of Jack's wife Amy in California.

Jack and Amy had lost two children to miscarriages in the first five years of their marriage. After the second, they decided not to try anymore. The buildup, the anticipation, all the hopes were too painful when they were dashed by the early-term endings. They lived full lives with their twin careers—Jack as a journalist, Amy as a part-time college art instructor and artist, each the other's best friend.

Memories of Amy were whirling for Jack since Devon moved in. He had blocked out so much from their twenty years together. Moving east had helped that. There was nothing from California to remind him of Amy, except for when his writing ended up with California references or needed to use sources there for columns.

Conversations in the evenings with Devon were helping Jack deal with Amy's loss, too, a continuation of things that started in the bed-and-breakfast up on Seneca Lake.

Devon confessed after one evening's chat that she had

worked very briefly as a grief counselor before becoming an environmental activist.

"I'm not sure I was very good at it," Devon told Jack.

Jack disagreed.

"You probably should add counselor to your resume, right there with environmental consultant and journalist. At least for me," Jack said.

Since moving in, Devon and Jack had made—and sometimes broken—a no-chat rule for weekends about hydrofracking.

Saturdays and Sundays they would sometimes bring it up briefly in terms of planning for the next week's research, stories, and Jack's column. It was hard, especially when Walter or Eli dropped by.

Devon would often take off on adventures with Shania or Shania's mother.

But mostly Jack and Devon spent time exploring, traveling around the Finger Lakes to places Jack had known growing up. They tried, with sometimes limited success, to stay out of the offices of the *Horseheads Clarion* on the weekends.

Of course, they had their laptops and Internet connection at Jack's house, and could dive into work any time they wanted.

Sometimes they ran into hydrofracking stories while driving around and the rule was suspended.

Belle was a partner in their travels and rounded out the family. Jack and Amy never kept dogs in California. Most of their homes were in urban settings where dogs had to be leashed. And California had so many people and dogs that it would have been a problem.

Plus, neither Jack nor Amy thought having a dog locked up during the day when they were off working was fair to the animal.

Belle was so human in her behaviors that it was spooky. When Jack or Devon talked to her, Belle appeared to be listening intently. And she was so well-trained that it never occurred to either Jack or Devon to put a leash on the dog when they visited anywhere.

But one day hiking in national forest land a dozen miles from Jack's friend Oscar's Lakeside Winery, Belle ran ahead of them as they walked a trail, heading for a 150-acre swampy wetlands area known as Fuzzy Tree Swamp. It bordered a county road, famous for birdlife and harboring largemouth bass in its deeper pond pockets. Belle had lifted her nose, caught a scent and was off in rush, ignoring Devon's command to turn back.

That remote area of the forest was a favorite with real estate agents because the land contiguous with the forest made development unlikely at best. People who could find a private lot to buy could use the county road to get in but be almost completely surrounded by protected forest.

After fifteen minutes of calling and searching for Belle, they rounded the corner of the trail, bringing the swamp into sight.

The smell hit them first.

It was a faintly petro-chemical odor like diesel, co-mingled with the stench of dead fish.

And they could see Belle circling an obviously ill black bear cub sitting on the ground. The bear was swatting at the air like there were flies or bees buzzing it, except there were very few insects around. Belle was panting as if she had run a dog marathon. On the edge of the swamp, Jack could see hundreds of dead fish floating.

"I think we need to suspend the no-frack talk rule," Devon said. "Somebody dumped something here and it was big. I bet it was fracking-related."

Jack moved gingerly towards Belle, who was staying out of reach of the seated bear.

"Oh shit. We don't have cell phone service here," Jack said, frowning while he checked his phone. "We need to get the fish and wildlife people up here to deal with this sick bear. Maybe the sheriff, too.

He looked at Devon who had turned pale.

"Devon? You ok?"

Devon nodded slightly. She was standing very still, looking over Jack's shoulder across the swamp to a small rise of dry land maybe a hundred yards away.

There, in a copse of brush and trees, was another bear cub sitting on the ground looking sick, too, swatting at the air.

But just behind the cub Devon could make out a full-grown adult black bear, probably the mother, Devon thought, who was swaying from side to side.

And she was looking across the water directly at Devon and Jack and Belle standing next to her sick cub.

The immediate problem wasn't so much the bears or the smell or the dead fish, for Jack. It was how to get Belle away from the pond and the three bears.

He knew that he and Devon could withdraw and be safe—the mother would not leave her cubs, especially in their condition.

But getting Belle to quit the scene was proving difficult.

The mother black bear pushed the sick cub on the rise with her into the trees and started lumbering around the end of the swamp, her intent obvious—to get to her sick cub being harassed (she thought) by this dog and two humans.

"She can run faster than we can so we have to move. NOW," Devon said.

While Jack ineffectually tugged on Belle's collar to move her away from the cub, Devon slipped her belt off and reached over, pulling it through the ring on the collar, making an impromptu leash.

Belle immediately calmed when she realized Devon had the leash on her. They moved away from the swamp in a half-trot and back on the trail, watching the mother bear head for her cub.

The mother bear had slowed her approach as she saw the humans moving away.

But Jack could see the mother bear seemed ill too, as she turned the corner and walked over to her cub.

"I'm not a vet, but I've seen lots of animals who ate rat poison," Devon said. "People in the suburbs in Denver would put it out to kill cats, too. Assholes. But that swatting at the air reminds me of the cats and dogs when they ate the stuff."

Jack kept walking fast, intently staring at the screen of his cell phone until he could get at least a tiny sliver of a signal. The mother bear was not pursuing them and Belle was pulling on the leash, looking at Devon wondering why she couldn't go back.

"We have to get back to the trailhead here or somewhere where we can call someone. Some fool is going to come along that county road with a fishing pole and get a helluva surprise. I need to get Eli on the phone, too."

In the excitement neither Jack nor Devon had taken a single photograph, though both had the *Clarion's* Canon cameras in their day-hike backpacks.

"Let's get some people out here who know how to deal with the bears and somebody to check out that fish and water. Shit. We needed to take a water sample, too."

They slowed their pace when they were a half-mile away, but kept alert.

It occurred to both of them there might be other sick animals—maybe even other bears.

"You're right, I'm pretty sure we had cell service when we first started hiking," Jack said.

They heard the roar of the mother bear a few hundred yards away, just as they crested a hill and were able to dial 911.

The story about illegal chemical dumping in Fuzzy Tree Swamp got national attention, thanks largely to the three sick bears that state fish and wildlife rangers took off to a veterinary clinic for diagnosis and treatment after knocking the animals unconscious with tranquilizer darts.

"Three sick bears found, Goldilocks missing," read the headline in one New York City tabloid.

"Bears get sick in the woods, too," another headline said.

Jack and Devon were quoted in the *New York Times* and in news services, including CNN and the Associated Press. They all avoided suggesting any direct connection to hydrofracking, except in some of Jack's quotes.

"That area is near wineries and small farms," Jack was quoted as saying. "Somebody dumped a lot of something pretty foul into that big swamp to kill that many fish and make the bears sick. I don't think just diesel fuel would do that. Plus, think about it. Why would anybody dump diesel, considering what it costs?"

The television footage of the dead fish couldn't capture how big the kill was. But the on-site TV reporters all commented on how bad the smell was, and sounded as if they were gagging as they filed their reports from the side of the swamp.

Jack was characterized in the *Times* as a "crusading anti-hydrofracking journalist," a nice sobriquet that unfortunately raised his public profile high enough that he turned off his home telephone while the *Horseheads Clarion* started getting even more nasty phone calls.

The Tuesday after finding the dead fish and the sick bears, the *Clarion* also received a nasty letter from Grand Energy Services corporate lawyers, demanding that the *Clarion* cease and desist from publishing anything that linked the incident to GES.

"Considering that our web story didn't say anything about GES, just speculation that it was fracking fluid, makes you wonder doesn't it?" Jack said.

The front page of that day's *Clarion* also had the story about the bears and the fish. It also included comment from state environmental offices that the bears were sick because of eating the fish, but expected to recover. The state labs were testing the water but so far had found high concentrations of toluene, benzene, xylene and several other toxic chemicals at levels considered dangerous to anyone who drank the water.

"I can hear GES already. Who would drink swamp water?" Walter said. "GES is particularly touchy because I bet someone is going to need to drain that swamp to get rid of that water. Hello Ohio!"

Devon and Jack were particularly grateful that they hadn't decided to run into the swampy water to escape from the bear. If they had, they might have absorbed some of the chemicals through their skins.

To be safe, they had bathed Belle thoroughly when they got home that night and took her to the vet for a checkup.

After the staff meeting Tuesday, Jack found a note on his desk to call Oscar Wilson at the Lakeside Winery.

The note said "Meeting tonight of concerned citizens. Can you come?"

Jack decided to check his email before calling Oscar.

He also knew he needed to get started on his column for Friday, and was really looking forward to a quiet dinner with Devon again that night.

A meeting, he thought. *Maybe*.

He had two emails from Oscar that had stacked up while he was in the staff meeting:

Jack, a bunch of people are really pissed about the swamp dump. We need to talk.

And

Hey Jack, come tonight to the winery, after 6. Bunch of people want to talk about the dumping and the GES goons. Might be a story.

From the *Horseheads Clarion*

Column One
The Horseheads Clarion

Poisoned water
—a warning

By Jack Stafford

HORSEHEADS, New York — The chemical spill that killed hundreds of fish and other aquatic wildlife in Fuzzy Tree Swamp—and the likely agent that nearly killed three black bears—has people questioning if the uncontrolled industrialization of hydrofracking of natural gas and the development that comes with it is a good idea for New York.

Actually, that's not accurate. Anyone who has driven into Pennsylvania, where hydrofracking companies have had free rein and little regulation for years, can see how well it's been working for that state.

And now the Fuzzy Tree disaster just adds that much more evidence.

It's not a good idea, no

matter how much or how loud hydrofracking gas companies yell. No matter how loud landowners bellow who have signed gas leases thinking they will get rich.

The cleanup costs are hard to estimate right now. But at a meeting at Seneca Lake early this week, it seems clear the swamp probably needs to be drained, the water hauled off somewhere (Hello Ohio! Here's some more toxic stew for you to swallow!) and the soil tested on the edges and at the bottom.

State environmental officials have agreed, in concept. But right now Fuzzy Tree just has thousands of yards of yellow crime scene tape around it to warn people to keep out while the state decides what to do.

Too bad the animals roaming the national forest don't know what that tape means. Or that the water in the swamp will make them sick, maybe kill them.

There was more than a little yelling at this week's meeting, some of it over the spill, some of it over the need for jobs, some of it just because people were mixing alcohol with politics.

What was interesting was that state environmental officials are calling the problem at Fuzzy Tree a "spill," which by most measures means that it happened by accident.

We won't know until the tests are all done what's in that water, though standing downwind the water reeks of diesel, has hints of other toxic chemicals, and makes eyes water. The fish and game officers who came to tranquilize the bears ended up having their eyes flushed out by paramedics.

But was it a spill? Or was it a deliberate dump?

Could it be that someone with a load of toxic water in a truck decided to cut their day a little short and head home early after pumping thousands of gallons of something horrible into the swamp?

The swamp appears to be quite deep. But it isn't. It's not a lake. In spots, it's only a foot deep.

And so one full tanker truck of, say, for the sake of argument, fracking wastewater, would be a pretty big dose of chemicals for the swamp to swallow.

At this point, no one in officialdom is pointing any fingers. Grand Energy Services went so far as to threaten a lawsuit against this newspaper a few days ago if it mentioned them in connection with the spill (or dump).

So we won't do that. Mention GES, that is.

We don't know what foul chemicals or poisons ended up in that swamp, except whatever killed the fish and other water creatures—and nearly did in two bear cubs and their mother—was not something natural that burbled up from the muddy basin.

State officials have asked GES and other natural gas companies to produce the official highway logs for their wastewater dump trucks for the last month. The few people who live in that area have been canvassed about whether they saw anything unusual.

A good first step.

But they need to drain the swamp and start the cleanup, too.

And we all need to consider how many of these incidents we want to put up with.

Because it is just starting.

Jack Stafford is an investigative columnist and reporter for The Horseheads Clarion *and has worked as an investigative reporter for metropolitan newspapers in California and Colorado.*

The draining of Fuzzy Tree Swamp proved to be more complicated than it first appeared.

The water's tentacles spread in many directions, and as the pumps began to draw off the water, it stuck in pools here and there, trapped by brush and debris and a small beaver dam at one end on a tiny creek that no one had noticed.

The family of beavers that built it were gone, leaving behind one dead beaver, maybe only a few months old.

Grand Energy Services had stepped up and offered its wastewater trucks to help haul the water off to Ohio, where one of its subsidiary companies had agreed to pump the water into injection wells to get rid of it.

Eli had gotten a great photo of a line of about twenty of the yellow trucks on the county road bordering the swamp, waiting their turns to fill up.

After the photo was published on the front page of the *Horseheads Clarion*, people began to chatter about how many of these trucks were coming through the area. They also began asking questions about where in New York they might be dumping toxic loads on normal wastewater dump runs.

Jack and Devon were pressing state environmental

officials on whether GES was donating the cost of hauling the water or charging the government for the service.

It looked like they would have to file a Freedom of Information Law request, which told Jack GES was likely charging and the amount they were charging was probably enough that the taxpaying public would not be pleased.

Water samples were still being tested, though preliminary results had been released by state environmental officials showing that there was some diesel, xylene, toluene, benzene and, to the surprise of officials, "significant traces" of DDT and Lindane, both pesticides.

How much fluid had been spilled—or dumped—into the swamp was difficult to tell, because whatever fluid was spilled or dumped had been diluted by the water already there.

The pumping took three days, mostly because of having to chase down the small pools that got stuck in the backwaters as the main swamp was lowered. An afternoon rain shower that dumped a half-inch of rain slowed things, too.

But as the last of the water was sucked out, three workers from a Rochester, New York company specializing in soil testing came in to take samples.

Eli got excellent photos of them, too, dressed in full protective gear as they waded knee-deep in soupy mud that made it very difficult for them to walk. They used a boring tool to go down a foot or two to take core samples as well as samples closer to the surface, popping the half-inch sized samples into test-tube-like containers, carefully marking each one and from what part of the swamp it was taken.

As with the trucks, Jack and Devon were asking who

was paying for the work, but county officials said it was "being negotiated"—but with whom they wouldn't say.

As the soil samples were being taken at Fuzzy Tree, Jack, Devon, and Walter were interrupted by a phone call during their strategy meeting at the office.

The whiteboard they used for notes and as a brainstorming tool showed a half-dozen in-progress stories, photos and proposed columns. They were adding more, and what had started as a simple diagram was turning into a nightmare of lines, arrows, and circles.

Roy Bonder Jr. was about to be returned from a psychiatric hospital to county jail, presumably for more legal proceedings. Ron Bonder Sr. and the hydrofracking wastewater truck he had been driving were still missing. Three GES workers had been arrested in a bar brawl in Rockwell Valley that put two other patrons in the hospital. And the family of the schoolteacher killed at Rockwell Valley High School by Bonder Jr. was filing a civil lawsuit against the school district.

"Walter, Eli has some news from the swamp cleanup," Jack said. "You have to hear this. I'll put it on speakerphone."

A garbled voice came through, the sound of wind howling in the background.

"So guess what they found?" Eli shouted. "One of the soil samplers pulled it up. I got a picture of them holding it."

Walter gave Jack a raised eyebrow look.

"I'll guess, Eli," Walter said. "A body. They found a dead body in the swamp. I hope it's Jimmy Hoffa and not Amelia Earhart."

Jack, Devon, and Walter all laughed, their voices blocking Eli's voice from coming through for a moment.

"Did somebody already call you? Weird. They didn't find a body. But they pulled up a skull. It looks like maybe a human skull. I'll send my photos right now. Maybe we can get something up on the web."

Jack grabbed a red marker pen and wrote on the whiteboard in all caps: ELI FINDS BIGFOOT!

"Send the photos, Eli, and try to get a closer look before we commit to anything, okay?" Walter said. "That swamp has been there forever. Jimmy Hoffa could be in there."

As Walter turned off the phone, Jack drew a line with an arrow from BIGFOOT up to Roy Bonder, Sr., with a big question mark.

"Only in the movies, Jack," Walter said. "Only in the movies. Or maybe a crime novel. But just in case, let's find that mug shot we published of Bonder when his son was arrested. Just in case it isn't Bigfoot or Hoffa."

The story about the skull in the swamp drew even more attention to the *Horseheads Clarion* and its staff.

Suddenly, out-of-state and Canadian newspapers—particularly in places where hydrofracking was taking place—were interested, running stories about the mysterious skull and the chemical composition of the water in the swamp.

After the soil sample workers found the skull, the swamp area was sealed off again, with more thousands of yards of yellow crime scene tape, as sheriff's deputies and forensic specialists waded through the muck looking for any bones that might go with the skull.

As soon as Walter had seen Eli's photos of the skull, he

knew that it had been there a long time. It was clear there was no flesh or hair, and it was missing bits of bone.

Still a human skull was a human skull. Most of the media stories used the phrase "cold case" in describing the police searching the swamp and trying to figure out who the skull belonged to.

A week after it was discovered, Jack, Walter, Devon, and Eli were back in the conference room late in the afternoon, sorting through the barely understandable reports about the chemicals found in the water and some early toxicology reports on the mud. But the latest twist came when one of the soil samplers and water testers mentioned that fracking wastewater often had traces of radium and other radioactive substances picked up from deep in the earth.

The soil and mud seemed clean of that. But some of the water samples they had taken in—the water already sent to disposal wells in Ohio—showed well-above background levels in radiation. And they were salty, too.

"They are pretty sure that the water that ended up in the pond can be labeled as hydrofracking wastewater, though they won't say it yet officially," Jack said. "Christ, it might be months before the state issues a formal report. And who knows how much politics might get played by then."

The whiteboard was cluttered again, but some themes were taking shape: chemical spills and dumps, skull identification, gas company wastewater truck logs, and a long column named "legal shit," with a list of stories that might require filing court documents to get authorities— and GES—to give them the information they needed.

One item—a lawsuit over Jack's mention of GES in column—was crossed off. Walter said the company probably decided it didn't want to be embroiled in a lawsuit and then find out later that the pollution could somehow traced back to them.

"The good news is the mud seems pretty clean," Devon said. "But that means the water was probably not in there that long. There are only a couple of houses along that road anyway. And they say they haven't noticed anything unusual. Of course, GES trucks use that road as a shortcut going north all the time, they said. And all kinds of other trucks and big rigs."

Walter suggested that they start using the newspaper's morgue—the old paper copies of the newspaper dating back nearly one hundred years—to check for missing persons who might have lived in that area.

"That skull makes this a real mystery," Walter said. "You can have some fun with that in your column, Jack. The police haven't been very good at sharing information on this. Be fun if we figured out who it might be first."

Eli suggested that they put together a list of everyone who was missing in the area for the last twenty-five years, a suggestion that dovetailed with what was computerized and would not require going into non-indexed paper copies that were stacked in the storeroom, or going through the old microfiche system that some of the papers had been filed on.

"That's a good idea, Eli. Start with that. But let's put the rest of our staff on going through the microfiche and the hard copies, too. We might all have to get our hands dirty for while on this."

Jack wrote "Bigfoot" on the white board again next to the skull.

"I would prefer looking for him than talking to anymore TV stations about this," Jack said.

"Him? Are you sure Bigfoot is a him?" Devon asked, her voice teasing. "And that skull might be a she, too. Don't rule out anybody."

"Sure," Jack said. "Mrs. Bigfoot maybe."

Eli was already to the door of the conference room when he turned around.

"Um, as long as we have Bigfoot up there. I want to add something. And I would appreciate not getting any laughs. Wolverines and *Red Dawn*. I haven't said anything, but there've been some incidents in Colorado and California that I think are connected. And there have been some postings on some sites about Roy Bonder, that maybe he wasn't kidnapped or something when his truck disappeared. Maybe he stole it."

Jack turned to the whiteboard and wrote "Bonder" and "wolverines," nodding to Eli.

"Kind of forgot about the Wolverines. Oscar asked me last weekend up at the winery if we were still pursuing that idea. But with missing trucks and drivers, skulls in swamps and mysterious chemical spills, who knows? Maybe we'll find Bigfoot, too. Where did you see this wolverine stuff?" Jack asked.

"A guy in Berkeley. He's been getting big-time involved in environmental stuff out west. It's like he just discovered hydrofracking," Eli said. "He connected some dots, too and just wrote a piece on a new blog."

"He have a name?" Jack asked.

"Oh, yeah. It's Wilson. Web Wilson. But he started using his full name so I wasn't sure it was the same guy as the one I remembered from some other reports. But it is," Eli said. "It's Noah Webster Wilson. And he mentioned the *Clarion* in his posting."

Jack looked over at Devon who was pressing her temples with her fingers like she had a headache.

"Devon? You know him? He's from Berkeley but he writes about Colorado, too."

"Yes," Devon said. "I know him. I was married to him once."

HEROES AND VILLAINS

Flathead, Missouri

Grayson Oliver Delacroix III checked himself in the mirror of his spacious top floor corner office at Grand Energy Services six-story headquarters before heading into the conference room where six vice presidents and a dozen staff members were nervously waiting for him.

He adjusted the Windsor knot on his red and white striped tie, noticing that the gray around his temples was spreading slightly farther back, a process that had started ten years before when he was in his early forties. He smiled as he remembered what his father had told him when he was lecturing him on clothing and style when he was still in high school.

"If you want people to think you're important, you have to look the part," Delacroix had said.

"Never look disheveled, unclean. Never. Always have your hair combed. Shave close. Someday you will be president of some big firm. Maybe you'll go into politics like me. Maybe a United States Senator. There has to be a consistent image of greatness seen in public. My daddy taught me that."

His father ended the lecture with a hard, open-handed slap to Grayson's cheek.

"There," he said seeing the anger blossom across his son's face. "That's the face you should project. You're a good-looking guy. But people need to be afraid of you, too."

Since then Grayson always gave himself a slap on both cheeks before going into any big meeting or confrontation. The redness was often interpreted as a touch of displeasure or willingness to explode. And remembering how that slap hurt helped set his jaw into the look his father said would strike fear. It had served him well all through college, then early in his career in the Louisiana oil industry, and now as president and chief executive officer of GES.

The chairman of the board of directors of GES once joked in a meeting that the board hired Grayson as CEO because he "looked just like the president of a big company." Grayson flushed red that day, not from the slaps he had given himself, but from genuine anger. And perhaps because he knew how true it likely was.

Today he didn't need a slap for his cheeks to be red.

One of his vice presidents was still out on a medical-stress leave after getting his hands burned with some caustic substance in the men's room on the floor below Grayson's office. His company was the target of increasing bouts of vandalism all over the country, with trucks being stolen and well sites and equipment targeted.

And now some goddamned environmental activist had started publishing a website that said these incidents were all being coordinated by some group calling themselves the Wolverines, and modeling themselves after some whack-job enviro-novel from the 1970s called *The Monkey Wrench Gang*.

It was the website that had Grayson the angriest.

For months GES had been getting reports from its offices and sites around the country that the word Wolverines was being spray-painted on equipment and sometimes contained in paper notes left at the sites of vandalism attacks.

GES had successfully kept most of the details of the vandalism secret, except for occasional newspaper and television reports.

But those reports were always local and didn't make a splash outside of the small circulation areas of the newspapers or broadcast areas of the stations.

Numerous attempts to make a big deal of it nationally by some pipsqueak, twice-a-week newspaper in Horseheads, New York had failed because of GES stonewalling.

But the Horseheads newspaper's persistence had bothered Grayson enough that he sent word down through the chain of command, ordering GES workers in the Finger Lakes region of New York to quietly start boycotting the newspaper's advertisers.

They were also to spread the word among the advertisers that the *Horseheads Clarion* had a vendetta against the GES because GES wouldn't advertise in the small newspaper.

The website was grabbing attention, though—lots of attention. There was plenty of detail, enough detail that national media had started calling the GES headquarters' press office for comments on the authenticity of the website's data and asking for more information about specific incidents from Maine to Seattle.

Grayson paid a consulting company $200,000 year to keep such things under control. But a few hours before, a reporter from the *New York Times* had managed to figure out

Grayson's personal—and he thought quite secret—email address and queried him directly, asking for an interview to talk about the burning-hands incident, the website, and most of all, this group calling itself the Wolverines.

The vice presidents in charge of operations, finance, and personnel, and the secretaries and support staff all stood quickly when Grayson walked into the room, offering a collective and nervously cheery "good morning, chief."

They kept standing, waiting for Grayson to sit in his chair at the end of the long conference table before taking their seats.

But Grayson Oliver Delacroix, the former Louisiana oilman, now a seven-figure CEO of a major American energy company stayed on his feet.

"Just who the *fuck* is Noah Webster Wilson?"

When Noah Webster Wilson was in college in California as a returning student in his thirties, he fell under the spell of a young female professor of environmental science who was interested in Noah's passion for saving the planet and his equally apparent passion for her.

He was about the same age as newly-hired assistant professor Devon Walsh, teaching her first semester fresh out of graduate school with her newly minted Ph.D.

The romance went from classroom to bedroom to wedding in Reno by the end of the semester with only a few of their mutual friends present, but it was doomed from the outset by Devon's conflict of interest as Noah's teacher.

It was also doomed by Noah himself, who went by Web Wilson then.

Even his friends thought Web had an ego the size of the University of California at Berkeley campus.

Maybe the entire San Francisco Bay Area.

In less than a month the marriage fell apart. Devon, no longer enchanted with the academic world either, packed her bags for Colorado, while Web stayed in Berkeley, content to play environmentalist, going to protests, organizing demonstrations, and generally being a nuisance to corporations that he believed were unkind to the environment.

Noah had visited Devon several times in Colorado in the next few years, but their short-time marriage barely even came up for discussion.

Growing up, Noah had hated his full name. The teasing he took and the bullying he endured had hardened him down so deeply that he frequently charged after wrongdoing well out of proportion to any perceived insult or wrong.

He flirted briefly with membership in a radical environmental group in which members talked about blowing up oil pipelines. But as much as he believed that big corporations were essentially evil and ruining the planet, he drew the line at violence.

On a trip to see Devon in Colorado, he got to see the effects of hydrofracking for natural gas up close, moving him from curiosity to alarm to full-blown anger.

In California, high volume slickwater hydrofracking was still mostly a dream of natural gas and oil companies, though in the Central Valley some activity was taking place. California's environmental regulators paid it little attention because of a shortage of staff caused by decades of budget cuts.

But in Colorado, drilling rigs were being set up in residential neighborhoods and near schools. Hydrofracking chemicals were polluting water wells. Methane gas was being vented directly into the air when it wasn't burned off in 50-foot flare stacks.

Scientists studying Colorado and neighboring states were also becoming increasingly alarmed at the amount of methane gas the wells were simply allowing to escape into the atmosphere. Collectively, the natural gas wells were providing more raw fuel for global warming than all the gasoline and diesel-powered vehicles on the road.

And the heavy truck traffic in many drilling areas had clogged the roads to the point where rural Coloradans were experiencing city-like traffic jams for the first time in their lives. And on country roads that usually were barely traveled.

After Devon left Berkeley, Noah completed an environmental science degree but continued taking classes—without enrolling, thanks to Berkeley's open door policies—with courses in geology, biology, hydro-engineering, and his new favorite, media.

The science coursework made him confident that he could argue the dangers of hydrofracking with anyone. The media classes gave him an idea: He would reinvent himself and take on the menace of hydrofracking as a champion for the environment.

The last time Devon saw Noah—then still going by Web Wilson—was in the same Colorado bar where she met Jack Stafford for the first time a few months later. Web had come to Colorado to tell her that he was going to launch a website titled *Fracking Serious,* to persuade people about hydrofracking's dangers.

He also told her he would be using his full name and planned to become an anti-fracking spokesman.

"My dad told me he named me Noah Webster Wilson because it was the kind of name people would remember," Noah told her in the bar. "I get it now. I get it. Really. I used Web all these years because I hated my real name. But now I can use it. It even sounds like a broadcaster."

Devon knew that what Web/Noah also wanted was for them to get back together. His charisma and good looks always made women fall all over themselves to be with him. Devon thought she might be the first woman who had ever rejected him.

"Web, I think the website is a great idea. Anything people can do to show how dangerous this technology is a good idea. But us? Together? Again? Web, please. I left California and came here because we're not good together. You're too needy, Web. But I don't want to revisit all that. Really. That's history. But good luck with this thing. I'll read it. I promise."

An unhappy Noah Webster Wilson left Colorado the next morning and headed back to Berkeley, more determined than ever to make the website something the world—and Devon—would notice.

A small cadre of his Berkeley friends had promised to help him with tech support, while others wanted to sign on just to wreak a little havoc against corporations from the safety of a computer keyboard.

But by the time he launched the website and was posting consistently, Devon had moved to New York. She logged on a few times, mostly out of duty, but also to see if he was actually going to shake things up. She thought that Noah's website was too much of a rehash of what other sites were publishing about chemicals, fracking-fluid spills, and the threat of earthquakes. He occasionally posted some interesting diatribes by scientists who predicted that hydrofracking would be the engine of an environmental doomsday.

Several times she started to email Noah to give him some advice about better ways to pursue the line of inquiry from the doomsdayers, but always balked at the last minute.

She didn't want to start even *that* level of an electronic relationship with Noah again and have him get the wrong idea.

He could be very persuasive.

Jack and Devon sipped wine as they rocked in metal chairs on the front porch of Jack's house in Horseheads, a house that Devon was domesticating one room at a time.

Jack's father had lived there as a widower long enough to turn it into a senior citizen's bachelor pad. And when Jack moved back in he simply used his childhood home as a shirt-drop for the most part since returning to work for Walter in the spring.

Now it was a full-on summer evening and the house seemed almost to sigh with relief that there were two people in it who enjoyed it and were taking care of it.

"I didn't say anything about Web—excuse me—Noah, because my marriage to him was such a mistake and so short. I wrote him off, really," Devon said. "And maybe I was embarrassed, too.

"It wasn't like what you have described about you and

Amy," she said. "I'm not sure what it was but it ended quickly when I got to know him well enough to see he was not good for me. Not at all."

Devon's announcement in the staff meeting that afternoon—that she had once been married to the increasingly well-known environmental activist Noah Webster Wilson—had stunned Walter, Jack, and Eli into silence.

"Do we say congratulations or condolences?" Walter had joked. "And on which? The marriage or the divorce?"

Devon had stood and walked out of the conference room, the redness in her cheeks screaming embarrassment. Her former husband's sudden emergence in New York had caught Devon by surprise, even though she knew he was also concentrating on hydrofracking and other environmental issues.

She decided if she was going to burst into the tears she felt welling up, she would do it on her own and not in front of the three men.

Jack rocked on the porch, petting Belle, who had started following him around all the time. Belle often went to the newspaper office with them, sitting in the floor space between Jack and Devon so she could keep an eye on them both.

"You sound apologetic and you don't need to be, Devon. Really. None of us knew you had a famous ex-husband out there. Or I guess it would be more accurate to say a want-to-be-famous ex-husband. And if you weren't doing the work you are doing for the newspaper, who would give a shit?" Jack said.

He rocked again, taking a sip of his wine, a full glass of

Oscar's Boot Riesling, compliments of Oscar, who brought a case of it the day that Devon had moved into the house. Once the weather had turned from wet spring to warm summer, Jack and Devon made it a practice to sit on the porch nightly to have a glass before dinner. And their wine of choice was anything made by Oscar's Lakeside Winery.

"I thought you might," Devon said, looking straight ahead, her jaw set slightly. "As in *give a shit* about whether I was married before or not. That's why I left the meeting so suddenly."

At the office, Devon had marched out to her desk, tapped on her keyboard for a few minutes, and then announced to no one in particular that she was leaving and heading home.

She had snapped a leash onto Belle, who looked confused when Jack stayed in the conference room, and headed out the door, walking to Jack's house.

"Okay. There're two things, Devon. But you have to look at me," Jack said.

Devon turned her chair so she and Jack faced each other a few feet apart.

"First, the professional side of this is that you're working at a newspaper that has at least a veneer of being objective. I don't have to be objective, particularly, because I write a column. But you've been writing news stories and Walter's worried that your marriage—make that *former* marriage, okay? Okay! Sorry! Walter is worried that it might somehow cast doubt on your ability to be objective. I know objectivity is a journalism myth, but it protects us and protects the paper."

Devon sat up straight in the chair ready to launch a response-defense, throwing her shoulders back. She stopped when Jack put up his empty hand with palm facing her.

"Wait! Please. Please. Before we get into a debate about professional ethics or any ethics, I do," Jack said. "I do."

He watched Devon's shoulders relax as a question-mark expression ran across her face.

"As in I *do* give a shit that you were married before. Not about that. Not the marriage. Not really. But I wish you had told me. That's all. Because I *more* than give a shit about you, Devon. I just haven't been able to get myself together enough to talk about it or even know what to talk about, not since that night up the lake at the bed and breakfast. Okay? Really."

Belle stood up and walked between Jack and Devon, looking back and forth between the two of them, trying to interpret from the tones of their voices what even she, as a dog, could tell was important.

She understood what happened next, and did her best to be a part of it.

Jack and Devon stood up and hugged each other, spilling some of that precious Oscar's Boot Riesling onto the porch, where Belle finally got a taste of the drink that her two human roommates seemed so fond of every night.

Belle didn't think it was such a big deal. But, being a Labrador, she made sure she licked up every drop anyway.

Grayson Oliver Delacroix got into the elevator, heading from his top-floor office to a meeting in the newly remodeled GES exercise center located on the first floor of the company headquarters.

The small conference room in the center had a window overlooking the six-lane lap pool Grayson used twice a day for exercise. He had been a swim team champion as a teenager and had brief moments of glory in college in Boston, even dreaming of getting into the Olympics for the 100-meter freestyle.

Now it was his daily exercise of choice, and any of his vice presidents who wanted to move up the corporate ladder learned quickly that swimming with Grayson was a required part of the path to promotion.

The poolside conference room was usually reserved for taking actions the company wanted to keep below the official GES radar. When Grayson had meetings there no minutes were taken or official records kept. It was understood that he used this place, as opposed to the conference room upstairs, when he had things he wanted done but not necessarily tracked back to him.

Officially, the poolside conference room had no recording devices. But Grayson made sure there were hidden cameras and microphones that he could access if he wanted a private record.

Today the *non-agenda* agenda was about the website run by Noah Webster Wilson, and how he was getting GES information for his rants against hydrofracking.

Since Grayson had summoned his vice presidents the week before to rail about Wilson, the GES director of Northeast field operations had discovered that some emails had been traced from a Rockwell Valley GES office to Wilson's tipster hotline, where people could send email messages or telephone in.

Whoever sent emails thought they had deleted them, but a copy remained of every email sent to and from GES on the company server in Flathead, nicknamed the Big Black Box.

GES had more than two dozen people working in the Rockwell Valley office, and any of them would have had access to the GES main email address, used mostly for replying to customer inquiries.

When Grayson walked in the entire group stood up quickly. Grayson was pleased to see that several of the vice presidents were dressed in exercise clothes with towels draped over the back of the chairs. He encouraged them to take two exercise breaks during the day. If they swam as part of that exercise, so much the better.

"So do we have some do-gooder in Rockwell Valley feeding stuff to this guy?" Grayson asked as he sat down. "And do we have any idea who it is?"

The vice presidents dropped to their chairs but shifted uneasily. They were all happy that they weren't directly in charge of that section of GES operations, though Bill Honer, the vice president for Human Resources knew it would land on his head at some point.

Honer's office had developed a series of sophisticated psychological tests for potential GES employees, to predict their likely loyalty to the company, willingness to follow orders, and most of all, belief that natural gas and hydrofracking were all positive developments.

The tests were only given to potential office staff and executives. The roughnecks who ran the drilling rigs, the truck drivers, and the men and a few women who ran the well-site equipment were assumed to be loyal, if only to their paychecks.

Honer nervously stood to speak, though he preferred to stay seated in case he had to face Grayson's wrath.

"We figured out the emails to Wilson came from the

main Rockwell Valley GES office," Honer said. "That much we know for sure."

As he tried to sit down, Grayson held up his hand.

"That's it? Jesus H. Christ. I knew that before I walked in here. We have somebody telling this asshole—who, by the way is getting a big play in the media in case you are asleep— about what goes on behind the curtain for us. We have to plug this now. Today. Yesterday. Is that clear Bill? *Yesterday.*"

Honer nodded and sat down, while Grayson drummed his hand on the table, his temper rising by the second. Seeing the two staff people who had started swimming laps raised his mood slightly. He knew he would hit the pool right after the meeting about this damned boondoggle.

"Who is our best man on the ground there in Rockwell Valley? I can't remember the guy we hired for acquisitions and leases. He's a Texas guy, isn't he? His name was like that guy in *The Godfather*, Luca Brasi or something like that?"

Honer stood again, thankful he could remember Luther Burnside's name.

"It's Burnside, Luther Burnside. Luke. And he's up in New York trying to get leases signed. He works mostly out of the office," Honer offered. "Should I contact him and tell him what's going on?"

Grayson stood quickly as if to leave, triggering a chain reaction of vice presidents popping up out of their chairs, with a few towels falling onto the floor.

"Yes, you should contact him, but do it in person, Bill. Fly up there. I want this solved quickly. Whatever needs to be done. Change passwords. Whatever. I bet there's some young college kid working in that office who slipped past your tests. But whatever. Get Luther on it."

Grayson started for the door, then stopped and turned around.

"And while you are there, Bill, I want everybody attached to that office retested with those fancy psyche evals of yours. In fact, hit all the roughnecks, too. Tell them it's a test to see if they have management potential. I want to find who's sending this stuff out."

Honer looked over and saw that the red light had started flashing on the wall telephone in the conference room. The only person who would dare ring that phone when there was a meeting going on was Grayson's executive secretary.

Honer grabbed the phone, grateful for a reprieve from Grayson's scrutiny. He listened, his mouth slowly opening, and then he hung up quickly.

"Earthquake," Honer said. "There's been a pretty big earthquake."

Grayson swore.

"Christ, Ohio is going to shut us down from ever dumping into those wells again. How many earthquakes is this? Five? Six? Shit."

Honer shook his head. "No chief, not Ohio. California. And they're saying it was triggered by gas-well drilling in the Central Valley. We just started some work out there. Mostly test wells."

Grayson shook his head and headed down the hall to the locker room.

A person leaking GES information, and now an earthquake that they would be blamed for.

He needed a swim.

From the *Horseheads Clarion*

Column One
The Horseheads Clarion

Hydrofracking shakes it up

By Jack Stafford

KERN COUNTY, California —
Early reports from seismologists this week projected that the Golden State was likely to experience a catastrophic earthquake in the wake of the earthquake that rocked the Central Valley the day before.

They backed off when the aftershocks of the quake settled down quickly. For two days now, there hasn't been a temblor of major concern.

California got lucky, at least as of this writing, Thursday morning.

People here in New York are familiar with the 1906 earthquake that destroyed San Francisco. Less familiar, but as frightening, was the 1989 Loma Prieta earthquake that killed 57 people and caused $6 billion in damages around the San Francisco Bay area.

That was known as the World Series Earthquake (Ah, now you remember it!) because it hit just as the San Francisco Giants and Oakland Athletics were about to start the third game of the 1989 World Series at Candlestick Park.

So, why am I writing about California earthquakes 2,500 miles away?

Because California seismologists are pointing the finger directly at the nascent hydrofracking drilling that's going on there, saying it is a prime suspect in the quake that shook the state.

Seismic meters from the Oregon border to San Diego registered the tremors, with property damage reported in San Francisco and Los Angeles. Only a few people were hurt by falling debris.

These cities are so used to earthquakes that their citizens generally take them in stride. But because both San Francisco and Los Angeles were hit simultaneously, everyone is nervous.

They should be.

California is crisscrossed with earthquake faults and because of it, state building codes to ensure that buildings can withstand fairly heavy shaking have been in effect for years, driving up all construction costs. A school in California costs many times more to build than a school in, say, Pennsylvania, because of having to withstand earthquakes.

California's environmental regulators are scratching their heads right now because hydrofracking started almost without notice. The state has virtually no rules. Several attempts to legislate regulations have been met with stiff resistance from natural gas exploration companies who say they have the situation under control and don't need anyone telling them how to run their companies.

Sound familiar?

Ironically, California has the stiffest water quality controls and laws in the nation. But its hands are tied by the same Halliburton Loophole in federal law that exempts gas companies from revealing what's in the toxic chemical cocktails they inject with millions of gallons of water to frack for gas. The various clean water laws that apply to you—and every other industry—don't apply to natural gas companies.

California should take a quick look at Ohio and other parts of the nation where earthquakes are becoming the new normal and gas companies are claiming total innocence.

Similar to the issue of polluted water wells at people's homes near natural gas well sites, the industry shouts that there are "no studies that definitively link" the injection of wastewater—or hydrofracking itself—to earthquakes. None, nada, zip, zilch.

Perhaps.

But even in our neighboring, pro-fracking state of Ohio, citizens are calling for a moratorium on injecting the wastewater into the ground, following a series of earthquakes that occurred for the first time in recorded state history.

Certainly the authors of building codes in Ohio and Pennsylvania never anticipated earthquakes. Why would they? Only a few have ever been experienced.

That's already changing.
You can feel the earth moving on this. Literally moving.

*Jack Stafford is an investi-
gative columnist and reporter
for* The Horseheads Clarion *and
has worked as an investigative reporter for metropolitan
newspapers in California and
Colorado.*

Noah worked on an email to Devon for a half-hour, changing words, changing phrases, moving the tone back and forth several times from really friendly to coldly professional.

His latest information from the Wolverines, whoever they were, put forth a theory about why the Halliburton Loophole to bypass federal clean water and air laws was pushed through, and it was outrageous. He knew he needed some mainstream media help to break the story if it was to have any credibility.

And although Devon's newspaper in New York was a small operation, it was getting national attention since the Fuzzy Tree Swamp incident. Plus, he saw that the number of hits on its website was soaring—way beyond anything that could normally be expected at a small, twice-a-week newspaper.

Most of the Wolverine messages detailed out stunts they had pulled in various parts of the country. They seemed to especially like to target Grand Energy Services with vandalism.

Not all of it was all that destructive, and sometimes they even showed a sense of humor.

Noah laughed thinking about the missive from them before this one, the details of which he was still trying to corroborate. The Wolverines took the lug nuts off two wheels of the Mercedes-Benz owned by GES president and CEO Grayson Oliver Delacroix while it was parked in the GES headquarters parking lot in Flathead, Missouri.

When Delacroix drove out of the lot that day, two tires popped off the car when he made a turn by the guard shack.

GES was saying it didn't happen. But Noah had a series of ten photos of a seemingly very pissed-off Delacroix standing next to his car, dressing down a security guard who wore a puzzled look on his face.

Noah knew he could simply publish the photos with a story on the *Fracking Serious* website. But he wanted to ensure the story would get picked up by other media. It was embarrassing for GES. More importantly, it showed the Wolverines were even more devious than Noah had thought. How they got into the parking lot and did that under the eyes of a guard was very James Bond. Maybe *Mission Impossible* would be a better analogy, he thought.

He put the finishing touches on the email and got ready to send, but then balked at the last second.

For the last week, Noah had started to get paranoid about his email communications, probably from dealing with the Wolverines. The group rarely used email or the telephone. At least not with him. He would find notes slipped under the door of his apartment and sometimes phone texts would pop up, telling him to go to a coffee shop where an envelope would be waiting with the cashier. The envelope usually held one or more flash drives with information and occasionally photos.

One time he had to go to the Oakland Zoo, where the fellow selling peanuts near the elephant cages had a paper bag for him with details in a note inside about what GES well sites the group had hit the week before.

The latest communication had come in the form of a typewritten note—ironically on what looked like official GES stationary—that said the Wolverines had found the real smoking gun behind hydrofracking. He wondered if Wolverines knew someone was spying on them electronically.

Noah's finger was poised over the send button on his email program again. He went back and took out two key sentences, leaving in an entreaty that he wanted to talk with the publisher of the *Horseheads Clarion* and Devon about what the Wolverines had just communicated to him.

Then he put them back in and swore at the computer.

He changed the subject line from "Gas company secrets" to "Tinfoil hats needed," as he sent the email to Devon, with a copy to *Clarion* publisher Walter Nagle.

He hoped she would open it, but was pretty sure Nagle would no matter what.

Walter grabbed Devon and Jack early Monday morning and suggested they go over to Millie's Diner for coffee and tea.

The general staff meeting to go over the planned content for Tuesday's newspaper went smoothly enough that Walter was confident they would make deadline easily, even with a little conference across the street.

And at the last minute, Walter grabbed Eli, too, suggesting he join them.

Eli almost dumped his chair over he was so eager to go along. He never got invited to go to Millie's by Walter, even though he had been working for Walter since graduating from college with degrees in computer science and journalism.

Eli wasn't sure why he was being invited into the tight inner circle of Walter, Devon, and Jack. Perhaps they needed his advice and wanted it out of earshot of everyone.

But it didn't matter.

Since a handful of local advertisers had started canceling their ads in the newspaper, Walter was becoming increasing cranky about money and paranoid about Grand Energy Services in general. One advertiser had confessed that he had been threatened by a GES employee that if he kept advertising with the *Horseheads Clarion,* he might find his propane deliveries slowed up the next winter when having propane for heat would be critical.

Thinking about that made Eli worry that Walter might be thinking about backing off on their coverage of GES.

It was a little crowded in their corner booth at Millie's, with Eli squished in next to Devon. Any discomfort for Eli was outweighed by getting to sit in such proximity to Devon, and then it was doubly outweighed when Shania came by with the coffee pot and made a fuss about Eli being in there.

"Hey Eli, are you a member of the Horseheads' Press Club now? That's what I call these guys. Tea or coffee?"

Shania poured coffee for Walter and Eli and headed back to get the tea setups for Devon and Jack, while Walter unfolded a printout of the email he had received from Noah Webster Wilson over the weekend. He shoved it over to Eli to read, then pointed to Jack when Eli was finished.

"I know it seems strange to want to talk about this outside the office, but I think some of the other staff members are feeling excluded. We're asking them to do hydrofracking grunt work, but not much real reporting. Not on that anyway."

Shania brought the tea and a menu for Eli, who she noticed had been eyeballing several of the platters of steaming food sitting on the cook's counter, ready to be taken to customers.

"Well, the four of us coming over here probably won't relieve any of their anxiety," Jack said, looking at Eli. "But what about this email? What do we do with it? Full disclosure? Devon showed it to me last night and we talked about it."

Walter smiled and took the note back, folding it up and putting it back in his pocket. He looked at Eli, who hadn't reacted at all when he read it.

"So, am I the only one who didn't read this and talk about it already?"

Eli raised his hand slightly.

"These guys called me at home last night and read it to me. It's not that new an idea. But if these guys have some proof? Wow. Double wow!"

Walter pulled out the email printout again.

D.

I have been talking with the W group who say that a major benefit to all big corps is that with the H. Loophole, they can dispose of all "manner" of liquids without disclosure. Any disclosure. They think it might be as important as getting the product out of the ground. Maybe more lucrative, even. They say they have numbers and proof, some of which I have seen.

Talk soon?
Noah

"This Noah probably thinks someone has a system monitoring his emails, using keywords like Wolverines or hydrofracking or toxic waste," Eli said. "But really, as clever as he thinks this email is, somebody could simply be reading all of his emails and this code could be figured out by a kindergartener. The NSA has been compiling emails since Bush the First."

Devon laughed and spoke for the first time.

"What he wants is for us to buy in—probably help authenticate whatever documents he has and use us as a way to promote this idea. It's not that wacky, really. But Noah likes conspiracies."

Walter nodded and suggested that they take back a bag of donuts and sweet rolls to the staff still working in the office.

"Devon, let's try to get your, um, friend Noah on the

phone this afternoon as soon at the Tuesday issue is put to bed," Walter said. "With the three-hour time difference, it should work out. I just hope he doesn't talk in code. I want to hear about this evidence before we make any commitment."

Bill Honer waited nervously for the connection to go through to the conference room at Grand Energy Services main office in Flathead, Missouri.

He was driving north from Rockwell Valley up a steep hill towards Ithaca, New York for a meeting with Luther Burnside, GES's best landsman, whose son was a computer technician at the Rochester Institute of Technology, helping them keep the geniuses who enrolled there from destroying RIT's mainframe computers with hacking and incredibly complex games.

Burnside hadn't nailed down who had fed the Wolverine organization—and possibly Noah Webster Wilson— information. But he had flagged a number of leaked emails that he thought Honer and the home office might want to know about.

One of those emails had made Honer gasp—a reference to an internal memo from 2004 that talked about a petrochemical company in Alabama that had been injecting toxic chemicals into deep wells.

The company's troubles had come to the attention of people in the federal government while they were working on a plan to make it easier for natural gas exploration companies to use the new technology of hydraulic fracturing.

That plan would amend federal law and exempt natural gas companies from various environmental laws. The GES memo suggested GES could contract to take some of the more hard-to-get-rid-of toxic liquids and add them to fluids they were already planning to use to hydrofrack the wells.

Local environmental groups screaming about the chemicals had gotten some press coverage.

Honer pulled off the highway in a narrow cutoff when he heard the speakerphone in his car start clicking, indicating the speakerphone at GES headquarters was on the line.

He didn't trust himself to drive if GES Chairman Grayson Oliver Delacroix started a rant aimed at him.

"Honer? Grayson. What do you have? Your email said Luther found some emails."

Honer opened a file folder on the passenger seat, shuffling until he found the one about disposing of toxic waste down gas wells as they were being hydrofracked.

"Chief, there're about a dozen that Burnside, er, Luther, found that he said look like they went to an email address that might be the Wolverines or that Noah guy running that website," Honer said. "The one that caught my eye says that GES had a meeting in 2004 with some federal people about the whole trade secrets provision of the law Bush was going to sign."

Honer paused, waiting for Grayson or whoever might also be in the conference room with him to react.

"That's it?" Grayson said. "We had a meeting with feds. So? Everybody knows about the trade secret stuff. What's in the other emails?"

Honer took a breath. "Um, the email references an internal GES memo that exists on paper only. My secretary had to go down into the archives to find it to fax it to me. Let me read the two paragraphs I thought may be a problem if they got out:

The names of chemicals injected down the wells can be called
trade secrets under the proposed amendments to the Safe
Drinking Water Act. There's
not going to be any monitoring so we can monetize this two
ways: in the fracking process
by charging a disposal fee for
non-fracking chemicals added,
and by charging a second fee
for wastewater disposal that
has these chemicals in it.

The wastewater can go to
regular sewage treatment
plants or injection wells. Either way, they won't be a GES
problem and what's in the fluid
is protected and confidential.
We need to develop a confidential fee schedule right away.

The line stayed silent. For a moment, Honer wondered if the phone connection had been lost. Then the static crackled.

"Bill, I want you to tell Luther we need to know who got the email that references this memo. And I want your secretary to go to the archives and pull the original and bring it to my office along with her copy. And Bill, get rid of that fax."

Honer agreed and said he would call Luther immediately, knowing he would be meeting with him in less than an hour.

But Honer was equally concerned about his lie about the fax.

He had not received a fax from his secretary. Instead, she had scanned the original memo, converted it to a PDF and then emailed it to Honer directly. Honer hated fax machines and thought they were too unreliable. Plus you could barely even find one anymore.

Still, he should have told the truth, even though he knew Grayson would go ballistic that an electronic copy had been made.

His copy of that email, with the PDF attached, was in his laptop, but it also was on her machine and in the GES mainframe computer. He immediately realized he should have alerted Grayson, but decided he would have his secretary dump her copies and tell the tech people to discretely delete the email from the Big Black Box mainframe.

Being head of human resources had its advantages when getting people to do these kinds of favors.

He pulled back out on the highway to Ithaca and was looking down to dial his cell phone to call Luther when his car drifted across the centerline into the path of a tractor-trailer propane tanker rolling down the hill into Watkins Glen.

Police later estimated the semi was probably going seventy miles per hour in a 55 mph zone—Honer's car was doing barely 40 mph uphill—when the two collided, killing Honer instantly, crushing his vehicle and shoving it off the side of a steep embankment.

Honer's car came to rest in a grove of trees and up against a sign protesting plans to hydrofrack in New York State.

The driver of the propane tanker was not cited for speeding, according to a news story published in the *Horseheads Clarion* several days later.

The teleconference call with Noah Webster Wilson, sitting in his Berkeley apartment/office combination, had gone as well as it could, considering that Noah was posturing for Devon, Devon was trying not to be exasperated with Noah, while Walter, Jack, and Eli were trying to push through the prevarications and barriers Noah was throwing up instead of getting to the point.

Eli had thought a Skype face-to-face would be best for the conversation, but Devon vetoed the idea.

"Noah. Look. I don't know you, though I have been reading your website postings and Devon speaks highly of you," Jack said.

Devon started to glare at Jack across the conference table as he was speaking, then closed her eyes.

"And I think I can speak for all of us that it is totally believable that there is some collusion on the part of chemical manufacturers with the gas companies to get rid of excess toluene or other chemicals by dumping them this way. For a news story, we need some documentation."

In his apartment, Noah rocked back in his chair and looked over at the computer nearest to him for a second. He was always checking to see how much traffic his *Fracking Serious* website was getting. That morning he had posted several commentaries by people who lived in Kern County near hydrofracking sites, the same sites geologists were blaming for the earthquake that shook most of California the week before.

"I understand. Completely," Noah said. "I'm trying to keep references to documents so I don't start sounding like the anti-fracking version of some nut-job NRA website. But these people are keeping these cozy deals way below the radar. In a lot of cases the big chem companies have an ownership stake in the gas drillers. So it's just as easy as shipping barrels of crap to the well heads. They might own the wells."

Jack scribbled a note to Walter, who pursed his lips then smiled, nodding approval. He spun the around for Devon to read, who shrugged her shoulders noncommittally.

"We have some excellent research people but haven't been able to pull up anything to prove what you are talking about," Jack said. "And so far, you haven't published anything on *Fracking Serious* about this, right? But I have an idea. Ship me what documentation you do have. Whether it's from the Wolverines or GES or the tooth fairy. Then let's coordinate on getting the story out—even it turns into a huge scream from GES."

Noah looked at the stack of materials he had received from the Wolverines, with a fresh set of three printed-out pages on top that he had picked up the morning before, slid under his door while he was sleeping.

"Okay, if we can agree to publish what I have simultaneously. I don't mean the same story, but the information. Yesterday the Wolverines gave me something that is as close to a smoking gun as we are going to get right now."

Walter leaned over to the speakerphone so Noah could hear him clearly.

"Noah, this is Walter Nagle again. As the publisher, I'll agree to some kind of deal like that, after we see what you just got. But I ask that you not name the *Clarion* in any story you publish on your website about this. Let us source you, instead."

Noah agreed to scan the Wolverines' latest missive and send it along via email.

"And really nice to hear your voice again, Devon," Noah said, just before hanging up.

Walter and Jack exchanged brief glances while Devon shook her head and looked up at the ceiling.

Then she stood up and headed back out to her desk.

"I think as soon as we see what he has, you should start writing your Friday column," Walter said to Jack. "And Eli. You should start digging into how some of these toxic chemicals are supposed to be disposed of. No matter what, if the companies are dumping chemicals in gas wells they don't need to just to dispose of them, it's news. But it's a pretty nasty charge to make. It better be true."

In Berkeley, Noah looked at the printed copy of an email that was sent from a GES secretary to a vice president at GES named Honer. It was hard to say how authentic it was. But if he attributed it to the Wolverines, given their recent track record of whistleblowing, it would be enough for him.

And maybe enough for Jack Stafford and the *Horseheads Clarion*, too.

Maybe.

He started writing an email to Devon about how it was great to be working together, but then decided to scan and send the GES documents first.

He would email the documents directly to her and Walter at the same time.

From the *Horseheads Clarion*

Column One

The Horseheads Clarion

The benefits of hydrofracking

By Jack Stafford

FLATHEAD, Missouri — Anyone who reads this column regularly probably just dropped their newspaper, and maybe spit their coffee across the table.

Benefits?

Since coming to the Horseheads Clarion in the spring, I have made no secret that I believe hydrofracking is a disaster for communities. The only ones who gain are wealthy gas company executives whose companies are raking in huge profits.

Oh. Sorry. The shareholders are doing well, too.

I've detailed out water and air pollution issues, the health impacts, transportation woes, increases in violence, and political conflicts of interest.

But this week, thanks in part to an anti-hydrofracking

website called Fracking Serious, there's a new reason to be concerned.

This scenario—still being unraveled and documented—is simple and explains one of the most difficult-to-understand things about hydrofracking: why the chemicals used in the process are kept so secret.

Since approval of the popularly nicknamed federal Halliburton Loophole, natural gas companies have been able to keep secret the names and amounts of the chemicals they pump thousands of feet down into the earth as part of their toxic hydrofracking cocktail to break loose natural gas.

That secrecy has been a puzzler and one that environmentalists (and most thinking people) rail about. The gas companies themselves say the formulas (and thus chemicals) are trade secrets. And to reveal them would give a competitive edge to other companies.

But the scenario Fracking Serious presents, based on documents now being studied by this newspaper, is that it's not just the fracking cocktail that's being pumped under pressure in the wells, it's other toxic chemicals, too. These are toxic chemicals that have nothing to do with the process—and aren't needed. These chemicals are in there simply to dispose of them.

Let me say that again. These chemicals are not in there because they help get the gas out. They are in there simply to get rid of them.

Apparently it's a lot cheaper to pump the chemicals several thousand feet down into the earth than deal with them on the surface where there are so many environmental regulations.

Worse, the composition of the chemical-laced water that comes back out of the wells is similarly secret. The non-fracking chemicals simply get trucked off to injection (disposal) wells or to municipal water treatment plants, plants ill-equipped to handle the chemical-laden (and sometime radioactive) wastewater.

How ill-equipped they are is hard to say, because no one (except for the gas companies) knows what's in the fracking wastewater.

This just-uncovered scheme is a great deal for any company that has a problem with toxic chemicals produced as a byproduct of their particular manufacturing. Just pay the gas companies a disposal fee and voila! No more toxic chemical waste. And whatever that waste is, it is a secret kept from environmental regulators, the public, and even most medical personnel if someone gets sick from exposure.

The scheme does sound farfetched. Multinational companies colluding with gas companies to use the legal secrecy of hydrofracked gas wells as cover to get rid of wastes that would be expensive—or almost impossible—to get rid of otherwise.

Yet within hours of the website Fracking Serious publishing its allegations, representatives of the federal government and environmental specialists from nine states contacted the site's editor and author, Noah Webster Wilson, demanding to see the documentation to prove gas companies were using their wells as hi-tech chemical dumps.

The gas companies, including Grand Energy Services, which has most of the gas wells in the Rockwell Valley area, are now in a complicated situation.

If the companies are asked to prove to officials they are not dumping toxic chemicals (unrelated to hydrofracking) in their wells, they will also have to reveal what chemicals they are dumping.

Further complicating the situation was an announcement by the Securities and Exchange Commission and the Environmental Protection Agency today that they would be conducting a joint inquiry about the alleged dumping, as well as trying to ascertain if any fiscal transaction rules were broken.

On the environmental side, the EPA noted that illegally disposing of toxic wastes is a felony.

Multiply one felony times the 5,000 or so wells hydrofracked in Pennsylvania alone and you have a crime wave of epic—and toxic—proportions.

Jack Stafford is an investigative columnist and reporter

> *for* The Horseheads Clarion *and*
> *has worked as an investiga-*
> *tive reporter for metropolitan*
> *newspapers in California and*
> *Colorado.*

The reactions to the *Fracking Serious* website's allegations were swift and brutal.

And although Jack Stafford's *Column One* had mostly repeated the *Fracking Serious* claims, the mention that both the website and the *Horseheads Clarion* had documentation sent the natural gas industry—as well as federal and state regulators—into a tizzy of finger pointing, accusations and finally, recriminations aimed squarely at the messengers.

While the federal government flapped on about how it was investigating, it was clear that the people who should have been on top of the issue were spending most of their time discrediting what *Fracking Serious* and the *Horseheads Clarion* had published.

And even large mainstream media organizations, which had been citing the *Horseheads Clarion* as an oracle about hydrofracking's woes, suddenly seemed to back off and began to suggest that the newspaper was slipping close to needing tinfoil hats by throwing in with Noah Webster Wilson's website and "its kooky conspiracy theories."

Walter's telephone had started ringing Friday within a few hours of Jack's column being printed. Over the weekend nearly 3,000 messages clogged the answering machine's digital memory.

"I wish I had kept the old machine hooked up. It could

only handle about 200 messages and then froze up," Walter told Jack Monday morning.

Jack laughed.

"But Walter, you realize that a lot of those are also from people who think what we wrote is not only believable, but true. They're ready to go to war. And did you check out some of the comments on the website after my column? There are some real whack-jobs on there. But I got comments from dozens of anti-fracking groups all over the U.S. supporting the theory. They also promised to demand a federal hearing. We kicked over a hornet's nest with this. A national hornet's nest, maybe."

Devon and Eli came in the front door bearing pastries from Millie's across the street, and cups of coffee from a new coffee machine just installed.

"I'd stay out of Millie's until all the GES trucks leave today, Jack," Devon said. "God, those assholes are nasty. They were telling everyone who would listen that your column is all just crap and that you made it all up."

Eli opened the bag on the table and snagged the maple bar before Jack could reach for it.

"Yeah. But I watched the other people in the diner and I think they know that the GES guys are full of it," Eli said. "They also didn't seem to know we worked over here. Lucky us."

The main phone line rang, rolling over to the answer phone, which Walter switched to speaker so they could all hear who was calling. It was before 8 a.m. and he steadfastly refused to answer the telephone until regular business hours.

The call was from an Oklahoma newspaper reporter who wanted a quote. She was writing a story about Jack's column and also wanted to get permission to reprint the whole column on their website.

Walter was about to pick up the call when the second line rang. It was another newspaper, this one in Colorado, where hydrofracking was being blamed for the illnesses of a half-dozen school children whose elementary school was across the street from a hydrofracked gas well. That reporter was doing a story on the health effects of hydrofracking and wanted to know if Jack could tell her the names of any of these toxic chemicals he had referenced in his column.

The next call came as Walter, Jack, Devon, and Eli had all retired to their computers as they munched pastries and sipped coffee or tea. A newly-hired young woman receptionist, a June graduate of Rockwell Valley High School, walked in and caught the call before the machine could pick it up.

After exchanging pleasantries with the caller, she looked at Devon expectantly, indicating the call was hers.

The official protocol the new hire didn't know yet was that phone calls were never routinely shipped directly to staff members. The receptionist was supposed to screen them and ask if the staffer would take the call.

And so it was that Devon's phone rang and she found herself talking to Noah Webster Wilson, who was barely awake in California, three-hours earlier than New York.

"Sorry to bother you, but I got my first really scary threat today," Noah said. "It was a text message to my cell phone. It came just a few minutes ago."

```
Leave this story alone. You
won't like the consequences.
```

```
You can't write if your fingers
are broken. And you can't talk
if your tongue is cut out.
```

Devon asked if he had gotten any other threats like that before. But Noah said the usual hate comments posted on the website, most of which he deleted, never hit this low or threatened him personally.

"And my cell phone is pretty private," Noah said.

Devon tried not to laugh. She knew that at least a half-dozen women probably had his phone number on speed dial and it would hardly take a professional spy to get it from any of them.

Still, it was troubling.

"So do you want to talk to Walter? Maybe we should put this on the speaker phone in the conference room so you can tell everyone," Devon said.

"No, no, no. I just wanted you to know, for now. Besides, I'm coming to New York and Pennsylvania in about two weeks. For the big Rockwell Valley anti-fracking concert and rally. You know about it, right?" Noah asked.

Walter had already been laying out a strategy for how to cover it, perhaps also making some revenue from it to make up for some of the advertisers who had bailed on the *Horseheads Clarion*. He had also started fielding requests from out-of-the-area media to provide some photos and possibly stories, requests that kind of irritated him, considering some of these same media had been calling the *Horseheads Clarion* a "fringe publication." He decided those media would pay dearly for exclusive stories.

"Yes, we've heard. I think the newspaper is going to

be running some special pages about it. Sounds like the Rockwell Valley organizers are bringing in some big guns from the colleges in Ithaca," Devon said.

The pause on the other end of the line gave Devon a hint about Noah's other reason for calling.

"Yeah, and it's going to be fun," Noah said. "They've asked me to give a speech, right after some memorial for that teacher who was shot to death. I'm working on it right now. I want to stir them up good. I'll see you there. You take care, okay? Ciao, Dev."

Devon eased the telephone back on the cradle and looked over at Jack, who was looking at her.

"Didn't mean to eavesdrop," Jack said. "But I got an email from some Rockwell Valley anti-fracking people. They are touting a talk at their rally by the famous anti-fracking activist Noah Webster Wilson. The title of his speech? "Fracking's Dirty Secrets.'"

Belle was sprawled out on Jack's front porch in her usual position at Jack's feet, watching him rock slowly in his chair. Devon was in and out of the house, bringing out some pre-dinner snacks of celery, tomatoes, and cheese.

They had been invited up to Oscar's winery, but after a tumultuous week they opted to sit at home, crack open a bottle of Oscar's Boot, and do very little.

The flap about the claims that natural gas companies were using their hydrofracking to dispose of toxic chemical waste was building momentum.

Virtually every environmental and anti-fracking website had either posted their own version of the story or linked to the *Fracking Serious* website and Jack's *Column One* in the *Horseheads Clarion*.

While newspapers' news sections and broadcast newscasters shied away from doing much with the story, newspaper and web columnists wrote about it, keeping the idea alive.

A few conservative television talk show hosts made jokes about the need for tinfoil hats, but the public, largely opposed to hydrofracking anyway, didn't bite, and the jokes had fallen flat by mid-week.

"I thought your column today about the need for more science and less politics in hydrofracking was great, Jack," Devon, said, putting a food tray on the small table between their chairs.

She slipped Belle a chew bone so the dog wouldn't spend her time begging for a piece of cheese.

Jack and Devon sat rocking, barely talking, just enjoying yet another warm summer evening. Climate change had altered summers since Jack's youth so much he barely recognized it.

When he was growing up, nights like this—dry, clear and warm-bordering-on-hot—were extremely rare. This summer it felt like living in California. Days and days of beautiful weather.

"I'm not sure I would have left here if the weather had been like this when I was a kid," Jack said suddenly. "I mean, I hated the snow and when that job came open in California it was getting out of the slush as much as it was going for the opportunity. But even summers could be pretty crappy. Humid. Lots of rain. And cold sometimes. Really cold."

Devon sipped her Riesling.

"So not to break the nostalgia bubble, but do you think you might leave here again? For a new job somewhere else? Or, I don't know."

Jack rocked, sipping before he spoke, trying not to grin.

"Actually Devon, I think you do know. And the answer is complicated. Walter needs me here. He wants me here. He's like a combination friend and father. He's like a father to you, too, in case you haven't been noticing. And when he asked me to come here, it was because he knows he'll be backing away bit by bit and needs someone to take over. Me? I don't know if it's me. I've barely even worked as an editor. But I would bet a bottle of this wine Walter thinks it should be me."

Belle put her nose in the air and dropped down off the porch, a squirrel on the ground somewhere near that she was going to chase up a tree—unless she accidentally caught it.

"That's almost what I asked," Devon said. "So I have to be blunt. If I leave when my six months are up, are you going to stay here in New York, or maybe head out with me?" Devon said.

Jack called to Belle, still circling a tree where several squirrels chattered at her from the high branches, scolding her for breaking up their summer nut-gathering on the ground.

He turned to face Devon, putting his wine glass down on the table, his hands on his knees.

"Devon, you have been a good friend to me. More than that. And I have been struggling with the fifteen-year age gap. No wait! Don't talk. Give me a minute. And I've been tearing my brain apart about Amy, too. My heart broke when she died, Devon. Broke. That's why I haven't even kissed you. I haven't been very good about all this. *Wait, wait*," Jack said, holding up his hand to forestall a verbal avalanche.

"I have to just let this all out here, okay? I probably should write a column called 'Jack and Devon.' It might be easier."

Devon smiled and relaxed back in her chair.

He paused long enough to take a gulp from his wineglass, looking at Devon who had put her hands in her lap like a child waiting for a scolding—or a birthday present.

"I wake up at night, staring out the window and I think *I love this woman*. There. There it is. But then in the morning, my brain says *don't hurt her*. I can't guarantee I won't go right off the rails if we...um... Christ! What do you even call it? My brain is like scrambled eggs. The only time it isn't is when I am writing. Or times like right now. Sitting here."

Devon let Jack stop completely. He blew out some air, then took in a deep breath.

Devon stood, grabbing both of his hands to pull him up, too.

"Jack, every one of these conversations seems to end up with us hugging each other. And it feels so good. I love you hugging me. And me hugging you. And it seems like neither one of us wants to let go. So here it is: I think we need to hug more. Right now would be good. And the next time you wake up in the night and think *I love this woman*, come into my room and tell me. And don't you tell me the next morning 'I didn't want to wake you up, so I went back to my room.'"

Belle came up on the porch as they wrapped their arms

around each other. She was puzzled because it seemed like they were doing that for an awfully long time, and it was Belle's time for dinner.

As an always-hungry Labrador Retriever, Belle had her priorities and hoped her humans would break it up soon. If not, well, the cheese on the food tray behind them was within easy reach if they weren't looking.

And they both had their eyes closed.

Grayson Oliver Delacroix was sick of fielding phone calls from the Grand Energy Services board members about the unfortunate release of the email and memo about including unnecessary toxic chemicals as part of the chemical cocktail used in hydrofracking.

But Bill Honer's death in a car accident took some of the heat off Grayson. He portrayed Honer to the board as a rogue employee with no sense of security, a situation Grayson had been trying to fix long before the accident.

Grayson was more concerned about damage done inside the company than externally, because his public relations minions were already having some success convincing every media type who would listen that the notion was lunacy.

And thanks to the Halliburton Loophole, there was no way to prove anything, he hoped.

Several years before, Grayson and a cabal of gas company executives had teamed up with oil producers and refinery owners to create an organization to tout the marvels of natural gas. *EFA —Energy First America*—was funded by the natural gas industry with some monies from oil companies, for the express purpose of counteracting anything negative about natural gas exploration or oil that activists came up with.

Among their tasks was convincing the public that the inexpensive solar panels and new, efficient wind turbines coming out of Chinese factories were a problem, not a solution. People had to be convinced that anything other than natural gas and oil couldn't possibly provide for the nation's needs for at least twenty years. Maybe fifty years.

It was the same twenty years the industry had been touting since the 1970s when the nascent solar industry starting making headlines.

The gas companies hired some of the sharpest young conservative college graduates to go to activist events, then write reports posted on *EFA's* website that attempted to debunk anything they had to say, regardless of how true. They also ridiculed anyone who criticized gas drilling, the gas industry, and especially hydrofracking.

EFA had been spectacularly successful in provoking the rage of hydrofracking opponents, who spent hours writing long diatribes in the comments section on the website in response to *EFA* postings.

The more they screamed, the more the *EFA* staff responded, tying up the activists' time even further—exactly what Grayson and the other companies wanted. If they were raising Cain on the website, they were not writing letters to the editor or to legislators and regulators.

The *EFA* staff was working overtime every day, pumping out articles about how the leaked email and memo were fabricated by hydrofracking opponents.

That was a total lie but hydrofracking opponents weren't as good at defending themselves.

Grayson's biggest concern today was a planned anti-hydrofracking, anti-natural gas development rally to be held on the field next to the Rockwell Valley, Pennsylvania high school where a teacher had been shot and killed by a student, the son of a GES employee.

That rally would likely draw lots of media attention. And because it came so close to the release of the email and memo, it was also likely that the issue could become a big part of the event.

His secretary had been fending off media inquiries about the email and memo since they were featured on the anti-gas website *Fracking Serious* and in the newspaper in Horseheads, New York that was always pestering GES with questions.

Now he was getting calls about the rally and a challenge the *Fracking Serious* website editor, Noah Webster Wilson, had made—that Grayson show up and tell people to their faces that hydrofracking was safe and also explain the email and memo.

Grayson squeezed a rubber ball he kept on his desktop to strengthen his grip.

I'd love to squeeze that bastard's neck, he thought.

Grayson logged onto the *EFA* website and browsed through two articles the staff had just published, suggesting that the rally was likely to draw a lot of people who would use drugs and that anyone who attended should be ready to be frisked by local police who were concerned about potential violence.

Neither was true, but it stirred up people and would make activists even more cranky and paranoid.

The *EFA* pieces did give Grayson an idea.

Normally, Grayson filtered any orders through executive levels so that nothing could be directly traced back to him. But with Bill Honer dead, he wasn't sure who to use, and asked his secretary to get their field man Luther Burnside on the telephone.

When the phone rang a few minutes later, Grayson had just logged off the *EFA* website after posting a comment— using a pseudonym the *EFA* director had created for him— suggesting that one of the key female leaders was a lesbian and insinuating that she was acting inappropriately with some of the younger female anti-fracking crowd.

He knew it would send her off chasing his posting.

"Um, Mr. Delacroix, this is Luther. Luther Burnside. Your secretary said you wanted to talk to me. I'm sorry about Bill. Bill Honer? He was a good guy, really. He hired me."

Grayson chose his words carefully, knowing that Burnside was sharp at getting farmers to lease their land to GES for gas drilling, but perhaps not as intuitive at understanding that his job was to protect the CEO of the company.

He pushed the record button on his telephone to ensure he had a verbatim record of what was said.

"Luther. Thanks for getting back to me so quickly. I know you're busy out there representing us to the New York farmers. I have a problem right now with this rally that's going to take place Saturday in Rockwell Valley. In Pennsylvania? I'm sure you've heard about it. They are going to make a big stink about our work. They are even going to try to exploit the death of that poor schoolteacher who was shot by that deranged teenager. Shameless bastards. Shameless."

"Mr. Delacroix, what can I do to help?"

Grayson flexed the rubber ball again before he spoke.

"Luther, I'm concerned that our point of view—how good this development is for Pennsylvania—isn't going to be represented. I wonder if you know some good people who might be willing to go and maybe show some support. Just to be fair. Do you understand?"

This time it was Luther who didn't speak for a moment. But when he did, Grayson recalculated Luther's capacity for understanding subtlety.

"I think I know exactly what you mean, Mr. Delacroix. I know just the folks, and I think I will ask a few of our GES guys if they know anybody who might want to go wave the flag. How's that?"

Grayson took a deep breath and silently thanked the late Bill Honer for hiring Luther. Luther was not only good at signing New York State leases at a record clip, but was likely going to prove useful in lots of ways.

"Luther, thanks for your help on this. I won't forget it.

"Oh, and Luther, until we get everything sorted out, I want you to answer directly to my office, through my secretary, of course. Bill Honer always spoke highly of you."

Grayson logged back onto the *EFA* website. He had an idea to put up a posting that Noah Webster Wilson might be gay that was sure to get people buzzing.

The first thing Jack noticed when he and Eli pulled up near Rockwell Valley High School was the bigger-than-life-sized photo of Anne Kovach, the 26-year-old chemistry teacher shot to death earlier that year by one of her students, Roy Bonder, Jr.

Bonder was still in a psychiatric facility, his mental state still an issue that needed to be resolved before the district attorney's office would move ahead with a murder trial.

But Anne Kovach was a centerpiece because Bonder Jr. shot and killed her in an apparent pique over Kovach's insistence that hydrofracking fluids were toxic.

Jack made a mental note to check and see if police had any leads on the boy's father, Roy Bonder, Sr., a GES employee who was still missing since driving a tanker truck loaded with fracking wastewater to an injection well site in Ohio.

The photo of Anne Kovach was a studio shot and showed a beautiful dark-haired woman with a smile that was heartbreaking to see. The photo and a table with cards, flowers, and other memorial items were at the far edge of the parking lot, where students were clustered in two groups. One was dressed in a style best described as hippies, the other looked like athletes, some wearing Rockwell Valley lettermen jackets.

But beyond them, in a large field, the actual anti-hydrofracking protest and rally was set up with a big stage in front and a sound system that looked like a rock concert was on tap.

Several second-tier musicians and groups were slated to be part of the event, but speeches were the mainstay. Nearly 3,000 people were already milling around the site, shooed away from the actual school grounds by local and state police and what looked like a dozen private security guards dressed in dark blue almost-military style uniforms.

They carried batons, radios and canisters of what looked like pepper spray, but no guns.

They also were all wearing mirrored sunglasses, making them look more like Mexican Federales than private guards.

"Take some photos of those security guards when you get a chance, Eli, okay? And some close-ups of their ID badges if you can. I'm going to ask the Rockwell Valley PD who hired them. I'll bet it was GES."

Jack and Eli parked Eli's SUV and headed into the throngs. It was almost a carnival atmosphere with lots of music here and there, tons of people carrying signs, and hints of marijuana smoke in the air.

Jack hoped the Rockwell Valley Police and state troopers would cut the protestors some slack today.

As they approached the stage, they saw a tall sturdy-looking man in his forties bustling about, his hair tied back in a ponytail. Jack recognized Noah Webster Wilson from photos, though in person he was much taller than Jack expected.

Even from 200 feet away, Jack thought he could almost feel Webster's nervous energy.

"There's Wilson, Eli. Walter said to be sure to get a good mug shot of him besides the action shots."

Eli rolled his eyes as he looked back at Jack, waving as he walked off into the crowd.

"Got it Jack. You take the notes. I take the pictures."

Jack scribbled some notes as he watched Eli walk towards the center of the protest, mentally noting that he needed to just let Eli do his job. He was a great photographer, really. And his reporting and writing were improving so fast he hoped he wouldn't be recruited by another newspaper or magazine.

The top of Eli's head was still in view as Jack spotted a young man in dreadlocks carrying a tray like a cocktail waiter would in a crowded bar. On the tray were about thirty two-ounce paper cups with yellow fluid that he was offering to people to drink, always getting a big laugh from everyone he stopped.

There were no takers.

From the corner of his eye, he saw three of the private security guards converging towards the man, closing in from different directions. The crowd parted and formed a circle around the man just as the guards braced him, asking what he had in the cups.

Jack had trouble hearing as he pushed through to get a better look, and then heard the man in dreadlocks say, "Just some tasty fracking fluid. Like a sip?"

The people in the circle laughed and started to taunt the three security guards, setting up a chant of "drink, drink, drink." As Jack finally got a good view, he realized one of the guards was the GES employee named Tom who had braced him and Walter several times at Millie's Diner and had been involved in an altercation at Lakeside Winery.

Tom turned towards the people in the circle and away from the man with the supposed-fracking fluid. Tom seemed startled when he spotted Jack. He was close enough that Jack could read his full nametag: Tom Fletcher.

Jack looked over Tom's shoulder and saw that the other two security guards—probably GES employees, too, he thought—were ordering the man to put down the tray of paper cups, drawing a chorus of booing from the people in the circle. More people were coming over as they heard the booing.

There was a lot of muttering as the carnival mood disappeared.

Then Jack saw the young man's face turn from a vacant-happy-hippie smile to anger just as he launched the entire tray at the two guards in front of him, dousing both of them with the fluid in the cups, the yellow fluid running down their dark uniforms.

The flying tray landed in front of the guards who both fell backwards down onto the ground trying to avoid the fluid. The gasps and laughter from the crowd drew even more people over to see what was going on.

Jack wanted to call Devon and Walter right then. They were both back at the office waiting for photos and a story. But he decided to wait to see how this all played out. As the two doused security guards got up, they unhooked their batons, and Jack realized that Tom Fletcher had left the circle.

Eli had arrived and was taking photos when the guards attempted to grab the young protestor. He was too quick.

He kicked the first guard solidly in the crotch, dropping the guard to the ground. The second guard aimed a swing with his baton at the young man's head, but missed, clumsily falling down to the ground from the effort.

From behind him, Jack could hear more shouting as a phalanx of a dozen burly-looking men carrying pro-hydrofracking signs pushed their way towards the circle, lead by Tom Fletcher. Tom had a canister of pepper spray held out in front of him and his lips curled in his usual snarl. He was about to let loose with a blast into the protestors when Jack saw the meaty hand of his friend Oscar Wilson clamp on to Tom's arm tight enough that he dropped the canister on the ground.

Then just as quickly, Tom tripped over the leg of Oscar's niece Lindy Karlsen, landing face first on the ground.

Oscar looked over with a huge grin on his face and yelled to Jack.

"Payback's a bitch isn't it?"

It took nearly two hours to get a semblance of order at the protest, with only a dozen arrests in the end.

One of them was GES and security company employee, Tom Fletcher, who was carrying a .32 caliber pistol for which he did not have a permit.

He might have even been forgiven that, except that in the confusing melee that ensued among the anti-hydrofracking protesters, the pro-hydrofracking people, the security guards, and local police, Tom managed to punch a Rockwell Valley police officer in the mouth hard enough to loosen a front tooth.

The officer was trying to stop Tom from choking the young man who had been carrying the tray of what turned out to be harmless liquid.

A later analysis showed it was tap water with yellow food coloring in it.

Jack and Eli had mostly stood back documenting the action, which proved rougher on the security guards and pro-hydrofrackers than the other protesters, who were younger and in seemingly better physical shape.

Oscar had waded in at one point to convince a security guard who was holding his niece Lindy to let her go. She wanted to jump in and pound Tom Fletcher to a pulp.

Jack shepherded Oscar and Lindy away and gave them

several business cards that said "STAFF *The Horseheads Clarion*" in case the police or security guards gave them any trouble.

"It's amazing what a press credential will do," Jack said. "I just hope they don't cancel this whole thing."

The rally and protest organizers had nearly two dozen volunteer marshals of their own wearing orange vests who cordoned off the fight area quickly, though it was clear that some of the pro-hydrofracking people wanted the confrontation to keep going and were ready for a lot more of a fight.

To their credit, the Rockwell Valley Police and state police noticed the same thing and a half-dozen pro-frackers ended up being arrested and taken away when they refused to calm down, continuing to attack the volunteer marshals even after police warned them to stop.

"We heard that GES was planning to disrupt the place, so Lindy and I decided to come down for the fun," Oscar said. "Nice to get a chance to squeeze that asshole Tom's arm. Would've preferred his skinny neck."

The television crews had shot plenty of footage of the fight and the arrests, and Jack shuddered to think how this would play on the screen. There were even some national cable TV outlets there, though most of them had shown more interest in the pro-fracking side of things than what the protesters were trying to get across.

The crew from one local cable channel was already packing up its gear when Jack caught up with the woman anchor, a recent college graduate who had an annoyingly-high-pitched voice.

"Um, Miss Millicence? Jack Stafford, *Horseheads Clarion*. I watch your newscast all the time."

She was pretty sure he was lying, but flattery from a real journalist kept her attention. Plus, he was kind of good-looking, in an older-guy sort of way.

"Why, thanks. What a fight, huh? The GES people said the protesters attacked the security guards, but the police say both sides are at fault," she said.

Jack decided he could do double duty—keep her and the local cable cameras there for the speeches and maybe correct what she would report.

"Actually, I was standing right there and the attack came from the GES guys. I mean security guys. I said GES because I recognized one of them by his nametag. He was one of the guys arrested? He had a gun and punched a police officer. Almost knocked out a tooth. Do you want his name?"

Amber Millicence, her broadcast journalism degree barely six-months old, was flabbergasted. The police hadn't mentioned anything to her about the police officer being attacked or that the security guards might also be gas company employees.

She was doubly mad because the police lieutenant she had talked with spent most of his time trying check her out.

"Could I interview you? On camera? Just for a few quotes about what you saw? We're packing up. I want to get back to the studio and go through all this tape."

Jack heard an announcement over the loudspeaker asking people to come to the stage.

"I would love to, but can it wait just a few minutes? I heard this guy Noah Webster Wilson has some real news about what the protesters are going to do next. And I need to be sure to hear it all."

Amber nodded okay. "But it has to be within the next half-hour. For sure?"

Jack nodded and held up his hands to agree as he turned and headed off towards the stage, smiling as he saw the cameraman pulling his equipment back off the cases as Amber fluffed her hair.

"Ladies and gentlemen," a voice called from the stage. "We are going to skip the preliminaries here. I think we have already seen the face of how ugly the natural gas people can be. Please give a round of applause for the editor of the website *Fracking Serious* who promised to be just that, *fracking serious,* today. Here he is, Mr. Noah Webster Wilson."

Jack made a note that the crowd had thinned from before the fight, but there were still probably 2,000 people on their feet cheering and waving signs when Wilson walked out on the stage.

And the cheering got louder and louder as he raised his right arm above his head, his fist clenched, his head dipped down.

"Are you ready to STOP these bastards from ruining OUR earth?" Noah Webster Wilson shouted.

"Are YOU ready?"

Jack noted that nearly everyone in the crowd had their fists clenched in what was once called the "power to the people" salute.

He was pretty sure Eli would have a great photo of that for the front page of the newspaper, even without asking him to get one.

Oscar Wilson prowled the crowd, watching carefully for people who might be GES shills ready to cause trouble. A GES employee had been at Oscar's winery a few days before and bragged he and "some of the boys" had been told to come "stir things up" at the protest.

After his fourth glass of wine, the GES worker said that if they did stir things up, they were guaranteed some overtime bonus money in the next few weeks.

The crowd was a mix of old and young, with even a sprinkling of elementary school age children. And although Noah Webster Wilson's speech was getting people worked up, the sense that a fight might break out at any second seemed to have passed. Many people were sitting on blankets. Quite a few sat comfortably in lawn chairs.

Looks like a modern Sermon on the Mount, Oscar thought.

Jack and Eli had taken up positions close to the stage. Eli wanted to get good photos of Noah. Jack wanted to hear and also be able to see crowd reactions.

They had already filed one story and a dozen photos about the fight and arrests electronically with Devon and Walter back at the newspaper office. Devon said she wanted to stay behind to help Walter with the mysteries of the website, though Jack was pretty sure she mostly wanted to avoid seeing Noah in person. Walter said he hated crowds anyway and preferred to stay in the office.

A photo of Oscar wrestling Tom Fletcher to the ground was generating a lot of hits, many of them from several Flathead, Missouri I.P. addresses, Devon said.

Major national news media outlets were contacting Walter about getting some exclusive stories and photos. Walter agreed. He also planned to bill them for the exclusive photos and stories at a rate five times higher than normal after they had publicly scoffed at the *Clarion* for its stories about the deliberate dumping of chemicals in hydrofracking wells.

The newspapers and television stations in the United States' Southwest and West were particularly interested in Noah Webster Wilson's speech. Wilson was fast becoming an environmental icon in the western states. In Wyoming, newspaper columnists and radio talk show hosts dared him to visit the state.

Jack tried hard not to like Noah—or be impressed by his oratorical skills—but failed at both.

Noah had an almost Kennedy-like way of speaking, his cadence perfect for driving home his points. And his smile—perfect damn teeth, Jack noted—gleamed across the crowd when he broke into a grin, making it hard not to smile in return.

The weather was perfect, too. A late August day, warm but not stifling hot or humid. Just a few puffy-looking clouds giving occasional shade. Even the breeze was mild, just enough to keep people sitting in direct sun from doing little more than lightly fan themselves with the anti-hydrofracking literature that was being handed out everywhere.

Jack realized he was letting his digital recorder do all the work instead of listening carefully and taking notes. There was something mesmerizing about Noah's voice as he hammered the gas companies for greed, lying and deliberately fouling the environment.

We've come to a crossroads
as a nation. Not just about

natural gas, but about the old ways of using up the earth. The time of that exploitation is over. Over.

For hundreds of years we have exploited nature. And this latest abomination, hydrofracking, is going to be the end of it all. And it will be the end of us, too. That's why we have to stop it. We have to stop it now.

We are polluting our drinking water beyond repair, pouring toxic chemicals deep into the earth without knowing what may happen. We are causing earthquakes in places where earthquakes have never happened.

Did I say we are causing this? Are we doing it? Are we? Are we? Are we?

A resounding NO! rose, followed by a chant of NO! NO! NO! NO! NO! NO! from across the entire crowd.

The NO! NO! NO! NO! NO! NO! morphed to a chant of NO FRACKING! NO FRACKING! NO FRACKING! NO FRACKING! that gradually had the crowd whipped into such a frenzy that some of the protesters nearest to Jack started doing a version of the St. Vitus dance as they screamed NO FRACKING! at the tops of their lungs.

Noah was screaming NO FRACKING! NO FRACKING! NO FRACKING! into the microphone, too, helping make the noise nearly deafening.

Jack didn't hear either of the gunshots through the roar. He turned slightly—just in time to see Oscar bull through the front of the crowd, tackling a middle-aged man in the first row who held a pistol in his hand.

The man looked like he was trying to get the gun up to his mouth when Oscar slammed into him.

Oscar punched the man in the head savagely until he was sure the man was staying down. Then he crouched over the man and the gun and shouted for people to call the police and an ambulance.

Jack turned and saw Noah Webster Wilson lying on his side on stage. Screams from the crowd of GUN! GUN! GUN! HE'S GOT A GUN! started a stampede that made it difficult for police to get to Noah or the man on the ground who Oscar was protecting so the crowd wouldn't trample him.

Jack tried to spring up onto the stage but was stopped by several of the protest volunteer marshals who were ringing Noah's body, unsure if there were other people with guns. Jack later wrote in his *Column One* in the *Horseheads Clarion* that the volunteer marshals looked like terrified school children.

Eli stood at the bottom of the stage, his camera held down at his side, his entire body frozen.

He later told Jack he had always wondered what photographers felt like when they witnessed an assassination.

He said he wished he had never had to find out.

Grayson Oliver Delacroix sat in his office, hardly believing what he was reading on his screen.

Just hours before, Noah Webster Wilson, a environmentalist and a particularly irritating thorn in the side of natural gas development and Grand Energy Services, had been shot at an anti-gas, anti-hydrofracking rally in Rockwell Valley, Pennsylvania.

Rockwell Valley—the same place where someone for months had been leaking GES information to a radical environmental group called the Wolverines, Grayson thought.

Details were sketchy, but police had a man in custody. They were not releasing very many details except that Wilson had been struck in the head by a bullet and was at Rockwell Valley Hospital.

Grayson read the account again, filed by a reporter/columnist named Jack Stafford, the same fellow who had been dogged in his pursuit of information about an earlier incident at GES headquarters in which one of Grayson's vice presidents burned his hands while washing them in the men's room.

Grayson almost admired how professionally and fairly the news story was written, especially when comparing it to a story filed earlier in the day about a brawl that had broken out.

A security company had hired some GES employees to work at the rally and somehow they had ended up tangling with the protesters.

Worse, Stafford had recognized one of the GES employees—the one who had been arrested for assault on a police officer and illegal possession of a firearm. Stafford's story prompted other media outlets to lean on the security company, which in turn quickly offered up that the men were hired as temporary workers for the event at the suggestion of another GES employee.

Grayson knew that was probably Luther Burnside, who had been trying to call him since the first incident. But Grayson was trying to get in touch with one of the other vice presidents to talk directly with Burnside. He didn't want any of his fingerprints on this.

Grayson's secretary had come in when he called her at home so that she could run some interference for him. He had turned off his cell phone, since every media outlet in the country could now dial him directly. The week before, Wilson had posted the number on his website, along with a picture of Grayson.

When his GES phone rang he expected one of the vice presidents to be on the line but instead got Burnside, who was still in Rockwell Valley.

Grayson made a note to chew his secretary out for letting Burnside's call through.

"Luther, what the fuck is going on there? GES employees arrested, masquerading as security guards? And now this Wilson schmuck gets shot. Please, please tell me that the guy who shot Wilson had no connection to us."

Grayson heard Luther Burnside take in a breath and Grayson braced for the worst.

If the person who shot Noah Webster Wilson was another GES employee, his presidency was probably over and the reputation of GES headed down the express natural gas toilet.

And Wilson would become a martyr to the anti-hydrofracking cause, even bigger than he already was in states where small environmental movements had been gaining momentum.

"The GES people there didn't seem to know him. Nobody seemed to. I caught a glimpse. But when I saw him, he had already been punched in the face and beaten pretty bad by some big guy. It was pretty crazy after Wilson got shot. People screaming, running. But it's worse."

Grayson rubbed his temples with one hand.

"Worse?"

"I'm outside the hospital. A nurse whose husband works for us got word out that Wilson died about a half-hour ago. It hasn't been announced yet. The police are keeping a tight lid on everything."

Grayson didn't say anything. He just hung up the phone and stared out the window.

Jack and Devon sat in the dark on a long rattan couch on the front porch at Jack's house in Horseheads late that night, their arms wrapped around each other as Devon wept and Jack did his best to console her.

While Devon was years divorced, it didn't mean she didn't have a place in her heart for Noah.

The suddenness and savageness of his death stunned her so much it was hard for her to breathe.

Walter had caught Devon as she nearly fainted after the phone call came through to the office from Jack that Noah had died. A Rockwell Valley police lieutenant had pulled Jack aside outside the hospital to tell him, asking that he wait until the official announcement to publish anything.

But the officer told Jack that Noah Webster Wilson, in the moments before he died, had asked for someone named Devon Walsh.

Jack thought it might have been the worst news he ever had to give to anyone.

And in this case, to someone he loved.

They hadn't spoken much after he got back to the office while he filed a carefully written story about the shooting with what details were available.

Walter then pushed them both out the door of the newspaper, with stern instructions to go home and not to show their faces until Monday morning.

He and Eli would handle anything that came up with the shooting over the weekend.

The light dinner Jack had fixed went almost untouched. Belle, sensing something was wrong, was very subdued, even eating the leftovers quietly.

Jack and Devon had finished off a bottle of Oscar's Boot Riesling and were just sipping on glasses from a second bottle. The conversation bounced back and forth between anecdotes about Noah Webster Wilson and Jack's late wife Amy.

"He was an egomaniac, Jack. A real egomaniac. I couldn't live with him. But for him to have been killed? I just hurt. I just feel like I was kicked in the stomach."

Jack confessed that while he listened to Noah's speech, just before Noah was cut down, he could see that, egomania aside, Noah's heart was in the right place. And Jack also confessed that he was afraid Noah was heading back into Devon's life and he didn't want that.

"I can't explain why," Jack said, "but I feel so guilty

about loving you and jealous since he came here. I thought I might lose you. Really."

Devon snuggled closer to Jack, her head on his shoulder, almost asleep after hours of cathartic talk and the wine.

"Maybe this is where we start our story, Jack. You lost Amy. I gave up Noah, but now I've really lost him, too."

Jack kissed Devon lightly on top of her head and hugged her tight, hoping to freeze the moment in his memory. Tomorrow was Sunday, and even though Jack hadn't set foot in a Catholic church in so many years he couldn't remember, he thought he would try to drag Devon to church tomorrow to at least light two candles —one for Noah, and the other for Amy.

"Let's go upstairs and get some sleep," Jack said.

"Only if it's in the same bed," Devon said. "Otherwise, we are sleeping right here on this couch. I really don't want to be alone."

Jack hugged her tight and kissed her head again.

"Well, I was going to suggest the same thing."

Belle wagged her tail looking back and forth at Jack and Devon as they stood up, still half-tangled in a hug as they went in through the front door.

She could tell the mood had shifted and bounded ahead of them to the top of the stairs, waiting to see which way she should go.

The death of Noah Webster Wilson sparked a firestorm across the nation from gun control advocates, hydrofracking opponents, and environmentalists in general.

Wilson had lived for several hours after being shot in

the torso and the head. Either wound would have likely proven fatal, the doctors said. He had already lost so much blood by the time he got to Rockwell Valley Hospital that it was hopeless.

The firestorm was stoked further by the revelation that the man who shot Wilson was a former employee of a natural gas company headquartered in Texas. Delmar Ogilvy, 44, had lost his job as a landsman in Colorado after Wilson's website, *Fracking Serious,* named him in a story about how landsmen often cheated landowners in the leasing process.

Ogilvy had become a poster child on the pro-hydrofracking website *Energy First America* as an example of persecution and entrapment by environmentalists.

Wilson had learned that Ogilvy was trying to sell an environmentally savvy rancher on leasing his land to a gas exploration company. Wilson set up a hidden camera in the living room to film Ogilvy's pitch and gave the rancher a series of pointed questions to ask about the lease.

The video was a devastating indictment of how gas company landsmen often lied to get people to sign complicated lease agreements.

And after the video went viral on the Internet—and showed up on a national cable news broadcast—Ogilvy was out of a job.

Even at that, *EFA* continued to staunchly defend Ogilvy's sales pitch on its website, using a heavily edited video of the sales pitch to claim he was doing a professional job.

EFA web pages and the edited video were hastily pulled down a few hours after Ogilvy was arrested.

But thanks to quick work by Eli at the *Horseheads*

Clarion, the web pages were saved on the newspaper's computers along with *EFA's* heavily edited video of Ogilvy.

"Eli, I think we need to weave all of that in the story for Tuesday," Walter said. "And let's run the original video and the *EFA* video side-by-side on our website to show what *EFA* did to manipulate it. Those people have no conscience."

The Monday morning staff meeting was nearly over and Eli headed out to his computer to start putting things together by deadline. Jack and Devon started to get up, too, but were motioned to stay put by Walter, who closed the door to the conference room.

"Devon, I wanted to say how sorry I am about Noah. I know you weren't married to him anymore. But to lose somebody like that, well, it's beyond awful."

As Devon's eyes started to water, Jack reached for her hand, prompting a smile from Devon and a smile from Walter.

"This is a sad time, I know," Walter said. "But if you two can stick together, I think it will be good for both of you. That's my fatherly advice."

Jack and Devon looked slightly surprised, though the emotional rollercoaster of the weekend had drained them so much they were semi-sleepwalking. They had quietly talked all day on Sunday. They stayed in the same room most of the time, leaving only for three long walks around town and to the park, walks so long they even exhausted Belle.

"There's never a right time for things, so let me just say this. Jack. When you came here in the spring, you were a wreck," Walter said. "A damn good writer, a damn good columnist. But you were a wreck. And when Devon got here, you started to get that spark back. That spark you had when we used to call you JJ all the time. And when Devon moved in with you, the two of you started seriously kicking the gas companies' asses. And unless I'm missing something, you two have figured out you're good together. Everybody else in town knew it the first time you walked into Millie's."

Jack felt his eyes welling up slightly, too.

"So, I'm guessing that's an endorsement that it's okay for two of your key staff members to date?" Jack said.

"Date? Jesus Christ, Jack. You are so obtuse sometimes. You already live together, work together, and spend nearly every waking hour within fifty feet of each other. If you don't get married one of these days, just adopt each other. All right?"

At that Walter, Jack, and Devon all broke out laughing, laughing hard enough that the rest of the staff outside could hear.

"Now, without further adieu and any more Ann Landers' advice from this old-fart publisher, we need to get Tuesday's paper out and I hope we can do something special for Friday about the rally.

"Thank God that guy didn't shoot anyone else. Oh shit. I'm sorry Devon, that was a pretty crass thing to say."

Devon smiled as she stood up.

"No harm, Walter. I spent the weekend crying. Jack's my witness. Now I'm getting back to being angry. *EFA* is starting to run comments on its website from people saying 'good riddance' to Noah. That's the only tame way I can say it."

Walter paused, looking directly at Jack.

"Perhaps the *EFA* people need a little light shining on them for their role in all this. Damned assholes. Know anyone who would like to ruin their day, Jack?"

"Yes," Jack said. "I know a guy with a newspaper column who has a girlfriend he wants to impress."

Devon looked at Jack.

"You mean impress again?"

Jack face blushed so red he stayed in the conference room for ten minutes before walking back out to the newsroom.

From the *Horseheads Clarion*

Column One
The Horseheads Clarion

There's a snake
in the gas

By Jack Stafford

At one time in this nation's history, deliberately telling a lie was a bad thing. A really bad thing.

Then at some point, some bright light came up with the word "disinformation," the notion of deliberately spreading false information to mislead people. Disinformation sounds so much cleaner than the word lie.

The idea of disinformation was usually associated with international espionage and showed up in spy novels, on television, and in movies.

But now we see disinformation all the time here in New York and Pennsylvania in the efforts of a group funded by the natural gas industry and oil companies.

The group is called Energy First America—EFA.

In this space, I will not use the polite term of disinformation. I'll call it lies, because that's what it is—lies.

Tuesday The Clarion ran a story and photos about the tragic shooting death of Noah Webster Wilson, a nationally known environmental activist gunned down less than a week ago at a rally held adjacent to Rockwell Valley High School. He was killed 200 yards from where Rockwell High chemistry teacher Anne Kovach was shot to death earlier this year by a student.

Both deaths are directly related to the gas industry.

Miss Kovach was killed because a student (whose father works for Grand Energy Services) was incensed that she was teaching her students that hydrofracking fluid contains toxic chemicals and is polluting groundwater.

For the record, both things are true.

Mr. Wilson was shot to death last week by Delmar Ogilvy, a former landsman for a Texas-based gas company, because Ogilvy blamed Mr. Wilson for getting him fired from his landsman position. Mr. Wilson posted a damning video on his website, Fracking Serious, that showed Ogilvy lying repeatedly as he tried to persuade a Colorado rancher to sign a gas lease.

Those are the facts.

But EFA has been hard at work twisting these facts, denying these facts, and even allowing people to post on its website comments like, "Wilson deserved to die," and "Good riddance to that fag hippie."

Despicable barely covers it.

Comments on the EFA website must be approved by the EFA chief spokesman and editor, Rod Mayenlyn, a former executive with Grand Energy Services, who declined to comment for this column.

Allowing these types of comments is unfortunately part of an all-too-often repeated pattern with the EFA site that maintains in its "About Us" information section that EFA "… is an independent journalistic voice telling the truth about natural gas, natural gas extraction, and oil in the Northeastern United States."

The truth is EFA uses its website to denigrate, disparage, and destroy.

And independent? Please!

The entire operation is funded by the natural gas and oil industries.

Every time there is rally or event opposing hydrofracking, the minions of Mayenlyn attend, shoot video, take photos, and post sarcastic stories on the website, touting that they are publishing unbiased news.

These same EFA minions frequently go to town meetings at which natural gas is discussed, posting the same condescending stories, photos, and heavily edited videos on EFA's website.

Anyone who dares ask even the most responsible questions at a public meeting can count on being the target of ridicule. And God help any person who suggests some form of alternative energy might be better for the planet in the long run than the foul technology of hydrofracking.

Likewise, after pro-hydrofracking events, these same EFA employees write fawning syrupy reports in praise of all fuels carbon-based.

So far, citizens are more concerned about the dangers of hydrofracking—and getting natural gas companies to clean up their messes—than to worry about what's being published on the EFA website.

But even a cursory review of what EFA has published in the last two months shows dozens of instances where citizens were clearly libeled—clear enough that a libel lawyer should have easy pickings.

After seeing comments allowed by Mayenlyn regarding the late Noah Webster Wilson, let's hope someone takes EFA to court.

We know the companies funding it have pockets as deep as the gas wells they are drilling to extract gas— and where they are disposing of toxic wastes.

> *Jack Stafford is an investigative columnist and reporter for* The Horseheads Clarion *and has worked as an investigative reporter for metropolitan newspapers in California and Colorado.*

When Rod Mayenlyn first read Jack Stafford's *Column One* in the web edition of the *Horseheads Clarion*, he spewed his coffee all over his computer keyboard, screen, and desk at his office at *Energy First America*.

He grabbed some tissues from a box on his desk to wipe the screen off so he could reread what Stafford had written.

Libel, he thought. *Jesus Christ! What the fuck do you think you just did to* me?

Mayenlyn picked up the phone to call Grayson Oliver Delacroix at home, then decided not to. It was a Saturday and Delacroix would likely have read it already. Nearly all the Grand Energy Services executives and staff had the podunk newspaper as must-reading when it came out on Tuesdays and Fridays.

And lately Mayenlyn had started logging on four or five times a day to see what was popping up on its website. The *Clarion* had started publishing a lot of web-only content, then referring to it in its print editions.

He noted grimly that the website was brimming with ads and the last two print editions he had seen were considerably fatter than normal.

So much for the GES boycott-the-Clarion program, he thought.

Mayenlyn was already piqued over Tuesday's edition that carried a big story about *EFA* with reprinted columns of really nasty comments that he had allowed to be posted. Luther Burnside had told Mayenlyn to ramp things up and whip up the faithful in anticipation of the rally at the Rockwell Valley High School. But he worried that he might have gotten carried away in what he let in before the rally.

And he was still puzzling over the comments about Wilson. He barely read most of the comments on any stories, preferring to approve them quickly. Anyone who tried to complain about them—by themselves commenting—he just deleted.

But he could not clearly remember approving a half-dozen or so particularly venomous things that were on the website, all of which popped up Sunday in a flurry from four different posters.

One of the *EFA* staff writers—a conservative 22-year-old who had graduated from a private Christian college in California in May—called Mayenlyn at home Sunday night when he logged on to the *EFA* system to file his story about a memorial service for Wilson.

He saw the "Good riddance to that fag hippie" comment and thought that something was amiss.

Still, Mayenlyn thought he might have missed it, and others, and so he quickly started deleting comments as fast as he could.

But apparently not as fast as some goddamned computer whiz kid at the *Horseheads Clarion*.

He nearly spewed his coffee across the desk again when the phone rang. He saw it was a GES number and hoped it was not Delacroix. Although the *EFA* funding was kept separate to maintain the appearance of independence, Mayenlyn never doubted that he could be out of a job in seconds if Delacroix wanted him dumped.

The call wasn't from Delacroix, but from Luther Burnside, who had been assigned full-time to damage control after the Wilson shooting. He sounded as cranky as Mayenlyn felt.

"Rod? Luther. I'm sure you already read that asshole's column in the paper. He knows we won't do anything right now. We have too much heat on us. Did you know that the gun the Ogilvy jerk used to belong to a GES employee? Some dipstick landsman in Ohio gave it to Ogilvy a month ago when Ogilvy was visiting him. The guy called me to tell me. He wants to say it was stolen. What a pile of shit we are in. Christ."

Mayenlyn breathed easier, realizing that he wasn't the target at the moment. But Luther's call was coming in because Delacroix and the other gas companies were expecting him to use *EFA* to help repair the damage.

"Well, I have two ideas for this, Luther. Three really. First, we run a story about Wilson and how terrible it is that he was killed. We can spin that we support reasonable dialogue on this stuff. We can put in about all the attacks GES and other companies have had to deal with. We can even bring up the missing wastewater truck drivers to try to get some sympathy. Big media might bite on that if we do it just right."

Mayenlyn waited to hear Luther grunt agreement, then kept going when the line was silent.

"The second is we need to hire a computer guy, somebody who can figure out if we got hacked. I don't think we were. But in a week or so, after Wilson's been buried and things calm down, we can claim we were. Act totally outraged. But we shouldn't throw out the hacking defense too early. It's too pat. People will be suspicious. Everybody who gets caught on the Internet claims hacking. Remember that Congressman guy? Weiner?"

This time Luther grunted agreement and told Mayenlyn to finish.

"Third thing is we need a miracle. Not a real one, just a believable miracle. Maybe a new study can come out that says there is a new process under review that will clean up fracking wastewater and make it glacier pure. We need science spin besides the politics."

Luther agreed to take all three ideas directly to Grayson Oliver Delacroix, but gave Mayenlyn the okay to start drafting the story about how terrible the shooting was and to find a computer guru to put on a show of looking for hackers.

"But Rod, pull in the dogs a little bit, okay? I see a comment posted below a story that went up on the website this morning about the shooting that says it's surprising Wilson didn't get shot in Colorado. The comment says lots of people there are cheering his death."

Mayenlyn agreed and got Luther off the line as quickly as possible.

Mayenlyn had most definitely not approved any comments yet today on the *Energy First America* website.

And he was afraid who might have.

The late Monday afternoon staff meeting and planning session was a little unusual for the *Horseheads Clarion*, partly because it was Labor Day but also because when the Tuesday edition was sent off electronically to the printer, normally everyone on the staff headed off for a drink at a nearby saloon or for a cup of coffee at Millie's.

But Walter thought it was time to chart out the newspaper's hydrofracking coverage again so they wouldn't be simply reacting to events.

He had sent the receptionist, bookkeeper, and the other staff members not directly involved with the fracking stories home as soon as he pushed the button on the final pages.

Tuesday and Wednesday the paper would have a skeleton crew when they took time off in exchange for having worked the Labor Day holiday.

"Devon actually suggested we convene to do this, and so I am going to turn over the floor to her," Walter said. "It makes sense. We've been reacting a lot lately—with a lot to react to. But I know there are some areas we need to get into and I want to see if we can set some publication dates and assign some research to all of our staff."

Devon pulled a white board up from behind the table and set it up so Jack, Eli and Walter could see it.

She had put a bulleted list of ten items on the board.

"I could have put fifty, but it's a small board," she joked. "And I didn't make this list up all by myself. It came in an email from Noah a couple of days before he was killed. He thought we were doing really good work. If he hadn't been shot…"

Jack stood up quickly and put his arm around Devon's shoulder. Eli and Walter sat very still.

"What Devon was going to say, I think, is that we want to call this Noah's List, as our in-house nickname. It will be best that we don't announce these are targeted stories, though anyone in the gas companies with half a brain should know we have them on our plate."

The half-a-brain description got a good laugh.

Devon motioned for Jack to sit down and drew a breath.

"Okay, take a look and then let's tinker," she said. "And if we can, let's give some dates to these stories."

NOAH'S LIST

- *Well-casing failures (data and projections)*
- *Shortage of deep injection wells (where will wastewater go?)*
- *Earthquakes (historical data pre-HF and post HF)*
- *Collateral damage already documented (roads, bridges, water supplies)*
- *Community impacts (rental shortages, crime, traffic, costs associated with)*
- *Destruction of microorganisms with biocides*
- *Air pollution (largely ignored because of more pressing water concerns)*
- *Declining real estate values (compare pre-HF to post HF, Dimock, et al)*
- *Corporate threats to democratic process (lawsuits against bans)*
- *Methane leakage – how much and impacts?*

Walter raised his hand, waving it like a child might. He wanted—and got—a smile from Devon.

"Yes, Walter, and what is your question?" she asked, laughing.

Walter laughed too.

"I like all these and now we need to start juggling and assigning research. I think on the collateral damage piece, we need to add taxpayers' costs. That is going to get people's attention. But I am curious about the microorganisms. What is that all about?"

Devon motioned to Eli to speak. Eli, as usual, was busy on the keys of his laptop.

"Well, when they frack they put down a lot of biocide with each well. Like, oh at least fifty gallons or more per million gallons," Eli said. "At least that's how much they say they are putting down. It could be a lot more. A lot. The reason is some of the life down there is a problem. And if there isn't any biocide killing them, they can clog things up and the gas and oil won't come up. They slow it down anyway. And faster recovery means more gas or oil, which means more money."

Walter looked puzzled.

"You said life. Are we talking bacteria? And other than clogging up the gas pipe, are they dangerous?"

Eli bit his lip before he answered.

"Well, these organisms are neither bacteria nor viruses. They are a third classification for microbes. Some of the more far-out theories say they are the remnants of comets hitting the earth. Some of the farther-out theories say they might be where life came from in the first place. But are they dangerous? Not from what I read. They sometimes find them everywhere. Even in sheep stomachs. I'm not kidding."

Walter looked puzzled again, but then decided they all needed time to think.

"This is a good start and I don't want to keep everybody," he said. "Let's agree to think about this list and meet as a group, maybe Wednesday. We can flesh out more on how to approach them and researching. We already put out a newspaper today and I spent a half-hour with a slimy attorney who claimed he represented *Energy First America* about Jack's column. So I'm tired. But Eli, one final question: Do these life forms down in the shale have a name? A pronounceable name, I hope?"

Eli grinned and spun his computer around with the name and a brightly colored photo of one of the microorganisms filling the screen.

"Archaea," Eli said. *"Archaea.* But I call them *Archies* for short."

Walter snorted. "Jesus, Eli. *Archies?* Okay. But Eli, you look like you have something else."

Eli hesitated for a second and then ~~and~~ spun his computer back around and tapped his keys for about ten seconds, then spun it back around so they could all see.

On the screen was a picture of a fierce-looking animal and beneath it in big letters a caption: *Coming soon to a gas company near you.*

Eli said he had gotten the photo in an email during the meeting, forwarded to him from an anti-fracking group in Pennsylvania.

"Recognize that animal?" Eli said. "That's a wolverine. A real wolverine."

Grayson Oliver Delacroix waited impatiently for the arrival of Rod Mayenlyn and Luther Burnside at Grand Energy Services headquarters.

Delacroix had summoned both men to come in to talk face-to-face with him about the situation in Rockwell Valley and across the border in New York, where GES was staging a lot of equipment and housing many of its workers.

Rockwell Valley's meager rental market had been flooded with GES workers, driving up prices concomitantly and forcing many of the workers to live miles away in Elmira, New York, and many of the neighboring towns.

The driving up of rental prices was a bonanza for landlords but a disaster for the less-affluent in the towns where unemployment was high, especially the younger people just leaving home.

The infusion of gas drilling money hadn't done much for employment—the majority of GES workers were coming in from Texas and Oklahoma, blending southern accents with New York nasal inflections and Pennsylvania's unique rural twangs.

Delacroix had a short list of items for the two men, starting with Jack Stafford's column and the *Horseheads Clarion*'s persistence in publishing well-researched and largely on-target critiques of GES operations and missteps.

He also wanted to talk about Mayenlyn's admission that the *EFA* website had been hacked, the arrest of GES employee Tom Fletcher, and how to distance GES, *EFA,* and the entire gas industry from Delmar Ogilvy, the man who had shot and killed Noah Webster Wilson nearly two weeks before.

Since the Stafford column, Delacroix decided he didn't

need to keep up the pretense that *EFA* and GES were totally separate. If need be, he decided, he would start telling the press that *EFA* was doing the work of public education that was beyond what a natural gas company like GES could do.

Delacroix buzzed his secretary and told her he would be going down to the lap pool for an hour, and that Mayenlyn and Burnside were to sit tight when they arrived.

"You can tell them I'll be down at the pool if they want to get some exercise," he said.

He liked having company in the pool when he swam, competing in both the speed and number of laps he would put in.

Two vice presidents he sometimes swam with had called in sick that morning. And the company's newest hire, a 30-year-old woman in the accounting department, was busy in a meeting trying to work out a creative way to make the declining gas well yields look better than they really were. They had started swimming together nearly daily, missing yesterday when she was too busy. Delacroix had to skip yesterday, too.

Just as he was about to head down to the pool, he got a call from a GES field agent that the Pennsylvania GES fracking wastewater truck that had disappeared a month before near the Ohio border had been found by police in a grove of trees only twenty-five miles from Delacroix's office. There was no sign of the driver, Roy Bonder Sr. Police had cordoned off the area, treating it as a crime scene because Bonder was still missing.

Delacroix's secretary buzzed his phone to tell him that Mayenlyn and Burnside were at the airport and had been picked up by the GES limo. That put them a half-hour away at most.

"Okay, fine. I'm going down for a swim now. Tell them to come down to the pool. And turn on the recording equipment in the pool conference room and pool."

In the elevator going down, Delacroix shared the ride with an unfamiliar maintenance worker, whose hair was an inch longer than Delacroix liked in GES workers, even janitors.

He chatted pleasantly with the worker, but made a mental note to tell the head of building maintenance to get his staff cleaned up.

The GES Human Resources Department had quietly warned Delacroix that grooming issues were a potential legal nightmare. But Delacroix didn't really care. If someone wanted to work for GES, by God, they would follow his standards.

In the locker room, Delacroix went from unhappy to angry when he saw some work-boot footprints on the otherwise gleaming light gray tiles. The boots led to the service room for the pool filters where the door was ajar and Delacroix could hear some clanking.

Pool maintenance was supposed to be done at late at night so as not to disrupt any swimming schedules and give the filters time to back-flush and reset.

Irritated, Delacroix slipped into his bathing suit and went out onto the pool's edge, did a few stretches and then dove in, swimming hard from the minute he entered the water. He had completed about twenty laps when he saw that Mayenlyn and Burnside were in the conference room, looking out the window at him. Both men looked stricken, which Delacroix took as a sign that both men knew their jobs were on the line.

Then he saw that a maintenance worker was in the conference room with them, too. All Delacroix could think of was that if it was whoever had been doing pool maintenance, they had likely tracked water and dirt on the hypoallergenic conference room pool carpet.

He decided to swim another few laps. Keeping Mayenlyn and Burnside waiting would only make them more eager to please. He was only a lap into that when he realized that the pool filter was not running. There was no water coming out of the pool jets at the end, which normally had enough power to massage muscles, like a hot tub.

Delacroix did another lap and noticed when he turned that all three men—Mayenlyn, Burnside, and the maintenance worker—were staring at him. He stopped and stood up in the waist-deep water, motioning for the two men to join him. But they just looked at each other and then at the maintenance worker.

Delacroix was already pulling himself up out of the pool when the worker waved for him to get out of the pool. Delacroix was furious. He surmised that the worker had started shocking the pool with chemicals, but then stopped when he realized someone was swimming.

He wrapped a towel around his middle and started for the conference room but was met in the hallway by Burnside.

"Mr. Delacroix. Sorry. About being late and everything," Burnside said. "Um. This maintenance guy here told me he got called this morning that the pool filter wasn't working right, making a lot of noise."

"And that means exactly what, Luther?" Delacroix asked. "I was swimming in dirty water or what?"

Mayenlyn came out of the conference room, the

maintenance worker in tow. The maintenance worker looked sheepish.

"He explained to me a line in the filter was plugged up," Mayenlyn said. "That's why he shut it off."

Delacroix felt a headache coming on.

"So, it's fixed. Why do you look like someone just kicked you in the balls?"

Mayenlyn took a plastic pool filler tube from the maintenance worker's hands and pushed out a smaller plastic tube with a cap on it.

"That's how he found it. It was in the tube and that's what caused the filter to overheat and quit working."

Delacroix looked at the tube curiously.

"And?" he asked.

Mayenlyn pulled the small plastic tube out and popped the cap, handing the small piece of paper inside to Delacroix.

In neatly printed letters, all in caps, was the word WOLVERINES.

Delacroix turned his head and threw up, thinking as he did he was glad he was puking on the pool tiles and not the hypoallergenic carpet in the conference room.

The video of Grayson Oliver Delacroix vomiting alongside the Grand Energy Services lap pool went viral on the Internet. It was a special favorite in Japan where the chatter in staid corporate boardrooms was all about how easily Americans frighten. That was usually followed with a second conversation about company security and limiting video camera feeds.

If a Japanese executive got caught puking like that,

it would mean such a loss of face that he might have to resign—or worse.

The same people who had slipped into the GES headquarters and placed the note blocking the pool filter had bounced the video feed from the pool cameras through a series of computer servers around the world. After making the rounds of popular anti-hydrofracking websites, and those who trolled for just plain funny or weird stuff, it ended up on most major news organizations' websites and newscasts.

And Grayson Oliver Delacroix became an immediate late-night television comedic punch line.

At GES headquarters, staff members who regularly used the pool were dispatched to be examined at a private medical facility.

"These bastards put lye or something in the men's restroom. God only knows what they might have slipped into the swimming pool," Delacroix said when he ordered the tests.

The tape shown on the Internet focused on Delacroix's sudden Linda Blair imitation. But many news channels carried a much more extensive clip of the nearly fifteen-minute video, which included Delacroix, Burnside, and Mayenlyn in a shouting match about the Wolverines and the empty wastewater truck that had been found twenty-five miles from GES headquarters.

It was a telling piece of video because it made it clear that *EFA* was a front for the gas companies and that Wolverine pranks—and much more serious vandalism—were a lot bigger concern to GES than it had been claiming.

At the *Horseheads Clarion* office, it was vindication of much of what the newspaper had been publishing, particularly since Jack had come on board in the spring, followed shortly by Devon.

"So do you think these Wolverines might have put something nasty in that swimming pool?" Jack asked Eli. "The people at GES had the pool drained that same day and, no surprise, won't say anything about the water. I saw that a couple of cable news channels have some water experts on saying some of the water from that fracking wastewater truck they found might have been put into the pool. And GES is calling this 'domestic terrorism.' Pretty ugly."

Eli tapped the keys on the computer, listening to Jack and web surfing at warp speed on a half-dozen anti-fracking websites almost simultaneously. Since receiving the one email about the Wolverines just days before Grayson Oliver Delacroix made his flash-vomit debut, he hadn't received any more missives. Many anti-fracking websites had received the same email—or something similar. They were all poised and ready for something when the GES pool incident happened.

"I told Walter this earlier," Eli said. "They could have dumped some fracking fluid in, of course. But I think the truck was in the area to make them think that. Anyway, GES keeps saying that wastewater is okay to put on roads for washing them down. So why not swim in it?"

Walter walked over and pulled up a chair.

"You two might not be old enough to remember this expression: 'The object of terrorism is terror.' Can you imagine what those people must be thinking? The ones who have been swimming in that pool? Every headache, rash, upset stomach they have had, or will have, is going to send them running to the doctor," Walter said. "Maybe it will be years of doctor visits, given how toxic the chemicals are in wastewater. It was classic monkey-wrench tactic. Classic."

Devon breezed in through the front door, a plate piled high with pastries from Millie's across the street.

"I'm not sure how I got to be the donut girl around here. But here's your dose of unhealthy food for today. By the way, I got through to that clinic in Missouri where all the executives and other people had to go? After the pool thing? Anyway, the doctors all had to sign non-disclosure forms. You'd really think normal medical records secrecy was enough. Well, I got one guy on the line who, believe it or not, knew Noah years ago. When I told him who I was he recognized my name and remembered that I had been married to Noah."

Eli, Jack, and Walter all leaned in to listen as Devon let a little suspense build while she pretended to be intently arranging the dozen donuts and pastries on a plate.

"I'll get the donuts next time. I promise," Jack said. "But for Chrissakes, what did he say?"

Devon cut a maple bar in half, taking a bite before answering.

"On the record? Not much. And they didn't test the water itself, just the people. He said they gave blood tests, took urine samples, the usual stuff. MRIs, too. That was kind of curious, he thought. But off-the-record? He doesn't think any of them show signs of chemical exposure or poisoning. Right now anyway. But he said he would love to know the composition of the water in that pool. Of course, GES won't say anything."

Eli starting tapping on his laptop keys again, then let out a little laugh and whoop.

He turned the computer around so Walter, Jack, and Devon could see a video already playing.

An anti-fracking website had posted a video of Delacroix speaking at a national natural gas supplier conference earlier that year about how fears about fracking fluids and wastewater were way overblown. Then the video faded into Delacroix vomiting and saying in the video, "Those bastards have poisoned me with my own fracking fluid."

Walter asked Eli to replay the short video, watched it again, then grabbed a Danish pastry.

"How they will wiggle out of this, I can't imagine," Walter said. "But today I really feel old and cynical. They'll probably figure some way to spin this."

Devon walked over and gave Walter a napkin to put underneath the pastry that was dropping crumbs all over the newsroom floor. Then she put her arm around him.

"Old? Please, Walter. What was it you told me when I got here? Wasn't it something like, 'your job is to kick big gases' asses'?"

And with that Walter, Jack, Eli, and Devon all sat down in front of their computers again, donuts nearby.

The newsroom room filled with the sound of clacking keys and occasional snorts of laughter.

The Delacroix-vomiting video was pretty funny to watch, no matter how many times you ran it.

Summer slipped into fall along the Southern Tier of New York and across the border in Pennsylvania.

The hot days and often humid nights turned into gentle warm days and cool evenings, and by late October people were beginning to light fires in their fireplaces, eyeing their woodpiles for the winter that was only a month or less away.

For Jack and Devon, September and October were months of long weekend drives around the countryside, with conversations that drifted between the hydrofracking stories they were churning out at a furious pace and what was happening between them.

They had gone from professional colleagues to friends to people in love so fast they were struggling with the adjustment. But they were enjoying the struggle.

They had slipped into an easy routine at the *Horseheads Clarion*—at least from the outside.

Every Tuesday, there would be some new hydrofracking story full of revelations about the junk science promoted by the natural gas companies, the corruption, the pollution, and often the increase in violence reported across the country.

Fed up with regulators and governments that were not protecting them, there was an increasing number of instances of citizen arrests, and a few shootings, where rural residents were taking matters into their own hands to try to protect their land.

Protesters were being arrested at gas well sites, pipeline depots, and even gas company offices.

The anti-fracking movement had also started to meld with the most unlikely of political partners, Second Amendment supporters.

In a statement issued in late October, a group calling itself Americans For Clean Water and Liberty announced its formation. Its goal was to ensure that people had clean water, and were armed to protect themselves and their water sources.

Every Friday, Jack would use his column to blast some element of the hydrofracking industry, which was still growing with more and more wells drilled, even as the price of natural gas plummeted. Several national magazines published longish articles about the natural gas boom-going-bust, with more and more analysts concluding that gas companies were using the new wells simply as a vehicle to build up capital and pump stock prices

Jack had used the same term as the magazines in his column, "Fracked by Ponzi," in which Eli and Devon had provided data about how the wells in nearby Rockwell Valley had dropped in gas production by 400 percent in less than a year. But new investors were always presented with production figures from the very first days of drilling—the absolute most natural gas the wells would ever produce.

The gas industry was still moving ahead with purchasing leases for drilling and mineral rights and drilling new wells. Drill rigs showing up on sites now frequently had a phalanx of security guards arriving at the same time, sticking around long enough to be sure that the landowners would go along with the terms of their leases.

As fall marched on, the story about the gas companies using hydrofracking as a way to dispose of otherwise un-disposable chemicals faded from the consciousness of most news organizations. Like the missing wastewater trucks, drivers, and the pollution of the Fuzzy Tree Swamp in New York, a weary public grew fatalistic about hydrofracking and demonstrations became fewer and fewer.

Efforts to get gas company records stalled in the courts, too, prompting Jack to write a column about conflicts of interest in which he listed the names of every judge within a ten-county area who had signed a gas lease. He only found a single judge who did not have a gas lease or some connection to the gas industry through a relative, friend, or close business associate.

The headline on that column by Jack read, "One honest judge."

Only the organization called the Wolverines seemed to grow, its pranks turning sufficiently violent that law enforcement authorities began more serious investigations. Walter and Jack were waiting for a subpoena for their email records and notes, as in stories and columns it was obvious that the *Horseheads Clarion* had some contact with whomever was behind the Wolverines.

Just before Halloween, Walter called a general meeting of the entire staff—the people in the newsroom, his part-time ad sales people, the distribution drivers, and even the mother and daughter who came in three nights a week to clean.

Jack and Devon had been in Rockwell Valley, interviewing high school classmates of Roy Bonder, Jr. He had been judged sane and would likely stand trial sometime in the next six months for the murder of Rockwell Valley High chemistry teacher Anne Kovach.

Walter hastily announced the meeting only the day before, and left the office without talking to Jack or Devon or Eli. Jack thought it was likely something about money. Ad sales had been good, but in the last few weeks Walter had seemed distracted, and left the running of the news section almost exclusively to Jack and Devon.

Devon worried about Walter's health. He was a robust 75-year-old but Devon had noticed in the last two weeks that he was sitting in his office for hours at a time, not bouncing in and out every fifteen minutes or so to chat with everyone in the building.

When Jack and Devon came in, Walter was sitting on a desk in the newsroom, obviously waiting impatiently for them.

"Sorry, Walter. We got hung up at the high school," Jack said. "And it looks like it's going to snow tonight."

His snow comment elicited a groan from everyone.

"That's okay. This won't take long," Walter said.

His tone was ominous enough that Jack and Devon's faces showed their concern.

"Thanks everyone for coming. We're all pretty busy. No, we are all really busy. But I wanted to make an announcement and I wanted to tell everyone at the same time. We're in the news business and I have no illusion about how skewed stories get when they get passed around through a bunch of people. Even among us.

"I'm going to Rochester tomorrow to check into the hospital. And if my doctor is right, I'll be there for a week or two. He said he's 95 percent sure I need heart bypass surgery. This didn't happen yesterday. He's been worried since Christmas. He told me two days ago that I can't avoid this. Some of you might remember I had a heart attack fifteen years ago. It was a small one. Well, my doctor says it's finally time for a full overhaul."

Walter held up his hand to forestall the questions and offers of help that were started to spill out immediately.

"As of this moment, Jack Stafford is acting editor in chief and publisher of the newspaper. He's the boss while I'm gone. Completely. And if the surgery goes well, I'll arm-wrestle him to get my job back after I recuperate. That's it. Thanks everyone. And good luck."

Walter turned and walked back into his office, grabbed

his coat, and headed for the door while everyone remained sitting, stunned.

He stopped at the front door and turned around to smile at everyone, then left without saying another word.

Jack looked at Devon and then at the door Walter had just walked though.

Jack noticed that it had started to snow.

ARCHAEA RISING

Grayson Oliver Delacroix was not used to begging, but it took something just short of that for him to keep his job as CEO of Grand Energy Services.

Now, months after his Internet puke debut and the collateral damage from statements made public from that entire poolside episode, he was still at the helm of GES, but being watched very closely by the board of directors—a board split on keeping him around.

"Thank God for the short attention span of the news media," Delacroix told Luther Burnside and Rod Mayenlyn in a conference call early on Halloween.

Besides Delacroix's embarrassment, the media had somehow found out that the in-house GES nickname for Burnside was Luca Brasi, after the muscle-bound enforcer from Mario Puzo's famous novel, *The Godfather*. And Rod Mayenlen's role as a shill for natural gas with the *Energy First America* website had also grabbed some headlines about industry-funded PR operations.

But that all was fading slowly, with only the most tenacious of journalists keeping the spark alive.

In most cases, where that spark existed, a few well-placed letters to the editor at a newspaper—or email to a TV news director—complaining that the journalists were beating a very dead horse would stop the continued mentions of flash vomiting, references to *The Godfather*, or use of the words "industry shills."

And the reading public was drifting somewhat, too, more concerned about the coming holiday season, NASCAR, and professional football.

Delacroix had no illusions that the opposition to hydrofracking had disappeared, however. The tension was mounting in Colorado, California, and other states where environmentalists were organized and active. Alarming reports of violence were also trickling in.

More and more protesters were choosing to be arrested as they blocked gates to gas facilities or stood in front of bulldozers getting ready to clear land. Public opinion was shifting in favor of the protesters, but very slowly.

Nor was Delacroix ignoring the group, the Wolverines, who had spiked his lap pool at GES headquarters.

GES and other gas companies were having a hard time keeping the incidents of vandalism and destruction hidden from public view.

But today Delacroix was hopeful they had found a magic bullet to diffuse some of the opposition.

"Rod, run this by me again, slowly," Delacroix said. "Particularly about how it will help with our PR problem."

"Well, from the PR standpoint, the biggest single problem has always been the water thing," Mayenlen said. "People think hydrofracking is ruining well water. Sorry, claim hydrofracking is ruining well water. Another bunch is worried about how much wastewater is produced and that we can't get rid of it safely. Then there's a third group that sees us sucking off too much fresh water. This Hydro-Green System can counter all three if we play it right," Mayenlyn said.

The Hydro-Green System wasn't really a system at all—it was mostly an idea with a sexy label, born in a laboratory in Ohio. There, a university researcher working on how to deal with the microscopic *Archaea* organisms that had been clogging gas and oil wells discovered that a food-products researcher in Michigan was busy splicing genes to help *Archaea* gobble toxic chemicals more quickly from factory-processed foods and raw farm products.

Traces of various toxic chemicals from agricultural operations were showing up in increasing amounts in harvested grains and vegetables. Even the United States Food and Drug Administration, normally a paper tiger about enforcing even its own relatively lax standards, was making noise about cracking down.

The food products researcher discovered that after the genetically modified *Archaea* metabolized the chemicals, they would die off within a few days, or sometimes even hours, with the toxic chemicals broken down into relatively safe, non-toxic basic elements. The harvested crops were then arguably safe.

"The Ohio project got started because of how much of our money gets spent on biocides to kill these little bastards in the wells," Mayenlen said. "We're just lucky this university researcher reads the journals about food product GMOs, too. Those food guys are doing some amazing stuff. You should see this pig they bred in a lab. Christ, it's bigger than a cow."

Delacroix rolled that idea around for a moment, and then asked Luther Burnside for his opinion. Burnside had become a good sounding board for Delacroix since the death of GES vice president Bill Honer.

"I guess we need to know if it really works, I mean, if it works outside a goddamned test tube. I don't know the PR stuff but if this could mean cutting down on the biocide and maybe cutting back on what's in the wastewater? We could then start dumping wastewater into city reclamation systems again. Or right into the sewers. We could save a ton of money not having to truck it and inject it in wells," Burnside said. "And it would slow down the bitching about big trucks and highway damage. People hate those trucks rolling through town."

Delacroix calculated the amount of non-fracking-related toxic chemicals that GES and other companies were putting down gas wells, and how much the other non-gas companies were paying GES for the disposal. Luckily that issue had faded from public sight too. He wondered for a few minutes whether the companies would even want to use GES wells as dumpsites. If the GMO really did what it seemed, the companies could just use it themselves.

"Well, at this point, let's see if we can get some testing going with this food researcher. Luther, bring him on board. Offer him some money, but get a non-disclosure form signed first," Delacroix said. "We will want to roll this out very carefully. We can just buy this whole Hydro-Green Systems if we need to. It's probably not even patented yet."

The three men agreed to talk again the next day. And Delacroix cautioned both Burnside and Mayenlyn to be very discreet.

"We need to know more specifics about what these GMOs eat and don't. Not a word to anyone outside. But I never thought I would say this, gentlemen. It seems Grand Energy Services might be going green. 'GES Goes Green.' There's a slogan for you, Mayenlyn. That ought to stick in the craw of those anti-frackers."

D evon looked in Walter's office and saw Jack fussing over papers on the desk—financial reports, she was pretty sure. It was the only time Jack would furrow his brow, as most of it was complicated and organized in a way that only Walter probably really understood.

She thought that for every week Walter was gone, Jack was aging six months. And it had been two weeks now since Walter had gone in for his heart surgery, ending up with a stay in the intensive care unit when things went south in the operating room.

What should have been a routine bypass operation turned into a more complicated procedure when doctors found several suspicious nodes in his chest, unrelated to his clogged arteries.

The biopsies had slowed the operation, which kept Walter under the anesthetic much longer than doctors had originally planned. And they turned out to be cancerous, though exactly what that really meant was still murky.

"All in all, it was medical cluster-fuck," Jack told the staff after Walter's surgery.

Walter was out of the intensive care unit and in a special unit for heart patients. But he was weak and doctors were concerned at his slow pace of recovery. They hadn't even started to talk about how to deal with the cancer. The nodes they removed likely had relatives.

"But the priority is to get Walter's heart working good again," Jack had said. "He's a tough guy, you know. If Vietnam didn't kill him, I think he'll be okay. He said that he wants you guys to keep up the good work. To keep fighting the good fight."

Devon knew that Jack was putting up a front for the staff and was less than optimistic about Walter. They had made the three-hour drive to Rochester to visit him twice, both times getting lectured by Walter that it was more important for them to keep the *Horseheads Clarion* healthy than hold his hand in the hospital.

The robust 75-year-old publisher had lost fifteen of his two hundred pounds during the short hospital stay. He also had an unhealthy pallor that doctors said was normal. Jack didn't think so and was pretty sure they weren't telling him everything.

Walter had listed Jack as his son on the admittance forms and Devon as his niece so they would have no trouble getting into the hospital.

Devon walked into the office and sat down quietly, waiting for Jack to break his concentration on the papers on Walter's desk. He looked surprised when saw Devon sitting in the chair. "I'm sorry," he said. "I was spaced out on this advertising report. The print side is doing okay, but if I read this right, we are actually making a pretty good profit on the website. That's almost unheard of."

They agreed to draft a brief, understandable synopsis of the financials to take to Walter on their visit in two days. The doctors had said that Walter was not to be bothered with details from the newspaper. But after several days of occasionally watching cable television newscasts, Walter had asked Jack to come ready to talk about the newspaper on his next visit.

"The finances are one thing. Maybe we will have some other good stuff to share," Jack said.

Eli came to the door and waited for Jack to motion him into Walter's office. He had a printout of a news story in his hand and was obviously agitated.

"It's starting," he said, breathlessly. "In Colorado. Just like the Wolverines said it would. Kind of. Right now, the wire services say. It's all over cable TV, too."

Jack held up his hands.

"Slow down, Eli. Slow down. What's starting? What are you talking about?"

Eli sat down and handed Jack the story. It focused on the governor of Colorado's press conference just a few hours before. He had been asked by several natural gas companies to call out the Colorado National Guard to force protesters to stop blocking gas company access to drilling rigs and newly designated well sites.

"These protesters aren't just waving signs," Eli said. "A lot of them are armed and waving guns. And not just pistols. Shotguns, AR-15s, that kind of stuff. The local police and sheriffs are standing back. I just saw a TV video of a deputy outside of Boulder who was filmed getting into his car. He said he wouldn't tell anybody to move—or draw his gun. The TV guy who interviewed him said the deputy told him off-camera that the gas companies are ruining the state."

Jack read the story and handed it back.

"You left out the best part, Eli. The police are refusing

to arrest the people for trespassing. And they're saying they won't enforce a court order from a Colorado judge to arrest these protesters."

Devon stood up and took the story from Jack.

"You don't have to ask, I have it. We'll contact local police for a comment and find out what they will do. And won't. And we'll publish on the website right now, right?"

Jack sat back in his chair and nodded a yes, thinking about how it was exactly how he and Walter interacted on stories like these. Walter barely had to suggest. And here Devon was doing the same thing.

"Okay... but Eli? You watch the wires. Angry people waving guns is not going to end well. And police refusing to enforce a legal court order? Jaysus."

"If the governor does agree to send in his National Guard, that's huge," Jack said. "We could have the National Guard staring down police and sheriff's deputies. It sounds like Latin America in the 1950s."

Eli and Devon headed out to their computers while Jack fiddled with the financial papers on his desk for a few minutes, then gave up and logged onto a news summary website that carried a half-dozen short bulletins about the Colorado situation.

Police had started making arrests—but of gas company employees who were trying to force their way onto gas company properties, brandishing their weapons.

"Eli. Pull those file photos of the local GES guys with their pistols. The photos we ran a couple of months ago? They may come in handy."

From the *Horseheads Clarion*

Column One

The Horseheads Clarion

The Guns of November

By Jack Stafford

ROCKWELL VALLEY, Pennsylvania — Faith in government at all levels has been eroding steadily for many years. It's hard to pinpoint exactly when it started diminishing.

Maybe it was in the 1970s with the late President Richard Nixon's ungraceful exit from the White House.

Maybe it was the 1980s Iran-Contra arms revelations.

Maybe it was going to war with Iraq because the federal government claimed there were weapons of mass destruction that threatened the U.S.

The American people don't like to be lied to, particularly by people who they support with taxes.

But across the country today we are facing the most serious crisis in generations—maybe since the Civil War.

Fed up with governments at all levels that are unable—or more likely unwilling—to protect the citizenry from the rapaciousness of hydrofracking by natural gas companies, people are taking up arms to defend their land, their homes, their environments, and their health.

As this is written, no shots have been fired—yet. But in Colorado, California, Ohio, Michigan, Texas—even here in New York—natural gas companies are being denied access to properties where they want to begin hydrofracking for natural gas.

Existing well sites generally have not been the main targets, though in some places protestors are denying entry to gas company properties where hydrofracking has been started.

Law enforcement is generally waiting and letting the protesters stand their ground while this drama plays out in courtrooms. But in numerous jurisdictions, courts have already issued orders saying that the protesters are illegally blocking access. A few months ago, the smart money would have bet that police would have gone in and arrested everyone in sight who refused to let gas company employees go in to drill.

But in some cases, they're not.

And it's not just because the protesters have guns. It seems the police are questioning the very legal system they are sworn to uphold.

Uh-oh.

We got to this place because the natural gas companies have wreaked havoc on the environment and on people's lives. They seem quite unrepentant and in complete denial about the damages they have caused. All manner of normal legal protests—pleas to legislators, regulators, petitions, marches, appeals to logic, lawsuits —have failed.

There is simply too much money on the table for democracy to triumph over greed here. Add to that deluded true believers who really think that no matter how many children get sick, animals die, wells are polluted, or millions of gallons of fresh water wasted, the natural gas taken from the earth is worth it.

They also ignore that most of it is planned to be shipped overseas. And when that happens, natural gas prices will soar in the U.S.

In Pennsylvania, at farms where protesters are carrying out armed vigils to prevent attempts to enter private properties, the atmosphere is like a cowboy saloon late on a Saturday night.

It feels like a fight could break out any second.

In the past week, a fight almost did break out at one Colorado drill site where an employee of Grand Energy Services whipped out a pistol and tried to force armed protesters to give way.

He was arrested by police for brandishing a weapon in a threatening manner.

Ironically, witnesses said he had at least five hunting rifles leveled at his chest when he pulled his pistol out and police arrested him.

This newspaper has written on occasion about a shadowy group called the Wolverines who are taking credit for numerous pranks, incidents of vandalism, and more serious attacks against natural gas companies across the country.

This week it issued a chilling manifesto that made headlines across the country and had cable news bobble-heads chattering like monkeys.

"Enough," it said. "We, the People, have had enough.

"If the government won't protect us, we will protect ourselves from the greed and destruction of our communities. It's that simple."

Simple? Maybe. Bloody? We can hope not.

Jack Stafford is an investigative columnist and reporter for The Horseheads Clarion *and has worked as an investigative reporter for metropolitan newspapers in California and Colorado.*

Jack and Devon eased their way into Walter's house, the first real snow of the season filtering down.

Even Belle was a little subdued as she followed them into the dark living room.

Walter had asked Jack to pick up some papers from his home office, most of them insurance-related, he said.

But Jack felt like he had snuck into his father's private study—something he did as a child and for which he was usually reprimanded when he did.

Now with the lights on in the large study, he and Devon felt like they had walked into a journalism museum. Every wall had photos of Walter with famous people or accepting awards from some journalistic organization. A roll-top desk sat open, its flat area covered with magazines and a few copies of the *Horseheads Clarion*. Pinned above it on a bulletin board were dozens of index cards, some with story ideas, some with phone numbers of people. In the middle was a photo of Walter's late wife, Andrea, taken probably when she was in her late thirties.

"Wow. Walter's wife was a stunner," Devon said, peering closely at the photo. "She could have been a model."

Jack had spent more than a few afternoons on the porch at Walter's house with Walter and Andrea when Jack was at the newspaper. Walter liked to bring his staff by the house to see that he also had a human side besides the role of tough-guy publisher, particularly when he was young.

"They never had children. And Walter never talked about it, really," Jack said. "He kind of adopted a lot of us who worked for him. He sometimes wrote me letters when I was out in California. He followed what I was up to out there. Publisher friends, I think, were keeping him in the loop about me. They never told me. But his letters always seemed to be pretty much on target."

Devon looked at Jack and decided to wait until later that night to bring up the topic of children again. The evening before she had briefly brought up the topic of children while they snuggled in bed. Jack got quiet and muttered something, and then joked about being an "old man" before changing the subject.

The insurance documents were right where Walter had

said they were, in a folder placed neatly in alphabetical order in the side drawer of the desk. And paper-clipped to it was a sealed envelope with "To Be Opened When I Am Dead!" written in Walter's scrawl on the front.

"Even money that's Walter's will, Jack," Devon said. "And I don't think it's any accident. He wanted you to find that. Insurance papers? He's worried about dying."

Jack took the file folder out to the dining room table and turned on some lights in the house. Like Jack's house before Devon arrived, it was decorated in "aging bachelor" motif. But on the wall there was a huge framed map of the South Pacific with pins in it, similar to the pins Walter used at work to show natural gas-related problems.

"He was in Vietnam in the sixties. He went back with Andrea and some other guys from his unit," Jack said. "They traveled for a month, I think. Only about a week was in Vietnam. They were in Australia and New Zealand, too. He wrote about the development of a free press in some of those countries. And he loved the diving in Tonga and Samoa. He was a scuba diver when I first started working for the *Clarion*. He and his buddies would go diving in the rivers and lakes in northern Pennsylvania. Too damned cold for me, even in the middle of the summer."

A map of the Kingdom of Tonga dominated one wall, with a circle drawn around the northern group, Vava'u.

"He and Andrea were supposed to retire to Fiji, or maybe it was Tonga, he told me, ten years ago. I think he even owned some land someplace over there."

Jack traced his fingers over the circle drawn around Vava'u, noting the protective reefs that encircled most of the islands.

"This might be a nice place to live someday. No hydrofracking there," he said. "You couldn't run away much farther from the U.S."

Devon stood behind him, resting her hands on his shoulders and studying the map as Jack thumbed through the insurance file quickly with a reporter's eye.

The insurance folder had data about Walter's medical coverage, medical history, and copies of various tests. The records showed that he had a litany of illnesses over the years, even a bout with prostate cancer five years before.

Over Jack's shoulder, Devon could read that there was also a copy of a letter referring to a paid-up $100,000 insurance policy Walter had taken out twenty years before through a local insurance agent, a friend of Walter's who had died just that year.

The insurance policy named Walter's deceased wife Andrea as the main beneficiary.

Jack Stafford was named as next in line when Walter passed away.

Grayson Oliver Delacroix slapped his face with his usual quick snaps before going out of the men's room to the press conference in the Grand Energy Systems auditorium downstairs, just a few steps from the athletic facilities and the now-infamous swimming pool.

Several of the television stations attending had asked to be allowed to shoot some footage of the pool, now reopened.

But Delacroix had sent word that no press was allowed in there. He told his public relations people to tell the TV crews he wanted to ensure the privacy of his staff who were back doing laps in the pool every day.

It had soured an already somewhat skeptical press, called out two days before by GES officials who had promised a big announcement about a new technique that would "revolutionize hydrofracking."

Television reporter Amber Millicence was in Flathead, Missouri for the press briefing. Millicence had become famous overnight when she anchored a series of live broadcasts from the protest near the Rockwell Valley High School at which Noah Webster Wilson was shot and killed. She was quickly promoted to be the roving science and hydrofracking reporter for a chain of television stations in the Midwest.

About twenty-five journalists were waiting for Delacroix when he took the podium—half of what he and Rod Mayenlyn had hoped for. But the list on the podium with the names and affiliations of the people had several representatives of national news organizations. Plus, Mayenlyn's own *Energy First America* staff was videotaping and would blast his remarks and announcement across the Internet though YouTube and a dozen friendly, industry-funded websites.

Seated to his right were Mayenlyn, Luther Burnside, and several other GES staff, all holding official-looking folders with GES stamped in bright letters on the outside. To his left sat a middle-aged man and woman, both of whom looked uncomfortable, partly from being in front of a group and partly because the man pulled at his necktie repeatedly, tipping off the journalists that he was unaccustomed to dressing up. The woman had forgotten a small price tag dangling from the sleeve of her ill-fitting dress.

"First, I would like to thank all of you for coming today to hear our announcement," Delacroix said. "We at GES are very excited to tell you about a new development that is going to help make hydraulic fracturing even safer and cleaner than it already is. We've maintained all along that our science and technology is sound, safe, and secure. Today, we will unveil something that will take us into the next century of gas exploration."

Amber Millicence watched her cameraman rolling video on Delacroix, simultaneously checking his phone for text messages. Delacroix's long-winded introduction to his big announcement was boring nearly everyone in the room, including the two people seated next to him who obviously had a part to play in the show.

Rod Mayenlyn, the person responsible for the industry *EFA* website had told her that Delacroix and GES would not be taking any questions about anything outside of this announcement today. But she planned on asking him on camera about the armed protests at GES sites anyway, even if all she got was bluster. In fact, a blustering Grayson Oliver Delacroix would be just the ticket for some good video, particularly when wrapped with footage of the armed people in Colorado and Michigan who were keeping gas company workers from getting on site.

She looked back at Delacroix when she heard him introduce Arnold and Loretta Simms, parents of Erica Simms, who had died two years before. The Simms claimed at the time that then 9-year-old Erica died because she was poisoned by chemicals from hydrofracking fluids that had leaked into their family well, chemicals that had sickened them, too.

"What the fuck?" she muttered under her breath, hoping the microphone hadn't picked it up.

"As you know, Arnold and Loretta have formed a group to help ensure that hydrofracking is conducted even more safely than it already is," Delacroix said, pointing to the couple. "It's called ERICA, Environmental Reform Initiative Care Actions. And as you know also, it's named after their daughter Erica, who passed away. You might also be aware that at one time, the Simms and GES were involved in a disagreement over the death of their daughter. We at GES don't believe our hydrofracking operations had anything to do with her death. And the Simms now understand and believe that too. But today's announcement should help show how hard we are working to ensure safety."

Millicence flipped open her smart phone to check on who the Simms were. She was still in college when the child had died. But what Delacroix called a disagreement, she quickly discovered, was a $5 million wrongful death lawsuit that had been settled out of court.

Millicence noted that the father of the dead girl was having a hard time holding back his scowl at Delacroix's remarks, tugging on his collar again. His wife was using a handkerchief to dab at her eyes.

She saw that one reporter was scrawling "paid off" in big letters in his notebook. Several others looked bored.

Then they starting paying attention again.

"That's all important background before I unveil the breakthrough we believe will remove the questions people have about the safety of hydrofracking and also make it more palatable for those of us interested in protecting the environment.

"Ladies and gentlemen of the press, I'd like to ask my associate Luther Burnside to come up and explain to you all about the Hydro-Green System. Those of you who have been asking so many questions about the chemicals used to bring the public natural gas should take special note. Hydro-Green is just that. It's a green technology for recovering natural gas. It's all about keeping our water clean and usable. It's the future."

Eli sat at the conference table with Jack, Devon and the two young reporters Walter had hired on the same day six months before Jack came on board at the *Horseheads Clarion* as investigative columnist, Stanley Belisak and Jill Nored.

Walter had initially dubbed them Jack and Jill because they seemed to practically finish each other's sentences.

But when Jack came on board, Walter dumped the sobriquet.

One Jack in the building was enough.

Today the five of them were vacillating between being glum and analytical after reading wire service reports about the GES announcement and its Hydro-Green System.

The *Clarion*, not surprisingly, had not been invited nor had it received information about the announcement.

GES claimed that it would soon start on-site testing of genetically modified *Archaea* organisms added to the fracking fluids it was injecting into the ground as it hydrofracked for natural gas. The *Archaea* were supposed to break down the toxic chemicals targeted by environmental groups, including benzene, xylene and toluene. In a lab setting, GES claimed, the *Archaea* organisms had shown they could basically eat the chemicals, breaking them down into simpler, non-toxic substances that would be essentially harmless to humans, animals, and plant life.

GES stopped short of saying precisely what the chemicals were in fracking fluid, but claimed the *Archaea* would be cleaning up fracking fluid so well so that wastewater could be treated and put back into the water system.

"I just didn't see this coming. At all," Eli said. "It's brilliant, when you think about it."

Jack had been ruminating for nearly a full day since GES made the announcement that was greeted by mostly positive press.

Television announcers in particular were enthusiastic, running some stock lab footage provided by GES that showed a beaker of normal wastewater extracted from a hydrofracked well, then a second to which *Archaea* had been added.

The first beaker looked sort of muddy, with particles floating on the surface. The second appeared like it had scooped up water from a pristine, high-elevation mountain stream.

"I can't believe they just run that footage without checking it out," Devon said. "Good grief. And besides, the toxic stuff isn't visible. You need a lab to test for it. God!"

Devon put her head in her hands and looked very tired, Jack thought.

The GES announcement had been just what the public and many members of the press were waiting for—a *miracle* that would make it possible for the rich natural gas reserves to be tapped, but without all the increasingly well-documented pollution problems. The public wanted the natural gas and the jobs the industry promised. The press was tired of getting criticism from the public when it ran stories questioning the pollution and other problems. And the pressure from the gas companies was also being felt in newsrooms all over the country, thanks to friendly government officials who were quietly lobbying owners of media to find other stories to chase.

"You know one TV reporter was pretty skeptical," Jack said. "Amber Millicence? She used to work locally but got her big chance after her broadcast from the rally. She did some good reporting."

Eli leaned in and spun his computer around to show a chart put up by an environmental group that had been warning about the dangers of hydrofracking for nearly a decade.

"See this last bar on the chart? It's an estimate of how radioactive the water is coming back up from some of these gas wells," Eli said. "They don't address radiation at all. They never have. They just say it's naturally occurring and so it has nothing to do with them. But the *Archies* aren't going to get rid of radioactivity. If they could, it would solve the problem of nuclear waste. Well, maybe."

The two young reporters were doodling on their notebook pads while Eli talked, looking like they wanted to say something, but were slightly intimidated by being brought in on an actual planning session. Walter had kept them out of the meetings, mostly because they were writing the majority of the non-gas-related new stories in the newspaper.

"Jill, what do you think?" Jack asked. "You, too, Stan.

How do we play this newspaper? And the website? Right now we're just putting up other media's reports. We need to check this ourselves, don't you think? But how?

Jill gave a sideways look at Stan and then reached down into her backpack for a book, which she held up for everyone to see.

The title was *Intelligent Design: How Human Cleverness Doomed the Planet.*

"I just got done reading this. It's like two weeks out. The author makes a pretty good case about how tinkering with untried techniques like this *Archaea* isn't the solution. It's the problem."

Jack remembered that when he first arrived Jill and Stanley had written a series of articles about genetically modified foods and its effects on people, using local farmers' efforts to avoid growing GMO crops as the news angle. The series was exceptionally well done, exceptional enough that the biochemistry and genetics labs of several universities had written flaming op-eds in national publications when the *Horseheads Clarion* had published the stories online. The *Clarion's* articles got picked up all over the country by media outlets.

"So what about the genetic altering part of this? Is that what you mean?" Jack asked.

"Yes and no. I don't know much about these microscopic *Archaea,*" Jill said. "But based on everything I've ever read, I bet these gas companies know even less. This whole thing might not work at all. But I'd be more worried about what it could do to the environment. This is being brought to us by the same people that are pumping diesel in the ground and act shocked when water wells are polluted."

Jack motioned to Jill, who slid the book across the conference room table to him. The picture on cover was a blowup of the tar sands oilfields in Alberta, Canada.

On the back, there was a brief synopsis of the book and a photo of the author, Kenneth MacInerery, a British historian and scientist who had several other books to his credit about the Industrial Revolution and culture.

"Can I borrow this?" Jack asked? "A little light reading? Just from the title I agree with his premise. Might give me some ideas."

Jack's cell phone vibrated on the table. Then Devon's made a chiming noise.

The hospital in Rochester had placed both calls from different nursing stations.

Walter had had "an episode," a nurse said. He was being taken in to emergency surgery right away.

Jack cursed the snow that was falling steadily as he and Devon made their way north to Rochester.

The roads were slippery and every so often, Devon would let out an involuntary "ooooh" as she felt Jack's SUV skid slightly.

The nurse at the hospital said Walter was going to be taken in to surgery right away because his blood pressure had dropped precipitously and the doctors were afraid that there was bleeding from the surgery.

That call had been nearly two hours ago, and Jack and Devon were resisting the urge to call the hospital every fifteen minutes for a status update. Being taken right in could mean right in or be taken in for surgery several hours later, given surgical schedules and Walter's actual condition.

Devon had started scanning *Intelligent Design: How Human Cleverness Doomed the Planet* as they careened along the highway. She needed to take her mind off Jack's driving and how hard the snow was coming down.

It was depressing reading.

The author had pulled together nearly all the threads that environmentalists had been harping about for decades: climate change, genetic tinkering, nano-particles, over-use of antibiotics, industrial and commercial pollution, rapid depletion of natural sources, food shortages and—in a chapter all by itself—the technology of hydrofracking.

"For a scientific-type, this guy writes extremely well," Devon said. "Listen to his introduction:

> Mother Nature is about to give the collective human ass a swift and painful kick. And she will do so suddenly, not gradually, like timid, government-funded scientists claim. They are afraid to tell the truth. The truth is the human species is in danger of extinction, not from some nuclear holocaust—although that should not be ruled out. The danger is all around us and also in us.
>
> Most scientists write about a 'tipping point' among the various environmental, social, and cultural problems we have to face. The chapters that fol-

> low show that we are not fac-
> ing a tipping point at all.
> We are really facing an elabo-
> rately-constructed arrangement
> of toxic and dangerous dominos
> standing on end that, once set
> in motion, cannot be stopped
> until the Earth as we know it
> no longer exists.

Jack tried to concentrate on the road while he digested some of what MacInerery had written. In California, Jack had written a lot about environmental issues but it was hydrofracking that had caught his attention, thanks to Devon. In the course of their research about fracking, he and Devon, and Eli had come to many of the same conclusions as MacInerery.

"I don't know about you, but that kind of stuff just makes me want to run away," Jack said. "Go find a corner of the world and hide out. This snowstorm makes the South Pacific look pretty good."

Jack's cell phone rang and he handed his phone over to Devon to answer. He had gotten a ticket for talking on his cell phone while driving and in this snowstorm he didn't want to take a chance that a state trooper might be lurking.

Devon only spoke in short bursts. "Okay, yes, sure." Then before she hung up she said, "How long?" followed by a final "Okay" and then "Thank you so much."

"The hospital?" Jack asked. "Walter out already or going in?"

Devon closed the book in her lap and gave Jack back his cell phone.

"Neither. When Walter's heart doctor got to the hospital, he vetoed the whole idea of surgery and changed Walter's meds. Walter's back in his room, sleeping the nurse said. And his blood pressure is back to normal, at least for someone who just had bypass surgery."

Jack eased back on the accelerator and let out a deep breath. They were well past halfway to the hospital from Horseheads and could have turned around. But after another mile Jack and Devon decided to go ahead and drive the rest of the way, see Walter, and have a talk with the doctors.

It would likely mean a night in Rochester at some hotel, given how hard it was snowing. But they knew that Walter would like getting caught up on some of newest news and might even have some ideas about how to proceed with the latest wrinkle in the hydrofracking stories.

"You know what he'll say, Jack?" Devon said. "Talk to this Kenneth MacInerery fellow for a column."

In Rockwell Valley, Eli noted with irony that the new gas well being used as a test site by Grand Energy Services for its Hydro-Green System was only two miles from the home of the late Muriel Dogg and late Delbert Dogg.

Delbert had been murdered while working at a GES well and no one yet had been arrested. Muriel had died from cancer, a cancer she blamed squarely on GES and hydrofracking.

In front of the heavy equipment and drilling rig, GES had set up a small stage with loudspeakers. In front were about one hundred chairs and even some tables and chairs off to one side, labeled "Press Only."

A ceremony was to begin in about fifteen minutes, at which GES President Grayson Oliver Delacroix was to preside. Various local and state politicians were buzzing about, too. Banners with green lettering were fluttering around, all printed with the GES logo and the new Hydro-Green Systems logo as well.

The snowstorm from the day before—a whopper of an early winter storm that had stranded Jack and Devon in Rochester—had ended, and although it was well below freezing, the sun had come out and it was quite a nice day, certainly for late November.

Eli noted that television reporter Amber Millicence was on site, but she and her cameraman were placed in the back of the crowd from where most of other TV crews had been allowed to set up.

The placement was probably payback for some aggressive reporting she had been doing about the havoc wreaked by the Wolverines at GES sites—plus, in recent weeks she had gotten and broadcast some graphic footage of GES employees in a shoving match in Michigan at a gas well where citizens were blocking the entryway.

That footage gave her a news angle to mention GES employee Tom Fletcher, arrested at the rally at which hydrofracking foe and environmentalist Noah Webster Wilson was killed. Fletcher had requested a jury trial.

GES was furious with Fletcher for calling attention to himself and GES.

Besides the politicians, media, and GES-related folks, a small cadre of about fifteen protesters carrying large placards and signs were standing along the edges. Besides the normal anti-hydrofracking signs, now there were some protesting the use of genetically modified organisms—the very heart of the GES Hydro-Green System.

"NO, NO, GMO," one sign read. Another, "Don't Screw with Mother Nature."

When Delacroix walked to the podium, the protesters started a chant, "GMO GOTTA GO, GMO GOTTA GO, GMO GOTTA GO."

The chanting drew angry looks from a crew of hard-hatted GES drill workers who had stopped their tasks when Delacroix first tapped the microphone to get people's attention.

The public address system and Delacroix's booming voice covered up most of the chanting, though some of the TV crews kept their cameras trained on the protesters and not the CEO of Grand Energy Services as he began to speak.

"Ladies and gentlemen. Welcome today to the first public unveiling of our new Hydro-Green System. It's the latest in technology to help us safely hydrofrack for much-needed natural gas. We had originally believed when we set up this event today that this would be the very first well using this new marriage of gas drilling and biology to make for even safer natural gas extraction.

"Well, our staff in the past week asked me if they could move ahead and start adding the genetically modified *Archaea* —boy is that hard to say!— to the fracking fluids on a few newly-drilled wells here in Pennsylvania, Michigan, Ohio, and Colorado.

"So even as we ceremonially start the process here, you should know that in three other states, GES gas rigs are already in the process of, or getting ready to usher in the future, just like you are with us.

"In all, by the end of this month, we hope have at least

one hundred wells using the Hydro-Green System, which we think is going to remove the environmental concerns that have been roadblocks to fully exploit this valuable natural resource."

Eli snapped photos from every angle he could as Delacroix and two men in white lab coats ceremoniously poured an 18-inch diameter, three foot tall glass beaker containing a clear fluid into an open pipe that went from the stage to a tank next to the silent drilling rig.

Behind him someone shouted, "Is that water from the GES pool?" drawing laughs from the protesters.

The three men struggled to lift the beaker, eventually pouring it in a rush down the pipe.

There was some mild applause from the crowd when Delacroix held up the beaker over his head like a trophy, grinning wide for the cameras. The applause was followed by a huge gasp when the beaker slipped from his hands and bounced off his shoulder, shattering when it crashed on the stage, sending glass in every direction, even out into the laps of people seated in front.

"Oh-my-God! WOW! That's the money shot," Amber Millicence said. She motioned to her cameraman to stop filming. "We've got plenty now. Let's pack up and go back to the station. I wonder if I'll be able to get away with saying 'butterfingers' on air?"

Eli kept shooting stills of Delacroix and the pained look on his face as some GES staff members sprang to the stage and were using their shoes to move the glass shards away.

Eli was already writing captions in his head for the photo of Delacroix trying to smile while all around him people were brushing glass off themselves.

If GES had wanted to get lots of publicity for the unveiling of its Hydro-Green System, it was going to get it.

Eli just hoped the *Archaea* sent down these wells were steadier than Delacroix.

B y the time Jack and Devon had gotten to the hospital the prior night, Walter was asleep and his doctor suggested they come back early the next morning. Walter's blood pressure was still a worry, but mostly he needed to rest.

And the doctor said he should not have any visitors until the next morning.

The snowstorm Jack and Devon had driven through was forcing the closure of roads, so they opted to spend the night in a hotel just a short drive from the hospital.

There was a small restaurant next door where they got a light dinner, drank several glasses of wine, and then hoped for a good night's sleep before seeing Walter the next morning.

In just the few months of their relationship, Jack and Devon had already fallen into many of the same easy routines of a long-married couple. Their relationship ran the gamut from close friends to newlyweds and back. They didn't question it. They simply went about lives that had become intertwined through the newspaper and their routines at home.

But Kenneth MacInerery's gloomy book prompted them to start an uncomfortable dialogue about the future, a subject generally off-limits, an unspoken agreement as they stumbled their way along. Jack's late wife hovered in the background of his thoughts; Devon had to contend with the ghost of her late former-husband, Noah.

And the age difference haunted Jack, though Devon only laughed when he brought it up. She thought age-difference issues were overrated.

With snow swirling outside the window and Walter in the hospital just a few blocks away, Jack and Devon were propped up on the bed with pillows behind their heads, still awake at midnight.

"It's just the end of the world, that's all," Devon said, half-flippantly, but wondering herself how serious she was. "It's not just the book. Look at what we've been uncovering and writing about. I mean, I have known about a lot of this for years. We live in a corrupt, greedy society. Okay. But now I wonder if we really are about to get to a tipping point. I mean, just think about water? How much clean water can we afford to waste, even here? I just read that fracking a single gas well in Michigan used 21 million gallons of water, Jack. *Twenty-one million gallons.* God!"

Jack flipped through a few pages of *Intelligent Design: How Human Cleverness Doomed the Planet*, settling on the section about hydrofracking for a few minutes.

"Well, here's part of his take on fracking. See if this cheers you up," Jack said.

```
    High    volume,    slick-water
hydrofracking    is    likely    to
prove  one  of  the  most  disas-
trous  natural  resource  extrac-
tion  processes  ever  developed.
The  discovery  of  how  to  make  it
work,  coupled  with  a  declining
regulatory  environment  (thanks
```

> to politics and corruption), along with an ever more ener- gy-hungry world created a per- fect storm for hydrofracking to burst into general use. Had hydrofracking been proposed even twenty years before, it would not have been able to find such easy acceptance.

"He has a lot more cheery stuff. But it's this idea—that all of these things are going to come together, that's the big bang of what he says. Fracking might be the last gasp of carbon industries, trying to hang on. And maybe the earth's last gasp, too."

Devon slid over and snuggled up next to Jack.

"Turn off the light and let's try to get some sleep. It will be nice to see Walter tomorrow. Maybe surviving his surgery will have brightened him up. And brightened me up, too."

Jack switched off the lamp and watched the snow blowing hard against the window.

When he fell asleep, he dreamed that he and Devon were running, dodging giant dominoes as they toppled onto the ground right behind them.

Jack and Devon walked down the hospital corridor, sunlight streaming through the windows. The snowstorm had passed, and although it was mounded up all around, the sun made the even normally grumpy nurses smile.

As they rounded the corner to Walter's room, they saw a Catholic priest leaving. He was kissing the Crucifix in his hand before he replaced it into a small bag he was carrying.

He smiled as he passed Jack and Devon, who hurried to get into the room where Walter was sitting up, reading a Rochester newspaper.

"What are you guys doing here? Isn't anyone minding my newspaper?"

Jack and Devon looked at each other, their blood pressures dropping back down to normal.

"So, what was the good Father doing here, Walter?" Jack asked. "You just took a year off my life."

Walter laughed and closed the newspaper on his lap. On the table next to his bed, there was a tray with orange juice and some toast.

"He was just stopping by. Yesterday one of the nervous-Nellie nurses had called him because my records list "Roman Catholic" and she thought he should stand by in case I needed last rites. Turns out he was once the priest in Rockwell Valley, but he's up here near Rochester these days. We had a nice chat about Rockwell Valley. He agreed the place is a mess. The priest who took over is dealing with a lot. People are sick. People are angry."

Devon stood close by the bed, checking Walter over carefully with a studied eye. He looked very pale, but better than someone doctors had nearly taken in for emergency surgery the day before. He was still wired up to a variety of monitors, but if she was reading them correctly, they were steady. And he seemed nearly as alert as if they were sitting in the newspaper office in Horseheads.

Jack quickly filled Walter in on the Hydro-Green System that GES had announced and what the newspaper had printed. Walter sat quietly, looking distracted while Jack talked. Then Devon showed Walter the copy of *Intelligent*

Design: How Human Cleverness Doomed the Planet that *Clarion* reporter Jill had given to Jack and Devon.

When they were done talking, Walter took the book and flipped through it for a moment, then laid his head back on the pillow and looked up at the ceiling.

He closed his eyes, and it was a full minute before he spoke.

Jack and Devon thought he had fallen asleep.

"I would expect you already have a column in mind about this book, Jack. Maybe you'll be able to get an interview with him. But consider taking a closer look at this green solution they have for hydrofracking. I worry about applying complicated biological solutions to industrial problems. I have read way too many science-fiction novels."

"Lying here in this bed has gotten me thinking," Walter said. "If there is any way to give people some hope, we need to start doing that. We've been hitting this thing so hard. I have had some time to think about it. People need hope, Jack. And maybe solutions, too."

Jack apologized for forgetting the personal documents Walter had asked for.

"We left in a hurry and barely had time to arrange for Eli to feed our dog. I'll bring everything next time. I have some finance stuff for you too."

Walter waved his hand in the air to indicate the papers left behind were unimportant to him.

"If I'm lucky I'll talk my way out of here soon and read them at home," he said.

A nurse came in and announced that Walter had to be wheeled down to the hall to a lab where they kept the MRI machine. "If you want to visit with Mr. Nagle, you'll have to come back this afternoon. I think he'll be there until well after lunch," the nurse said.

Devon and Jack said their goodbyes and at Walter's urging, called the staff to say they would be back by afternoon at the *Clarion* office. It would be a quicker trip now that the snow had stopped falling.

"Hope and solutions for our readers, okay?" Walter said as the nurse unhooked the wall monitors.

"Hope and solutions, you two."

They moved out of the way when a burly attendant came in and wheeled Walter out into the hallway on the bed.

He was half-sitting up reading the newspaper again, muttering about something he was reading as he turned the corner.

They heard him shout one last time: "Hope and solutions, Jack!" as he continued down the hallway.

It was the last time Jack and Devon saw Walter alive.

From the *Horseheads Clarion*

Column One
The Horseheads Clarion

Clarion says goodbye to Walter Nagle

By Jack Stafford

HORSEHEADS, New York — This is one column I wish I didn't have to write.

Two days ago, the *Horseheads*

Clarion's publisher of nearly 40 years died of a heart attack at a Rochester Hospital. He had checked himself in, had bypass surgery, and by all measures was recovering.

Then suddenly in the night, Walter Nagle's big heart stopped beating and he was dead.

Walter had a love affair with this community and this region that never dimmed his entire life. He used his newspaper as a tool for good, a tool to help people, and as a positive force.

Just days before he died, he asked that in this column and in the pages of the Horseheads *Clarion* that we provide the community with hope and solutions.

In fact, those were his last words to me and to my *Clarion* colleague, Devon Walsh:

"Hope and solutions."

Walter's full obituary, detailing a career full of awards and recognition, is printed on page 3 of today's issue. Walter never wanted his personality to overshadow the newspaper or his staff. And so in keeping with his wishes, that death notice is where he placed the death notices and obituaries of all people, famous and non-famous, during his long career.

But I am writing about him in this prime space on the newspaper's front page because as his friend, as a colleague, and as someone who owes him an entire career as a writer and journalist, I get to break his rules.

Sorry Walter, but that's the way it is, because you deserve to be honored on the front page of the newspaper you so dearly loved.

In the 30-plus years I knew Walter Nagle, he had many offers to purchase the Horseheads *Clarion*. All the offers came from large corporations he called "print predators" who were interested in using the newspaper as a cash machine, not in serving the community.

Walter wasn't interested. He believed a community newspaper is a sacred trust. When I was a young reporter starting out at the *Clarion*, he told me that telling the truth, fighting for the underdog, and helping the helpless was our goal. And by reporting the news honestly and fully to the best of our ability, we could do that.

He lived that philosophy, and lived it until the moment of his death.

When Walter's wife Andrea died, Walter said he felt as if a big hole had been blown through his soul. His surviving colleagues here at the newspaper feel that very same thing today. And the community outpouring of grief at his passing indicates Walter Nagle's legacy is secure.

The *Horseheads Clarion* will continue to publish. We will continue the good work of Walter Nagle even as we all struggle with the grief of his death.

And we will continue to chronicle the ongoing threats to the community's well-being from the outside forces of greed and the unthinking, uncaring corporations that Walter fought against every day of his life.

Walter Nagle might have left the building. But his spirit is still with us and stronger than ever.

Jack Stafford is an investigative columnist and reporter for The Horseheads Clarion *and has worked as an investigative reporter for metropolitan newspapers in California and Colorado.*

The staff of the newspaper posted the "closed" sign at 4 p.m. New Year's Eve, just after Oscar Wilson, his niece Lindy Karlsen, Shania from Millie's Diner across the street, and a dozen other friends trickled in to the *Horseheads Clarion's* office at Jack and Devon's invitation.

Eli was busy setting up a table with some cheese, crackers, and a few other good eats. Staff reporters Stanley and Jill were popping champagne corks along with Jack and Devon's favorite Finger Lakes Riesling, Oscar's Boot.

Jack had learned the tradition from Walter that New Year's Eve was a good time to celebrate early and go home. "It's amateur night out there on New Year's Eve," Walter would say. "Everyone in six counties who barely touches a drop all year seems to think they need to get plastered New Year's Eve. Too ugly for me to watch."

At home, Belle was lying on the floor, smelling the aromas from the crockpot of chicken and vegetables brewing for dinner, which Jack and Devon planned on eating at the table by the front window.

Oscar took a glass of champagne from Jillian, took one sip and scrunched up his face. He put the glass down, reaching over to replace it with a glass of his own vintage.

"I have a toast, in case no one else does right now," he said. "Everybody got a glass?

"To Jack, the publisher of the *Horseheads Clarion* and the best man I know. Cheers!"

The group all lifted their glasses high, a few clicking with each other.

The late-afternoon party was the first really festive event at the newspaper since Walter Nagle had died. Jack's attempts to make Walter's wake and funeral into a celebration of life had fallen flat in the community. They knew that they had lost a giant when Walter had passed.

But the staff of the newspaper was adjusting and the community was taking slowly to the idea of Jack running the newspaper with Devon at his side. Jack's hometown roots helped. Devon's charm rounded out what the community needed to hear and think about in a newspaper in which they felt a lot of ownership and community pride.

Jack grabbed Devon's hand and walked to where everyone could see them, and raised his glass.

"I want to make a toast and an announcement," he said.

"First, the toast... To Walter, for building this newspaper to what it is, and to thank him for entrusting it to me. I am still stunned that Walter left this place, lock, stock, and barrel to me as part of his trust. Like I wrote a few weeks ago, I am honored. When I started here chasing high school sports right out of college more than thirty years ago, I never thought I would be standing here as publisher. Here's to Walter. Here's to the *Clarion*. Here's to all of you!"

This time the toast also drew some applause and a wolf whistle from Eli, who had already slammed down two glasses of champagne and was eyeing Shania across the room, mustering up the courage to ask her out.

Shania was having similar thoughts. She had been asked out by many of the Grand Energy Services gas workers who frequented the diner but she turned them all down. She had felt their eyes trying to peer down the front of her uniform too many times to believe they all wanted ~~was~~ to go out dancing. Or talk.

"Okay, Jack, let's hear this announcement. Pay raises for the staff, right?" Oscar joked, generating a big laugh all around.

Anyone watching closely saw Jack take Devon's hand and squeeze it before he spoke.

"Well, I think the *Clarion* will use Lakeside Winery as a way to calibrate raises this year Oscar. We'll follow your lead," Jack said, getting an even bigger laugh.

"No, my announcement—our announcement—is personal.

"Devon and I are engaged and sometime this spring, we are going to get married. Maybe right here in the office."

The announcement brought out a babble of chattering from nearly everyone in the room who rushed forward to congratulate the couple, with champagne and wine spilling in the process.

The handshakes and kisses and hugs went on for nearly fifteen minutes, with Oscar finally tapping his wine glass with a spoon to get everyone's attention again.

"I want to say that I predicted this the first time I saw Devon and Jack together. They were arguing over a story Jack was working on. And because Jack actually was listening and not simply blowing Devon's beautiful black hair off her head, I knew they would get together.

"So, another toast—my last, I'm afraid, because if I drink anymore, I can't drive home up the lake. To Jack and Devon, the nicest people I know, and now the nicest couple I know. I am calling dibs on being best man, Jack. And please, please… if you guys have any boys, name them Oscar, not Walter."

The glasses all were raised high while Devon and Jack blushed deeply, partly from the wine and partly from Oscar's reference to children. Jack was 55, soon to be 56. Devon was 40, nearly 41. Children had been coming up in their late-night discussions since Walter's death—more debates than discussions.

But that issue wouldn't be settled for some time, not until the *Horseheads Clarion* had published several horrific stories about children and hydrofracking that made headlines around the globe.

The tradition at the *Horseheads Clarion* was to publish a roundup of news from the previous year on New Year's Day, or as close as the Tuesday and Friday publication schedule would allow.

And because the New Year fell on a Tuesday, Jack was busy in the office, overseeing the pick-up of the newspapers by delivery drivers getting ready to take them out to stores and business. Many delivery drivers were suffering from bell-ringer hangovers but game to get their papers delivered.

Today's carriers would be picking up some New Year's tips from customers, in addition to the earned money for every subscriber. Many customers had already tipped them around Christmas Day but more would come today.

The front page carried a column by Jack—not his normal *Column One,* but one with the title "From the Publisher's Desk," a rubric Walter used infrequently, but one that Jack decided would be a nice tribute on the first day of the first year after Walter's death.

Jack was pleased with the way the paper looked, even though the front page and inside pages were rehashes of what had happened in the community that year.

One entire page was taken up with updates about hydrofracking news, very little of it encouraging.

Reporters Stanley, Jill, and Eli had produced most of the stories and photos. A photo of Roy Bonder, Jr. stared out at Jack. Bonder Jr. was still going through the court system for shooting Anne Kovach, the teacher at Rockwell Valley High School. All indications were the former high school student would go to jail for life. His father, Roy Bonder, Sr. was still missing, though his fracking wastewater truck had been found the same day as the GES pool incident.

Tom Fletcher, the pint-sized bully from General Energy Services, had been convicted of illegal possession of a firearm and assaulting a police officer at the Rockwell Valley High School protest and rally. He was awaiting sentencing. And Delmar Ogilvy, who shot and killed environmental leader and activist Noah Webster Wilson while he addressed the crowd at the same rally, was still in custody awaiting trial.

Jack grinned when he read the paragraphs explaining that Ogilvy's legal bills were being paid by GES. Devon had sat in on several of Ogilvy's court appearances and recognized one of the attorneys as being a GES associate.

A few phone calls to the court clerk confirmed the connection.

GES had been furious at the initial story—even more so at the headline on the story: "GES funds lawyer for accused murderer of anti-fracking leader."

Eli had shown a real flair for producing graphics in recent months. He had produced a graphic to go with the story about the Wolverines and the shadowy group's various assaults on gas company facilities across the country. Devon had thought the original graphic looked a little too much like an often-published sketch of the Unabomber.

With a few changes, Jack approved it but still, it was a chilling image, perhaps more so to anyone working around gas rigs, the primary targets now for Wolverine activities.

The caption under that graphic was sure to prompt a phone call or letters from GES, Jack thought. "Got gas? We got you."

Jack noted sadly that the third female bladder cancer victim in Rockwell Valley had died just a few weeks before. In today's edition, Eli had updated the story about the murder of the husband of one of the other three cancer victims, Delbert Dogg.

Since Dogg had been shot and killed one year before at a GES well site, Rockwell Valley Police said they were now close to making an arrest in that case, hinting that there was likely some connection with the Wolverines.

The most disturbing story on the page, for Jack, was the one about growing civil unrest around the country. In some foreign countries, citizens were being arrested for blocking hydrofracking well sites.

In many locales, police were allowing the well sites to

be blockaded, stepping in only when goons hired by gas companies got violent when they tried to break up largely peaceful protests and force their way onto the gas company property.

Police departments in two cities in Colorado were being sued in civil court by GES and a consortium of gas companies for failing to evict people they said were trespassers. GES promised lawsuits against more.

One story that didn't make the paper was an update on the Hydro-Green System that GES had been using since just before Walter died. The company was being uncooperative about providing any factual information about how effective the genetically modified *Archaea* were at breaking down toxic fracking fluids.

The system was now in use at hundreds of wells—maybe more, because they claimed even saying where the company was using it was akin to a trade secret.

But it seemed strange to Jack that the company was not pushing it more, even in pro-gas media or its house PR promo site, *Energy First America*.

When Eli and Devon hadn't been able to put together much except for a rehash of a month-old story about Hydro-Green, Jack decided they should spike any mention of it in the New Year's Day edition.

Jack and Devon had just finished reading Kenneth MacInerery's *Intelligent Design: How Human Cleverness Doomed the Planet,* and they were concerned about the potential long-term effects of Hydro-Green.

In a longish section about antibiotics, MacInerery graphically detailed the history of antibiotics and the generally well-known notion about how bacterial diseases adapt to medicines, with some strains eventually becoming immune through survival of some small portion of cells.

In a similar chapter on pesticides, he warned that doomsday predictions about pests like grasshoppers and cockroaches taking over the earth weren't that far off, given that pesticides were proving to be more toxic to humans than initially thought.

But one of his most damning sections was on genetically modified organisms and industrial geneticists.

"We joke about scary monsters like Frankenstein, from Mary Shelley's famous book by the same name," MacInerery wrote in a chapter called "Shrinking the Genes."

> "The truth is the men and women working in labs today are creating all manner of arguably strange crossbreeds, and have very little understanding of the longer-term impacts of what they do. GMO food is already clearly wreaking havoc on the human digestive system. Think about the wild increase in gluten allergies alone. GMO crops look beautiful in a field but have 10 percent of the nutrition of non-GMO foods. And the tinkering with bacteria and viruses is beyond dangerous."

Jack had been hounding MacInerery to talk on the phone about *Archaea* and how the gas companies had modified some of the life forms so they would munch down toxic chemicals in fracking wastewater. That technology/gene modification had started after MacInerery's book had gone to the publisher. Jack was sure MacInerery would have some thoughts worth publishing but they hadn't connected yet.

He folded up the *Horseheads Clarion* and put it on top of the large stack of papers already on the corner of his desk. The last delivery driver waved as he spun his tires leaving the parking lot.

Jack was putting his coat on for the walk home when he heard his email alert go off. He was pretty sure it was Devon who had stayed home to relax and cook. She said she wanted to be domestic on the first day of the New Year, and the first day of them being officially engaged.

Jack leaned over and saw that it was not from Devon but from author Kenneth MacInerery.

Mr. Stafford: We can talk next week. I have some ideas about Archaea and what GES has done. It's uglier than I guessed.

Michael Ahlbright fidgeted in his chair in the conference room at Grand Energy Services. He had been hired just before Christmas and he was still sorting out his job as a special consultant on water and chemicals.

He had sat through nearly an hour of mid-morning discussion led by Grayson Oliver Delacroix and his executive staff about GES operations, profits, and public relations problems.

The snowy scene he could see outside was nothing like what he was used to in his native Sacramento, California, and he already had caught a nasty cold from not dressing warmly enough.

He had almost dozed off when he realized that Delacroix was ushering people out of the conference room.

"Michael, you stick around. You too, Luther, Rod," Delacroix said.

Ahlbright blew his nose and reached for his cup of now-cold coffee. In his first two weeks, he had figured out that Luther Burnside, a former landsman and now a vice president for special projects, and Rod Mayenlyn, a public relations vice president who ran a website aimed at squelching opposition to hydrofracking, were Delacroix's closest confidants.

Alhbright wasn't sure either of them were the sharpest tools in the shed, but they certainly had Delacroix's ear—and Delacroix had their absolute loyalty.

"Michael, I know you have some information you said is very preliminary about Hydro-Green, but I didn't want the rest of the staff to hear it just yet. So, you have the floor."

Ahlbright shuffled through his file folders and opened the one with a label *Archaea* on it, frowning when he couldn't find the summary pages right away.

"Well, I'll give you exact numbers in a minute, but the wells where the modified *Archaea* have been added to our fracking fluid are showing some problems. The yields from the wells are lower than expected, even given how these wells peak early and taper off quickly," Alhbright said.

Delacroix waved his hand in the air, as if to erase Ahlbright's words.

"Michael, Michael, Michael. That much I knew when I hired you. That's why we hired you. But what is going on? The developers of Hydro-Green said that all their tests showed was significant lessening of toxicity in the fracking water that came back up when they added these GMO, well, things. They said the water was almost clean. They said production would go up, not down. Answers Michael, please. Answers."

Ahlbright found his summary pages and spread them out in front of him, frowning again.

"Okay, Mr. Delacroix. I understand. But this is still preliminary. I'm having trouble getting all the data I need, even from our own people.

"The *Archaea* are doing what they are supposed to do, but not anything like the numbers the developers said they would," Ahlbright said. "Some of the chemicals—toluene for one—are not being touched by these bugs. Others are, but at far less than what we expected."

Delacroix waved his hands in the air again, obviously frustrated.

"But that doesn't explain shit," he said. "What is causing the lower yields? Should we go back to not using these in the mix?"

Ahlbright looked at his notes, weighing whether to throw out his theory today or wait until he had more data to back it up. Then he looked at the expression on Delacroix's face and decided he needed to roll the dice. His old job at the consulting firm in California was still open—his bosses had pleaded with him to stay there anyway. And if Delacroix got pissed enough to fire him, well, he had already had enough of the crappy Missouri winter weather anyway.

"Well, this is just my theory, based on what little I can find and get from well managers. It's been too soon since it was introduced," Ahlbright said. "Most of these wells are bringing up less gas because we are having a much higher incidence of well-casing failures than normal. So we are losing the gas before we get it. Plain old venting—sometimes a lot of gas, like in California last week right before that explosion at the well."

Rod Mayenlyn leaned in and raised his hand to speak.

"Well, I would like to say that particular incident has been a goddamn mess to handle. We're lucky it was so far out in the boondocks in California. Plus that area of the central California Valley has all kinds of toxic waste issues and strange smells anyway. Had that been in Pennsylvania or Ohio, oh Christ! We would have been all over the front pages and on TV."

Delacroix motioned for Ahlbright to continue.

"That's just it, Rod. The problem, I mean. What happened in California? Well, it might start happening more. Maybe. I'm just not sure."

This time Delacroix stood up, shaking his head. "Michael. I know you are new. I know you don't want to make a mistake. But I want you to tell me what you do know. What you think. And I want it right now, without the waffling. Please, cut to the chase."

Ahlbright flipped his file folder closed and spoke slowly. He could tell that all three men needed to hear what he thought he had discovered. But for a moment he flashed on the expression "don't shoot the messenger."

"Okay, in a nutshell, I think that the GMO *Archaea* isn't gobbling the toxic chemicals as fast as predicted. But that's not that big a deal. The big deal is it seems to have developed a taste for something in the concrete well casings.

The casings. The numbers for failures on those wells is four, maybe fives times the number of normal failures. And these aren't just cracks. These casings are crumbling, turning to powder at a couple of wells. The *Archaea* is the only variable I can figure. I think it's eating the casings."

Delacroix sat back down and leaned back in his chair, closing his eyes.

"Rod, I want you to start thinking about how to be creative about how to make us look like we are victims. Maybe we can blame the inventors of this. But we better stop using Hydro-Green right away, very quietly, until we figure this out. I don't want a word out there yet. It's been the first decent PR we've had in years."

Ahlbright leaned in to the table to give Delacroix the balance of his bad news.

"If I am right. That's IF. Any well that used this stuff is likely at risk of having full failure of its well casings. So yes. I would recommend the company stop using it, or at least reformulate. And we need to look at every well that had Hydro-Green as part of fracking.

"But there's something else."

Ahlbright saw Delacroix's face redden. Luther and Rod put their heads in their hands.

"The suicide gene in the *Archaea?* The genetic modification designed to get rid of it after it had broken down the chemicals? It's not working very well. At least in the handful of samples I saw. The samples show high levels of *Archaea* in the water when it should be just part of the chemical stew and not detectable."

Delacroix hit the intercom button and told his secretary to order some food for the four men, that they would be in the conference room while they wrestled with this.

Ahlbright relaxed slightly, staring at the last page of his notes, wondering when he should give the final piece of information, the part of which he was the least certain, but which was likely to send Delacroix through the roof when he found out.

Delacroix was composing himself again, his face no longer red as he started chatting about Hydro-Green and how to handle cutting back on using it while making it appear it was still viable.

"Except for us, no one is testing that flow-back wastewater when it comes up anyway," Delacroix said. "We'll be okay. But we have to get control over this casing problem," Delacroix said. "We need more gas, not less. If our numbers drop, so will our new investors. Shit, this could not have come at a worse time."

Ahlbright decided his last bit of bad news could wait a few days until he had time to lean on the lab that had done the original gene splicing on the *Archaea* to be sure his information was correct.

He slid the sheet titled *Archaea-E. coli* back into his file folder.

Failed well casings could be the least of their problems.

Eli sat in Millie's Diner, admiring Shania from his perch at the corner table that had become the unofficial *Horseheads Clarion* press club, at least for coffee and tea.

Their New Year's Eve casual encounter had grown into a dating friendship that seemed like it might go places.

At least Eli hoped so.

Shania didn't seem to mind Eli's geeky computer habits—in fact, she was asking him for help almost daily on some of her junior college work. And Eli could sit for hours and watch her waiting tables.

Since Walter had died, Jack continued to come to Millie's mid-morning for tea and sometimes breakfast, even though Devon was slowly weaning him off high cholesterol foods like bacon and eggs. And Eli was now welcome to join them, part of an alliance of three that was making most of the news decisions about the newspaper.

Eli was finding Jack to be a lot easier to approach than Walter had ever been.

Eli had cultivated a handful of sources about GES and other gas company operations, all of them online. He had never met any of the people in person, but the information seemed solid most of the time. And when he got what seemed like a good lead, he would either chase it himself or have Jack or Devon pick it up.

Today he had some information about the sudden resignation of Michael Ahlbright, a highly respected California environmental consultant who had worked for GES for a little over a month, then suddenly left the company.

The official GES announcement said that Ahlbright was returning to California to be closer to his family and that he had done some "important analyses" for GES in his short time with the company. "Michael made some important contributions in his short time here," Grayson Oliver Delacroix said in a press release. "We are sorry to seem him leave Grand Energy Services."

But Eli discovered in fifteen minutes of Internet searching that Michael Ahlbright didn't have any family in California at all. In fact, he had been adopted, and his adoptive parents had died several years before—in Kansas.

Then the *Energy First America* website published an article about his leaving that implied that Ahlbright was not able to deliver what he had promised when he was hired by GES. The *EFA* story was interesting to Eli because the site almost always parroted the official GES line. More interesting was that Ahlbright had posted a comment on the site saying the *EFA* people should be careful about printing false information.

"Eli, you're staring and making Shania uncomfortable," Devon said as she and Jack walked up to the table. "Now she's blushing."

Jack and Devon ordered tea, while Eli tried to keep his eyes focused on his two co-workers and away from Shania as she walked away. He was unsuccessful and drew a laugh from Devon.

"So Eli, you said you have something about Ahlbright and GES that might be a story?" Jack asked. "We could have talked in the office. Oh, of course." He looked up to see Shania approach with their tea, and refill Eli's coffee mug, giving Eli a smile as she walked back over to the lunch counter, conspicuously absent of any GES workers.

"Well, the thing is, I'm sure Ahlbright signed a non-disclosure form with GES. They all have to. Even the line grunts that drive trucks do now," Eli said. "But after that snarky *EFA* posting about him and then his response, I thought he might be willing to talk about what he was hired to do."

Jack stirred some honey into his tea, thinking for a minute about how many of these conversations he had with Walter since moving from California.

"Sure, but do you have any idea what he was hired for? We can't call him cold and go fishing for information. But I agree. One month on the job and he leaves that quick? And the cover story is pretty funny. Still, that could be just corporate politics, insider baseball."

Eli flipped open his laptop and scrolled down through his messages, finding the one labeled "Hydro-Green" from a Hotmail account that one of his sources was using to feed him information.

"Let me read you this."

Ahlbright was looking into well-case failures and Hydro-Green Systems. Whatever he found got him fired. LS.

"LS?" Jack asked.

"Um, yeah, Land Shark," Eli said. "It's all these avatars people have and stuff. I'm pretty sure he's one of the Wolverine people. But I don't know for sure."

Jack looked at the screen for a minute, then at Devon.

"So he found a link between well-case failures and Hydro-Green. We've been publishing about these failures and the failure rate since before I even joined the staff. People either don't believe it or are outraged," Jack said.

Eli nodded as he clicked the keys.

"Here's a report I ran across posted by a Rockwell Valley blogger about well-case failures. He doesn't say who his source is, but he says that since GES started using Hydro-Green, there have been a lot more leaks. And more serious leaks. He says that explosion in California was because of a well-casing failure," Eli said.

"GES said that was a leak in a transmission pipeline," Devon said. "We reported it that way. They said it was a faulty valve and a spark set it off."

Jack signaled to Shania for more hot water.

"Eli, first let's see if we can find out if Hydro-Green was used to frack that California well," Jack said. "If it was, then let's talk to this Michael Ahlbright. I nominate Devon to talk to him if we need to. All in favor?"

Jack and Eli raised their hands while Devon folded her arms across her chest.

"Of course," she said. "I accept the nomination. And maybe the newspaper can fly me to California to talk to him directly. I've had enough cold and gray to last me for a long time. And it's not even February yet."

It was the first week in February—almost always a bitter cold time in upstate New York—before Eli could confirm that the California gas well that had exploded had been using the Hydro-Green System as part of its fracking fluid three weeks before when the skies lit up and two GES employees were almost burned.

Devon's half-in-jest request to fly to California ended up with a Skype interview instead.

Ahlbright had agreed to the online conversation after *EFA* had published a second article mentioning him, obliquely indicating that he had given GES bad advice about how to monitor well casing integrity and water quality.

He was furious when he read it. His attorney said while

he was legally bound by the non-disclosure form he had signed, he could certainly give some hints about what he was really working on at GES. And in the meantime, Ahlbright's lawyer was watching the *EFA* site carefully for the possibility of a libel lawsuit.

Ahlbright had not been hired back yet at his old company. His conversations with former workers were uncomfortable and he was pretty sure GES was spreading rumors that he had done a poor job for them.

Devon arrived at the newspaper office just before the scheduled Skype interview, drawing a totally unintentional wolf-whistle from Eli when she walked through the door.

He started apologizing halfway through the whistle.

Devon was wearing a stylish red dress, a pearl necklace, with matching earrings. She was considerably more formally dressed than Eli had ever seen her.

But it was her makeup and hairdo that had drawn his whistle. Eli had always thought she was attractive. But with the makeup and styled hair framing her face, she looked ten years younger, and even more gorgeous.

"We're set up in the conference room with the big monitor," Jack said. "You look great."

Devon blushed, noticing that the handful of other people had quickly dropped their gazes back to their computers.

"Well thank you, Publisher Stafford. I thought it might help loosen the tongue of Mr. Ahlbright today."

Jack made a face before he spoke.

"Um, you do know he's gay, right?" Jack said.

Then he laughed.

"Just kidding! Do you think Eli and I should sit in on this or not?"

Devon and Jack rolled the interview strategy around several times. Not knowing Ahlbright was a disadvantage. But it was clear from brief email dialogues that he was unhappy with what was being published on the *EFA* site. Jack and Devon were sure he had signed a non-disclosure form, but his willingness to even have this conversation said something was really amiss for him to risk the legal exposure.

Most likely his non-disclosure said he was not to have any contact with the press about anything related to GES or its subsidiaries.

The Skype connection came through cleanly and crisply, with Devon sitting in a chair in the conference room while Jack and Eli sat off-camera.

On the screen in front of Devon, Michael Ahlbright appeared, dressed casually in khakis and a golf shirt, as if he might be sitting in his home. Jack thought he could see a bookcase in the background.

Ahlbright looked about 35, but could be older. Jack always thought Californians who lived a healthy lifestyle often looked ten years younger than they really were. When Jack first moved back to New York, people guessed he was younger than his 55 years. He wasn't sure that would still be the case.

"Good morning, Miss Walsh. I wanted to tell you right away that my attorney is listening in and I want to record this whole conversation. Is that a problem?" Ahlbright asked.

Devon gave Ahlbright her best smile and tried to look completely cooperative. "Not at all. I would like to record this too, if that's all right. And please, call me Devon."

She fingered the pearls at her neck, waiting for him to offer to let her call him Michael.

"Um, sure Devon. I want to read a statement and then I will answer questions, but I am under some legal restrictions, as you know.

"Okay, here it is. 'I left the employ of Grand Energy Services voluntarily and after doing a variety of analyses for the company. I have a professional reputation for thoroughness and excellence as demonstrated by my work here in California. I have been distressed by the lies and innuendo published by the *Energy First America* website. The people at *EFA* have damaged my reputation and I am considering legal action against them. Not against GES.'"

Devon glanced briefly over at Jack, regretting it immediately. She had forgotten to tell Ahlbright that there were other people in the room with her.

"Devon? Can I assume there are other journalists listening in on this?" Ahlbright asked.

"Yes, Mr. Ahlbright, I am sorry. I meant to say so at the beginning. We have our editor and publisher Jack Stafford and IT consultant and reporter Eli Gupta here. Mr. Stafford was interested in listening and Mr. Gupta keeps the lights on around here."

For the first time, Ahlbright seemed to relax and even gave a small chuckle at her description of Eli.

"Those 'keep the lights on' people are critical," he said. "And please, call me Michael. I'm sorry, this whole thing has me worried."

At the word "worried" Jack's interest started to ramp up. Was Ahlbright worried about his own reputation or something else?

Jack almost got up to go sit by Devon, then decided that she would be offended. Plus, it might break the flow of the just-started conversation.

It proved to be a good decision.

Devon simply waited for Ahlbright to speak again, offering an encouraging smile. She had used the tactic of silence many times in interviews as an environmental activist. Most people can't stand what radio and TV people call "dead air."

"What I am going to tell you is not anything about GES, just some speculation on my part. And I do not want to be quoted on this. And I want you to agree to keep me and what I am going to tell you separate from any reference to me. I need your word on that. All of you listening in, too. Your word."

Devon shot a glance over to Jack who gave her a thumbs up, then motioned to ask if she wanted him to speak.

She did.

"Mr. Ahlbright, this is Jack Stafford speaking. What you are asking is quite reasonable. We just need to know what you are worried about and anything you are willing to tell us. We have some good researchers here. And if you can pardon the expression, if you tell us where the bodies are buried, we can dig them up."

Ahlbright looked away from the camera for a moment then back.

"I'm taking that as your word about anonymity. So, okay. Here's what I'll say. I think the Hydro-Green System has some serious problems. The problems are not coming from GES. I think you need to look into the work done at the labs and companies that did the original genetic modifications," Ahlbright said.

"I really don't want to say much more than that."

Eli wiggled in his chair, frantic to get Devon's attention. Then he scribbled a word on a notepad for Jack to read: "Modifications to what?"

Devon saw the exchange out of the corner of her eye. "Um, Mr. Stafford, did you want to ask Michael a question?"

Ahlbright shifted his eyes away from Devon, almost as if he could see Jack and Eli sitting off-camera.

"Well, thanks Devon," Jack said. "Um, Michael. Without stepping outside of what you are willing to talk about, I'm assuming you are talking about the changes to that *Archaea* life form so it will eat toxic chemicals. We think there may be some link with the well-casing failures. Can you confirm that? Even with a nod of your head?"

Ahlbright ran his hands through his hair, the first time he had broken from his pose on screen. He did it again.

"That sounds like proprietary information," Ahlbright said. "What *Archaea* does or doesn't do. But as I said, I think you need to look at the labs and the original genetic modifications."

Devon leaned forward before she spoke, trying to tease out what Ahlbright was really trying to say without saying it.

"Because we would be interested in what *Archaea* might do in the future, right?"

Ahlbright closed his eyes before he spoke.

"Yes. The future," he said. "What it might do in the future."

From the *Horseheads Clarion*

Column One
The Horseheads Clarion

Don't tinker with Mother Nature

By Jack Stafford

ROCKWELL VALLEY, Pennsylvania — When Grand Energy Services announced that was going to use its newly developed Hydro-Green System in the hydrofracking process, it seemed like a good idea.

It was going to use the same toxic fracking fluids—the names of which we still don't know, thanks to various gas company exemptions to nearly all clean water and air laws. But thanks to a miracle of modern science—genetic engineering—a life form called Archaea was "slightly modified" (those are GES's words, not mine) so that it would quite literally "absorb or eat" (GES's words again) most, if not all, of the toxic chemicals, breaking them down into simpler, non-toxic substances.

And best of all, the Archaea would itself simply die after doing its dirty work.

It's not working out that way, of course.

While GES refuses to confirm or deny reports that Archaea organisms are affecting the stability of concrete well casings, there has been a quadrupling in the number of well-casing failures in the last month. An analysis of those by the *Horseheads Clarion* shows that in each case, GES most likely used its Hydro-Green System additives to its fracking fluid. I say most likely, because GES refuses to confirm or deny which wells are using or have used Hydro-Green.

If the system is a serious problem, I suppose I would not want to broadcast it either.

Those well-casing failures have resulted in large volumes of natural gas venting into the air, numerous explosions, complaints by neighbors of overpowering chemical/gas smells, and more than a few hospital visits by persons who have been overcome by the sudden rush of methane and airborne toxic chemicals.

And many scientists now say that vented methane—the gas that isn't captured and leaks out—might provide the tipping point in accelerating global warming even faster that it currently is progressing.

Just this week, one of the first wells in Rockwell Valley to use the highly touted Hydro-Green System suddenly started venting natural gas so fast that emergency crews from three counties were brought in. Hundreds of people were evacuated in a 10-mile radius.

GES said it was just a broken pipeline. But emergency services officials who responded to the call said the gas was escaping from cracks crisscrossing the entire concrete well pad at a rate so fast they feared it would ignite.

A science-fiction writer could have a field day with this real-life scenario.

But it isn't science-fiction.

GES genetically modified a life form that is not all that well understood by the experts. The company had to know that when it started this project. If it didn't, it's just that much worse. Prior to Hydro-Green, GES and other gas companies were adding many gallons of toxic biocides to kill the Archaea in their gas pipes and wells because the Archaea would slow the flow of gas.

The laboratories that did the original work on Archaea to turn it into a toxic-waste antidote are not saying anything about their work. Admittedly, it's complicated, this gene-splicing business.

And almost always a mess.

On a number of occasions I have written about how genetically modified foods are not the panacea food companies would like us to believe. Good for profits? Yes. Good for people? No.

And now we have a GMO that has turned out to not behave the way its human creators expected.

Will we ever learn?

Most frightening is those human creators won't comment about the modified Archaea. They should. Environmental regulators should stiffen their spines to require these scientists to reveal exactly how Archaea was modified and why the life form keeps living way beyond its modified life expectancy.

Suppose, for example, if gene splicers borrowed some genetic material from an un-friendly bacteria or virus to make this toxic-waster gobbling Archaea? Imagine an Archeae-E. coli-Ebola blend. Crazy, you say?

Maybe.

But maybe not. How would we know?

Jack Stafford is an investi-gative columnist and reporter for The Horseheads Clarion *and has worked as an investiga-tive reporter for metropolitan newspapers in California and Colorado.*

Jack's column was reprinted in its entirety in nearly three hundred daily newspapers and even more weekly news-papers across the country.

The *Horseheads Clarion* website had a record number of hits over the weekend, too.

Many of the comments posted on Jack's column—and many commentators—blasted him for his speculation that the Hydro-Green System was creating a micro-monster that could be harmful to people.

The *Energy First America* website was particularly shrill, calling Jack a "leftist lunatic" and said that he was a "scientific ignoramus."

"If he knew anything about genetic engineering, he would not have made such incendiary, inflammatory statements," *EFA* sniffed.

GES itself declined to comment, of course.

But Monday morning Jack opened his email to find a note from the author Kenneth MacInerery, congratulating him for his column and suggesting they talk that morning.

MacInerery was staying in Denver but suggested they finally have their first Skype conversation.

Jack had come in before the paper was officially open for business and left the "closed" sign up so he could do some writing. He called Devon at home and asked her to bring in their copy of MacInerery's book so he could take a peek at it again before they talked.

The book had profoundly affected both of them. Devon said it was probably the most depressing book of its kind she had ever read.

Still, MacInerery optimistically predicted that despite the incredible environmental and cultural disasters looming, he was confident that civilization—a chunk of it anyway—would survive.

"Civilization is carried on from generation to generation by only a tiny percentage of any population," he wrote. "I would like to take credit for that statement, but someone told me the late Gore Vidal said it first. I think he had a point."

When Eli came through the front door a half-hour later, Jack told him about the Skype call and asked Eli to set things up in the conference room as they had with Michael Ahlbright. Eli was as enthusiastic as if it had been Christmas. He had just finished reading MacInerery's book too and said he had lots of questions.

"We'll see how long we can keep him on the line," Jack said. "He said he wants to talk about the modified *Archaea*."

Devon came in through the front door, flipping around the sign from "closed" to "open" and was followed by the balance of the writers, ad staff, and receptionist.

The receptionist told Jack that there were more than 400 phone messages to be picked up and transcribed.

"Well, I think we will say we had a phone malfunction," Jack said. "Erase them all. I don't want you to spend all morning listening to people crank about my column. Or congratulate. If it was important, they'll call back."

Jack knew that if Walter were still alive, he would normally have had every single call transcribed and responded to. But Jack had learned that a tactic of the gas companies was to have stooges call in in big numbers to keep the media busy anytime something critical was published.

When the receptionist hesitated to delete the messages, Jack told her that if they were busy chasing those phone calls, they wouldn't have time to get on to the stories they knew they needed to cover.

MacInerery's Skype call came in just before noon. The morning had flown by getting Tuesday's newspaper ready for the printer, but Jack, Devon, and Eli had by then caucused about a few areas they wanted to ask Devonshire about, particularly the *Archaea*.

The connection was poor at first, with MacInerery

freezing on the screen during the first few minutes as they were going through introductions.

But when the connection became solid, MacInerery congratulated Jack again for his column.

"I'm not a journalist, though I certainly read what enough journalists have to say," MacInerery said. "And there are times I absolutely abhor the little trick you used—that sort of tongue-in-cheek speculation about *E. coli* and *Ebola*. But this time, my hat is off to you. Nicely played. Very nicely played."

Devon started to scrawl a note to Jack, then decided to simply ask MacInerery herself. This Skype dialogue was such a sharp contrast to the tight-lipped Michael Ahlbright's. MacInerery seemed happy to chat.

"Mr. MacInerery. I thought it was a nice touch too, maybe to flush the gas companies out about Hydro-Green," Devon said. "But we had a debate before that column was published last Friday. I was one of the people who wondered if Jack was making too strong a point by using the *E. coli* and *Ebola* references, even if just to be provocative. There's been a lot of blowback that he was trying to create panic. Do you think it will help force GES to say what's really in there?"

MacInerery looked puzzled at the question.

"No, no, no...I'm afraid you misunderstood, Miss Walsh. "I think the GES lab may have used some *E. coli* genetic material as part of its beefed-up *Archaea*.

"I would bet the royalties from my book on it," he said. "I would bet them indeed."

Grayson Oliver Delacroix wasn't sure he dared fire Rod Mayenlyn for the screw-ups regarding criticism of Michael Ahlbright and the hacking of the *Energy First America* website.

Mayenlyn had been in on too many confidential conversations, and besides, now that they had installed additional security on the firewall protecting the website, it was unlikely they would have trouble again with non-*EFA* people being able to post.

When Mayenlyn told him that the site had been hacked again, this time to use the website to make it look like GES was attacking Ahlbright, he wanted Mayenlyn's head on a pike.

Probably by those damned troublemaking Wolverines, Delacroix thought. *Smart bastards.*

And no matter how much money Delacroix waved at Ahlbright to try to rehire him, Alhbright refused.

"We need to move on, gentlemen, to the report on these leaking wells," Delacroix said.

He had filled the conference room with his executive staff, including Mayenlyn and Luther Burnside. In addition, he had set up a teleconference with four other regional GES sites around the country to coordinate dealing with the concrete-eating *Archaea* and sealing the natural gas wells that were collapsing at a rate of one or two a day.

"Let's hear from the California and the West first," Delacroix said. "I counted eleven wells down and needing major work to seal them. Is that right?"

Each of the four other GES sites were shown on separate television screens placed at the end of the room, with California and the western states at the far left, the other regions moving to the right, just as their geography dictated.

"With the eleven and the four that crashed before it, I think we are done with all the wells we used Hydro-Green in, boss," Melvin "Mac" Norhouse said. "That's the good news."

"And the bad?" Delacroix asked.

"Well, we think we have another well, about a quarter-mile from the one we just sealed, showing signs of concrete degradation," Norhouse said. "But it's a full quarter-mile away. I don't see how it could have been contaminated. I don't see how the *Archaea* could have migrated that far."

Delacroix cut off Norhouse's feed and asked the other regions about whether things were under control and if they had experienced any similar incidents.

He felt a headache creeping up the back of his neck as the other regions reported similar experiences. The coordinator for the Rockwell Valley area of Pennsylvania, which had nearly 1,000 wells, a third of which had used Hydro-Green, said production was dropping rapidly and that they were having difficulty containing leaks. Flare stacks were burning methane day and night to lower the pressure so they could attempt to fix cracks in the concrete. Sometimes they were simply venting methane, if the wind was right.

And some workers were getting ill from breathing too much gas.

Delacroix had visions of *Archaea* somehow migrating to the concrete foundations of people's homes. He made a note to call the GES labs again. They seemed puzzled by what the *Archaea* was doing, which had Delacroix moving from concern to near-panic.

When Norhouse got the floor again, he told Delacroix and the conference that they were starting to use biocides that weren't legal in the United States to try to kill the *Archaea*.

"If we don't kill it —and it seems to thrive on the concrete—it doesn't matter how much we cap these wells," he said. "Whatever genius said it had a suicide gene in it should consider offing himself."

His remark drew the only laugh during the whole meeting and conference.

After another half-hour, Delacroix called an end to the discussion with the simple caveat that all current supplies of Hydro-Green were to be quietly disposed of. Efforts to get new wells drilled and producing was top priority.

"We're getting pressure from China and India to be able to ship gas as soon as the new coastal ports are approved. We have a golden market there but we need the gas to sell them, gentlemen. If not, I don't need to tell you what our investors are going to think—and do," Delacroix said.

"The Saudis just found some accessible natural gas offshore in the Red Sea," he said. "But it's going to take time to build rigs and get to it. If we don't have gas to ship before they do, the Saudis will eat our lunch. Those bastards will be able to send it by pipeline. The good thing is our ships should be arriving in Asia long before they can get a pipeline in place."

Delacroix adjourned the meeting but asked Mayenlyn and Burnside to stay behind.

He fussed with the papers on his desk, until he found the note from his secretary about Michael Ahlbright's getting his old job back with a new title: director of Natural Gas and Environment.

"Rod, I want you to write a story about Ahlbright being back on the job in California and what a fine job he did for us. I don't give a shit if it means the website has to eat it. We can't have a libel lawsuit along with everything else. Plus, maybe he'll stop talking to people.

"And Rod, make it good. Really good."

O scar popped the cork on the second bottle of his signature Riesling.

An impromptu Saturday night party was underway at Jack and Devon's house after Oscar and his niece Lindy spontaneously showed up that afternoon.

The mid-March weather had turned from gorgeous spring-like weather back to sleeting rain, dropping business at the winery to the occasional drive-by customer. Oscar knew the few tourists willing to brave icy roads could be easily handled by the two college girls from Ithaca he had hired as extra weekend help.

And right after Oscar and Lindy arrived, Eli and Shania from Millie's Diner had shown up.

Devon declared they would have a dinner party.

"Do you carry around cases of that wine in your trunk, Oscar?" Jack said. "Jaysus, it's like when we were kids and always had beer in a cooler."

Oscar poured wine all around, topping off glasses.

"I am a much higher-class drinker now, thank you very much. And by the way Devon, whatever you and Shania have cooking out there, I want it. It smells great."

Shania and Devon had gotten to be good friends when Devon first moved to Horseheads and lived with Shania and her mother. It was there Devon realized that Shania was a marvelous cook. Her waitressing at Millie's Diner was a waste of talent, Devon thought. But tonight she was using some vegetables, pasta, and a bottle of off-the-shelf tomato sauce to make a fabulous pasta casserole. She dispatched Eli to run across town to a bakery. He had come back with three loaves of still-warm French bread.

"Tonight we feast and celebrate," Jack said.

Since announcing their engagement, Jack and Devon had started laying plans whenever they could, often getting excited, then sliding back down into depression because of the increasingly bad news about hydrofracking they reported on day after day.

But late Friday afternoon Eli learned that police had found a rifle at the home of Tom Fletcher that they believed was used in the murder of GES employee Delbert Dogg.

"I'm not sure why I feel good about that," Jack said. "That guy is such a turd. But it's a helluva turn of events," Jack said. "Who would have thought that he would be killed by one of his co-workers?

"Police think that Fletcher murdered Dogg because of something to do with GES," Jack said. "I think it might have been over the documents his wife gave us. Dogg might have stolen them from the GES office."

Devon came out of the kitchen with Shania to get their glasses refilled while the dinner cooked. She slipped her arm through Jack's while they sat on the couch, Belle slumbering at their feet.

"I knew that guy Tom was a total creep," Lindy said. "Always harassing most of us at the wineries. Maybe he'll have to be somebody's girlfriend in prison. Now that would be justice."

They all swirled their wine, lost in thought for few minutes, until Eli raised his glass in a toast.

"Hey, I want to toast next week's interview," he said, drawing cries of 'boooooo' from Jack and Devon.

"Eli, we said no talk about the newspaper. Remember? It's Saturday. Come on," Jack said.

Eli look chastised, but had had just enough wine that he was not going to give it up.

"Ok, not a toast. But it's big deal. Right? We are going to do a three-way conference with the guy who wrote that end of the world book, MacInerery. You know, *Intelligent Design*? And Michael Ahlbright will be on at the same time. Ahlbright might talk about the labs that did the genetic engineering for those *Archie* things that are causing so much trouble. I feel like something big is waiting around the corner," Eli said.

They all laughed at the "waiting around the corner" phrase. Walter had used that expression all the time when he thought they would be making a breakthrough in a story. And his sense of news was good. They almost always did find something significant when he felt it coming.

"I hope you're right, Eli. It's tough to get the whole story. But the little pieces we make into something bigger," Jack said. "You might be right. These guys are smarter than anyone in the gas industry. We will try to get the big picture. Walter used to say that a lot, too."

Devon and Shania disappeared into the kitchen then came out with two steaming pans and a basket filled with French bread, which from the smell of it had butter and garlic on it.

As they sat down to eat, Devon turned a little green and held her stomach for a second as she sat, hoping no one noticed.

"To a future free of fracking and fracking problems," Oscar said, raising his glass.

"To the future anyway," Jack said. "To the future."

From the *Horseheads Clarion*

Column One
The Horseheads Clarion

The time for fracking secrets is over

By Jack Stafford

Since I speculated in this column that Grand Energy Systems might be using some harmful bacteria as part of its much-touted Hydro-Green System for hydrofracking, the Horseheads Clarion has received more than 5,000 emails, mostly protesting what was published.

The newspaper is causing unnecessary panic, the emails say.

I am not encouraging panic—necessary or unnecessary. I am encouraging GES to do the right thing and let the public know what is going on, in what may be an incredible threat to our health and wellbeing.

In case you tuned in late

to this latest hydrofracking nightmare, Grand Energy Systems teamed up with a laboratory involved in genetic modifications, primarily with foods such as corn. GMOs have found their way into nearly every food on the shelves of our grocery stores.

GES wanted to find something that would rid it of a pesky ancient life form called Archaea that clogs gas pipes and slows production. But the company also thought it would be swell to use this Archaea, genetically modified, to break down the toxic chemicals that are pumped into the ground in the hydrofracking process. Toxic wastewater is a major issue.

It has, pardon the expression, all gone to hell.

Virtually every well that used the Hydro-Green System has been shut down—and even at that, the concrete caps placed on top of the wells are cracking, leaking gas and making anyone in the vicinity sick.

GES says this isn't true, but anyone driving by GES well sites can see concrete trucks working 24-7 to cap wells. And the smell of methane is over-powering.

From California, we have received reports that other already-operating natural gas wells are showing more-than-normal leaks in concrete casings, leading California environmental regulators to be alarmed that the Archaea used in hydrofracking might, so to speak, be on the march.

Rockwell Valley, Pennsylvania is experiencing problems, too. The hospital there reports seeing a dozen patients in the last few weeks, all complaining of headaches and dizziness from natural gas in the air, all coming from leaking well pads.

So why is disclosure of what is in the Hydro-Green System so important?

Hydrofracking wastewater.

The water that came back up from those hydrofracking wells using the Archaea-fracking fluid cocktail contains this new Archaea that was supposed to break down the toxic chemicals. Then the Archaea was supposed to die off, the result of a suicide gene spliced in.

Apparently the Archaea organisms (genetically modified with, well, something) didn't get the memo and now—with an apparent appetite for normal concrete—have been trucked to various water treatment plants all over the United States.

You don't need to be a geneticist, engineer, or structural specialist to see that there may be a problem.

Grand Energy Services and many other gas companies who started using the patented Hydro-Green System might be responsible for unleashing something that is going cost billions of dollars to repair.

Billions.

No doubt this column is going to draw more thousands of comments and criticism that I am trying to causing panic.

Nonsense.

I am trying to get GES to publicly state everything it knows about the biological composition of Hydro-Green Systems and tell a worried public what it plans to do to clean up its mess and make sure it doesn't continue.

Who would have ever thought that an effort to clean up the toxic waste problem of hydro-

fracking would end up causing an arguably even greater
threat to the environment and
our health?

Not this writer.

Grand Energy Services,
please, do the right thing.
Stop hiding behind your claims
of trade secrets.

Please do so before your
genetically modified Archaea
starts cracking the concrete
bases of buildings. Maybe even
those at your headquarters in
Flathead, Missouri.

*Jack Stafford is an investi-
gative columnist and reporter
for* The Horseheads Clarion *and
has worked as an investigative reporter for metropolitan
newspapers in California and
Colorado.*

Jack was grumpy.

It was a Monday morning and his column from the
week previous had, predictably, drawn the wrath of Grand
Energy Services and a lot of other people.

Their main complaint was that he had no evidence to
prove that it was the genetically modified *Archaea* that was
causing the problems. GES said it was mostly a problem
caused by the manufacturers of the concrete. And that they
were reformulating.

"Hydro-Green Systems is undergoing some modifications to make it more efficient," CEO Grayson Oliver Delacroix said at a well-attended press conference.

But Jack's particularly dour mood was because GES had done half of what he wanted. The company claimed that the labs that had genetically modified *Archaea* were not using either the *E. coli* bacteria or the *Ebola* virus as he had speculated in an earlier column.

"The *Horseheads Clarion* has a long history of antipathy towards the natural gas industry, even as its boom has help fuel more money for the newspaper and its readers," Delacroix had said. "But to say that Grand Energy Services would even consider using something as dangerous as anything genetically connected to either *E. coli* or *Ebola* is unconscionable. Writer Jack Stafford needs to apologize to all the hardworking people at GES who are working to keep the environment clean as we produce clean natural gas and set this nation on a course towards energy independence. *E. coli? Ebola?* Where do these crazy ideas come from?"

Jack had timed his column, thinking that the same day it was published he would be having a conversation with both Michael Ahlbright and Kenneth MacInerery. Both men were working on figuring out what GES's labs might have done in the genetic modifications. And both had given him the idea to pressure GES with his column.

Jack expected the blowback, gambling that Ahlbright and MacInerery would be able to back up his call for complete disclosure.

But at the last minute, first Ahlbright, then MacInerery, had canceled their Skype interviews.

Both pleaded they had scheduling conflicts but Jack

found it too convenient that both men had pulled out. He was beginning to wonder if Ahlbright's earlier conversation was a setup to get the newspaper to stick its neck out.

And the *Energy First America* website had suddenly started singing Ahlbright's praises. *Damned odd*, Jack thought.

Devon went into Jack's office and closed the door.

"Still no word from either Ahlbright or MacInerery? Well, Eli is working on getting a source at the lab, but he said security there is very, very tight. Plus, the people at the lab are not real happy that we are saying they may have created a monster," Devon said.

Jack ran his hand through his hair, a new mannerism he had developed since jumping into Walter's chair.

"The problem is I know that Hydro-Green System is at fault and I can't let these people get away with this. I can't. I just can't," Jack said. "They say that they have reformulated but no one is watching them. There's no oversight."

Devon stood up slowly from her chair, and started to walk back out into the newsroom.

"We'll catch a break soon enough, Jack. We have an opinion piece coming in from a Cornell economist about what the new Saudi gas fields in the Red Sea might mean for us here. It could mean that big overseas market will disappear, at least for American natural gas. That would take the pressure off GES to produce more gas for export."

Jack smiled for the first time that day. "Or maybe it will put more pressure on them to compete. I never thought shipping our natural gas overseas was a good idea, so I guess that's sort of a win. But I am not going to say so in a column for a while. I think I'll write about baseball this week. Spring is upon us."

Jack turned to his computer, noting another batch of hate mail had come in since he had last looked at his screen a half-hour before.

Then he got an instant message from Eli, who was in Rockwell Valley taking photos at a well site where GES was pouring concrete on top of a huge steel slab it had put down to cap a well.

```
    Ahlbright emailed me. Says
  he's ready to talk — Wolver-
  ines, Archaea, too.
```

Jack smiled for the second time and waved to Devon, pointing at Millie's diner.

It was time for tea and to get out of the office for a few minutes.

Plus, he wanted to ask Devon why it seemed like her stomach was upset again today.

The Rockwell Valley Hospital was uncooperative when Devon first called about a report of a Grand Energy Services employee being admitted for what was reported as chemical burns. She had gotten an email telling her about the worker being taken in for treatment.

"You need to check this out," the email said.

And so it was that Devon and Eli were sitting in the parking lot of the Rockwell Valley Hospital, pumping themselves up for going into the hospital to get answers and to try to get to see the man, now identified as Alberto Defines, one of a handful of Mexicans working for GES in the area.

Defines had been brought in two days before, a few hours after a valve popped loose on a fracking wastewater truck that had just loaded water from a holding pond.

Eli had checked his list of natural gas wells and he was 95 percent sure this one had used the Hydro-Green System. He shouted "Bingo!" in the office when the area where Defines was working showed several Hydro-Green System wells and only a single large holding pond for wastewater.

A battered pickup truck came into the hospital parking lot, a woman driving and two elementary-school age boys in the front seat. Mexican banda music blared out the open car windows until the woman turned the truck off.

Eli and Devon both jumped out of Devon's car.

"Disculpeme, Señora Defines. Soy Eli Gupta, del periodico de Horseheads¿" Devon looked at Eli and wondered where this upstate New York, New Delhi, India-born boy had ever learned Spanish.

Mrs. Defines quickly offered that her name was Lourdes. She told her two boys to wait inside the hospital front door.

"I speak English. My husband is very hurts. Hurt. I need go in. Thank you."

Devon scurried to her side while Eli trailed them, his camera held loosely down low and out of sight.

"Mrs. Defines, we would like to talk with your husband, just for a few moments? Do you think we could do that? It's important. I know this is a bad time," Devon said.

Mrs. Defines slowed her walk slightly, glancing to her right and left. Growing up in Mexico had made her extremely suspicious of authority and the press. But she was angry that no one from GES had even bothered to come by the hospital or call her since Alberto had been brought in from the worksite.

Another GES employee had walked Alberto into the hospital, and then left right away, even before the emergency room doctor took a look at Alberto. Alberto was treated in the ER, then moved to a burn-unit isolation room.

"I think is okay. You come. Not him," she said, motioning to Eli. "You come to the room with me and talk with Alberto."

Eli hung back, waiting to get a good shot of Mrs. Defines walking into the hospital. He hoped Devon still had the small point-and-shoot camera he had given her when she first came to New York. It was half the size of a smart phone but took excellent photos. Eli had set it up so it was silent, too. No shutter sound at all.

He got off a great shot of Mrs. Defines opening the door to the hospital.

Devon and Mrs. Defines walked through the lobby chatting about the accident and family. The two Defines boys trailed a handful of steps behind. They were ecstatic about being out of school, even if their papa had been hurt. There were few Latinos in Rockwell Valley schools and they had already had a number of playground scuffles.

At the nurses' station, the head nurse took one look at Devon and stood up. "Excuse me. Family only can see Mr. Defines," she said. "No media." She glowered at Mrs. Defines too, as she sat back down.

"Excuse me," Devon said. "But I am here as a friend of Mrs. Defines to check on how her husband is being treated at your fine facility here. I don't want any trouble. I will be in and out."

The nurse's jaw dropped. She reached for the telephone.

"If you call anyone, call the hospital administrator," Devon said. "My photographer is waiting outside and it would make a such a great photo if you had some security officer escorting me out when all I wanted to do was visit a patient," Devon said.

The nurse put the phone down, her face red. She went back to shuffling papers on her desk while Devon, Mrs. Defines and her two boys walked into Alberto Defines' room just a few doors down from the nurses' station.

The shriek from Mrs. Defines startled the head nurse, who stood up quickly and headed for the room at a faster clip than any of the nursing staff had ever seen her move.

Alberto Defines was trying to smile, but the left side of his face was red and raw and looked like it had been hit with sulfuric acid.

"Dios mio, Dios mio," Lourdes Defines said, her hands held against the sides of her face. "Yesterday morning his face no look like that. Alberto, Alberto!"

The head nurse ran back to the station to pick up her desk phone to get the on-call doctor up right away.

Although she hated to do it, Devon pulled out her camera and took three quick photos, then excused herself.

She needed to find a bathroom right away where she could throw up in private.

Jack decided that the photos of Alberto Defines' face were too gruesome to publish, particularly as the *Horseheads Clarion* had no official information from the hospital about his injuries.

Grand Energy Services claimed that Defines' injury came

from getting sprayed with some caustic cleaning chemical, even though the GES worker who dropped Defines off at the hospital told the emergency room doctors that Defines had been knocked flat by the force of the water pouring out the back of a hydrofracking wastewater truck.

The force of the flow had pushed him back into a shallow depression in the ground where he lay stunned for a few moments, bathed in the pouring water until other workers saw what was happening.

Unofficially, the hospital had told Eli that doctors were treating Defines for burns over most of his body. Mrs. Defines said whatever they were doing wasn't helping and his burns were getting redder and uglier every day.

"The hospital is still just saying his condition is guarded," Eli told Jack and Devon. "They are still pretty tweaked that Devon got in and saw Mr. D."

The three of them were sitting in the conference room, waiting for Michael Ahlbright to come online for a Skype chat. Kenneth MacInerery was supposed to join them, but because he was in Australia, Jack had doubts the increasingly famous author would actually be awake.

"Whatever is going on, it seems proof that the wastewater is more toxic than ever," Jack said. "Christ, they used to spray the stuff to salt the roads before they used Hydro-Green."

Eli fiddled with his computer keyboard, checking for MacInerery and Ahlbright's online status.

"I saw a report from Pennsylvania about increased radioactivity in the wastewater they're pulling up. Of course, that could be because they just started looking for it," Eli said. "Until people started squawking about the pollution in wells, I don't think GES or anybody paid much attention."

Eli's computer gave off a loud beeping noise like a telephone and a moment later, the large screen display showed a somewhat rumpled-looking Michael Ahlbright sitting at a desk.

It was 10 a.m. New York time which made it 7 a.m. where Ahlbright was. But he had chosen the time.

"Good morning Michael. I'm here with Devon and Eli. Thanks for taking the time to talk," Jack said.

Unlike their first conversation, this time Ahlbright was chattier.

"Yes, yes. I apologize for not being able to talk with you when we first scheduled. My life has been crazy since getting back to work here. I wanted to double-check a few things. And besides that, someone who claims to be a member of that Wolverine group has contacted me multiple times by email. He—well, I think it's a he—says he has information about the genetic work done on the *Archaea*. I think you will be very interested."

In the last issue of the *Horseheads Clarion*, the newspaper published an eight-page special section about hydrofracking and the growing opposition around the country. The section included a longish story about the Wolverines, their sketchy history, their likely connection to a group calling themselves the Monkey Wrench Gang and the various incidents they claimed to have caused.

Most of the section was taken up with stories and photos of less-shadowy hydrofracking opponents who were protesting daily in thirty states, camping out in state legislature hallways, trailing lawmakers and environmental regulators to their homes. They also were being arrested in record numbers, causing a panic among government officials who wondered how far those people would go, and how determined they were.

The anti-fracking movement had in just a few years gone from a few fringe environmentalists to a populist group that drew membership from all ages and across the political spectrum.

"I just saw on television that a group of nervous National Guardsmen in Colorado accidentally opened fire on a crowd of protesters," Ahlbright said. "Did you hear about it? It looks like four people might dead. One is a 9-year-old child who was there with her mother. I can't believe it."

Jack and Devon had seen the report. Already the networks were comparing it to the fatal shootings at Kent State University in Ohio in 1970. Ahlbright had seen an early report. The death toll was now estimated at seven. About twenty-five people had been hit by either rubber bullets or live rounds.

"I read something about it just before you came on, Michael. You know there is a citizens' militia in Colorado that's been denying gas companies access to some well sites for months," Jack said. "They've been waiting for something like this. Idaho, too. There are a lot of people in harm's way."

"Well, I don't have children," Ahlbright said. "But I can't even begin to imagine what I would do if someone shot my child. I don't know. But I don't want to talk about that.

"I have something I got from the Wolverine contact," Ahlbright said. "I checked with someone I trust at the GES lab, someone who can be discreet. They wouldn't confirm, but they didn't deny this either. Mostly they wanted to know who had told me what they have been doing.

"I am pretty sure they did not use any genetic material from *E. coli*. By the way, this has to be off the record, too. Okay? This can't be connected to me. I have a non-disclosure agreement with GES and I don't want any more legal hassles. Okay?

Jack looked over at Devon and Eli, mostly for show. Jack didn't trust Ahlbright entirely.

"Sure, Michael. We had that agreement before and it still stands. We just need to know what you think you know."

Ahlbright sat back in his chair, then slowly leaned forward into the camera.

"Again, this comes from these Wolverine people. Have you heard of *Aeromones hydrophila*? You might hear a lot more about it soon, if that's what they spliced with *Archaea*. A lot more."

Eli tapped on keys, frowned, then tapped again, this time opening his eyes wide.

"You're kidding?" he blurted out, staring at the screen. "Sorry! Sorry, Jack."

Jack reached over and looked at Eli's computer screen, then up at Ahlbright.

"It's a good question, Michael. Frankly, it's more far-fetched than my *E. coli-Ebola* reference," Jack said.

"I understand. And I can't verify it," Ahlbright said. "But like I said already, when I contacted someone in the lab, someone who has helped me before, they didn't tell me I was wrong. She would have. I trust her. You might think about it and then see if you can get the doctors to look at the guy in the hospital, that fellow who got thoroughly soaked with wastewater? They might be able to offer some evidence based on his injuries. He could be your proof."

Devon got up and stood behind Jack to look at the sentence in a medical listing for *Aeromones hydrophila* that Eli had highlighted. She let out her own "You're kidding?" as she grabbed the top of her head. "You're kidding."

"In very rare cases, *Aeromonas hydrophila* can cause necrotizing fasciitis."

"Flesh-eating disease? They pumped million of gallons of water laced with an *Archaea* hybrid into the ground that has genes from a flesh-eating bacteria?" Devon said. "A flesh-eating bacteria?"

Ahlbright jumped back in, shaking his head.

"I know. I know. But from what I was told about that particular bacteria, if linked properly with the *Archaea,* it could do just what the gas companies want. It could destroy the toxic chemicals. The emphasis is on could," Alhbright said.

Devon went back and sat down, shaking her head, while Jack and Eli chatted for a moment longer with Ahlbright about how *Energy First America* had suddenly started running very positive stories about him. Ahlbright reminded them that his comments were off the record.

Then they thanked Ahlbright for the conversation and logged off.

For a few moments, all three of them sat quietly, not saying anything. Then Jack spoke.

"You know, it might not be true at all. We've chased our tails before. We've gotten good feedback from our special section, and I don't want to join in the crazy club on this," he said.

Devon closed her eyes as she spoke.

"But suppose it is true, Jack? Just suppose it is. We have to chase this. You know we do. We have to. Just suppose they did this and created some nasty God-awful thing.

"Then what, Jack? Then what?"

She held her stomach as she sat down, while Jack stared out the window.

THE WHEELS ON THE BUS

Devon had gotten nowhere for three weeks with the genetic labs about how the *Archaea* had been genetically modified to supposedly break down the toxic wastes in the fracking fluid pumped into the gas wells.

But at Rockwell Valley Hospital she had made friends with the wife of Alberto Defines, the GES worker whose fracking wastewater bath had caused so much damage to his face and body that doctors were sending him to a hospital in New York City, where they hoped specialists could do more.

Antibiotics had slowed the deterioration of what doctors had first thought were chemical burns.

Now, because of the response to the massive doses of the medicine, they knew there was a biological agent at work.

But the doctors weren't talking either. The Pennsylvania gag law on doctors kept them from disclosing what they did know about Defines' case. All they would say was that he was responding well to the antibiotics, a statement that blew a hole in claims by GES that he had been burned by caustic cleaning chemicals.

"I have some more bad news," Eli said, walking into the conference room where Jack, Devon, and reporters Stanley and Jill were having a summit meeting to chart out the next week's issues of the newspaper. "It looks like Colorado isn't going to charge any of the National Guardsmen who fired on that crowd and killed those people. The governor just made a statement that said it was the official investigation finding that the guardsmen felt they were in danger and were protecting themselves."

Jack's exhale was loud enough that everyone turned towards him.

"Kids, they shot children," Jack said. "Justified. My God. How? How?"

In the weeks since the shooting incident, news organizations had published how much money had been given to Colorado politicians by the natural gas industry in campaign contributions.

It was a massive amount, with the governor getting the biggest chunk.

"This is going to cause riots," Devon said. "Riots. People are going to go totally nuts over this. I feel like going crazy myself."

Jack stood up and walked over to the white board where they had sketched out the stories for the next week, with a mix of fracking news and other local happenings.

He wrote "reaction to Colorado shootings" and then put his own name next to it.

"I don't think we need anything but a short wire service piece in the news section. We'll get it up on the web right away. Right, Eli?"

Eli nodded and then shrugged, indicating that he had already posted something.

"Good," Jack said. "Why am I not surprised you already did it? This week I'll do my column on the shootings. I still can't believe it. Kids. Okay. We're done here…"

As the others filed out, Devon stood up and walked over to Jack, putting her arm on his.

He was still facing the white board as if he was studying it.

She knew he was close to crying. Anything to do with children had him on the edge these days since she had admitted that she thought she was pregnant.

Thaddeus Bartholomew Peck popped another Vicodin and took a swig of Mountain Dew to get it down.

It was mid-morning and he was halfway from Rockwell Valley on his way to Long Island with a tanker full of hydrofracking wastewater from one of the wells with concrete failure.

The water had been contained as it came back up the well, mixed with the escaping gas. It had been channeled into a shallow pond where Grand Energy Services trucks had been picking it up for several days, most of it being hauled west to Ohio's deep injection wells. A few trucks were going out to Long Island.

The Long Island water treatment facilities had started taking the hydrofracking water shortly after GES announced that its Hydro-Green System was stripping out 99 percent of the toxic chemicals in the water. Before that, municipal water treatment plants wouldn't take it because they said they couldn't clean the water. Added to that, GES and other gas companies wouldn't say exactly what the toxic chemicals were in the wastewater, making reclamation impossible.

When GES started paying the municipal plants in excess of $2,000 per load, and promised the water was just salty with some bacteria in it, the wastewater plant managers happily took the money and stopped testing. They simply ran it through their filtration systems and then dumped it into either Long Island Sound to the north, or the Atlantic Ocean to the south.

Most of the trucks were carrying more than 5,000 gallons of wastewater.

But after GES worker Alberto Delfines had taken a thorough soaking with the fluid and ended up in the hospital, orders had come down straight from GES corporate headquarters in Flathead, Missouri to get rid of every drop of the hydrofracking wastewater from that site as quickly as possible. The contents of the 55-gallon drums of Hydro-Green on site were also being added to the wastewater destined for disposal.

Peck was doing his third round-trip load in as many days, sleep-deprived and hurting, but needing the overtime.

He slid around in his seat to ease the pain while fumbling in his jacket to see how many Vicodin he had left. His hernia was acting up and his doctor had warned him that continued driving would likely be painful.

Still, he hated the idea of getting an operation, plus, his GES health benefits would cover only half of the cost.

He found his pill bottle and decided one more wouldn't hurt. He had an hour before he would get to New Jersey and then head across New York City to Long Island in what could be really bad traffic.

His other runs had been timed for the middle of the night when there were fewer cars and less chance that some environmentalist was waiting with a video camera, ready to post something on YouTube. But dispatch told him to get this load out right away.

The GES wastewater trucks were painted plainly and carried the legally required minimal markings. Even Peck's truck log simply said 'wastewater for disposal' under the section "Cargo."

He shook his can of Mountain Dew and looked at the pill bottle on the seat.

His groin was killing him and he had hours to go.

But he couldn't remember if he had taken a second pill or not.

Thelma Laverne Washington looked at the maple bar on the dashboard of the school bus, weighing whether to eat it before the school children came out of the museum, when they would head back to school.

More than an hour before, she had brought thirty-three nearly vibrating St. Savior's Elementary third and fourth grade students from West Haven to the Sandia Glass Works for a tour of the shop and demonstration of glass blowing.

Washington hoped the kids came out pretty soon. She had to pee but the school's rules wouldn't allow her to leave the bus unattended.

The teacher and two Spanish-chattering moms had taken the kids in, promising to come back in fifteen or twenty minutes to stand by the bus so Washington could use the bathroom.

She cursed the school for its arcane rules, which included keeping all the windows closed tight, even though the air conditioner on the ten-year-old school bus barely worked. Although it was late April, it was already 80 degrees and not yet noon.

The trip back to the school would be a nightmare without some ventilation, she thought.

She had just taken a bite out of the maple bar when she saw one of the mothers coming to the bus. Washington opened the door for her, feeling a cool breeze come in along with the woman whose English was barely up to the task of asking Washington if she needed a break.

"Yeah. I'm going in to pee. But open some of the windows, okay? It's too hot in here and when the kids get back on they will roast their little butts," she said.

From the look on the mother's face, Washington could tell that most of what she had said wasn't understood.

"Ventanas¿ Abiertos¿ Comprendes¿"

The mother smiled a big grin and started down the rows opening every second or third window.

Washington got out of the bus and headed into the shop. She noticed that traffic was already starting to stack up on the elevated freeway. She thought she'd better call the school to tell them they might be getting back a little later than expected.

Then she remembered she could take a short cut along the beach on a two-lane road paralleling the highway, one used primarily by heavy trucks and construction crews.

She would be breaking another school bus rule to do it, but if she got the kids back past their appointed time to leave school, there would be hell to pay, too.

Washington looked back over her shoulder at the bus and saw the mother finishing the uneaten portion of Washington's maple bar.

She would deal with that after her bladder.

Jack watched as Eli, Devon, Stan, and Jill wrote their stories and assembled photos for Tuesday's issue of the *Horseheads Clarion*.

He was still stunned by the apparent callousness of the state of Colorado in dismissing any further probes into the shootings of the protesters.

Seven people had been killed, three of them children. And most of the twenty-five other protesters who had been hit by either rubber bullets or live rounds were still nursing their injuries.

Jack could see a raft of civil lawsuits headed towards Colorado.

He tried to get his column for Friday started early. He wanted to be sure of all his facts and to be able to scorch state officials and take a solid swing at Grand Energy Services at the same time.

Without proof of what they were using in the company's Hydro-Green System, it was hard to be very specific. Yet after all of his dealings with GES he thought it was almost impossible to underestimate the company's lack of regard for health and safety, and their willingness to outright lie about everything related to their business.

Jack decided he was probably too distracted to write his column and set it aside for the moment. He pulled up the *Clarion* website to reread the wire service reports about the Colorado shooting and about the state's decision not to prosecute.

The news accounts from several different media outlets had only minor differences.

All indicated that about twenty Colorado National Guardsman had been dispatched to a Grand Energy Services hydrofracked gas well where protesters—as many as 300 to 400—had surrounded the well and were denying the gas company employees access to the rig.

Local police had come, talked to the protesters, and then moved to a nearby parking area, saying as long as the protesters remained peaceful, there would be no action taken.

The well was within view of an elementary school. Many of the protesters had children with them who were carrying their own hand-lettered signs with slogans like "Don't Frack our Schools," and "Save our Schools from Gas."

Several National Guard units had been called out weeks before as protesters were systematically closing off access to drilling sites all over the state. Local police were standing back.

The small unit of National Guardsmen arrived as police withdrew. No one seemed to question why the local police left the peacekeeping to the platoon of weekend warriors.

Grayson Oliver Delacroix was quoted in one story as saying the shootings were "tragic and avoidable."

"Our hearts at GES go out to the victims in this incident," he said. "But these people, these people protesting, need to understand that they are trespassing and interfering with legitimate and legal business," he said.

Jack looked up to see Devon sitting in the chair across from his desk. She had slipped in while he was reading.

"You were moving your lips," she said. "And I think you were swearing."

Jack leaned back in his chair. Their marriage plans were on hold for the moment. And because news events were taking up so much of their time, it felt like they ate meals standing up.

The conflict about hydrofracking was turning even uglier on both sides across the country. The anti-hydrofracking protesters were blocking natural gas wells and getting arrested in numbers not seen since the Vietnam War protests of the 1960s. The gas companies were trying to use local police to force access but increasingly were hiring private security companies or getting states to bring in the National Guard.

And the Wolverines—fast becoming a household word—were making statements through friendly journalists about people being ready to launch a real civil war to stop the destruction of the environment and the poisoning of water.

"With the whole world crumbling, we pick this time to fall in love," Devon said.

Jack's jaw dropped slightly.

"You remember that line from *Casablanca*? I'm impressed," he said.

"Actually, I just looked it up before I came in here. I knew you needed some cheering up. I know it feels like we are carrying the whole world. We're doing a great job, Jack. Walter would say that if he were here. You know that," Devon said.

Jack smiled for the first time that day, forgetting for a moment the deaths in Colorado and the other bad news that the *Horseheads Clarion* was packaging at the moment.

He and Devon had just decided that a cup of tea across the street at Millie's might be in order when Eli's eyes opened wide while looking at his computer screen.

Sometimes he lit up that way when Shania sent him an email. But there was no smile on his face now.

He looked up at Jack and Devon and walked over to Jack's door.

"More Colorado news. It's just hitting the wires," he said.

The guy who was the squad leader of that National Guard unit that killed the people? He used to work for Grand Energy Services. It's been confirmed."

Jack's stomach rolled and for just a moment, he thought he was going to be sick.

Thaddeus Bartholomew Peck rolled along slightly over the speed limit on the interstate, the pain from his hernia held at bay by the Vicodin, though every few minutes he would get another twinge.

He kept alert enough to drive by sipping Mountain Dew.

Peck was still in Pennsylvania but hoped to be out on Long Island dumping his load by 2 p.m. at the latest. Traffic was still light and he was pushing the speed limit a little, alert for state police as he got ready to cross from Pennsylvania into New Jersey.

Jersey police worried him more than Pennsylvania troopers.

The Mountain Dew was filling his bladder, the added pressure from having to pee also pushing on his hernia.

He felt a little dizzy from fatigue. And he was hungry, too.

He decided a fifteen-minute pee and snack break at the next rest stop would be okay. He was going to get stuck in traffic crossing New York City anyway. Fifteen minutes, one way or the other, wouldn't make much difference, he thought.

He was wrong about that.

Thelma Laverne Washington stayed inside for a half-hour, enjoying the cool temperature in the Sandia Glass Works factory, enjoying being out of the hot bus, and watching the demonstration on glass blowing.

When she was young, art had been her favorite class and she had flirted with the idea of being an art teacher when she grew up.

The children loved the glass blowing demonstration and several came up and wrapped their arms around Washington while watching.

She had driven some of these children for several years and was as fond of them as they were of her. Her maple bar had been a present from one of the children whose Lebanese father owned a bakery.

Washington watched the glass blower making an ornate animal —she couldn't tell exactly what it was just yet—but the gasps from the children and screams of "giraffe," then "dog," then "bird" made her smile. Her four children, all adults now, would have loved to see this.

She checked her watch. They still had nearly two hours before they had to be back at school, but that included a side trip to a fast-food restaurant for lunch. The restaurant was owned by a parent of one of the children in the class and was on the way back to the school.

To get there, though, Washington knew she would have to maneuver the school bus up onto the elevated freeway and then back down a curvy off-ramp near the beach that had been under construction for months.

The ramp was narrow and banked poorly in its temporary condition. But to avoid it meant a long trip around. And in traffic, it could add maybe an extra forty-five minutes driving.

Neither alternative appealed to her, but she decided to enjoy the show and let the mother who had relieved her sit roasting in the bus.

"Giraffe!" the children started to scream, looking at the almost-finished product. "Giraffe!"

Thelma Washington peered at the colorful, long-necked glass creation but couldn't quite see a giraffe in it. It looked to her more like one of the orange construction cranes she had to pass on that steep ramp on the way to the restaurant.

And thinking about the restaurant made her hungry and just a touch angry at the mother sitting on the school bus who had eaten her maple bar.

Cabrona, she thought.

J ack and Devon got into Millie's diner just ahead of the lunch rush and decided to go ahead and eat instead of just having some tea.

They had been going home for lunch most days, but with the pages being laid out for Tuesday's paper right then, Jack said he needed to stay close by in case he was needed.

Plus he wanted to postpone the inevitable conversation about the baby they had confirmed was growing inside of Devon.

Since Devon had shown positive on a home pregnancy

test, she and Jack had been pushing off the discussion.

In Jack's case, he had serious doubts about his ability to be a good father at his age. Devon was concerned that she was on the edge of being too old to have a child. She had read a dozen articles in the last week about problems older mothers had with births, and sometimes how the children were more likely to be born with problems, too.

Shania dropped their lunches and checked on their tea.

"I know you haven't set a date yet for your wedding, but can you give me any kind of hint?" Shania said. "Eli and I... Well, I shouldn't speak for him. I want to take a vacation trip to Canada this summer and I don't want to miss your wedding. Neither does Eli, but then he has to ask for vacation from you."

Jack shrugged his shoulders and looked at Devon who made the same motion, who without thinking touched her stomach for a moment.

"You okay, Devon?" Shania asked. "Your face is flushed. I'm getting my springtime allergies big-time. Really big-time. Maybe you have some."

Shania stepped back two steps and stared at Jack and Devon for a full thirty seconds. Then she smiled broadly at Devon and walked back over to the window where another lunch order had come up.

Devon reached across the bench seat and took Jack's hand.

"I don't think our secret will be secret for very long, Mr. Publisher. What do you think?"

The snack-and-pee break for Thaddeus Bartholomew Peck took almost exactly fifteen minutes.

As luck would have it, the vending machine at the rest stop had Mountain Dew, so Peck grabbed four cans, downed one inside the building, then grabbed his hastily-assembled meal of potato chips, peanuts, and bag of pretzels to take them to the truck.

The best part was taking a pee before lunch, then a second pee afterwards and a last-minute one before he climbed back into the cab of the tractor-trailer.

He was pretty sure the hernia was somehow pushing on his bladder, making him have to go so often.

As he swung up into the cab of the truck, a stab of pain made his eyes water as he eased himself into his seat. He popped the lid on a Mountain Dew and gulped another Vicodin.

With a stomach full of carbohydrates, another painkiller might sit just fine, he thought.

The sun was getting warm and he switched on the air conditioning, listening to the fan start to rattle loudly. He banged the dash twice, then gave up and cranked up the stereo as he headed towards the George Washington Bridge.

The AM news channel on the radio was reporting explosions at three different GES facilities, one in California, one in Colorado, and a third in Pennsylvania.

The newscaster said a group called the Wolverines was taking credit. Peck remembered hearing something about them from his boss.

He switched on his CB radio, crackling with good traffic reports from truckers who said the GW Bridge was running pretty smoothly, though traffic on the Cross Bronx

Expressway and traffic out onto Long Island was starting to get backed up.

The south shore water treatment plant was on the Atlantic Ocean near Kennedy Airport. He decided to take the same shortcut from his trip a few days ago.

Peck eased the truck into gear and started rolling back out on the highway towards New York City. He punched in a music playlist put together by a fellow GES wastewater trucker called *Driving Like Crazy*, which included "Foggy Mountain Breakdown," "Thunder Road" and a half-dozen rocking songs by Bob Seger and other country favorites that made most truck drivers put the pedal right through the floor.

The pain in his groin gave him another jolt. Peck looked at the Vicodin container on the dashboard and couldn't remember if he had actually taken one or not.

He took a swig of Mountain Dew as he pulled into traffic, then reached for the open container.

The presentation in the glass factory was dragging on. Thelma went out twice to check on the bus, where the Spanish-speaking mother seemed quite happy to listen to the bus radio, tuned to a Spanish music station.

Thelma was heading back in after her second bus check when she heard someone on the radio say something about "una bomba" in Pennsylvania.

She couldn't make out too much more, except that it seemed there had been three explosions, all at natural gas facilities. And although she couldn't be completely sure because of the pronunciations, she thought the announcer said it was "el grupo Wolverine" that was responsible.

She knew if she went back in and switched the radio over to the English news station, she was likely to lose her bus sitter. And it was getting damn hot out there even with the windows open.

When Thelma went back in, the glassblower was taking some questions from the now close-to-bored children. Thelma signaled to the teacher and the other mother that they needed to get going, pronto.

There was still lunch to be eaten, and the traffic looked like it was going to be a bitch for maneuvering the school bus through.

B oth Stanley and Jill looked tired when Jack said they had to rip up the front page layout for Tuesday's paper to put in a story about the bombings at three GES facilities, one of them in Rockwell Valley.

That explosion had been at the same site where Delbert Dogg had been murdered last year.

Jack made a note to have Eli follow up on the status of the case of former GES employee Tom Fletcher, at whose home a rifle had been found that police were using as evidence. They believed it was one of the guns used to kill Dogg.

The almost simultaneous explosions in California, Colorado, and Pennsylvania all targeted gas-drilling rigs owned by GES. There was no information about the bombs themselves from authorities, or the extent of damages. But no one had been hurt at any of the sites in the blasts.

Eli had rocketed out of the office for Rockwell Valley to take some photos the minute he heard. But he had run across the street to Millie's long enough to tell Jack and Devon what had happened.

"The Wolverines are taking credit for all three bombs," he said. "They have some kind of declaration that they sent to GES and a dozen other big gas companies. It pretty much says they are done playing nice."

Jack rushed back to the office and now was digging through the notes from his earlier columns that mentioned the Wolverines. He also put in a call to Oscar at the winery.

"I just heard. Sounds like these people have decided to make this a real fight," Oscar said. "Remember that night when we all watched *Red Dawn* here at winery? Nasty pranks are one thing. High-powered explosives are something else."

Jack asked Oscar to keep his ears open at the winery for any people chattering about the bombings. He had his suspicions about some Seneca Lake folks who had vowed that they would defend the land with their lives and their rifles if any gas company attempted to drill on their property.

Jack couldn't imagine any of them being bomb makers, or bomb throwers. But some of them were Vietnam, Iraq, or Afghanistan veterans. They certainly knew how to make things go *boom*.

Oscar hung up and Jack went back to reading the wire service stories about the bombings. The bombs appeared to have all been detonated within minutes of each other. The declaration from the Wolverines had been sent out moments later and came just short of declaring a guerilla war on all the natural gas producers who were using hydrofracking.

He looked out in the newsroom and realized Devon wasn't sitting there.

He had rushed out of the diner so fast when Eli gave

him the news that he had left Devon sitting there. She wasn't back yet.

And he had forgotten to eat his lunch.

Traffic on the George Washington Bridge had been as light as the other truckers had said, making Peck's drive across easy.

It was so easy he nearly nodded off twice mid-span, prompting him to grab another cold Mountain Dew.

Now in city traffic and working his way towards the south shore of Long Island, he had to keep more alert, challenging given his lack of sleep, long driving hours, and the uncounted number of Vicodin coursing through his system.

The hernia pain was back, a dull throb. Peck decided he could bear it until he delivered his load.

He figured even with traffic he was maybe only about an hour from pulling in. He could take another pill then and a good nap in the truck once the 5,000 gallons of fracking wastewater was out of his hands.

The news channels were buzzing with stories about the explosions at gas facilities—all three owned by his employer. Peck was used to seeing people with picket signs in front of GES sites. Employees had orders to ignore the protesters unless they got violent. If they did, GES employees had been directed to figure out who might have a video camera and deal with them first, as quietly as possible.

Then they had company permission to crack heads.

He was listening to the radio announcer reading something that this group called the Wolverines had handed out about their demands. Most of the talk-radio stations had people calling in saying the Wolverines were terrorists. Occasionally a caller would say the Wolverines were patriots, trying to save the environment.

Peck thought about the load right behind him and shook his head.

Then the pain in his groin stabbed again, this time so violently he nearly threw up.

He slowed the truck and tried to downshift, the motion of his leg making his groin area and hernia hurt even more. He knew he had to make it to the wastewater disposal plant no matter what.

Peck took a deep breath, then a swig of Mountain Dew, scanning the slowing traffic.

It might take one more Vicodin to make it the rest of the way, he thought.

It took nearly twenty minutes to get all the children out of the glass works and back aboard the school bus, despite the urging of the teacher, both helper-moms, and even Thelma Washington.

It wasn't until Thelma told them that lunch was waiting for them at a restaurant that she suddenly faced a swarm of bodies trying to cram in through the front door.

It also reminded her how hungry she was.

She yelled back to the children to buckle up into their seats as she closed the door. Since she was already breaking a school rule having some windows open, she figured she better follow protocol and have the children strapped in.

The teacher sat near the front, with the two moms strategically placed in the middle and back of the bus.

She was glad she was driving elementary school children, not the trouble variety that Thelma occasionally had to deal with when she was driving junior high kids.

Still, driving in heavy traffic occasionally meant slamming on the brakes and she did not want to take any chances on some half-pint catapulting from the back of the bus and getting hurt.

Plus, she could see that traffic was just light enough that she could grab the elevated freeway and take the under-construction ramp if she hurried.

The bus wheezed its way up the ramp onto the expressway where traffic was moving faster than it had any right to, she thought. Just a few miles ahead was her exit, which would take them to the frontage road and the back way to the restaurant where they were scheduled to arrive about ten minutes ago.

She pushed the bus up to 50 miles per hour, about as fast as she ever liked to drive the old girl. The brakes were good, tires fair. And on the straightaway, the bus was almost comfortable to ride in.

The heat was creeping up but Thelma didn't even bother turning on the air conditioner. She smiled when she saw that the teacher had started fanning herself. And smiled again when she heard the song start from the back of the bus and work its way forward until everyone, Thelma included, was singing as they rolled down towards their exit.

Oh the wheels on the bus go round and round,
Round and round,

The Wheels on the Bus

Round and round,
Oh the wheels on the bus go round and round,
All the day long...

The children and the adults were working on a third chorus *"the babies on the bus go waa, waa, waa,"* when Thelma took her foot off the gas and began to brake as she started down the steep ramp, dodging construction cones and potholes.

She could see the frontage road down below, bordering a shallow ditch that ran alongside of it.

Just two miles past that was the restaurant where lunch for everyone was waiting.

Thaddeus Bartholomew Peck put pressure on his groin with his right hand, steering his big rig with the other, the 5,000 gallons of hydrofracking wastewater sloshing around in the tanker behind him.

The traffic had been light enough that he didn't have to maneuver too much. That was a good thing because the pain was worse. The Vicodin was barely touching it, and the drugs had fuzzed his brain to the point where he had trouble remembering where the exit was. When he drove through with a full load the last time, there was construction on the ramp. But because it was the middle of the night, he breezed through, bouncing over the potholes and knocking over a row of orange cones when he swung a little wide.

At least he thought he remembered knocking over cones.

He was staying tight in the right lane today behind some slower traffic, to be sure not to miss his exit.

He had sloshed down another can of Mountain Dew since getting off the George Washington Bridge, and now it felt like his bladder was going to simply explode.

He had an emergency pee bucket in the cab within reach, but he needed the truck to be stopped to use it without pissing all over the place.

A sign for his off-ramp popped up into his vision, about a half-mile ahead, and traffic was still moving along near the posted speed.

He thought he could see the back of a yellow school bus leaning into the curve as it made the turn down the ramp.

He grimaced as he let go of his aching groin to shift up a gear to catch up with the truck ahead of him. The talk-radio station was still yammering away about the Wolverine people.

He had gotten so distracted by the pain that he had forgotten to turn his music back on.

He flipped the switch and the cab filled with the booming sounds of Flat and Scruggs' classic "Foggy Mountain Breakdown."

Traffic was moving fast now, and he gritted his teeth as he shifted up one more gear. The blaring music seemed to help a little, he thought.

Jack checked over the new front page of Tuesday's edition, waiting only for a photo from Eli, who was now at the scene of the explosion in Rockwell Valley.

Devon had already pieced together a short story from

wire service reports to include the bombings in Colorado and California. For the local incident, she had quotes from several Grand Energy Services' employees who were working at a nearby well site and heard the explosion.

The bombings marked an escalation that Jack had been expecting. The events seemed more like they belonged in the Middle East, not rural Pennsylvania.

Other newspapers were calling the three bombings "terrorist activity," hinting that the Wolverines had some non-American connections.

Jack insisted they not speculate in any stories about that, knowing full well that the gas companies were pushing that line.

"As soon as the photo comes in, put it on the page and then we'll send the package to the printer," Jack said, loud enough for Stan and Jill to hear.

Devon had come back from Millie's looking somewhat confused. When Jack bolted out the door, she assumed he would come back, finish his lunch, and they would then proceed to deal with the need to fix the front page.

She hadn't ever seen him quite so distracted. But then again, since they had realized they were going to be parents, he was inside his head a lot.

Jack came out of his office and sat down in the chair next to Devon's desk where he sheepishly apologized for not coming back to Millie's for her. Belle had followed them into the office and was sitting patiently under the desk.

"I was in a such a panic that we might miss getting something into Tuesday's paper that I lost track of everything," he said.

Devon laughed. "I've been stood up on occasion but

never in a diner." She put her hand on his arm. "It's okay. Really. Now breathe. Please."

The photos from Eli popped up on Devon's screen and showed a twisted tangle of pipes and equipment.

"It's amazing no one got hurt in this," Devon said. "Amazing."

Jack reached over and enlarged the photo, where in one corner a building not affected by the blast could be seen.

Scrawled on the side of it in red letters was WOLVERINES.

"We better call Eli to check all his other photos. I want that showing on the cover," Jack said.

Thelma Washington was a confident driver, used to maneuvering this particular school bus around busy streets and in tight quarters.

But she had no illusions she was driving a sports car.

One of her colleagues once opined that piloting these buses was like "driving a bar of soap," an analogy she didn't think fit that well but was pretty funny, considering how sloppy her steering wheel often seemed.

As she started down the poorly-banked curve, she thought about the soap comment as she felt the back wheels of the bus sliding ever so slowly towards the edge of the ramp the farther down she went. She cranked the steering wheel to straighten out.

The road didn't look oily or slippery, but it didn't feel right to her as she tried to correct the motion.

She took her foot off the brake to see if it was a problem with the brakes locking up. She was traveling barely 15 miles per hour. But the motion continued, and as she wrestled the steering wheel to straighten out, the back wheels kept heading for the edge.

She pushed the brake pedal down again, harder this time. It went right to the floor.

Off to her right of the ramp was a steep dirt bank, ending at a ditch filled with water, one of many tidal channels that crisscrossed this part of Long Island near the ocean.

She realized that the steering column was gone, maybe the connector rods below, too. And now blown brakes.

The children in the bus were deep into singing "Wheels on the Bus" and didn't have any hint of what was happening.

She had just a few seconds to act.

If she continued on, the bus would likely pull left and maybe roll over in the traffic lane. She was sure the bus would be slammed into by the traffic behind her.

Or she could try to wrestle the bus to the right with what little steering she had left, drive it into a flimsy temporary guardrail, and hope it held enough to stop the bus or at least slow it down. If it didn't, the bus could slide down the bank, she thought.

Both relatively ugly alternatives were running through her mind when she grabbed the wheel tight with both hands and swung it as hard as she could to make a right turn, knowing that one of the steering rods below was likely bent, or even broken. She hit the horn at the same moment to warn any motorists.

But the steering suddenly returned.

Instead of gently banging into the guardrail, the bus burst through it, jumped a four-inch concrete curb, skidding down the dirt bank at an angle towards the ditch.

"Hang on!" Thelma screamed as loud as she could.

The bus kept moving forward, flipping over to the right in slow motion, rolling onto its right side, gently sliding until it rested halfway in the ditch.

The last thing Thelma heard before she hit her head was the screams of the children and the Spanish-speaking mom by the back door. Thelma was unconscious when brackish water began pouring in through the open windows.

Thaddeus Bartholomew Peck had never been quite so happy to see an off-ramp as he took his foot off the gas pedal, swinging a little wide onto the steep off-ramp to the frontage road.

He had maneuvered his emergency pee bucket to the floor by his feet, thinking he might need it before he could pull over. But once he got to the bottom of the ramp and onto the frontage road, there was room for him to simply stop.

He pulled the Vicodin bottle off the dashboard tray and tossed it onto the passenger seat, noting that he had about a half-dozen pills left. The pain had flared up twice driving across the city and felt like it was about to give him another sharp blow to the belly.

Peck shifted his eyes back from the Vicodin bottle and suddenly realized that there was a car stopped in the left hand lane and people were standing near the bottom at the edge of his lane, looking over the edge at the ditch.

He quickly tried to downshift. His reward was a pain in his groin as sharp as if he had been kicked. He had managed to pull the rolling truck out of gear, but now the rig was freewheeling down a steep ramp and the pain almost paralyzed his clutch leg.

His right foot collided with the emergency pee bucket as he struggled to get his foot over on the brake pedal.

And as he feebly kicked and tried to get his rig under control, an electric shot of pain ran through a heavily drugged, bladder-filled Thaddeus Bartholomew Peck, just seconds before Peck, his truck, and payload of 5,000 gallons of toxic hydrofracking wastewater went straight through the guard rail where Thelma Laverne Washington's school bus had gone moments before.

The first reports that came into the newsroom at the *Horsehead Clarion* were that there had been a shooting on a school bus in New York City.

The initial report had come from a bystander who climbed down to the school bus, which was wedged underneath a tanker truck. The bystander saw the truck driver's bloodied head and a handgun sitting on top of the overturned bus.

The handgun, police later said, had fallen out of the truck when it slid into the school bus at the bottom of the slope.

Jack and Devon held the newspaper for about an hour while they waited for wire service reports.

But as soon as they learned that it was a traffic accident, they sent the newspaper on electronically to the printer, opting to go online with more timely updates than what they could provide in the print edition.

"It looks like there were thirty or more kids on the bus," Devon said, reading from her screen to Jack. "What a mess."

Jack's phone buzzed with a text from Eli who had left the site of the bombing in Rockwell Valley to go to the hospital to check on the GES worker who had been bathed in fracking wastewater.

> Defines died today. Hospital says he will be cremated. No autopsy.

Jack reached for the phone to call the Rockwell Valley Police Department.

Thelma Washington regained consciousness just as the big rig slid down the hill, slamming into the side of the bus and pushing the bus further into the water.

Even with the screams of the children she could hear people yelling somewhere outside the bus.

The water had stopped rushing into the bus from the ditch, but the emergency windows on the high side of the bus were blocked by the tanker. The front door on the right side of the bus was underwater.

The only exit was the back door which the Spanish-speaking mom had popped open. She was yelling *"Ven¡ Ven¡"* to the kids to climb out into the water. But it was slow going as half the kids couldn't get their seat belts unbuckled and were dangling like marionettes.

Thelma struggled to get out of her seat, an awkward maneuver as the bus was lying entirely on its right side with a downward angle. She gingerly worked the release knowing that when the belt let loose, she would have to hold on tight to the pole behind her head or else fall down into the bus stairwell.

She nearly gagged from the smell of the water leaking from the big rig.

As she unclipped her belt she looked in the rear view mirror and saw water was starting to stream in from the tanker truck, which had cracked its silvery-looking tank when it landed on top of the bus.

The heavy construction of the old school bus had saved the children from being crushed by the weight of the rig, but it had also put a gash in the tank where water was spraying out like a geyser.

The children were trapped in the seats by their belts, the liquid pouring over them through the open windows, making them scream that much louder.

Thelma pulled the snap on her belt and fell into the water, grabbing onto the nearest seats to stabilize herself. She started working her way to the back, unbuckling the children one by one, pushing each towards the back where the Spanish-speaking mom was handing them out to several Good Samaritan bystanders who had raced down from the off-ramp and jumped into the water.

Midway down the bus she found the teacher facedown in the water, her face a mass of blood. She had not been buckled in when the bus rolled.

Thelma heard sirens of police and arriving rescuers just as a seam on the tanker ripped open another ten feet, sending a wall of fracking wastewater into the bus through the open windows, cutting off visibility, and prompting a new round of screaming from the dozen children still struggling to get free.

The water was coming in so fast that it was rising inside the bus quickly, unable to drain.

She held her breath as she fought her way back along the aisle to free the children, trying not to swallow any water as it poured over her head.

J ack and Devon watched the television footage late into the afternoon back at their house.

They marveled at the tenacity of the bus driver coming to the back door of the bus several times with a child tucked under each arm, handing them to rescue workers.

A traffic helicopter had caught the action on video as fire and rescue teams arrived.

It looked like Thelma Laverne Washington was on her way to becoming a hero.

Jack turned the sound off on the television as he and Devon headed out to the porch, each with a glass of Oscar's Riesling in their hands. They perched on the big glider couch, where Jack angled himself so he could still see the television screen and the news coverage of the bus accident.

"I know what you're thinking, Jack. Suppose that was our child on the bus. I can't stand even imagining it. What a world we're living in."

Jack took a sip and watched Belle chase a squirrel in the yard.

"It's that," he said. "It's that I'm feeling really old these days. I never wanted to be publisher. But I understand what Walter wanted.

"Amy and I were young and pretty broke when we got married. After the miscarriages, the doctors told us Amy could have children. But she just never got pregnant again."

Devon slid up close and put her arm through his.

"Well, remember how Walter used to say it's never too late for anything? It isn't. And even as horrible as that bus crash was, we have to live, Jack. We can't be afraid all the time. Of buses or trucks or anything else."

She felt Jack kiss the top of her head, then looked up to see that he was staring intently at the television screen in the living room.

He stood up and walked quickly inside. A moment later she heard him on the telephone.

"Eli, you back at the office? Check out the photos of that tanker truck. I'm looking at the footage from the helicopter right now. The TV people are saying it's a wastewater truck. You tell me what you think. I think it's a *goddamn* fracking wastewater truck. I think I'm looking at recovered water pouring out of it."

Devon heard Jack pause for a moment.

"I thought so. Okay, you call GES right now. And pull any file shots you have of their wastewater trucks. We'll need them."

From the *Horseheads Clarion*

Column One
The Horseheads Clarion

The death of school children uncovers the truth

By Jack Stafford

NEW YORK CITY, New York — It took the deaths of six young children and their teacher to finally force the natural gas industry to admit just how poisonous, just how toxic the chemicals and biological agents really are that are being used in the hydrofracking process.

On Monday a school bus on Long Island, filled with third and fourth grade students, was nearly crushed by a Pennsylvania-registered tanker carrying fracking wastewater. In the course of that horrible accident, the children, the bus driver, the teacher, and two mothers along to help shepherd the kids on a field trip were soaked with the fluid from the leaking truck.

Emergency responders took the children to area hospitals to be treated, but were unaware that the truck contained water recovered from hydrofracked gas wells. It took nearly 12 hours before Grand Energy Services would admit that was the cargo.

And because of the secrecy allowed by federal law, it took another 12 hours before New York

State authorities were able to force GES to reveal the exact chemical composition of what the children were exposed to.

That delay in treatment is likely part of the reason that six children gave up their lives, doctors say. And some of the others may die. They certainly will suffer much more than they would have if GES had given the doctors the information they needed immediately to treat the children, the driver, and the mothers.

The bus driver and the two mothers are heroes, getting the children off the bus as quickly as they could. All of them remain seriously ill.

Two days after the school bus accident, a laboratory owned by Grand Energy Services revealed the chemical formula used in fracking and the composition of the newly-introduced genetically modified organism GES had touted in the Hydro Green System. This was the GMO that was supposed to break down toxic chemicals and make the wastewater safe and treatable in commercial treatment plants.

We know now that was a sham

on the part of GES. If anything, the wastewater was made even more toxic by the addition of the GMO.

So far six children have given their lives because of that lie. So did Alberto Defines. Who knows how many others have died—or will die—because of the overarching greed exhibited by this company, and others, who care nothing about the health, safety, and welfare of people? They do care about company profits.

The deaths of the children and the injuries overshadowed the news this week about a series of bombings of natural gas facilities in Pennsylvania, Colorado, and California by members of a radical environmental group called the Wolverines. The Wolverines have announced they are declaring a guerilla war to stop hydrofracking and its rapacious destruction of the environment.

This newspaper in no way endorses bombings or violence.

But at the same time, the destruction of the environment and the incredible toll hydrofracking technology is

taking on the health of people
must be stopped.

The level of anger and
frustration has risen to such
a boiling point among many
normally peaceful citizens
that local, state, and federal
officials can no longer ignore
the issue. There is a need to
take action to protect our
citizens, not take action
against citizens who have been
poisoned, cheated, and lied to.

While we mourn the deaths
of these six children and
their teacher and perhaps more
victims in coming weeks as the
poisons they were exposed to
destroy their lives, we need
a full accounting from GES and
other companies involved in
this.

A full accounting.

*Jack Stafford is an
investigative columnist and
reporter for* The Horseheads
Clarion *and has worked as an
investigative reporter for
metropolitan newspapers in
California and Colorado.*

Eli was nearly vibrating as he reread a wire service story
about Roy Bonder, Sr.

Las Vegas Police had nabbed Bonder that morning as he was attempting to squeeze out a tiny bathroom window of a low-rent motel room a few blocks off the main Vegas strip. Police said he was clutching a laptop computer and a satchel full of what they would only describe as "anti-gas political materials and documents about a company called Grand Energy Services."

He had been living in the motel for a month with a 45-year-old swing-shift cocktail waitress who turned him into the police when she read that there was a $10,000 reward for information about his whereabouts, put up by Grand Energy Services.

Two weeks before Bonder was taken into custody, former GES employee Tom Fletcher claimed in a statement to police investigators in Pennsylvania that it was Bonder, not him, who had shot and killed GES worker Delbert Dogg on January 1 the year before near Rockwell Valley.

But police earlier had tied Fletcher, who was in jail on a charge of assaulting a police officer, to the shooting by finding the two rifles that killed Dogg at Fletcher's house.

The wire service story detailed Bonder's mysterious disappearance, along with his fracking wastewater truck.

It also mentioned Bonder had a brief career in Hollywood as a child actor. He worked as an unnamed extra in three movies, the story said. But his film days ended when his family moved to Pennsylvania in 1985.

That piece of the story prompted Eli to madly chase every Internet lead he could to find out which three movies Bonder might have been in. Locating the names of actors working as extras, particularly child extras, in thirty-year-old films was proving almost impossible to track down as Eli bounced from website to website, going through cast lists and actor listings with theatrical agents.

Calls to several theatrical agencies in Hollywood came up cold, as did a phone call to the wire service reporter who filed the story.

The reporter told Eli her information about Bonder had come directly from the Las Vegas Police Department's report. And the reporter said she couldn't say if Roy Bonder, Sr. had used that name when he worked as a child actor.

But Eli was willing to bet one of the movies Roy Bonder had a bit part in as a child was *Red Dawn*. And if Eli's hunch turned out to be correct, Eli was even more certain he had found his first, real-live, honest-to-God Wolverine.

G rayson Oliver Delacroix's nightmare woke him up with a heart-pounding start.

In his dream he had been using a big knife to carve the flesh off a small dog—a cocker spaniel—peeling the meat off in strips and eating them. He could feel blood running down his cheeks and neck.

The dog didn't seem to mind the carving and was looking away from him. And Delacroix knew he should stop. But he couldn't. It just tasted too good.

In his dream, someone came into the room just as he stuffed a long stringy piece of dog meat into his mouth.

Then he woke up, wondering if it was the dream or if he had heard something.

He sat up in his bed upstairs in his two-story house built one hundred yards back from the road on the front side of a carefully manicured five-acre hillside estate in Flathead, Missouri. It was four miles from the Grand Energy Services corporate headquarters where he had been CEO up until he was shown the door by a unanimous vote of the corporation's board the week before.

His carefully constructed wall of deniability crumbled quickly when the truth about Hydro-Green Systems was revealed and the corporation needed someone to take the fall.

Delacroix understood the logic of it, almost admired it in a way. It was just as ruthless as he had been while at the head of GES.

But it still pissed him off when he thought about all the money he had made for stockholders, the board and other corporate executives who were now clucking their tongues, blaming Delacroix for every problem GES had ever had. As if they had any intention of changing how they were running the business.

And that worm Rod Mayenlyn! He was using the *EFA* website to crucify Delacroix. And the media were lapping it up, quoting from the *EFA* tirades. Luther Burnside wasn't much better, having issued a statement when he was named acting CEO that promised "openness and a course correction for the company."

Assholes, Delacroix thought.

The day he was ushered out of the building by security guards, Delacroix had considered having his attorney weigh in to fight for his job and reputation. But on reflection he realized that he had nearly $25 million in stock and bonuses still on the books that would be at risk if he got into a pissing contest with GES.

The lawyers for GES reminded him that his non-disclosure agreement laid that out in excruciating detail. Too much noise, or a lawsuit, would likely cost him everything. Everything included forfeiting a $10 million off-the-books cash payout to his Grand Cayman Island bank account.

Delacroix fumed about that again for a moment and looked across the room where his digital clock was flashing. Flathead had been having power outages for weeks and it seemed like another blip would now require him to reset a half-dozen electronic things in the house.

Delacroix popped out of bed and slid on his red silk monogrammed bathrobe. He walked over to check the status of his home alarm system. He was relieved to see it was on and had rearmed itself immediately after the power outage. The outage had to have been for less than ten seconds or his emergency generator would have kicked in.

His two bodyguards hired by the company after the Wolverines had pulled the stunt with the GES headquarters' swimming pool had been taken away when Delacroix was shown the door.

And since the Wolverines had set off bombs at three gas wells and were making bold threats about blowing up liquid natural gas terminals, Delacroix had started sleeping with a loaded gun on his nightstand.

For a fraction of a second Delacroix missed his ex-wife who had slept so lightly she was better than any watchdog. He shook that thought away quickly, reminding himself to call his former executive secretary for a quiet liaison and a chance to catch up on what was going on at the company.

Unless she's turned on me, too, he thought.

He looked out the window and saw it getting to be first

light and decided he might as well get up. He could see a layer of moisture on his expensive cobblestone driveway paved with stones imported from South America. And he could also see his newspaper hanging inside a plastic bag on the wrought iron gates of his driveway.

Delacroix was about halfway down the stairs, still fussing to get the knot tied just right on the front of his red silk monogrammed bathrobe when he caught the faint whiff of natural gas.

You're kidding. A fucking gas leak? he thought. *Jesus Christ.*

The Saturday afternoon staff meeting at the *Horseheads Clarion* was almost festive.

Millie's Diner provided platters of food. Oscar came by with enough Lakeside Winery wine to ensure there would be a lot of people walking home or catching rides with designated drivers.

At Jack's insistence, nearly everyone who worked at the newspaper—writers, production people, delivery drivers and circulation workers—had caravanned in a dozen cars and trucks to a community meeting in Rockwell Valley that morning. Oscar, his niece Lindy, and Shania from Millie's went along, too.

So did Belle the Labrador Retriever.

The event at Rockwell Valley High School was called "Fracking: Today and Tomorrow" and was one of many similar meetings being held in several parts of the country in the wake of the New York City school bus tragedy and the revelations about GES and Hydro-Green.

And unlike most other such events where pro- and anti-fracking forces would end up in shouting matches, this time the conversation in Rockwell Valley was civil and as close to productive as could ever be hoped.

Jack was one of the main speakers, talking for nearly a half-hour about the role of media. Whereas he once might have been booed for scathing comments about the industry, this time he drew several rounds of loud applause from a crowd that had at least one hundred people directly associated with Grand Energy Services sitting and listening.

After his speech, several GES line workers who Jack recognized from frequent breakfasts at Millie's walked up to the podium to thank him for the newspaper's dogged pursuit of the truth.

Another speaker was Michael Ahlbright, who had been rehired as a special consultant to GES. His main job, it seemed, was to reassure communities that GES would from this point forward be dealing honestly with everyone and government entities in the future.

"The company fell prey to putting profits over people," Ahlbright said. "We need profits, but not at the expense of the communities we are supposed to serve."

Some people in the crowd grumbled at the attempts at public relations, but Ahlbright still got polite applause.

At the *Clarion* office later that afternoon, the staff meeting turned into a block party as passersby saw the party overflowing the office and came in to see what was happening.

Jack and Devon decided to simply make it an unofficial open house.

Finally, at 5 p.m. Jack asked Oscar to start moving people out while he asked the *Clarion* staff to stay behind.

In the months since Walter's death, Jack had gradually assumed the mantle of leadership of the newspaper. He felt like his speech at the Rockwell Valley meeting, and warm welcome by the audience had been like his graduation.

No one wanted to leave the *Clarion* office. They all wanted to hear what Jack had to say.

Oscar locked the door when the last of the community members headed out. He went to the cooler and pulled out the last two bottles of the Riesling he had brought down from Seneca Lake.

"I really thought I would have about eight or ten of these left," he said. "Next time you are going to invite the whole county, Jack, you need to give me a heads up."

Jack took a refilled glass from Oscar and stood up in front of the newsroom, the same place he stood when he had offered up a eulogy for Walter earlier that year.

The group fell silent as people noticed Jack was standing still. He surveyed them all for a moment, noticing that even Belle had sat at attention and seemed to be waiting.

"I want to thank you all for going to the community meeting today, especially those of you who work here but don't always get to see what kind of impact we have. That meeting came about in good part because this newspaper, and all of you, worked hard to get the word out about hydrofracking. It wasn't easy. It wasn't pretty," Jack said. "But you did it. We did it."

He drew a round of applause and more than a few half-drunken catcalls and wolf whistles before he raised his hand to quiet people down.

"So today, we party. Absolutely. Walter would agree. It was a victory to hear somebody from GES finally admitting to so many things. And for our reporting on a lot of those things, we took a lot of crap in the last year. Even though every word of what we printed was true.

"Companies don't admit that stuff lightly. What the GES reps didn't mention is they are facing wrongful death suits filed by the parents of those children killed on the school bus. And lots of other lawsuits, too. GES will likely go bankrupt. That's actually going to be our lead story Tuesday, right Eli?"

Jack held his hand up to cut off another rising round of applause and whistles.

"No. No. Please. No. We shouldn't take joy in that, as tempting as it is. For every son-of-a-bitch like Grayson Oliver Delacroix, there are thousands of GES workers who will find themselves out of a job if the company goes belly-up. That's nothing to celebrate."

People started looking down into their glasses or at the floor.

"But, well, what I wanted to say, and I don't think Oscar's Riesling is helping me much at all—is that there are plenty of other dragons out there we need to slay. GES was one gas company that ran amok. Multiply them by a hundred. Maybe by a thousand.

"Those other gas companies are still pumping toxic chemicals into the ground. They're still planning on shipping a lot, if not most, of this gas to Europe and China. They still want to keep hydrofracking fluid toxins a secret. And we've barely even scratched the surface dealing with the air pollution from fracking. Barely."

"Did I miss anything, Devon?"

The room stayed silent for a moment as she shook her head. Then from the back, a burly circulation truck driver shouted, sounding exasperated.

"Well Jesus H. Christ, Jack. What else can we do? Really. What now?"

Jack took a sip from his glass before he spoke.

"Elegantly put. Especially putting the H where it belongs in Jesus H. Christ," Jack said, getting a laugh.

"Let me answer that the way Walter might have: We can swear about it. We can pray about it. We can get drunk over it. Maybe we should do all three things.

"But when we get done with those we can get back to work publishing this newspaper. That's what we do. We publish a newspaper. And by God, by *Jesus H. Christ*, if you want, we will continue to do so and do the right thing for our readers and our community."

Jack waited to let his comments sink in for a moment.

"So, I have a question for everyone in this room. An important question.

"Who is with me?" Jack asked.

The people in the room looked at each other, unsure how to respond.

"*Who is with me?*" Jack asked, again, this time raising his voice a notch.

The third time, he put his wine glass down and raised both arms up in the air, clenching his fists shouting **Who-is-with-me?**

His face was flush from an afternoon of wine and emotion.

After a few heartbeats of silence, the entire crowd started clapping, whistling, and cheering in a building wave of noise that went from simple approval to a roar that had passersby on the sidewalk in front of the *Horseheads Clarion* stopping to peer inside to see what the heck was going on.

It was a raucous roar that made Jack's eyes tear up.

The roar was almost as loud as the explosion that had blown Grayson Oliver Delacroix III up the stair case, out through his roof and onto the expensive cobblestone driveway where Flathead, Missouri fireman found him sprawled in a shattered heap.

The coroner's report noted that the knot on his expensive monogrammed red silk bathrobe was still neatly tied around his waist, his initials —GOD— boldly displayed on what was left of him.

EPILOG

Two-year-old Noah Walter Stafford toddled unsteadily along the ocean's edge of the sandy beach on Lata Island, a ten-acre tropical dot of land in the Vava'u group of islands in northern Tonga across the equator and International dateline in the southen Pacific Ocean.

Puffy clouds drifted slowly overhead. A mother humpback whale and her calf frolicked nearby in the strait that separated Lata from its nearest island neighbor two miles away.

On the beach just behind Noah, a grizzled-looking Australian shepherd mix named Tokanga kept watch on the child. He had been Noah's beach dog and protector since Jack, Devon, and Noah had come to the island when Noah was six months old. If Noah stepped too far in the water, Tokanga would gently tug on the child's diaper to pull him back, a game Noah enjoyed from the very first time he crawled to the water and Tokanga yanked him to safety.

Jack and Devon sat holding hands on the porch of their shore-side Tongan thatch home in the shade of the palm trees, back from the water, watching Noah and the whales.

Close to Noah on the beach, their Tongan friend

Gideon sat on the sand splicing a new anchor line for the 24-foot sailing catamaran moored just offshore. The boat provided their inter-island transportation and occasionally brought paying guests to the island.

When Jack made inquiries to an old American friend of Walter's living in Tonga about coming for a visit, Gideon's name had popped up in conversation. He and Walter had been friends since Walter and Andrea had taken their first trip to the South Pacific and Gideon was a young man working on scuba diving boats.

Five minutes into the conversation, Jack found out that Walter had been paying on a lease for Lata Island for more than ten years.

And Gideon's family was willing, and quite eager, to change that lease over to Jack and Devon's names, particularly if they were willing to put some money into refurbishing the half-dozen single-room buildings that had once been an eco-resort run by a German family.

It seemed to Jack and Devon like the right place to spend some of the $100,000 Walter had left Jack in his life insurance policy.

"Are you going to write today, Jack? It is Sunday," Devon asked.

All Tongans took Sundays very seriously, reserving it for church services, families, and feasts. No work was allowed anywhere and Jack was surprised Gideon was even working on the anchor line.

"I don't think so," Jack said. "I already told Eli to run one of the backup columns I sent a week ago."

When Jack and Devon left New York for an open-ended stay in the South Pacific, they put Eli in charge of the

Horseheads Clarion and gave him a generous budget to hire additional staff.

Eli was proving to be a very competent and popular community newspaper editor, even more so since he and Shania had gotten married and temporarily adopted Belle the Labrador.

"I meant work today on your book, Jack," Devon said. "You haven't mentioned it in at least a week. And you've barely touched your computer, either. Is everything okay?"

Jack watched Tokanga stand and gently pull Noah back from the edge of the water.

Okay? Jack thought. *I wonder.*

After the public outrage surrounding the Grand Energy Systems revelations, it seemed the United States was actually considering ways to wean itself off oil and natural gas and move toward renewable energy sources—the direction much of the rest of the globe was already heading.

But now that idea was fading as some United States law enforcement agencies, with political arm twisting by the oil and gas industry, were clanging alarm bells, warning that eco-terrorists were lurking behind every tree, bush, and protester's sign.

"No writing today," Jack said. "It's family day. We should take the catamaran with Gideon. Go visit his family in Neiafu. The wind is perfect and I know they will have a great feast."

Before the Staffords left New York for Tonga, Jack had wanted to write a companion volume to Kenneth MacInerery's *Intelligent Design: How Human Cleverness Doomed the Planet.*

Jack wanted to take MacInerery's glass-mostly empty

theories and match them up with ideas for solving the depressing problems MacInerery's book presented. It had been slow going. And yet Jack had found that for all the doom, gloom, politics, and seemingly intractable problems the world faced, there were solutions, almost all of which depended on increased and consistent citizen pressure that challenged politicians and corporations to do the right thing for people, not profits. Pressure that was greater than corporate pressure.

When he pitched the idea to Devon, along with moving to Tonga while he wrote the book, Devon had come up with a title, based on Walter Nagle's last words: *An Endless Quest for Hope and Solutions.*

Kenneth MacInerery liked the idea so much he offered to co-author the book with Jack, an offer Jack agreed to without hesitating.

Lost in his own thoughts for a moment, Jack snapped to attention when he heard Noah shout from the shore, his tiny two-year-old voice straining.

"Da! Da! Da! Whale! Whale! Da! Da!" Noah shouted.

He pointed a tiny finger at a spot a hundred feet from the beach where a whale calf the size of an SUV had rolled on its side, its huge whale eye peering at the child on the shore.

Devon and Jack walked down to the water's edge, where Jack scooped up Noah into his arms, and then waded waist deep into the water.

They all waved to the whale calf, which had started flapping its fin at them, as if to wave back at the three strange-looking creatures.

"I'm thinking about going back to New York," Jack said.

"Thinking, anyway. Eli said the newspaper could use me at the helm again as publisher."

Jack paused and took a deep breath.

"And, well, I finished the book a week ago."

Devon put her arm around Jack and kissed him lightly on the cheek.

"I guessed the book was done. I was just waiting for you to tell me. Congratulations. You must feel relieved. I'm relieved."

Their retreat to these far-flung islands had worked. It had taken them far enough away from the madcap world of hydrofracking so that they could regroup, reflect and become a real family.

They stood quietly watching the whale calf for another few minutes until it gave one final fin wave and disappeared, surfacing a few hundred yards away, just past the catamaran anchored where the mother whale waited.

"If we go, we can always come back here," Jack said. "Maybe I'll write another book."

Devon kissed Jack again, then Noah.

"Nothing has to be decided right now," Devon said. "That's one of the most beautiful parts of this life, these islands. One of the parts I've loved the most here. Time is so different. It's doesn't seem that important."

Jack waved to Gideon and pointed at the catamaran, signaling that they wanted to head out for a sail to one of the other islands.

"Well, I've decided one thing," Jack said. "Let's go with Gideon to his family feast. Suddenly I feel like celebrating."

They watched Gideon dive into the water, quickly swimming out to the catamaran to get it rigged. The grin on his face made it clear he knew where they would be sailing.

"Are we celebrating the book being done?" Devon asked.

Before Jack could answer, Noah started waving his arms, pointing out to the water just past the catamaran. Behind them on the shore, Tokanga started barking wildly.

Then Jack and Devon heard a huge whooshing sound as the mother whale heaved her entire body out of the water in a spectacular full-body breach, crashing down and creating such a huge splash in every direction that it nearly sprayed Gideon as he climbed up on the deck of the catamaran.

"That's what we're celebrating today," Jack said. "Everything. My book being done, sure. But really the whales. These islands. Gideon. And what Walter helped me see. Maybe mostly what Walter finally helped me see."

Devon moved in to hug Jack and Noah closely, while Tokanga barked, wanting to be included.

"Let me guess—it's hope and solutions, right?" Devon said. "Hope and solutions."

CPSIA information can be obtained at www.ICGtesting.com
Printed in the USA
BVOW11s0415280314

348990BV00004B/7/P